T0359184

LYNNE   KIM   TINA   KIM
GRAHAM   LAWRENCE   BECKETT   FINDLAY

Valentine's Day

Collection 2025

MILLS & BOON

VALENTINE'S DAY COLLECTION 2025 © 2025 by Harlequin Books S.A.

THE BOSS'S VALENTINE
© 2003 by Lynne Graham
Australian Copyright 2003
New Zealand Copyright 2003

First Published 2003
Fourth Australian Paperback Edition 2025
ISBN 978 1 038 94072 8

RAFAEL'S PROPOSAL
© 2003 by Kim Lawrence
Australian Copyright 2003
New Zealand Copyright 2003

First Published 2003
Second Australian Paperback Edition 2025
ISBN 978 1 038 94072 8

THEIR REUNION TO REMEMBER
© 2021 by Tina Beckett
Australian Copyright 2021
New Zealand Copyright 2021

First Published 2021
Second Australian Paperback Edition 2025
ISBN 978 1 038 94072 8

A VALENTINE'S PROPOSAL
© 2021 by Kim Findlay
Australian Copyright 2021
New Zealand Copyright 2021

First Published 2021
Second Australian Paperback Edition 2025
ISBN 978 1 038 94072 8

Except for use in any review, the reproduction or utilisation of this work in whole or in part in any form by any electronic, mechanical or other means, now known or hereafter invented, including xerography, photocopying and recording, or in any information storage or retrieval system, is forbidden without the permission of the publisher.

This book is sold subject to the condition that it shall not, by way of trade or otherwise, be lent, resold, hired out or otherwise circulated without the prior consent of the publisher in any form of binding or cover other than that in which it is published and without a similar condition including this condition being imposed on the subsequent purchaser.

All rights reserved including the right of reproduction in whole or in part in any form. This edition is published in arrangement with Harlequin Books S.A. Cover art used by arrangement with Harlequin Books S.A. All rights reserved.

This is a work of fiction. Names, characters, places, and incidents are either the product of the author's imagination or are used fictitiously, and any resemblance to actual persons, living or dead, business establishments, events, or locales is entirely coincidental.

Published by
Mills & Boon
An imprint of Harlequin Enterprises (Australia) Pty Limited (ABN 47 001 180 918), a subsidiary of HarperCollins Publishers Australia Pty Limited (ABN 36 009 913 517)
Level 19, 201 Elizabeth Street
SYDNEY NSW 2000
AUSTRALIA

MIX
Paper | Supporting
responsible forestry
FSC
www.fsc.org   FSC® C001695

® and ™ (apart from those relating to FSC®) are trademarks of Harlequin Enterprises (Australia) Pty Limited or its corporate affiliates. Trademarks indicated with ® are registered in Australia, New Zealand and in other countries. Contact admin_legal@Harlequin.ca for details.

Printed and bound in Australia by McPherson's Printing Group

CONTENTS

The Boss's Valentine
Lynne Graham

MODERN
Power and passion

LYNNE GRAHAM was born in Northern Ireland and has been a keen Harlequin reader since her teens. She is very happily married with an understanding husband, who has learned to cook since she started to write! Her five children keep her on her toes. She has two dogs—one large who knocks everything over and a tiny terrier who has a big bark. When time allows, Lynne is a keen gardener.

CHAPTER ONE

IT HAD BEEN a hideous day at work.

On the way home, Poppy called into the corner shop and the first thing she noticed was that the big valentine card she had admired over a month earlier was still unsold. She couldn't understand why nobody had bought it for she loved its glorious overblown pink roses and simple sentimental verse. She wondered why all the cards her more fortunate friends received were joke ones with comic, cruel, or even crude messages.

On an impulse, Poppy lifted the card and decided to buy it. Why shouldn't she send a valentine card? True, nobody had ever sent *her* one, but that didn't mean that she couldn't use the card as a means of brightening someone else's day. As to the identity of that special, lucky someone, there was no doubt in her mind about who would receive the card...

Poppy had fallen head over heels in love with Santino Aragone in her first week working at Aragone Systems. She was all too well aware that Santino was as out of her reach as the moon. Santino was a hugely successful entrepreneur, blessed by spectacular sleek, dark Italian looks, and he had a never-ending string of gorgeous women in his life. But in an emergency Santino Aragone could also be incredibly kind. On her first day at work, when she'd got her finger trapped in a door, Santino had taken her to the hospital himself. When he had fainted dead away at the sight of a needle, Poppy had known he was the man for her...she had thought that was so sweet.

Starry-eyed over the idea that her small, anonymous gesture of a card might at least bring a brief smile to Santino Aragone's brooding dark features on what she knew would be a difficult day for him, she was unlocking the door of her bedsit before her thoughts roamed uneasily back to her own horrendous day at work.

Desmond, the slick new head of marketing, had asked her if she had been born stupid or perhaps she'd got that way with effort? Having spilt coffee on his keyboard, Poppy had cleaned it up without telling him and in the process somehow wiped his morning's work from his computer. Although she had made grovelling apologies, Desmond had still put in a complaint about her to Human Resources and she had been issued with a formal warning.

Her colleagues would have been surprised to learn that Poppy, famed for her laid-back nature, was even angrier with herself than Desmond had been. If she had not been so busy chatting, the coffee would never have been spilt. Time and time again, a lapse in concentration led to similar mistakes on her part. Sometimes she wondered if the problem had started when she was at school and her parents had, without ever meaning to, managed to undermine her every small triumph.

'I'm sure you've done your best,' her mother would say with a slight grimace when she scanned Poppy's school reports. 'We can't expect you to match Peter's results, can we?'

Her elder brother, Peter, had been born gifted and his achievements had set an impossible standard against which her more average abilities sank without trace. Punch-drunk with pride over their son's academic successes, her parents had always concentrated their energies on Peter. Poppy would have liked to go to university, too, but when she was fifteen, her parents had told her that, as further education was so expensive and

Peter would still be completing his doctorate, she would have to leave school and train for a job instead. It had seemed to her then that there was no point in striving for better grades. But it had been a conviction that she had since lived to regret.

Now painfully conscious that she didn't have much in the way of academic qualifications and that she had been lucky to get a position in a slick city business, Poppy worked hard as a marketing assistant. She was willing, enthusiastic and popular with her colleagues, but employees who made foolish mistakes were frowned on at Aragone Systems. In addition, the warning she had received that day was her second in six months and if there was a third, she could be sacked. Ironically, it was not so much the fear of being fired that sent a chill down her taut spine, it was the terrifying knowledge that if she was fired she would never, ever set eyes on Santino Aragone again...

'Is this someone's idea of a joke?' Santino Aragone demanded with incredulous bite when he opened the giant envelope two days later and found himself looking at the most naff of valentine cards awash with chintzy roses in improbable clashing pinks.

'I'm as surprised as you are.' His PA, Craig Belston, thought with considerable amusement that no woman could have chosen a worse way of trying to impress his sophisticated employer. Or indeed a worse day or even year to make such a declaration.

The staff Christmas party had been postponed after the sudden death of Santino's father, Maximo, and rescheduled to take place as a Valentine's Day event this evening. As bad luck would have it, Santino was attending another funeral of an old schoolfriend that very afternoon. Furthermore, it might be a little-known fact but Santino loathed Valentine's Day in much the same way that Scrooge had loathed the festive season.

Lean, strong face grim, Santino opened the card. A faint whiff of an eerily familiar perfume made his nostrils flare and he frowned. Floral...jasmine? An old-fashioned scent, not the type of fragrance worn by a stylish woman. But so taken aback was he by the candid message on the inside of the card that he forgot about the perfume.

'As always, I'm thinking of you and loving you today,' ran the screed.

Had he become the unwitting target of some dreadful school-girl with a crush? Wincing at the very idea while he mentally ran through the very few teenage girls within his social circle, he made no demur when Craig took the liberty of turning the card round to peruse it for himself.

'Tinkerbell…' Craig pronounced in a tone of raw disbelief.
'I beg your pardon?' Santino prompted drily.

'That dippy redhead in marketing. We call her Tinkerbell be-cause she's always flying about and putting her feet in it noisily. Well, Poppy's certainly stuck her silly head above the parapet this time,' the younger man remarked with an unpleasant smile.

'I'm certain she sent this card. That's her scent. She always wears it and guess who loves pink and flowers as well?'

Poppy Bishop, the marketing junior, hired six months ago by his late father in total defiance of HR's choice of candidate while Santino had been on vacation. Why? Maximo had felt sorry for her because she had confided that it was her first in-terview after fifty-odd job applications. Poppy with her shy but sunny smiles, explosive Titian corkscrew curls and her comical penchant for floral prints and insane diets. Even in a large staff, Poppy was hard to ignore and calamity did follow her around.

'Some women just *live* to embarrass themselves,' Craig re-marked thinly. 'Shouldn't someone have a word with her about this? The cheek of her too…a little nobody like her making up to the boss!'

Summoning up a recollection of how Poppy behaved in his vicinity, Santino decided she very probably *was* the culprit. He knew he made her nervous. Around him, she was more than usually clumsy, tongue-tied to the point of idiocy and envel-oped in a continual hot blush. She also had a way of looking at him that suggested that with very little effort he might walk on water. Other women treated him to the same look but where they were concerned it was deliberate flattery, whereas Poppy's expressive face paraded her every thought like a banner. He was relieved that she had not signed the card. She would not have appreciated that her trade-mark perfume and love of flowers might be a giveaway and would undoubtedly cringe if she realised that she was even under suspicion. Instantly, Santino regretted allowing Craig to read the card.

'I doubt that Poppy Bishop sent it,' Santino murmured in a bored tone of dismissal as he dropped the card straight into the bin. 'She's just not the type. I imagine it's more likely to have come from some schoolgirl, possibly the daughter of one of my friends. Now, since we've had our entertainment for the day, could you get me the MD of Delsen Industries on the phone?' Later that morning, Santino's attention wandered back to the bin where the card lay forlorn and rejected. A groan of exasperation escaped his wide, sensual mouth. What on earth had possessed her? His PA hated her guts and would do her a bad turn if he got the chance. Why? Craig was famous for hitting on the youngest, newest female employees, treating them to a one-night stand and then dumping them.

But when his PA had tried his routine on Poppy, she had turned him down and admitted that she had been told that he was the office romeo on her first day, a put-down that had hit Craig's ego right where it hurt. Craig would have been more humiliated, however, had he realised that Santino had been the one to issue that warning. He still didn't know why he had bothered. Maybe it was the fact that his father had warmed to the girl; maybe it was the sheer naivety he had seen in her blue pansy-coloured eyes...

Around ten o'clock that morning, Poppy had to stock up the stationery cupboard. She was glad that she had to trek down to the floor below to get fresh supplies. Anything capable of taking her mind off the valentine card she had sent was welcome.

To say that she had got cold feet about that card would have been a major understatement. It had been an insane impulse and she hadn't stopped to think about what she'd been doing. Suspecting that Santino could hardly be looking forward to the staff party when it would only remind him of his father's sudden demise at Christmas, she had overflowed with sympathy for, as far as she knew, Santino had no other close relatives. And although her own family were still alive, they had emigrated to Australia and she rarely heard from them.

Even so, her far-too-emotional frame of mind the night before last was no excuse for the personal message she had inscribed on that card. She also had the sinking suspicion that Santino, who was the very image of ruthless workplace cool and efficiency, might very much have disliked receiving a huge pink envelope at the office. Surely some of the executive staff must have commented on that bright envelope? And possibly laughed, which was not something she felt that Santino would have enjoyed either.

That idiotic declaration of love had been her biggest misjudgement of all. Why had she let herself get so carried away? Why hadn't she had the wit to just sign it with only a question mark? Then the card might have been interpreted in a dozen ways and even as a harmless joke. But her statement of undying love had put that crazy card into an entirely different realm and might well rouse much greater curiosity.

Clutching a sheaf of paper and several bags of pens, Poppy headed back towards the lift, her steps slowing when she saw Santino chatting to several other men in the reception area. Her heartbeat quickened, her chest tightened, her mouth ran dry, symptoms that always assailed her when Santino Aragone was in view or even within hearing. The dark, deep timbre of his honeyed, accented drawl sent a positive tingle down her backbone. Santino could voice the most prosaic statistics and make them sound like poetry.

While pretending great interest in the supplies she was carrying, Poppy glanced up and stole a look at him. *Bang*...the full effect of Santino just exploded on her. She was entranced by the commanding angle of his dark head, the gloss of his black hair beneath the lights, the sheer height and breadth of him in a dark formal business suit that exuded classic designer tailoring. Yet when he moved he was as fluid as a big cat, and as graceful. As he turned his head to address someone she caught his profile, strong and distinctive from his lean, sculpted cheekbones to the proud jut of his nose and the aggressive angle of his jawline. His golden skin was stretched taut over his superb bone structure.

He made her ache. Just looking at Santino made her ache. As one of the bags of pens escaped the damp clutch of her nerveless fingers and fell to the floor Santino swung round and she collided with his incredible eyes, black as sloes below these harsh interior lights but the same shade as polished bronze in daylight. His gaze narrowed, spiky black lashes curling down to zero in on her. Then, instead of looking away again as she expected, he stared almost as if he had never seen her before.

It was as if time stopped dead for Poppy. Her heart was pumping blood so hard, she was as out of breath as if she had been running. There was a singing sound in her eardrums and her whole body felt oddly light and full of leaping energy. She looked back at him, wide, very blue eyes steady for possibly the very first time, and sank without trace in the glittering golden intensity of his appraisal.

Someone stooped and swept up the bag she had let fall, blocking her from Santino's gaze and breaking that spell. She focused with dizzy uncertainty on Craig Belston, absorbed the sneer etched on his self-satisfied features and almost recoiled, her fair skin reddening.

'You're making a patsy of yourself,' Craig murmured very low. 'The old dropped hanky routine went out with the ark!'

Her face tightened in shaken disconcertion. 'Sorry?'

Faint colour demarcating the hard slant of his cheekbones, Santino strode into the lift, hit the button to close the doors and left all his companions behind without even thinking about it. Poppy Bishop's hair was a vibrant golden auburn and very un-usual. Just for a moment under the lights her hair had looked quite dazzling and she had beautiful eyes. For once, although he was quite certain that it would have been something that would have jarred on him, he had not noticed what she was wearing. But he was not attracted to her; of course, he wasn't.

Poppy was an employee, he reminded himself with relief. Not even if Cleopatra joined the staff would Santino have al-lowed himself to be tempted into an unsuitable liaison. That stupid card was still on his mind, that was all! He began with cool logic to list all Poppy's flaws. She was only about five feet three and he preferred tall blondes. She was twenty-one and he liked women closer to his own age. She had such dreadful dress sense that she stuck out like a canary bird among the suits at a meeting. She talked too much, knocked things over, messed up royally on the computer on a regular basis. He was a tech-nical whizz, a perfectionist, she was an accident that just kept on happening. She was also the kind of woman men married and he would die single. The prospect of the funeral he had to attend that afternoon was stressing him out. What he ought to have was a drink.

Poppy hurried back to the marketing department and went to fetch Desmond's coffee. She was in turmoil. Why had Santino stared at her that way? Or had that just been her imagination? She was so ridiculously obsessed with him that her mind had probably played tricks on her. Why had she got this horrible suspicion that he knew she had sent that card? How could he *possibly* know? He couldn't read minds, could he?

And why had Craig attacked her that way when he usually

behaved as though she was beneath his lofty notice? For goodness' sake, what had got into him? Craig Belston never deigned
to speak to her, at least not since that first week when he had
asked her out and badgered her to the point where she had been
tactless enough to say that she had been warned about him. 'The
old dropped hanky routine'? Did Craig suspect her feelings for
Santino? But how could he?

It was madness to let her discomfiture about that wretched
card work her up into a state, Poppy told herself in annoyance.
Short of dusting the card for fingerprints and matching them to
hers, there was no way that anyone could identify the sender.
As for Craig, well, he had few friends at Aragone Systems and
was pleasant to even fewer. Brainy he might be, but he had a
nasty tongue and a habit of smirking at other people's misfor-
tunes. So it would be foolish to read anything into those snide
comments of his... Wouldn't it?

CHAPTER TWO

'NO...NO...NO!' Desmond urged Poppy in loud dismay. 'Just leave the coffee over there. I prefer to stretch my arm out!'

Although Poppy smiled like a good sport at the tide of amusement that those pointed instructions roused, she was cut to the bone. Hadn't she suffered enough yet for the episode of the spilt coffee? A lecture about safety measures with liquids from the HR manager had set the seal on her shame while she had also been reminded of her first formal warning, which had resulted from poor timekeeping in her very first month at Aragone Systems. 'One more strike and you're out,' had been the message she'd received after the coffee incident and she really was determined not to make any further blunders.

'What are you wearing to the party tonight?'

Grateful for the interruption, Poppy glanced up with a smile from the unexciting graph she had been tinkering with on her monitor. It was Lesley, a tall, slim brunette on the market research team. 'Nothing special. Just a dress.'

She listened while Lesley described her own outfit. She knew that without a doubt it would enhance every slender curve of the other woman's enviable figure. As Desmond informed her that he wanted the graphs she had been working on for a meeting, she hurried into printing them, relieved that she had finished the last one in time.

'I heard that Santino got a valentine card,' Lesley continued, and as Poppy tensed she added, 'I was more surprised to hear he didn't get a whole sackful! I bet it was from his ex trying to get back in with him.'

'Ex?' Poppy queried, relaxing again.

'Don't you read the gossip columns? He dumped Caro Hartley a month back,' Lesley informed her with authority. 'I didn't think that would last long. She's quite a party girl and I suspect Santino got bored fast. He's a very clever guy.'

'I'm sure he'll not be on his own for long,' Poppy remarked, anxious eyes on Desmond, her boss, as he treated the printed graphs to a cursory appraisal. Had she changed the colouring of the one she had first done in pink for her own amusement? Yes, she was sure she remembered doing so. Even so, she didn't lose her tension until he had slotted them into a folder.

Never, ever again would she play around with the colours of the graphs, she swore as she went into the cloakroom to freshen up at lunchtime. If it killed her, she was going to erase her every bad habit. She gave herself only the most fleeting look in the mirror. At least she had grown out of the spots and her skin now looked great. But her rippling auburn curls were a constant source of aggravation, for the little tendrils that gathered round her face ensured that her hair never looked as tidy as other women's. However, cut short her riotous curls were even harder to handle, so she kept her hair long and wore it clipped back at the nape of her neck.

Her unfashionable curves were the biggest challenge, she conceded ruefully. She was in dire need of a new, inspiring diet. The banana regime had put her off bananas for life, and the cabbage soup one had ensured that she felt queasy just passing vegetables on a market stall. No, it was back to boring old salad and yogurt, which worked but meant that she spent most of her time fantasising about food and feeling so hungry she could have munched on wood.

When she returned to her desk, the email icon was flicking on her monitor and she opened it, hoping it was a cheering communication from a friend.

'Pink graphs are inappropriate in a business environment,' ran the email.

Poppy looked at the message in shock and then glanced around herself to see if anyone was looking at her, but nobody was. Who had seen her mucking about with that graph before lunch? Who was pulling her leg? It was unsigned and the address was a six-digit number and, as such, anonymous.

'Says who?' she typed in and sent the email back. 'I like graphs in dark colours.'

'That's boring,' Poppy told her correspondent.

'Rational. Pink is a distraction.'

'Pink is warm and uplifting,' she protested in reply, typing at full tilt.

'Pink is irritating, cute, feminine...inappropriate.' That awful word, inappropriate again. Her correspondent was a guy, she decided, and certainly not Desmond, who regarded email as a time-wasting exercise and who would surely have gone into orbit the instant he saw a pink graph.

'How did you see my graph?' she typed. 'Stick to the issue.'

Poppy grinned at that rejoinder. *Definitely* a guy.

'One more warning and you could be out of work. Be sensible.' That next message came in fast on the previous one without having given her the chance to respond.

Her grin fell off her lips at supersonic speed. 'How do you know that?' she typed.

But this time, infuriatingly, there was no answer. Thinking about her mystery correspondent, Poppy conceded that quite a few people would be aware of those warnings on her employment record. The very first time it had happened she had been so upset, she had talked about it herself and, after the coffee episode, Desmond had been so furious that he had announced his intent to complain about her in such ringing decibels that most of the department had heard him.

Intrigued by those emails, scanning her busy colleagues with intense curiosity, Poppy sent several more to the same address that afternoon but still received no further response. Then she began thinking about the party that evening and wondered what she would wear, since pink had become such a controversial issue...

'I'm *AMAZED* that you're still laying on large supplies of alcohol for your employees.' Jenna Delsen's exquisite face emanated shocked disapproval as she scanned the low-lit noisy room full of party revellers. 'Daddy used to help our staff to get sloshed at our expense, too, but not since *I* joined the company. Now we have a nice sober supper do. No loud music, no dancing, no drink and everyone behaves.'

'I like my staff to enjoy themselves. It is only one night a year.' Santino suppressed the ungenerous thought that the blonde could be a pious, penny-pinching misery, for she had been welcome company at the funeral that afternoon and he had enjoyed dining with her and her father at their home afterwards.

'I suppose that's the extrovert Italian in you. You threw some very riotous parties when we were at Oxford together.' Jenna gave him a flirtatious, rather coy look as she reminded him that they had known each other since university.

In receipt of that appraisal, all Santino's defensive antenna hit alarm status. 'Let me get you a drink,' he suggested faster than the speed of light, already mentally listing the unattached executives present on the slender but hopeful thought that she might take a shine to one of them instead. They had always been friends, *never* anything else.

Jenna curved a slender hand round his arm when he returned to her side. 'I have a confession to make...for the whole of the time we were at uni together, I was in love with you.'

Santino conceded that what had started out as an unusual day, and had gravitated into being a very long day, was now assuming nightmarish proportions. 'You're kidding me.'

'No.' Jenna fixed her very fine green eyes on him in speaking condemnation. 'And you never noticed. In four *long* years, you never once noticed that I felt rather more for you than the average mate.'

In one unappreciative gulp, Santino tipped back an entire shot of brandy meant to be savoured at leisure. He was transfixed and trapped by that censorious speech. There was no polite or kind way of telling her that, beautiful and intellectually challenging as she was—for she had a first-class brain—there had been no spark whatsoever on his side of the fence.

'And I had to sit back and watch you chasing girls who couldn't hold a candle to me,' Jenna continued with withering bite.

'Oddly enough, I don't recall you sitting home alone many nights,' Santino countered sardonically.

'Once I understood that I was in love with a commitment-phobe, I trained myself to regard you only as a friend—'

'Jenna…when you first met me, I was eighteen. Most teenage boys are commitment-phobes.' Santino groaned, thinking what an absolute pain she seemed to have become, still nourishing her sense of injustice over the unwitting blow he had dealt to her ego so many years after the event. 'I was no better and no worse than most—'

'Oh, don't be so modest,' Jenna trilled in sharp interruption. 'All the girls were crazy about you! You were spoilt for choice but you deliberately chose women whom you knew would only be short-term distractions. You always protected yourself from the threat of a steady relationship and you're *still* doing it!'

When Santino went back to the bar for another drink, Jenna was so taken up with her discourse that she accompanied him. Santino's temper was on a very short leash and his second drink went the way of the first. He was cursing the innate good manners that had persuaded him that he ought to invite the blonde to accompany him to the party. He was thinking of what a very much better time he would have had mixing with his staff. Then he glanced across the room and saw a figure hovering in the doorway and the remainder of Jenna's barbed criticisms washed off him because he no longer heard them.

Noticing that she had lost his attention, Jenna followed the direction of his gaze. She saw a youthful redhead with a vibrant mane of curly hair. Small, very pretty, but not at all Santino's style. Yet Santino was so busy watching the girl that he had forgotten Jenna was there.

Scanning the crowded room, Poppy finally picked out Lesley in her distinctive white and silver dress and began to move towards her, an apologetic smile on her lips. She was a little late but then some of her colleagues had opted to stay on in the city centre and warm up in a bar before attending the party. But Poppy loved getting ready to go out at home and had known that she didn't have enough of a head for drink to have sustained a lengthy pre-party session.

'I really like that dress,' Lesley said warmly as she flipped out a seat for Poppy's occupation. 'Where did you buy it?'

'It's not new. I got it for my brother's wedding,' Poppy confided, and then added in an undertone. 'To be honest, it's my bridesmaid's dress—'

'I wish my best friend had let me wear an outfit like that for her big day. At least I could have worn it again afterwards.' Lesley admired the strappy green dress that flattered Poppy's shapely figure and slim length of leg, then drew Poppy's attention to the drinks already lined up in readiness for her, pointing out that she was very much behind the rest of them, before continuing, 'It must have been an unusual wedding.'

'My sister-in-law, Karrie, wanted a casual evening do. She wore a short dress, too.'

Poppy's attention, which had been automatically roaming the room in search of a certain tall, dark male, finally found

Santino where he stood by the bar with a spectacular blonde woman clinging to his arm. She lifted the drink that Lesley had nudged into her fingers and sipped it to ease her tight throat, but she resisted the urge to ask the chatty brunette if she knew who Santino's companion was. After all, what was the point? Did it make any difference who it was? And it was none of her business either.

Indeed, she should not even be *looking* at Santino Aragone, Poppy told herself guiltily, because looking was only feeding her obsession. Having thought over Craig's sneering remarks earlier that day, Poppy had finally faced the unhappy fact that he at least suspected that she was rather too attached to their mutual employer. That conclusion had unnerved her for Craig's reputation for making others the butt of his cruel sense of humour was well-known. So, she would have to be more circumspect in the future, for languishing like a lovelorn teenager over Santino could easily make her a laughing stock at work. In fact, she would be much better devoting her brain to sussing out the mystery identity of her email correspondent, who had to at least *like* her to have gone to the trouble of trying to give her a warning word of advice, she reflected.

'Who is she?' Jenna enquired very drily of Santino.

'Who are you talking about?' Santino asked with a magnificent disregard for the direction of his own gaze.

'The little redhead with the pre-Raphaelite hair...the one whom you've been watching for at least *three solid minutes*,' Jenna completed between gritted teeth.

'I'm not watching her,' Santino murmured with cool disdain. 'But even though you employ hundreds of young women you know *instantly* who I'm referring to,' Jenna noted with rapier-sharp feminine logic.

'Did you get out of the wrong side of the bed this morning?' Santino drawled with his sudden flashing smile. 'Exactly *why* are you trying to wind me up?'

'Before I tell you—' Jenna gave him a grudging smile of approbation for finally registering that she had been set on evening the score for past injuries '—you tell me who the redhead is and I will give you ten very good reasons why one should never, ever date an employee.'

Santino drained his drink again and dealt her a mocking glance. 'I don't need them, Jenna. All ten of them are in my mind right now.'

Returning to her table after chatting to various friends, Poppy sat down again. Lesley and two other women were chatting about Santino's date, who was evidently the daughter of the owner of Delsen Industries.

'What do *you* think of Jenna?' another, less welcome voice enquired.

Poppy's head swivelled, her startled gaze only then registering that Craig Belston had joined their table during her absence. That question had been directed specifically at her and she was gripped by discomfiture. 'Why would I think anything of her?' she answered with a determined smile. 'All the boss's girlfriends are incredible beauties.'

'Now why did I get the idea that you mightn't have noticed that?' Craig rested his pale blue probing eyes on Poppy and her mouth ran dry.

'Santino's leggy ladies are rather hard to miss.' Lesley shot a frowning glance at Santino's PA and added, 'Come on. You've been keeping us all in suspense since we finished work. Who sent Santino the naff card?'

Poppy froze and then gulped down her drink as her colour heightened.

'Did I mention that it was an *inside* job?' Craig murmured with tormenting slowness and Poppy's heart skipped an entire beat, her every tiny muscle pulling rigid.

'No, you darned well didn't!' one of the other women piped up in exasperation. 'Who on earth working for Santino would be daft enough to send him a valentine card swearing undying love? I mean, come on, *yes*, he's hugely fanciable, but he's the last guy around who would respond to that kind of blatant invitation from a member of staff.'

'You said the card wasn't signed,' Lesley reminded Craig. 'So how could you know it was sent by someone in Aragone Systems? It didn't come through the internal mail, did it?'

'Just assume that in this particular case we're talking about someone who's not very bright,' Craig invited, and Poppy's tummy began to churn where she sat. 'Someone who assumed that only a name would expose her identity.'

'You recognised the handwriting!' someone exclaimed.

'I really don't think I like this conversation very much,' Lesley remarked suddenly. 'Valentine cards are just for fun.'

'It wasn't the handwriting. It was a combination of errors,' Craig explained to the table at large. 'A distinctive perfume, a predilection for a particular colour and a love of flowers.'

Poppy was now as pale as milk and feeling physically ill with humiliation. She could not bring herself to look at any of her companions and silence greeted Craig's last explanation, an awful uneasy silence that left Poppy's nerves screaming and her skin clammy.

'Now who do we all know who wears jasmine scent?' Craig murmured.

'I don't know anyone who wears that,' Lesley chimed in, and the two other women followed her lead to say the exact same. Painfully conscious that her companions were trying to throw sand in Craig's eyes and deflect him from his target, Poppy had to grit her teeth to prevent herself from lifting her drink and throwing it at her tormentor.

At the other side of the room, Jenna was still in full confiding mode, but Santino was having a hard time dragging his brooding scrutiny from his PA's smug expression and Poppy's pale, rigid face.

'So, I hope you'll forgive me for giving you a rough time tonight,' Jenna murmured in dulcet continuation, 'but I always promised myself that some day I would tell you the truth and make you sweat for a few minutes. Will you still come to my engagement party?'

Taken aback, Santino frowned. '*Engagement* party?'

'I'm so grateful I'm not in love with you any more.' Jenna sighed. 'Didn't you hear me telling you that I'm getting engaged to David Marsh and that he's picking me up here in five minutes?'

It had been a long time since Santino had heard that much good news in one sentence; he was genuinely fond of Jenna and relief on his own behalf and pleasure on her behalf sliced through his growing tension. Realising that the blonde had merely been set on claiming a small slice of revenge for his past indifference to her, he flung back his handsome dark head and started to laugh with genuine appreciation.

The sight of Santino splitting his sides with laughter, and Jenna equally convulsed and holding onto him for support, filled Poppy with paranoia. Immediately, she assumed that Santino had told the blonde about her pathetic card and that they were laughing at her, for if Craig had guessed that she was the culprit he was certain to have told Santino. Feeling as if she had just had her heart ripped out while she was still breathing, Poppy nonetheless rose from her seat with as much dignity as she could muster, for she could not bear sitting there playing poor little victim for Craig's benefit any longer.

'You're a real Sherlock Holmes, Craig,' she said flatly. 'I'm very impressed.'

Poppy walked away fast. Tears were stinging her eyes and blurring her vision, but she kept her head high and that was her final undoing. She didn't see the small table laden with drinks in her path. She hit it with such force that the table tipped over with an enormous crash that seemed to turn every head in the room. For an instant, Poppy hovered, staring in horror at the smashed glass and liquid everywhere, not to mention the startled dancers leaping back from the mess she had created. Then her control just snapped and she fled.

'Now,' Lesley said icily to Craig, who was sniggering at Poppy's noisy exit, 'while you're wondering why Poppy's friends aren't rushing after her to offer support, watch Santino and *learn...*'

'What are you talking about?'

'Upsetting Poppy is not a career-enhancing move in Aragone Systems. You see, if you were a woman and in touch with the *real* newsbreaking gossip in this building, you would already *know* that Santino fancies the socks off Poppy, too—'

'Rubbish!' Craig snapped. 'He binned the card!'

'Did you check the bin at the end of the day?' someone enquired drily.

'Santino doesn't know what's hit him yet,' one of the other women commented with immense superiority. 'He's more at home with his keyboard than his emotions.'

'But when a bloke like Santino, who likes everything done by the book, starts telling poor Desmond that pink graphs are fresh and creative, he's in *very* deep,' Lesley completed.

In companionable and expectant silence, the three women then focused pointedly on Santino, who had stridden forward the instant that Poppy had sent the table flying. He swung round to speak to Jenna Delsen and not thirty seconds later left in the same direction as Poppy. Witnessing that demonstration, Craig turned the greyish colour of putty and groaned out loud.

CHAPTER THREE

WHEN POPPY EMERGED from the function room at full tilt, several women were entering the cloakroom across the foyer and she wheeled away in the opposite direction.

Finding herself by the lifts, she stabbed the call button with a frantic hand and gulped back a sob. She had to find a quiet corner to pull herself back together again. Selecting the marketing floor, she slumped back against the lift's cold steel wall as the doors closed. Wrapping her arms round herself, she hugged herself tight. But it was no help, no comfort, because all she could think about was what a fool she had made of herself.

When she saw the dark reception area on the marketing floor, it looked eerie and she hit the door button again in a hurry and tried another floor. Her eyes flooded with burning tears. Of course, Santino Aragone would have laughed when he was told who had sent that card. Everybody would be laughing! After all, she was just a junior member of staff, the plump little redhead Craig had nastily labelled, 'Tinkerbell' and hardly competition for the gorgeous women Santino specialised in. Why on earth hadn't common sense intervened before she'd posted that stupid card to Santino at the office? Didn't she *have* sense like other people? Her throat aching, she could no longer hold back the tears and a sob escaped her. How could she have exposed herself to that extent?

In the foyer below, Santino was watching the lights that indicated which floor the lift was at. The light flicked through the levels in descent again, made several brief stops and then sank as low as the floor above before beginning to ascend again. When the lift finally reached the executive level, he waited in taut suspense to see if it moved on again.

When the doors opened on the top floor, Poppy blinked in confusion for she had lost track. But low lights were burning and the floor was not in darkness like the others. Dimly recalling that Santino's secretary had a private washroom, Poppy stumbled out. She needed to tidy herself up and fix her face before she could go home.

But shock was still setting in hard on Poppy. Only when it was far too late to change things did she see her mistake. She *should* have toughed out Craig's insinuations. Instead she had fallen right into his trap and confirmed his suspicions. He couldn't have proved anything, yet she had virtually confessed by saying what she had and leaving the table.

Taunting, wounding images were now bombarding her mind, increasing her distress. She had left the party with all the cool of a baby elephant let loose in a drawing room. She saw Craig's self-satisfied smile, Santino laughing, the stiff, disapproving faces of the other women. Craig might as well have stripped her naked in public. Her trembling hands braced on the edge of the washroom vanity unit and, letting her head hang for she couldn't stand to look at herself in the mirror when she hated herself so much for her own stupidity, she began to sob.

Santino had never made it from the lift to his secretary's office so fast. But then those heartbreaking sobs acted on him like a shriek alarm. He would usually have gone quite some distance to avoid a crying woman, but the curious automatic pilot now overruling his normal caution ensured that he strode right through the open door of the washroom and gathered Poppy straight into a comforting embrace.

The sheer shock value of a pair of masculine arms closing round her when she had believed that she was alone provoked a startled cry from Poppy. Then she looked up and focused on Santino and even more shock froze her from head to toe. Bronze-coloured eyes set below lush black lashes were trained to hers, the lean, dark contours of his handsome features taut with concern.

'It's OK,' he soothed in his gorgeous accented drawl.

'Is it?' Poppy's voice emerged on the back of a breathless sob, for she could not have got oxygen into her lungs at that instant had her life depended on it. What was happening should have felt unreal but, in actuality, being in the circle of Santino's arms felt very real and very right. Furthermore, it was something she had been dreaming of for so long that no power on earth could have sent her into retreat.

'Course it is,' Santino asserted, not really knowing what he was talking about, then deciding it was safer to confine himself to inconsequentials rather than risk reawakening her distress. Lifting a lean hand, he curved it round the back of her head to urge her face back into his shoulder where she had started out.

Poppy's tension evaporated and she subsided against him, feeling as boneless as a rag doll. The faint aroma of whatever shaving lotion he used assailed her and immediately became familiar to her: rather exotic, distinctively male. She sucked in a steadying breath, her fingers resting lightly against his broad shoulder, yet she could still feel the flex of his lean, powerful muscles beneath the expensive cloth of his jacket as he held her close. He could be so kind. How had she managed to forget how considerate he had been when she had hurt her finger and he had taken her to hospital? A little calmer, better able to think than she had been minutes earlier at the height of her distress, she saw how unlikely it was that Santino had been nastily indulging in a good laugh at her expense with his ladyfriend. He wasn't like that.

'Let's get out of here,' Santino urged with a faint quiver of wry amusement edging his deep voice. 'This is my secretary's inner sanctum and I feel like an intruder.'

In a jerky motion, she peeled herself from him again, her colour high, her eyes lowering, for she was sure she looked a total fright after giving way to all those tears. Her nose would be pink, her eyes swollen and her mascara might have run. Not that she felt that he would care either way, but she didn't want him seeing her at her very worst. He pressed a light hand to her tense spine and turned her back into the office beyond and on into what had to be his own office.

Abandoning her in the centre of the dark room, Santino strode over to the desk to switch on the light there and indicated a door to her left. 'You can freshen up in there if you like.'

Her eyes widened at the sight of the big luxurious office and then centred back on Santino where he was poised by his desk. The pool of illumination shed by the lamp shrank the large room to more cosy contours but simply emphasised his impact. He was so tall, so wonderfully dark and vibrant. Why was it that every time she looked at Santino he seemed more gorgeous than ever? As she encountered the onslaught of his mesmeric dark golden eyes her heartbeat thudded in what felt like the foot of her throat. She reddened, suddenly all too conscious of the emotions that had got her into such a mess in the first place. Dropping her head again, she went through the door he had indicated.

Santino released his breath in a slow, sustained hiss. He would chat to her for a while just to smooth matters over and then tuck her into a taxi to go home. Concerned employer? He grimaced, picturing her standing there in that green dress that defined her lush curves, the fiery luxuriance of her glorious hair tumbling round her face, bright blue eyes full of strain. He wanted to see her usual sunny smile replace that hunted look.

He just liked her, that was all. There was nothing wrong with that that he could see.

Poppy winced when she saw her tousled reflection in the mirror on the wall of Santino's opulent washroom. Breathing in deep because her head was swimming a little, she repaired her eye make-up but didn't bother to refresh her lipstick, lest he think that she was getting tarted up for his benefit. Don't think about that valentine card, she warned herself fiercely. What was done was done and, whether he knew she had penned that card or not, he was hardly likely to mention it. Having dried her hands, she emerged again.

'Take a seat,' Santino told her.

'Don't you have to get back to the party?'

'No. I don't usually stay to the bitter end. My presence tends to inhibit people,' Santino advanced with a wry smile that lent his lean, dark face such innate charm that for several tense seconds she simply couldn't take her eyes from him. 'Would you like a drink?'

'What have you got?'

'Just about everything,' Santino informed her, deadpan. 'Come and have a look…'

Madly self-conscious of her own every move, but enervated by the novel sensation of being alone with him, Poppy moved closer, peered into the packed drinks cabinet and opted for what she hoped was the most sophisticated choice. She backed away with the glass until her legs brushed the low arm of one of the comfortable leather sofas that filled one corner. She sat down on the arm, too skittish to seat herself in the more normal way.

She watched him pour a brandy from a cut-crystal decanter, light burnishing his black hair, accentuating his hard cheekbones and the very faint blue cast of stubble already shadowing his strong jawline. She hadn't seen him when he needed a shave before and she decided that it gave him a very sexy, macho look. As he straightened he shot a glance at her and caught her staring.

'So,' Santino murmured on a casual note intended to put her at her ease. 'Where did you work before you came here?'

'I was a nanny...that's what I trained for when I left school,' Poppy advanced, her face flushed, her voice tense as she strove to match his relaxation.

'A nanny.' Santino was initially surprised and then he saw her in his mind's eye surrounded by a bunch of children and it was like the missing piece of a jigsaw puzzle suddenly sliding into place for him. Kids would adore her, he thought. She would throw herself into their games, never mind when they got dirty, fuss over them and hug them when they got hurt. Thinking of the chilly, correct sourpuss of a nanny he had had to endure as a little boy, he felt positively deprived.

'How come you ended up in Aragone Systems?' Santino prompted.

Poppy sighed. 'My first placement was with a diplomat's family and I was with them for two whole years...'

'Did they make you work endless hours for a pittance?' Santino enquired cynically.

A brief smile blossomed on her lips at that idea. 'No, they were a lovely family. They treated me very well. The problem was all mine. I got far too attached to the children and when they left England and I was no longer needed, I was just devastated,' she admitted ruefully. 'So I decided it wasn't the job for me and signed up for an office skills course.'

Within an ace of remarking that he considered that decision a wrong move on her part, Santino thought better of it when he registered that he could not imagine the marketing department without her.

'The trouble is...the career change hasn't worked out very well,' Poppy commented rather gruffly.

Santino's ebony brows pleated. 'Everyone makes an occasional mistake—'

'I've managed to pick up two formal warnings in six months.' Poppy shrugged a slight shoulder, cursing her own impulsive tongue, her habit of being too candid for other people's comfort. All she had done was bring her own failings to his notice.

Santino had to resist a strong but unprofessional urge to tell her that her head of department had been guilty of an overreaction when he'd made a complaint about her on the strength of an accident with a spilt drink. She had been unlucky. Desmond Lines was in his first week in the job, keen to make his mark and show his authority, but he had chosen the wrong event and the wrong person to clamp down on. In fact, Poppy might not know it, but that misjudged warning had even been discussed in the boardroom with varying degrees of levity and incredulity. One of Santino's senior executives had looked in mock horror at the puddle of mineral water he had left on the table and had wondered out loud if HR were going to haul him over the coals, too.

Poppy tilted her chin. 'I didn't make mistakes as a nanny.'

'But people would miss you if you weren't here.'

Colliding with glittering dark golden eyes, Poppy felt dizzy. Did he mean *he* would miss her? For goodness' sake, what was she thinking? What difference would it make to him if she went off in search of another job and moved on? She was one very humble cog in a big wheel. He was just being kind again.

Quick to recognise when a subject ought to be changed, Santino asked, 'Do you have any family living in London?'

Poppy moistened her dry lips with her drink and sighed, 'Not any more. My parents moved out to Australia about eighteen months back. My brother, Peter, and his wife, Karrie, live in Sydney.'

'What's the connection that took them all to the other side of the world?' Santino enquired lazily, lounging back with indolent elegance against the edge of his desk.

'Basically... Peter. He's married to an Australian and he was offered a very prestigious teaching post at a university out there. He's a brilliant mathematician. He was doing algebra as a toddler.' A self-deprecating smile curved Poppy's lips. 'I was still struggling to do it at twelve years old.'

'There are more important things,' Santino quipped, opting for the sympathy vote and overlooking his own stratospheric success in the same subject. 'So why didn't you emigrate to Australia with your family?'

'Well… I wasn't *asked*,' Poppy confided with a rueful grin of acknowledgement at that oversight. 'Mum and Dad just worship the ground Peter walks on. They've bought a retirement home near where he and Karrie live. Mum now looks after their house and Dad keeps their garden blooming.'

'Free labour…not bad if you can get it. Does your sister-in-law mind?'

'Not at all. Karrie's a doctor and works very long hours. She's also now expecting their first child. As an arrangement, it suits them all very well.'

'Do you have any other relatives left in the U.K.?' Santino pressed with a frown.

'An elderly great-aunt in Wales whom I visit for the odd weekend. What about you?' Poppy questioned, emboldened by that dialogue.

'Me?'

'I suppose that if you have any relatives they live in Italy,' Poppy answered for herself. 'When did your mother die?'

Santino tensed, his jawline clenching. 'She's not dead. My parents were divorced.'

Disconcerted, Poppy nodded, thinking that that was a little known fact in Aragone Systems for most people had assumed that Maximo Aragone had been a widower.

Santino drained his glass and set it down. 'I haven't seen my mother since I was fifteen.'

'How *awful*!' Poppy exclaimed, her soft heart going out to him at the thought that he had been abandoned by some hard-hearted woman.

Santino shot her a look of surprise and then added drily, 'It was *my* choice to cut her out of my life.'

At that explanation, Poppy surveyed him in sincere shock, and when he went on with complete cool to ask her if she wanted another drink, she said no. Although she suspected that what he had just confided was rather private, she could not rest without knowing more.

'Was your mother cruel to you?' Poppy asked baldly.

'Of course not. She loved me very much but she was not such a good wife to my father,' Santino advanced on a forbidding note that would have warned the more cautious off the topic.

'Oh... I see. You took your *father's* side when they divorced.' Poppy spoke that thought out loud without meaning to.

Raw exasperation currented through Santino. As if it were that simple! As if it weren't possible that he had reached such a decision on the strength of his own judgement!

The silence seethed.

Recognising that she had got too personal, Poppy turned pink with discomfiture. 'I'm sorry. It's just...you said she loved you and yet you've been *so* cruel to her.' As she registered what she had said she actually clamped a sealing hand over her parted lips and surveyed Santino's set features and flaring golden eyes in dismay and apology. 'It's time I tucked my big mouth up for the night,' she muttered through her spread fingers.

'No... I will defend myself against that charge first!' Santino countered forcefully. 'Let me tell you why I hate St Valentine's Day...'

'You...*do*?' Her hand falling back to her lap, Poppy stared at him in a combination of surprise and confusion.

'I adored my mother,' Santino grated. 'So did my father. He flew her over to Paris to her favourite hotel to celebrate St Valentine's Day and do you know what *she* did?'

In silence and very much wishing she had minded her own business, Poppy shook her curly head.

'That's the night she chose to tell him she'd been having

an affair and that she was leaving him for her lover!' Santino
ground out like an Old Testament prophet reading out the Riot
Act, raw censure in every hard male angle of his striking features.

Poppy pondered that explanation. 'She probably felt so guilty
that she couldn't help confessing... I bet she didn't choose that
night or those circumstances deliberately.'

'Whatever... Maximo was *shattered*,' Santino stressed on a
note of decided finality.

'Was he...?' Poppy compressed her lips on the question she
was dying to ask, but then discovered that she was unable to
hold it in. 'Was he always faithful to her?'

It was an issue that Santino had never before discussed and
she was coming back at him on an angle he had actually never
once considered. He stilled in angry unease, looked at Poppy's
intent face and wondered why the hell he was suffering from
a sudden need to justify a decision he had not once wavered
from in fifteen years. It had been that little word 'cruel' that
had shaken him, disturbed him in a way he could not have believed. Dark colour marked his superb cheekbones.

'You're not sure he was...are you?' Poppy whispered, recognising the rare flash of uncertainty now lightening Santino's
dark gaze. 'Yet you still judged her and not him. But then I've
heard that it can be harder for boys to forgive their mother's...
er...mistakes.'

'Tinkerbell...the *oracle*?' Santino derided with all the cutting force of his own unsettled emotions. 'That's got to be a
new one.'

Poppy flinched as though he had slapped her and every ounce
of her natural colour drained away. He had never utilised that
tone on her before, much less looked at her with a pure dismissive contempt that bit right through her tender skin to her bones
and made her feel about an inch high. And, of course, he was
right, for what did she know about such a situation? Some of
her friends had lived through their parents' breaking up but she

had no personal experience. Who was she to tell him that he had been unjust and cruel?

'You're right…' Her voice emerged slightly thickened by the stark rise of tears threatening her again and she slid off the arm of the sofa in a hurried movement. 'I can't even solve my own problems, much less tackle other people's. A-and as you've already said,' she stammered in growing desperation as she turned round in a blind uncoordinated circle, 'you don't have a problem in the first place—'

'I'm sorry,' Santino bit out in a rather raw undertone. 'Never mind. I'm hardly the world's most diplomatic person…especially after a few drinks,' Poppy mumbled, narrowly missing a sculpture on a pedestal in her haste to reach the door. 'Maybe I was even a bit jealous.'

'Jealous?' Santino echoed in incomprehension as he tracked her the whole way across his office.

'Yeah…' Poppy had to force herself to turn back. 'You said your mother loved you very much. If mine had ever loved me like that she might answer my letters more often.'

Santino groaned something in Italian and reached for her hands to prevent her from getting any closer to the door. 'Come here…' he urged thickly.

CHAPTER FOUR

SUDDENLY EXTRAORDINARILY SHORT of breath, Poppy stared up at Santino and as she met his beautiful dark golden eyes she drowned there in her own reflection.

Santino inched her steadily closer until bare inches separated them. 'I want to kiss you…'

'Seriously…?' Her wide gaze clung to his.

'I want to take you home to my bed,' Santino confessed raggedly. 'In fact, I can't think of anything else…'

Poppy blinked. It was as if a little buzzer went off in her brain and allowed her to think again. But what he was telling her was still such an enormous surprise, she just ended up staring up at him again, dark pupils dilated, moist lips parted on her own ragged breathing. He wanted to *kiss* her? That revelation wholly enchanted her. But the second was too much to handle for as yet no man had contrived to persuade Poppy either to go home with him or allow him to come home with her.

'But I'll settle for a kiss…and then supper somewhere public, *cara mia*.' Santino noted the sudden anxious expression in her gaze and the rise of colour in her cheeks with the strangest, newest sense of protectiveness he had ever experienced. He didn't know what he was doing and, for the first time in his very structured life, he realised that he didn't care.

Poppy's heart was playing leapfrog with her ribs. He was attracted to her, too? She couldn't believe it. She was achingly conscious of his hands holding hers and such a flood of happiness filled her that she felt literally light-headed with it and her throat ached. 'Kiss...' she selected her favourite option, the one she could least bear to wait for.

Santino smiled, his heartbreaking, stunning smile that lit up his vibrant bronzed features and sent her pulses racing. 'Only one kiss...otherwise I might not stop.'

'One's a bit mean,' Poppy argued. 'I've been waiting a long time for this. Oh, good heavens, you've left your girlfriend downstairs!' she suddenly gasped, her expression one of comical horror.

'Jenna's just an old friend and she's already left,' Santino assured her with a laugh of appreciation.

As relief at that explanation travelled through Poppy, Santino was already drawing her back across the office towards the corner with the sofas. It was so cool and natural the way he did it, too, that she was helplessly impressed. She couldn't dredge her attention from his lean, strong face, couldn't quite accept that what was happening was really happening. Her legs went weak under her at just the thought of his wide, sensual mouth on hers and she was so keen for it to happen, she was ashamed of herself.

'What are you thinking about?' Santino murmured silkily.

'Kissing you...' Poppy told him, but in truth she was equally enthralled by the new and more intimate side of Santino that she was seeing. It occurred to her that he was in his element, she the one floundering and following his smooth, assured lead.

'Kissing me...' Santino repeated huskily as he tugged her down onto the sofa, wound long fingers through her hair, curving them to the nape of her neck to angle her mouth up to his.

'You're good at this,' Poppy muttered, trembling with the most wicked amount of anticipation.

'Ought to be...' Santino treated her to a slashing irreverent

grin that acknowledged his own experience and her eyes clung
to his lean, powerful face, her heart hammering. 'But I've never
got this close to a woman in the office before—'

'No?'

'Feels forbidden and...*fantastic*,' Santino growled in a throaty
purr of hunger.

Poppy quivered, every skincell leaping, and when he brought
his mouth down on hers, when he hauled her close, fantastic
was in her opinion a serious understatement. She fell into that
explosive kiss as though she had been waiting all her life for it.

He captured her lips with intoxicating urgency and with sensual slowness let his tongue slide into her mouth in a darting,
probing invasion that was unbelievably exciting. Poppy had
never felt what she felt then, not that rise of inner heat or that
sudden charged impatience for more that gripped her like a
greedy vice. She couldn't get enough of his hot, hard mouth.
Every so often sheer necessity forced them to break off just to
breathe but they welded back together again fast, Santino groan-
ing low in his throat and muttering fiercely against her swollen
mouth, 'You blow me away, *cara*.'

He pulled back from her to shrug free of his suit jacket and
wrench at his silk tie to loosen his shirt collar. Sucking in a shallow, shaken breath, Poppy slumped weak as water back against
the arm of the sofa and just watched him. The tie was discarded
on the carpet beside his jacket and as he straightened he swept
her ankles up so that she was lying full length. He slid off her
shoes and let them drop as well. Poppy collided with smouldering dark golden eyes and she had never been so electrified
with sheer excitement in her entire life.

Santino ran deceptively indolent eyes over her as she lay
there all of a quiver, his attention lingering with potent appreciation on her. 'I love your hair...it's incredible and you've got
a very, very sexy mouth...'

'Don't stop talking,' Poppy whispered helplessly.

'If I talk, I can't kiss you,' Santino pointed out thickly, scanning her feminine curves in a more bold and intimate appraisal that sent the blood drumming at an insane rate through her veins. 'Problem,' she agreed, barely able to squeeze that single word out.

'Not an impossible one, *cara*,' Santino assured her in his wicked dark drawl, his intense bronzed eyes signalling pure enticement and sensual promise. 'I can think of several very interesting pursuits that I can talk through.'

The atmosphere sizzled. His smile flashed out once more and she just ached so much for contact again that she sat up, grabbed his shoulder to steady herself and found his passionate mouth again for herself. A low moan of response was wrenched from her as he suckled at her lips and then parted them to invade her mouth again.

'Thought I had to talk,' Santino teased as he lowered her back to the sofa and unbuttoned the rest of his shirt.

'No…' Her mouth ran dry as she stared up at him. He looked so big and powerful. A haze of short dark curls delineated his broad, muscular chest and his skin was the vibrant colour of bronze. Her body tensed, wild heat snaking up inside her again.

'Last time I was on a sofa with a female, I was sixteen,' Santino confided with dancing amusement in his dark golden gaze.

He lifted her up to him with easy strength and curved her round him. Cool air hit her taut spine as he unzipped her dress. He brushed down the delicate straps on her slim shoulders and released his breath in a slow, sexy hiss of appreciation as he bared her lush, pouting breasts.

'Superb…every inch of you is a work of art, *cara mia*,' Santino swore with husky fervour as a tide of shy pink washed up into her cheeks. 'Without a doubt you are the perfect reward at the end of a lousy day.'

Then he touched her and she was immediately lost in the passion again. All control was wrested from her by the seductive delight of his skilled fingers on her tender flesh and the even more intense excitement of his knowing mouth caressing the almost painfully sensitive rosy peaks. With a whimper of tormented response, she surrendered to that world of wild sensation...

CHAPTER FIVE

SANTINO WAKENED TO the buzz of his mobile phone.

Disorientated in a way that was far from being the norm for him, he sat up, realised that he was still in the office and dug into his jacket for his phone. It was a very apologetic security guard calling up from the ground floor to ask if he was still upstairs working. *Working?* Santino stole a lingering glance at Poppy where she lay fast asleep beneath the suit jacket in which he had rifled for his phone. Shame and discomfiture gripped him.

'Yes, I'm here. I'll be a while, Willis.' Discarding his mobile again, he checked the illuminated dial on his watch. It was after four on Saturday morning. His teeth gritted as he attempted to come up with a viable plan that would enable him to smuggle an admittedly very small redhead past the security guards down in the foyer. Otherwise, Poppy's reputation was likely to be in tatters by Monday.

Santino swore under his breath. How much alcohol had he consumed yesterday? There had been the pre-dinner drinks with the Delsens, the wine over the meal he had barely touched and then several brandies in succession. That kind of boozing was not a habit of his. All right, he had not been drunk, but he had not been quite sober either. Alcohol had certainly released all inhibitions and slaughtered his ethics, he conceded grimly.

He looked at Poppy again. Her gorgeous hair was a wild tumble spilling across the leather, one pale bare shoulder and his jacket. She looked adorable, totally at peace and innocent. Only, as he now had very good cause to know, she was no longer *quite* the innocent she had been *before* he laid his womanising hands on her. In the midst of examining his conscience, Santino was appalled to register a powerful temptation just to grab her back into his arms again and kiss her awake. Drink was supposed to be death to the average male libido. *Dio mio*, so much for that old chestnut!

Raking angry hands through his tousled black hair, Santino suppressed a groan. He was furious with himself. How could he have taken advantage of Poppy like that? He struggled to work out how it had happened. They had almost had an argument. He had thrown that vicious comment. She had been leaving when he'd apologised. At that instant, it had somehow seemed unbelievably important to him that she did *not* walk out through that door. Then she had said that about her mother not answering her letters and…?

Ebony brows pleated, Santino gave up on that confusing angle to concentrate on the logical facts that he was more comfortable with. She *worked* for him. Affairs between staff were officially frowned on in Aragone Systems. And guess which smartass had laid down that ground rule for the greater good of interpersonal office relationships and morale? He grimaced. She had been a virgin. He hadn't taken a single precaution. It dawned on him that the last time he had been on a sofa with a woman he might only have been a teenager, but he had exercised a lot more caution then than he had demonstrated the night before. He had screwed up, royally screwed up. In the midst of that lowering acknowledgement, which sat not at all well with his pride, he wondered whether there were still any valentine cards for sale. Finding himself wondering something so inane and out of character unsettled him even more. He breathed in very deep.

Poppy wakened to the sound of a shower running somewhere and her sleepy eyes opened only to widen in dismay when the first thing she saw was her dress lying in a heap on the carpet. A split second later, she realised that she was actually lying under... Santino's jacket! Her heart skipped a beat as she finally appreciated that she had spent most of the night in his office. In *his* arms. As the events that had led up to that staggering development unreeled in her blitzed brain like a very shocking film, she leapt off the sofa like a scalded cat. Praying that Santino would stay in the shower next door long enough for her to make an escape, she dressed at excessive speed.

Tiptoeing to the door, her shoes gripped in one trembling hand, she crept out and then raced for the lift. How could she have behaved like that with Santino? She hadn't even been out on a date with him! Sick with shame and embarrassment, she emerged from the lift and slunk out past the two men chatting at the security desk and mercifully behaving as if she were invisible. The buzzer went, though, to unlock the door and let her out, and her face was as red as a beetroot by the time she reached the street.

'She's a right little looker,' Santino's chauffeur remarked to Willis, the head security guard. A long night of playing poker together had formed an easy camaraderie between the two older men.

'She's a nice friendly kid. That's the first time she's walked out of here without saying goodnight,' Willis said. 'I suppose I can recall the rest of my team now—'

'They'll be getting suspicious if you don't. I'd better get out to the limo and look like I've been dozing. Still, at least you got them shifted before the cleaners come on. Like I said, the boss doesn't usually carry on like this.'

Minutes later, Santino strode from the lift out of breath, black hair still wet from the shower, stormy golden eyes sweeping the foyer in search of Poppy. He couldn't believe she had walked out on him without a word. As if he were some sleazebag of a one-night stand she didn't want to face in daylight! He was outraged. That kind of treatment had never come his way before. Indeed, the clinging habits of certain previous lovers had driven him near to distraction. He had never had one who'd evaporated like scotch mist the first chance she'd got.

He had had hardly any sleep…he was going home, he was going to bed and he'd call on her in the afternoon, he decided. She'd be glad to see him then. She'd appreciate him by then. He hoped she spent the whole lousy morning miserable because that was what she deserved and, in that self-righteous and ripping mood, Santino strode out of the building.

Late that afternoon, Poppy sat on the train watching the countryside fly by with eyes that were blank and faraway. In her mind all she could truly see was a lean, dark, handsome face.

It was amazing how little time it had taken to pack up her belongings and give notice on her bedsit. Everything she possessed fitted into two suitcases. But then she never had been one for gathering clutter, and money to spend on non-essential items had always been in short supply. A fresh start was the best thing, she reminded herself painfully. She could not go back to work at Aragone Systems again. Yes, she could have steeled herself to live down the gossip about that stupid card and her own silliness, but *no*, she could not put herself through the agony of seeing Santino again. She imagined he would be relieved when word of her letter of resignation finally filtered through to him.

Well, she had surely taught herself one good, hard lesson about what happened when a woman flung herself at a man. After all, wasn't that exactly what she had done? Humiliation and guilt engulfed her, for she blamed herself entirely: that childish card telling him that she loved him.

Once Santino had known who the sender was, he wouldn't

have been human if that hadn't made him curious. Craig's malice, Santino's concern and her own distress had led to a physical intimacy that would never have developed in normal circumstances. There they had been all alone in the enervating quiet of his office. No doubt even the admiring way she had looked at him had been a provocative encouragement and invitation on male terms. And she might not have much experience with men but every magazine she read warned her that, while nature had programmed women to seek a relationship, men were programmed to seek something an awful lot more basic.

While the train was speeding Poppy towards Wales where her father's aunt, Tilly, lived, Santino was having a very trying dialogue with one of Poppy's former neighbours.

'Nah…haven't seen her for weeks,' the guy with an obvious heavy hangover groused, yawning in Santino's face. 'Maybe she's in there and just doesn't want to answer the door. I had a woman who did that to me. Do you mind if I go back to bed now?'

'Not in the slightest,' Santino breathed grittily.

Santino was now in what was totally unknown territory for him. Maybe Poppy didn't want anything further to do with him. Maybe she *was* in her bedsit not answering the door and praying that he would take the hint and leave her alone. It wasn't exactly a mature response, but a woman who had retained her virtue to the age of twenty-one might well hate his guts for having slept with her when she'd been in such a vulnerable state. If she was so keen to avoid him, and her flight from his office had already brought that message home once, did he have the right to crowd her? Or was he more likely to make a difficult situation worse by pushing too hard too soon? At the end of that logical internal discussion with himself, Santino was still fighting an almost irresistible urge just to smash the door down!

Three weeks later, Poppy was shouting at Tilly's pet geese for lurking behind a gate in an effort to spring a surprise attack on the postman. But the older man was even wilier than the web-footed watchdogs and he leapt into his van unscathed, honked the horn in cheerful one-upmanship and drove off.

Poppy went back into her great-aunt's cottage, clutching the post and the newspaper. Tilly, a small, spry woman with short grey curly hair, well into her seventies but very fit and able, set her book down in favour of the paper.

'Have you got some answers to that ad you placed?' Tilly asked.

'By the looks of it, several,' Poppy answered with determined cheer. 'With a little luck, you'll be shot of your uninvited house guest within a few weeks!'

'You know I *love* having you here,' Tilly scolded.

But her great-aunt's cottage was tiny, perfect for one, crowded for two. Furthermore, Tilly Edwards was one of those rare in-dividuals who actually enjoyed her own company. She had her beloved books and her own set little routine and Poppy did not want to encroach for too long on her hospitality. Within days of her arrival at Tilly's rather isolated home, she had placed an advertisement in a popular magazine seeking employment again as a nanny.

She would take anything—short-term, long-term, whatever came up. The sooner she was working again and too busy to sit feeling sorry for herself, the happier she would be. In the minuscule kitchen, she made a pot of tea for herself and coffee for Tilly. Of recent, she herself had gone off coffee. But then she had pretty much gone off food, too, she conceded wryly, thinking of the irritating bouts of queasiness she had suffered in recent days. Obviously a broken heart led not just to sleepless nights, but poor appetite and indigestion as well. So out of mis-ery might come skinniness. She couldn't even smile at the idea.

She was grateful that she had had enough pride and sense to leave Aragone Systems, but the pain of that sudden severance from all that was familiar and the knowledge that she would never see Santino again was unimaginable and far worse than she had expected. But then it was short, sharp shock treatment, exactly what she had deserved and most needed, she told herself.

'Poppy...' Tilly said from the sitting room.

Poppy moved a few feet back to the doorway. Her great-aunt held up her newspaper. 'Isn't that the man you used to work for?'

Poppy focused on the small black and white photo. Initially the only face she saw was Santino's and then right beside him, beaming like a megawatt light bulb she recognised Jenna Delsen. 'What about him?' she prompted as evenly as she could manage, for one glance even from a distance at Santino in newsprint upset her.

'Seems he's got engaged...an attractive woman, isn't she? Would you like to read it for yourself?' Tilly immediately extended the paper.

'No, thanks. I'll take a look at it later.' Poppy retreated back into the kitchen again and knew that the glimpse she had already had of that damning photo was more than sufficient. She felt incredibly dizzy and assumed that that was the effect of shock. Bracing unsteady hands on the sink unit, she snatched in a stricken breath and shut her anguished eyes tight. *Engaged?* To Jenna Delsen only weeks after he had referred to the beautiful blonde as 'just an old friend'?

Later she went out for a long walk. The strain of trying to behave normally around Tilly had been immense. So, the man you love isn't perfect, after all, she told herself heavily. Shouldn't that make it much easier to get over him? His engagement put a very different complexion on their night together. Santino had *lied* to her. He had lied without hesitation. He was a two-timing louse, who had simply used her for a casual sexual encounter. Clearly he had already been involved in a relationship with Jenna Delsen that went way beyond the boundaries of platonic friendship.

Three days later, Santino arrived in Wales. Finding out where Poppy's only relative lived had been a long and stony road, which had entailed ditching quite a lot of cool and calling Australia several times before eventually contriving to talk to Poppy's sister-in-law, the doctor. And if Karrie Bishop ever got tired of medicine, secret police forces everywhere would vie for her services. Santino had not appreciated the interrogation he had received, and even less did he appreciate getting lost three times in succession in his efforts to find a remote cottage that he had even begun suspecting Dr Bishop might have only dreamt up out of a desire to punish him!

But there the cottage was, a minute building hiding behind an overgrown hedge, the sort of home loved by those who loathed unexpected visitors, Santino reflected with gritty black humour. His tension was at an all-time high now that he had arrived and he had to think about what he was going to say to Poppy. Oddly enough, Santino had not considered that contentious issue prior to his actual arrival. *Finding* Poppy had been his objective. What he might do with her when he found her was not a problem for his imagination in any way, but what he could reasonably say was something more of a challenge. He missed her at the office? He couldn't get that night out of his mind?

Very unsettled by that absence of cutting-edge inspiration, but too impatient to waste time reflecting on it, Santino climbed out of his sleek car in the teeming rain. When a pair of manic honking geese surged out of nowhere in vicious attack, Santino could happily have wrung their long, scrawny necks, built a bonfire on the spot and cooked them for dinner. The confident conviction that the cottage might lie round every next corner had prevented him from stopping off for lunch and he was in a very aggressive mood.

Hearing the noisy clamour of the geese announcing a rare visitor, Poppy hurried to the front door to yank it open. The car was a startling vivid splash of scarlet against the winter-bare garden. But it was Santino, sleek and immaculate in a charcoal-grey business suit, who knocked most of the air in her lungs clean out of her body.

In the act of holding his feathered opponents at bay with his

car door, Santino caught sight of Poppy lurking in the doorway
and stilled. The pink sweater made her look cuddly and the floral skirt with the pattern that made him blink was *cheering* on a
dull day, he decided, rain dripping down his bronzed features.
He just wanted to drag her into the car and drive off with her.

Shock having made Poppy momentarily impervious to his
battle with the geese, she stared back at Santino, only dimly
wondering why he was standing in heavy rain and getting
drenched. What on earth was he doing in Wales? How could
he possibly have found out where she was? She met his beautiful eyes, dark as ebony and shameless in their steady appraisal,
and she knew she ought to slam the door closed in his face. Seeing him in the flesh again hurt. It only served to refresh painful memories of how much that one night, which had meant
so little to him, had meant to her. For just a few hours she had
been happier than she had ever hoped to be, but her happiness
had flourished in a silly dream world, not in reality, and pun-
ishment had not been long in coming.

'Are you planning to call the geese off?' Santino enquired
gently. 'Or is this supposed to be a test that picks out the men
from the boys?'

Forcing herself free of her nervous paralysis, Poppy lifted
the broom by the door and shooed the geese back to allow Santino a free passage indoors.

'Grazie, cara,' Santino drawled, smooth as silk.

Her soft mouth wobbled. With an inner quiver, she recalled
the liquid flow of Italian words she hadn't understood in the
hot, dark pleasure of that night. She turned her burning face
away, but not before he had seen the shuttered look in her once
trusting and open gaze. She was ashamed of her own weakness. She knew she ought to tell him to go away, but she just
didn't have the strength to do that and then never know why he
had called in the first place. At least Tilly was out, she thought
guiltily, and she wouldn't find herself having to make awkward
explanations for his visit.

As Poppy led him into the sitting room Santino bent his dark glossy head to avoid colliding with the low lintel. The room was packed to the gills with furniture and so short of floor space he was reluctant to move in case he knocked something over.

She could not look away from him. Her entire attention was welded to every hard, masculine angle of his bold profile, noting the tension etched there but secretly revelling in the bittersweet pleasure of seeing him again. He turned with measured care to look at her, curling black lashes screening his keen gaze to a sliver of bright, glittering gold.

The atmosphere hummed with undercurrents. Her restive hands clenched together, longing leaping through her in a wildfire wicked surge. Lips parted and moist, in a stillness broken only by the crackling of the fire in the brass grate, she gazed back at him and leant almost imperceptibly forward. Santino needed no further encouragement. Body language like that his male instincts read for him. Without a second of hesitation, he reached for her. Tugging her slight body to him, he meshed one possessive hand into a coil of her Titian red curls and tasted her lush mouth with a slow, smouldering heat that demanded her response.

She was in shaken turmoil at that sensual assault, and a muffled gasp escaped Poppy. His tongue delved with explicit hunger into the tender interior of her mouth. The liquid fire of need ignited in her quivering body faster than the speed of light. She was imprisoned in intimate, rousing contact with his big, powerful length, and her spread fingers travelled from his shoulder up into his luxuriant black hair to hold him to her.

And Santino? In the course of that single kiss, Santino went from wary defensiveness to the very zenith of blazing confidence that he was welcome. Indeed, he was totally convinced that everything was one hundred and one per cent fine. He would have her back in London by midnight. Mission accomplished. Simple, straightforward—why had he ever imagined otherwise?

Then, without the smallest warning, Poppy brought her hands down hard on his arms to break his hold. She wrenched herself free of him with angry tears of self-loathing brimming in her eyes. A wave of dizziness assailed her and she had to push her hands down on the dining table to steady herself and breathe in slow and deep. There was just no excuse for her having let him kiss her when he belonged to another woman. As for him, he was even more of a rat than she had believed he was. He was a hopeless womaniser!

'What's wrong?' Santino breathed in a tone of audible mystification and indeed annoyance.

Her back turned to him, Poppy finally managed to swallow the tears clogging up her vocal cords and she stared with wooden fixity out the window at his car. 'What are you doing in Wales?'

'I had a business meeting in Cardiff earlier.' Santino had decided to play it cool. He was a step ahead of her, he believed and he was already thinking of how to present his having phoned Australia as the ultimate in casual gestures.

But Poppy took the wind right out of his sails by saying, 'I suppose my landlady gave you my forwarding address.'

Infuriatingly, so simple a means of establishing her whereabouts had not even occurred to Santino, but, ignoring that angle, he cut to the chase. 'I wanted to see you.'

He had some nerve. Did he really believe that she was still that naive? In the area on business and at a loose end on a Friday afternoon, he had decided to look her up. Why? Well, she had been free with her favours before and why shouldn't he assume that she would be again? No man could think much of a woman who let him make love to her on his office sofa for a cheap, easy thrill. Poppy felt horribly humiliated.

'I would've thought that most men in these circumstances would've been glad *not* to see me again,' Poppy countered painfully in a small voice.

Santino wondered why it was that, when she had run to the

other side of the country to avoid *him*, he was being accused of not wanting to see *her*. Suddenly he too was asking himself what he was doing in Wales. Suddenly he suspected that he could well be within an ace of making a total ass of himself.

'Why would you assume that?' Santino enquired.

'Well, if you don't know that for yourself, I'm certainly not going to be the one to remind you!' Poppy condemned chokily, for she refused to lower herself to the level of mentioning Jenna Delsen's name. She refused to give him that much satisfaction. No doubt his ego would relish the belief that she was heartbroken at the news of his engagement. Or maybe he imagined that she was still in blissful ignorance of the true nature of his relationship with the beautiful blonde.

Unable to work out exactly where the unproductive dialogue was going, Santino decided that it was time to be blunt. 'Why did you send me a card telling me that you loved me?'

If the window had been open at that moment, Poppy would have scrambled through it and fled without hesitation. Aghast at that loaded question, she went rigid.

'I don't think that's an unreasonable question,' Santino continued, tension flattening his accented drawl into the command tone he used at work. 'And I'm tired of talking to your back.'

Seething discomfiture flamed hot colour into Poppy's cheeks, but pride came to her rescue. Flipping round on taut legs, she encountered brilliant dark-as-midnight eyes and forced a dismissive shrug. 'For goodness sake…the valentine card was a joke!'

The silence that fell seemed to last for ever.

Santino had gone very still, his strong bone structure clenching hard. 'A joke…?' A flame of raw derision flared in his gaze as he absorbed that demeaning explanation. The most obvious explanation, yet one that for some reason he had never considered. 'What are you…fourteen years old or something?'

'Or something…' Her nails were digging purple welts into her damp palms while she struggled to control the wobble that had developed in her knee joints. 'It was just a stupid joke…

and then Craig got hold of it and blew it up into something else and I ended up looking like an idiot!'

'I hope you don't also end up pregnant,' Santino framed with a ragged edge to his dark, deep drawl, wide, sensual mouth compressed, the pallor of anger lightening the bronzed skin round his hard jawline. 'I doubt very much that that would strike even you as a joke.'

Poppy gazed back at him in appalled silence, her tongue cleaving to the roof of her mouth, for not once since that night had she even considered that there might be consequences. She had, without ever really thinking about it, simply assumed that he had taken care of that risk for her.

'You mean, you *didn't*…?' she began shakily.

'I'm afraid not.' Brooding dark eyes acknowledging the level of her dismay and disconcertion, Santino released his breath in a slow speaking hiss of regret. 'But I do accept that, whatever happens, the responsibility is mine.'

CHAPTER SIX

AT THAT MOMENT, Poppy wanted to curl up in a ball like a toddler and cry her heart out, for what Santino had just revealed shed a very different light on what had motivated his visit.

Since when had she got so vain that she believed Santino Aragone was so bereft of females willing to share his bed that he had sought her out in Wales? The idea was laughable, *ridiculous*! Now she was remembering his tension when he'd first arrived. Had she precipitated that kiss? Had that been her fault once again? Or just one of those crazy mishaps that occurred when people were all wound up and not really knowing how to react or what to say?

Well, it scarcely mattered now, Poppy conceded painfully. Santino had come to find her and speak to her for a very good reason, and indeed the fact that he had made the effort told her much more about his strength of character than anything else. He had been worried that he might have got her pregnant. That was the only reason he had taken the trouble to seek her out again. Most men, particularly one who had just asked or had been about to ask another woman to marry him, would have done nothing and just hoped for the best. But Santino had *not* taken the easy way out.

'The night of the party...' Santino caught and held her swift upward glance '…we had both been drinking. I have never been so reckless, but then I don't have a history of that kind of behaviour and I know that you had no history at all.'

Feverish colour flared in Poppy's tense face. She was still in shock at her own naivety, her own foolish, pitiful assumptions about why he had come to see her. It took enormous will-power for her to confront the more serious issue. Might she have conceived that night? A belated rethink on what might have caused her recent bouts of nauseous disinterest in food froze Poppy to the spot. And what about the little dizzy turns she had written off as being the results of not eating or sleeping well? *Was* it possible that she was pregnant? She had never bothered to keep track of her own cycle. How long had it been since the party? A couple of weeks, *more*? Her brain was in turmoil, refusing to function. When had she last…? She couldn't remember. It seemed like a long time ago. Santino had just delivered what had to be the ultimate male put-down. He had come to tell *her* she might be pregnant!

Poppy shifted her head in a dazed motion. 'I really don't know yet if I'm…you know… I don't know…er…either way.'

Santino took a slight step forward. She looked so much like a terrified teenager. She couldn't even find the words to talk about conception. He wanted to close his arms round her, drive out the panic and uncertainty clouding her eyes, tell her that she had nothing to worry about and that he would look after her. And then he stiffened, sudden bitter anger flaring through him, making him suppress his own natural instincts. The valentine card had been a joke, a childish, stupid joke with no sense that he could see, but then someone might have dared her to do it for a laugh. How did he know? He didn't feel as if he knew anything any more about Poppy.

In fact, the more Santino thought of how she had behaved, the more alienated he felt. She wasn't in love with him, never had been in love with him. Even a little dose of infatuation would have lasted longer than a couple of weeks. Maybe she had slept with him because she had decided it was time she acquired some experience. Whatever, her behaviour ever since had spoken for her: she didn't want to see him and preferred to forget about that night. In fact, she could not have made her feelings clearer. She had jacked in her job, left London. Exactly why had he gone to such extraordinary lengths to locate her? Had he become such an arrogant jerk that he couldn't accept a woman's rejection?

'Presumably you'll know whether or not you're pregnant very soon,' Santino drawled without any expression at all. 'If you are, please get in touch with me immediately and we'll deal with it together. Obviously I will give you my support. You know how to reach me.'

His beautiful dark eyes were still level but his detachment was noticeable and complete. Poppy could feel that change like a wall he had thrown up between them. He wanted to leave. She could feel that, too. But then why not? It hadn't been a very pleasant visit for him to have to make, she recognised miserably. It had been a waste of time too when she had been unable to tell him that he had nothing to worry about. Naturally he would be praying that there would be no repercussions from that night and that awareness prevented her from sharing her own misgivings. Why say anything when she might well be fretting about nothing?

Santino strode towards his car and then swung back for one last look at her. 'Look after yourself,' he offered gruffly.

Feeling as if she were dying inside, Poppy stood like a statue watching the car reverse out. She had the most terrible urge to run after it and tell him that, even though she ought to hate him, she still loved him. But what would he want to know that for? He *had* to be in love with Jenna.

A couple of miles down the road, Santino brought the car to a halt, buzzed down the window and drank in a great lungful of the fresh, rain-wet air. *Mission accomplished?* A raw-edged laugh, empty of all humour, broke from him. Why was he chickening out of confronting the obvious: his success scores before the sofa, and on the sofa, had been nil. Everything that had struck him as fantastic and very special had left her distinctly underwhelmed. She hadn't even offered him a cup of coffee. All the way to Wales for the privilege of being shot down in flames in the space of ten minutes!

Thinking of the stupid, naff valentine card he had bought for her, a violent miasma of emotion lanced through Santino. He just wanted to smash something. He didn't want to think about her. In fact he was determined not to think about her. Of course, she wasn't going to be pregnant! Off the top of his head, he could have named three young, healthy married couples tying themselves in knots in a desperate effort to conceive a child. The chances of his having fathered a baby in one night were slim and surely she would have known by now? He would check into a hotel, get something to eat...only he wasn't hungry any more.

So he would check into a hotel and have a lost weekend. Why? He just felt like it! He wanted to drink himself into a stupor. He was off women, really, really *seriously* off women.

Three days later, Poppy learned that she was indeed pregnant.

During the weekend, she had had to content herself with purchasing a pregnancy test kit. When the test had come up positive, she'd barely slept for the following two nights. Unsure of how reliable a home test was, she'd made an appointment at her local surgery. When the doctor gave her the same confirmation and discussed options with her, she already knew that she didn't want a termination. She loved children, had always hoped that some day she would have some of her own, but that prospect had until then existed in some dim, distant future. Now that a baby, Santino's baby, was a much more immediate reality, she also knew she had some hard thinking to do about how she intended to manage.

At first, she believed that she could steel herself to phone

Santino to tell him that she was carrying his child, but when it came to the point she couldn't face it. Santino was engaged to Jenna. Like it or not, what she had to tell him was very bad news on his terms. She had her pride too and she didn't want to risk getting all weepy and apologetic on the phone, did she? As she wasn't prepared to consider a termination, she decided that it would be less painful all round if she wrote a letter spelling out her intentions.

So, Poppy sat in Tilly's narrow little guest-room bed and tried to write a letter. But she kept on sitting there and trying to write it and failing and scrunching up her every attempt and ended up in floods of miserable tears.

Finally, she stopped trying to save face and just let her own honest feelings speak for her in what she wrote. After all, did she really want Santino to go on thinking now that the valentine card had just been a cheap, silly joke? That their baby had been conceived as a result of such a joke? Poppy cringed at that image. Some day, she would want to tell their child that she had loved his father and that truth was surely more important than her own pride.

When it dawned on Poppy that she would have to send the letter to Aragone Systems because she *still* didn't know Santino's home address and he wasn't in the phone book either, she was careful to print 'Private and Confidential' in block capitals on one corner of the envelope. Once it was in the post, she tried not to think about it. The ball was in his court now. She would just have to wait and see what happened.

During the following week she was offered interviews with two families in search of a nanny, in fact *desperate* for a nanny. Qualified nannies, it seemed, were in even shorter supply than they had been when she had first emerged from her training. But did she admit she was pregnant or not? She decided that she would be happier being honest from the outset as she would need time off to attend pre-natal hospital appointments, and then of course she would have a baby in tow. At the same time, on every occasion that Tilly's phone rang, her heart would start banging like a drum and she would think that it was Santino calling her. But Santino *didn't* call and watching the post proved to be no more productive.

But then, had she but known it, Santino never received her letter. He was in Italy when it arrived and Craig Belston was working his last day at Aragone Systems. An astute operator, Craig had recognised that his promotion prospects were slim if he stayed; Santino had been cold with him ever since the night of that party. Although Craig had found lucrative employment elsewhere, his resentment at what a little teasing of Poppy Bishop had cost him still rankled. He examined the letter, his mouth twisting at the 'P. Bishop' and return address printed on the back of the envelope. Walking over to the tall drinks cabinet, which had of recent contained nothing stronger than soft drinks and mineral water, he dropped the letter down between it and the wall and he smiled.

Within a month Poppy had left Wales and started work as a nanny again. Initially shocked that Santino had not responded to her letter, she grew more cynical as time passed. After all, his silence was in itself an answer, wasn't it? Confronted with the worst-case scenario, Santino had decided that he didn't want to know about the baby. Why had she swallowed all that impressive guff about him being willing to take responsibility? Why once again had she begun thinking of him as an essentially decent guy?

After all, Santino had lied that night about Jenna to get her onto that sofa, so, why shouldn't he have lied again? She was on her own in *every* way and, for the sake of the child she was expecting, she reckoned that she had better get used to the idea.

CHAPTER SEVEN

'YES, THAT UNIFORM looks the thing, all right. Turn round,'
Daphne Brewett urged Poppy, her be-ringed hands clasped together, an approving smile blooming on her plump, attractive
face. 'You look like a *proper* nanny now, luv. No chance of
folk mistaking you for one of those au pair girls, who work for
pocket change! What do you think, Harold?'

Her balding husband, Harold, removed his admiring gaze
with reluctance from Poppy's slim black nylon-clad ankles.
'Does anyone but the Royals put their nannies in uniform these
days?' he enquired in his refined public school accent, his tone
apologetic.

Daphne stuck her hands on her ample hips and skewered him
with one warning glance. 'Poppy's wearing a uniform... OK?'
she rapped out loudly.

Harold nodded in submission and picked up his newspaper.
Poppy, who had been toying with the idea of mentioning that
she was afraid that the fussy white apron and the frilly little
hat were *definitely* over the top, thought better of it. Daphne
had a terrible temper and Harold might be a very astute and
respected business tycoon, but he was terrified of his wife and
knew when to keep quiet. Poppy reminded herself that she was
earning an enormous salary. If pleasing Daphne meant dress-

ing like a cross between a French maid and a Victorian nurse, she would just have to put up with it. After all, Daphne had been broad-minded enough to hire a nanny who came with a very young child of her own in tow. Indeed, Daphne had been warmly accepting of what had struck other potential employers as a serious drawback.

'Right...' Having vanquished Harold, Daphne turned her attention on Poppy again. 'You have the kiddies packed and ready for two this afternoon. We're off to Torrisbrooke Priory for the weekend. That'll be a treat for you. You can look forward to seeing some real landed gentry there,' she said with unhidden satisfaction.

Poppy walked out of the drawing room. Three children were seated on the stairs: Tristram, aged ten, Emily Jane, aged eight, Rollo, aged five, all blond and blue-eyed and very unspoilt and pleasant children. Daphne Brewett might be a very domineering personality but beggars could not be choosers, Poppy reminded herself squarely, determined to make the best of her recent employment with the family.

'Well, did you tell Ma how dumb you looked?' Tris asked with rich cynicism.

Poppy shook her head in wincing apology.

'I'm not going to be seen dead with you in that daft get-up!' Tris warned her.

'It's very uncool,' Emily Jane pronounced in a pained tone. 'You look funny!' Rollo giggled. 'I like your silly hat.'

With a rueful grin, Poppy went over to the pram parked below the stairs. Florenza was wide awake, big blue eyes sparkling beneath her soft mop of tiny black curls. Poppy reached in and scooped her daughter out to take her back upstairs again. Florenza was three months old, cute as a button, and the undeniable centre of her adoring mother's world.

'Who lives at Torisbrooke Priory?' Poppy asked Tris on the way upstairs.

'Dunno. But Ma thinks the invitation's really great, so it's probably somebody posh with a title. I wish she'd just leave us at home,' he grumbled. 'She's really embarrassing in other people's houses.'

'Don't talk about your mother like that,' Poppy reproved. 'I don't like people laughing at her,' Tris said defensively.

Ignoring that, for to deny that Daphne could be both vulgar and comical in her desire to impress all with the conspicuous extent of the Brewett wealth, was impossible.

At four that afternoon, the Brewett cavalcade of limousines drove at a stately pace up the long, wooded, winding drive to Torrisbrooke Priory. A vast and ancient building appeared round the final bend. It was built of weathered Tudor brick, winter sunshine glittering over the many mullioned windows, and Poppy gazed out at it with interest. Half a dozen big cars were already parked on the gravel frontage.

A venerable butler stood at the gothic arched front door in readiness. Daphne and Harold descended from the first limo. Florenza clasped in her arms and wearing the gabardine raincoat that went with her uniform, Poppy climbed out of the second limo in the wake of the children. The third limo was just for the luggage: Daphne did not travel light.

When a very tall, dark male strolled down the steps to greet her employers, Poppy's steps faltered. It couldn't be, it couldn't possibly be! But as her shattered eyes focused on the lean, devastatingly handsome dark features that still haunted her dreams on a shamefully regular basis, she saw that it truly was...it *was* Santino Aragone! Sheer, disbelieving panic afflicted her. Was he their host? Why else would he be shaking hands with Harold? Did that mean that the priory belonged to Santino?

Daphne summoned her children to her side to introduce them. In the background, Poppy hovered. There was no place to go, no place to hide. At the exact moment that Santino registered her presence, Poppy froze, heart thumping so hard she felt sick, her taut face pale as milk. His brilliant dark eyes welded to her and just stayed there, his surprise unconcealed.

'And this is our nanny, Poppy,' Daphne trilled in full swing. 'And little Flo.'

Her blue eyes achingly vulnerable, Poppy's chin nonetheless came up in a sudden defiant tilt. What did she have to be embarrassed about? Santino was the one who ought to be embarrassed! She noted that as his piercing gaze suddenly veiled, he did not succumb to the temptation of stealing so much as a glance at his own daughter.

'Poppy and I have met before. She used to work in Aragone Systems,' Santino remarked without any apparent discomfiture. 'Let's go inside. It's cold.'

While Daphne chattered cheerfully about what a small world it was, Santino was in shock but refusing to acknowledge it. A coincidence and life was full of them, he told himself. Poppy was the Brewetts' nanny and she would be busy with their children all weekend. It was almost a year to the day *since…* No, no way was he revisiting that memory lane. A baby wailed. As Santino hadn't noticed a baby in the party, he turned his head in bewilderment, following the sound right back to source: the small bundle cradled in Poppy's arms.

'I didn't realise you had a new baby,' he said to Daphne, struggling to act the part of interested host, endeavouring to force a relaxed smile to his taut features.

'Oh, the baby's not ours.' Daphne loosed a girlish giggle, flattered by Santino's misapprehension because she was pushing fifty. 'Three was quite enough for me! Flo is Poppy's kiddy.'

At the foot of the glorious oak carved staircase where the butler was waiting to show her upstairs, Poppy stared at Santino with very wide blue eyes. What on earth was he playing at? When his startled gaze zeroed in on her with sudden questioning force, she was at a complete loss. Why was he acting so surprised? Hadn't he appreciated that pregnancies most often led to births and little babies?

'Her name's Florenza,' Tris piped up. 'Flo's just what Ma calls her.'

'Florenza...' Santino repeated, ebony brows pleating. 'It's I-talian,' Daphne told him helpfully.

Santino angled a charged scrutiny at the little squirming bundle. He was suffering from information overload. Was Florenza his child? What age was the little girl? She was wrapped in a shawl and, the way she was being held, the shawl was all he could see. She might be a newborn baby, she might be some other man's child. She *couldn't* be his daughter! Poppy would have told him, wouldn't she?

Fabulous cheekbones prominent below his bronzed skin, Santino dredged his attention from the mystery bundle, encountered a speculative look from Daphne Brewett's keen gaze and hastened to show his guests into the drawing room.

Poppy climbed the stairs in a daze, beneath which a growing turmoil of emotions seethed. Santino had been astounded when Daphne had informed him that the baby was her nanny's. He had stared at Florenza much as though she were a Pandora's box ready to fly open and cause a storm of catastrophe. A tremor ran through Poppy and her arms tightened round her tiny daughter. Why was she shrinking from facing the obvious explanation for Santino's incredulity? Evidently, Santino had assumed that without his support she would *not* continue her pregnancy. Well, how else could she interpret his shocked reaction to Florenza's existence?

Was Jenna waiting in that drawing room downstairs? Jenna in her gracious role of hostess as Santino's wife? Had they got married during the last year? At that awful thought, a cold, clammy chill slid down Poppy's spine and her sensitive tummy clenched in protest. For the first time, she regretted not having allowed herself to check out whether or not that wedding had taken place as yet. But refusing to allow herself to seek any information whatsoever about Santino Aragone's life had been a necessary defence mechanism. She had brought down a curtain on the past and disciplined herself to live only in the present.

'Is this Mr Aragone's home?' she enquired of the elderly

butler, Jenkins, whose steps were slowing with each step up the stairs.

'Yes, madam,' he wheezed and, as he was so clearly in no fit state to answer any further questions, Poppy had to content herself with that.

Three hours later, having supervised a late and riotous tea with the children that had been served in a small dining room on the ground floor, Poppy set up Florenza's bright and cosy travel cot in the nursery and tucked her up for the night. Poppy was tired. Her days started at six when Florenza wakened and she was grateful that it was her night off. Although impressing that necessity on Daphne had been a challenge, she conceded ruefully. But she was painfully aware that live-in nannies had to define boundaries or she would soon find herself on call twenty-four hours a day.

The priory was a simply huge house. Poppy reflected that she might well contrive to stay the weekend without seeing Santino again. Unhappily, she was conscious of a dangerous craving to nonetheless throw herself in his path for a showdown. He *deserved* to be told what a rat he was! Removing her elaborate uniform with a grimace of relief, she ran a bath for herself in the bathroom beside the nursery and got in to have a soak.

In the library downstairs, undercover of having announced the necessity of making an urgent call, Santino was delving in frustration through a very old book on babies. All he needed to know was what weight the average baby was when it was born. Armed with that knowledge, he might then take a subtle peek at Poppy's baby and work out whether it was within the realms of possibility that Florenza was *his* baby, too. Why not just ask Poppy? That would entail a serious loss of face that Santino was unwilling to consider.

Convinced that Poppy would be down in the basement swimming pool supervising the Brewett children, Santino strolled into the nursery on the top floor. The grand Edwardian cot was unoccupied but the lurid plastic and mesh contraption set beside it contained his quarry. Breathing in deep, Santino advanced as quietly as he could to steal a glance over the padded rim. The first thing he saw was a downy fluff of black curls and then a pair of soft blue unblinking eyes focused on him. His first startled thought was that, for a baby, Florenza was remarkably pretty.

But it was hard to say which of them was the most surprised. Santino, who had paid only the most fleeting attention to friends' babies, fully believed that infants only operated on two modes: screeching or sleeping. He had *expected* Florenza to be asleep. Aghast, he watched Florenza's big eyes flash like an intruder-tracking device, her tiny nose screwing up as her little rosebud mouth began to open.

Santino backed off fast. But even though he was bracing himself, the threatened screech never came. Instead, Florenza turned her little head to peer at him through the mesh. When he dared to inch forward again, Florenza's tiny face tensed in warning. It dawned on him that lifting the baby to gauge her weight was not a viable option. She was a really sharp, on-the-ball baby, ready to shriek like a fire alarm at the first sign of a stranger getting too close, and he didn't want to frighten her.

Wrapped in a bath towel and barefoot, Poppy glanced into the nursery just to check on Florenza before she went to get dressed and could not credit what she was seeing. Her lips parted on a demand to know what Santino thought he was doing, but the manner in which her tiny daughter was holding him at bay was actually very funny. However, she only found it funny for about the space of ten seconds. For as she studied Santino's bold, masculine profile and switched her strained gaze to Florenza's matching dark eyes a wealth of powerful emotion overwhelmed Poppy without warning. Father and daughter didn't even know each other and never would in the normal way. Curiosity might have brought Santino to the nursery, but that did not mean he had suffered a sudden sea change in conscience.

As an odd choky little gasp sounded behind him, Santino

swung round and caught only the merest glimpse of Poppy's convulsed face as she spun away and raced into the bedroom across the corridor, slamming the door in her wake.

Sobs catching in her throat, she sank down at the foot of the bed and buried her head in her arms. She hated him, she *really* hated him! She was thinking of every bad experience she had had in the months since that night they had shared, not least having been the only woman in the maternity ward without a single visitor. In addition, her parents' initially shocked and censorious reaction to the revelation of a grandchild born out of wedlock had increased Poppy's distress. Although relations had since been smoothed over and gifts had been sent, Poppy remained painfully aware that once again she had disappointed her family.

When the door opened and Santino strode in, Poppy was astonished for she had not expected him to risk forcing a confrontation in his own home. But there he stood, six feet three inches of lean, powerful masculinity, apparently so impervious to remorse that he could face her with his arrogant head high, his stubborn jaw at an angle and without any shade of discomfiture. For a timeless few seconds, she drank her fill of looking at him. He was still absolutely gorgeous, she noted resentfully, and she was ashamed to feel the quickened beat of her own heart, the licking tension of excitement and the taunting curl of heat slivering through her. In despair at her own weakness, she veiled her gaze.

'I only have one question...' Santino breathed in the taut silence. 'Is Florenza mine?'

'Are you out of your mind?' Poppy gasped.

What was he trying to do? Portray her as some loose woman, who might not know the paternity of her own child? How much lower could a guy sink than to insinuate that?

Taut as a high-voltage wire, Santino was endeavouring to make sense of the incomprehensible while resisting what had become a predictable instinct when Poppy was upset: a need to haul her into his arms that was so strong only fierce will power kept him at the other side of the room. He was also working very hard at not allowing his attention to roam one inch below her collar bone, where an expanse of smooth, creamy cleavage took over before vanishing beneath the tightly wrapped towel.

'You know very well that Florenza's yours,' Poppy splintered back at him, her bright tousled head coming up, her blue eyes angry. 'So don't you *dare* ask me a question like that!'

Knocked back by that accusing confirmation that Florenza was his child, momentarily blind to even the allurement of Poppy's exquisite shape in a towel, Santino could not immediately come up with a response. He was a father. He had a daughter. His mother was a grandparent. He was an unmarried father with a baby sleeping in a plastic playpen. His baby's mother hated him *so* much she hadn't even been able to persuade herself to accept his support, financially or in any other way...

Poppy collided with his stunning dark-as-midnight gaze and tensed at the sight of the pain and regret that he couldn't hide. 'You don't even know what to say to me, do you?'

'No...' Santino acknowledged hoarsely, lean hands coiling into fists and uncoiling only slowly again.

'I've turned up like a bad penny in the wrong place.' Poppy said what she assumed he was thinking. 'Is Jenna downstairs?'

'Jenna?' Santino echoed with a frown. 'Jenna who?'

Poppy flew upright and threw the first thing that came to her hand. A shoe thumped Santino in the chest. The second shoe caught him quite a painful clip on the ear. Poppy blazed back at him in a passion that shook him even more, 'Jenna...*who*? Jenna Delsen, your fiancée, whom you described as *just* an old friend when it suited you! You lying louse, Santino Aragone!'

Santino cast aside the second shoe, brilliant eyes narrowed in astonishment. 'I'm not engaged to Jenna. She *is* an old friend and I was a guest at her wedding last summer.'

In wordless incredulity, Poppy stared back at him, but a hollow, sick sensation was already spreading through her trembling body. He had been a guest at Jenna's wedding? Such a statement had a serious ring of truth.

Lean, strong face taut, Santino moved expressive hands in a gesture of bewilderment. 'Where on earth did you get the idea that I had got engaged to Jenna?'

Poppy snatched in a stark, quivering breath. 'It was in a newspaper…a picture of you and Jenna. It said you were engaged… er…but I never looked at it that closely.'

Santino stilled then, black brows drawing together. 'An old friend did phone me to congratulate me on my supposed engagement last year,' he recalled with an obvious effort, his frown deepening. 'The newspaper he mentioned had used an old picture of Jenna and I together and he'd misread the couple of lines below about her engagement party. Her fiancé, David, *was* named but he hadn't picked up on it.'

Silence fell like a smothering blanket of snow.

Poppy was appalled at the explanation that Santino had just proffered. Tilly had only glanced at the item because she had recognised Santino and Tilly only ever skimmed through newspapers. When her great niece had failed to display any interest in the seeming fact that her former employer had got engaged, Tilly would, in all probability, not have bothered to look back at it again. And Poppy had been far too cut up, far too much of a coward, to pick up that newspaper and read exactly what it had said for herself.

'Tell me,' Santino asked very drily, 'exactly when did you see that newspaper and decide that I was an outright liar?'

Her breath snarled up in her throat. It had been too much to hope that he would not immediately put together what she had believed him capable of doing. Squirming with guilty unease and embarrassment and a whole host of other, much more confused emotions, Poppy admitted shakily, 'Before you came to Wales…'

A harsh laugh that was no laugh at all was dredged from Santino, bitter comprehension stamped in his brooding features as he turned sizzling dark golden eyes back on her in proud and angry challenge. '*Per meraviglia*...you had some opinion of me! You decided I'd been cheating on another woman with you. No wonder you were so surprised to see me in Wales, but you didn't have the decency to face me with your convictions, did you?'

Poppy gulped. 'I—'

'I didn't have a clue what I was walking into that day,' Santino framed in a low-pitched raw undertone, treating her to another searing appraisal that shamed her even more. 'But all the time that I was trying to make sense of your bewildering behaviour, you were thinking I was a two-timing liar with no principles and no conscience!'

'Santino... I'm *sorry*!' Poppy gasped.

His lean powerful face stayed hard and unimpressed. 'You tell our daughter you're sorry. Don't waste your breath on me!'

'No...you tell her you're sorry,' Poppy dared hoarsely. 'You're the one who decided you didn't want anything to do with her.'

'I didn't even know she *existed*!' Santino's temper finally broke free of all restraint. 'How the blazes could I have had anything to do with a child I wasn't aware had even been born?'

'But I wrote to you telling you I was pregnant,' Poppy protested.

'I didn't get a letter and why would you write anyway? Why trust an important and private communication of that nature to the vagaries of the post? Why not just phone?' Santino demanded, immediately dubious of her claim that there had ever been a letter.

Poppy closed her eyes and swallowed hard in an effort to pull herself together. It was obvious that her letter must have gone astray. Only then did she recall once reading that thousands of letters went missing in the mail every year. But why that one desperately important letter? Why *her* letter? She could have wept.

'Look, I have thirty-odd people waiting dinner for me downstairs,' Santino admitted curtly. 'I don't have time to handle this right now.'

'There *was* a letter,' Poppy repeated unsteadily.

Before he shut the door, Santino dealt her a derisive look. 'So what if there was?' he derided, turning the tables on her afresh. 'What kind of a woman lets her child's whole future rest on one miserable letter?'

CHAPTER EIGHT

STRIVING TO LOOK as though she had not passed a sleepless night waiting for the phone by her bed to ring or even the sound of a masculine footstep, Poppy knocked on her employer's bedroom door and entered. 'Tris said you wanted to see me.'

Still lying in bed, clad in an elaborate satin bed jacket, Daphne treated her to a rather glum appraisal. 'Yes. It's a shame about that uniform, though. I bet you it won't fit the next nanny.'

Poppy stilled. 'I'm sorry…er…what next nanny?'

With a sigh, Daphne settled rueful eyes on Poppy. 'Santino had a little chat with me last night. Didn't he mention it?'

Her colour rising, Poppy stiffened. 'No.'

'You just can't work for us any more, luv. Once Santino told me that little Flo is his, I saw where he was coming from all right,' Daphne continued with a speaking grimace. 'Naturally he doesn't want you running about fetching and carrying for my kids!'

'Doesn't he, indeed?' Her face burning fierily at Santino's most unexpected lack of discretion, Poppy was scarcely able to credit her own hearing.

'It wouldn't suit us either.' Daphne gave her an apologetic look. 'The point is, Harold and Santino do business together.

You're the mother of Santino's kid and you working for us, well, it just wouldn't look or feel right now.'

It was obvious that the older woman had already made up her mind on that score.

'You don't even want me to work my notice?'

'No. Santino's arranged for an agency nanny for what's left of the weekend. He's a decent bloke, Poppy...' Daphne told her bluntly. 'I don't see why you should be angry with him for wanting to do what's right by you and take care of you and that little baby.'

A minute later, Poppy stalked down the corridor and then down flight after flight of stairs until she was literally giddy with speed and fury. She arrived in a breathless whirl in the main hall. Santino appeared in a doorway. He ran his lethally eloquent dark eyes from the crown of the frilly hat perched at a lopsided angle in her thick, rebellious hair to the starched apron that topped the shadow-striped dress beneath.

'Good morning, Mary Poppins,' he murmured lazily. 'Remind me to buy you more black stockings, but you can ditch the rest of the outfit.'

'Yes, I can, can't I?' Poppy hissed. 'Especially when you've just had me thrown out of my job!'

Striding forward, Santino closed a hand over hers and pressed her into the room he had emerged from. 'We don't need an audience for this dialogue, *cara*.'

'I'm surprised you care! You had no trouble last night baring my deepest secrets to Daphne Brewett!' Poppy condemned.

'Why should Florenza be a secret? I'm proud to be her father and I have no intention of concealing our relationship,' Santino stated with an amount of conviction that shook her. 'And please don't tell me that you're breaking your heart at the prospect of taking off that ludicrous uniform!'

Poppy refused to back down. 'It was a good job, well paid and with considerate employers—'

'Yet the rumour is that the Brewetts still can't keep domestic staff. Do you know why?' Santino enquired sardonically. '*Daphne.* She's wonderfully kind and friendly most of the time. But she can't control her temper and she becomes much more abusive than the average employee is willing to tolerate these days. Haven't you crossed her yet? It doesn't take much to annoy her.'

Poppy paled, reluctant to recall the older woman's worryingly sharp reproof the previous afternoon when she had been five minutes late getting the children downstairs with all their luggage.

'But then you've only been working for them for a few weeks and she'll still be wary, but I do assure you that if you had stayed much longer, you would have felt the rough edge of Daphne's tongue. She's famous for it.'

'Well, I still don't think that that gave you the right to interfere,' Poppy retorted curtly. 'I can look after myself.'

'But unfortunately, you're not the only person involved here. I want what's best for all *three* of us.' Santino surveyed her with level dark golden eyes, willing her to listen to him. 'I don't see the point in a further exchange of recriminations. Life's too short. I also want to share in Florenza's life. For that reason, I'm willing to ask you to marry me...'

Shock held Poppy still, but the way he had framed that statement also lacerated her pride. He was 'willing' to ask her to marry him? Big deal! Her first marriage proposal and he shot it at her when she was seething with angry turmoil at the manner in which he had attempted to take control of her life. Now it seemed that he had taken away her security so that he could offer her another kind of security. That of being a wife. *His wife.* Her lips trembled and she sealed them.

'Possibly I messed up the delivery of that,' Santino conceded as the tense silence stretched to breaking-point. 'I *do* want to marry you.'

Poppy spun away to gaze out the window at the rolling parkland and mature trees that gave the priory such a beautiful setting. Of course, he didn't *want* to marry her! In Daphne's parlance, Santino was offering to do 'the right thing' by her. He had got her pregnant and he saw marriage as the most responsible means of making amends. He was really lucky that she wasn't the sort of female who would snatch at his offer just because he was rich, successful and gorgeous. Or even because she still loved him, she conceded painfully.

Poppy flipped round to meet Santino's intense dark scrutiny, her face tight with strain. 'Our relationship has only been an ongoing catastrophe,' she framed unevenly.

His jawline clenched. 'That's not how I would describe it—'

'When you called on me at Tilly's, you said pretty much the same thing,' Poppy reminded him. 'I ended up on that sofa because you had had too much to drink and you regretted it. That's no basis for a marriage and, anyway, I don't want to be married to some guy who thinks it's his *duty* to put a ring on my finger!'

'Duty doesn't come into this.' Santino groaned in sudden exasperation. 'We made love because I couldn't keep my distance from you, because I couldn't help myself, *cara*—'

'Yes, but—'

'Just looking at you burns me up. Always did…*still* does,' Santino intoned, striding forward to close his lean hands round hers. 'That's not a catastrophe, that's fierce attraction. If you hadn't worked for me, we would have got together a lot sooner.'

'I can't believe that…' But even so, it was an assurance that Poppy longed to believe.

Santino reached up and whisked the frilly hat from her hair and tossed it aside.

'What are you doing?' she whispered.

The sudden slashing smile that she had feared she might never see again flashed out, lightening his lean, dark features and yanking at every fibre of her resistance. He undid the apron, removed it with careful hands and put it aside, too. Then he unbuttoned the high collar of her dress.

'You want me to prove how much you excite me?' Santino

enquired with husky mesmeric intensity, molten golden eyes scanning her with anticipation. 'Ready and willing, *cara mia*.'

A little quiver of sensual response rippled through Poppy's taut frame. 'Don't...'

'Don't what?' Santino asked, flicking back the collar to press his lips to the base of her slender throat, sending such a shock wave of instantaneous response leaping through her that she let her head tip back heavily on her neck, her untouched mouth tingling, literally aching for the hungry heat of his. 'Don't do *this*...?'

He discovered a pulse point just below her ear and lingered there. She trembled, heard herself moan and she grabbed his jacket for support, feeling herself drowning in the melting pleasure she had worked so hard to forget. Then, he framed the feverish flush on her cheekbones with spread fingers and kissed her just once, hard and fast, demanding and urgent, leaving her wanting so much more.

'Now do you believe I really want you?' Santino breathed raggedly.

Poppy stumbled back from him, lips still throbbing and body still thrumming from that little demonstration against which she had discovered she was without defence. He could turn her into a shameless hussy with incredible ease, but he didn't *love* her. 'It wouldn't work...us, I mean.'

'Why not?'

'Don't you know how to take no for an answer?' Poppy muttered shakily from the door.

'I took it the last time. It gained me a daughter of three months old whom I have still to meet.' As Santino made that raw retaliation Poppy's discomfited gaze slewed from his and she left the room and was relieved when he didn't follow her, for he had given her a lot to think about.

Getting changed into jeans and a sweater, Poppy put Florenza in her buggy and went out for a walk. She was starting to see that all she had ever done with Santino was think the worst of his motivations and run away as fast as her legs could carry her. Twelve months ago, she had still had a lot of growing up left to do. So many misunderstandings might have been avoided had she not performed a vanishing act after the staff party. She had reacted like an embarrassed little girl, afraid to face reality after the fantasy of the night. Scared of getting hurt, she had ended up just as hurt anyway. She had assumed that everything that had happened between them had somehow been *her* fault and had denied them both the chance to explore their feelings.

Poppy sat down on a fallen log below the trees. In the same way she had just accepted that Santino was engaged to Jenna Delsen and had hidden behind her pride rather than confront him. But what she could forgive herself for least was the conviction that Santino was a liar and a cheat when he had never been anything but honest and straight with her.

How much could she still blame Santino for effectively getting her the sack? She understood all too well his angry impatience and his need to take control when she herself seemed to have made such a hash of things. He had made it clear that if she conceived his child, he would stand by her. What good had it been for her to talk about a letter that he had never received? Had he got the chance, he would have been a part of Florenza's life from the start. And that was why he was asking her to marry him. Her wretched pride had made her too quick to refuse that option. After all, she loved Santino, could not imagine *ever* loving anyone else...

Fifty feet away, Santino came to a halt to study Poppy on her log and Florenza snuggled up in her buggy. Poppy did not look happy. The marriage proposal had not been a winner. But then he had not promoted his own cause by depriving her of her employment, had he? However, an ever-recurring image of Poppy sailing away in a Brewett limo the following day never to return had driven him to a desperate act. He had known exactly what he'd been doing, he acknowledged grimly. He had cut the ground from beneath her feet in a manoeuvre calculated to make her more vulnerable to his arguments.

Glancing up and seeing him, Poppy froze. Dressed in tan chinos and a beige padded jacket that accentuated his black hair and olive skin, Santino looked stunning. Her mouth ran dry. Should she admit that she'd been a bit too hasty in turning him down?

'Won't your guests miss you?' she asked as he dropped down into an athletic crouch to look at Florenza.

'Country house guests entertain themselves and most of them are still in bed. As long as I show up for dinner, nobody's offended,' Santino told her, resting appreciative eyes on his baby daughter. 'She's something special, isn't she?'

In a sudden decision, Poppy reached into the buggy and lifted Florenza free of the covers. Santino vaulted upright, looking ever so slightly unnerved. 'I've never held a baby before. It might upset her.'

'She's a very easy-going baby. Just support her head so that she feels secure.'

Santino cradled Florenza in careful arms. He looked down into his daughter's big, trusting blue eyes and then he smiled, a proud, tender, almost shy smile that made Poppy's eyes glisten. 'She's not crying. Do you think she sort of knows who I am?'

'Maybe…' Her throat was thick.

'And maybe not, but she can learn.' Santino studied Poppy with sudden, unexpected seriousness. 'Let's hope that Florenza never does to me what I did to my own mother. I'm in your debt for what you said the night of the party about me having taken my father's side when my parents divorced.'

Poppy blinked. 'How in my debt?'

'I went over to Italy to see Mama and found out what a pious little jerk I'd been,' Santino admitted with a rueful grimace. 'I blamed her for the divorce and she didn't want to ruin my relationship with my father by telling me that throughout their marriage he'd had a whole string of casual affairs. I just wish he'd been man enough to admit that to me, instead of going for the sympathy vote to ensure that I chose to live with him when they broke up.'

Knowing how close he had been to his father, Maximo, Poppy muttered, 'I'm sorry...'

'No. Don't be.' Santino smiled. 'Thanks to what you said, my mother and I are getting to know each other again.'

Poppy was delighted at that news. 'That's brilliant!'

'I would never be unfaithful to you,' Santino informed her in steady continuation, and then his wide sensual mouth curved in self-mocking acknowledgement. 'I'm even working on my narrow-minded response to pink graphs...'

Poppy froze at that teasing conclusion. 'That was *you*...that emailed me the day of the party?'

'Who did you think it was?' Santino glanced at her in surprise before hunkering down to settle their sleeping daughter back into her buggy with gentle hands.

It meant so much to Poppy to know that that teasing exchange had been with him. Her heart just overflowed, and when Santino sprang back up again he was a little taken aback but in no mood to complain when Poppy flung her arms round him and hugged him. 'I think I might just want to marry you, after all,' she confided. 'Is the offer still open?'

'Very much,' Santino breathed not quite levelly, unable to drag his gaze from her happy, smiling face and absolutely terrified that she might change her mind. 'How do you feel about getting married next week in Italy?'

Her lashes fluttered up on shaken blue eyes. '*That*...soon?'

'I'm really not a fan of long engagements,' Santino swore with honest fervour.

'Neither am I,' Poppy agreed with equal conviction, her heart singing, for there was something very reassuring about a guy who just couldn't wait to get her to the altar.

CHAPTER NINE

WALKING BACK TOWARDS the priory, Santino said with smooth satisfaction, 'I'll feel a lot more comfortable when you sit down to dinner with my guests this evening.'

At that prospect, Poppy's eyes widened in dismay. 'But I can't do that. I came here as the Brewetts' nanny and what are people going to *think* if I suddenly—?'

'That you're my future wife with more right than most to grace the dining table.' Impervious, it seemed, to the finer points of the situation, Santino exuded galling masculine amusement.

'Well, it can't be done. I didn't bring any dressy clothes. I've got nothing but jeans!' Poppy exclaimed.

'If that's the only problem...we'll go out and get you something to wear right now, *cara mia.*'

Nothing pleased Santino so much as solving problems with decisive activity. The village a few miles away rejoiced in a very up-market boutique. It took him only twenty minutes to run Poppy there, stride in, select a short, strappy, soft blue dress off the rail, which struck him as absolutely Poppy, and herd her into the changing room, paying not the slightest attention to her breathless and shaken protests.

Inside the cubicle, Poppy stared at her reflection dreamily in the mirror and wondered how Santino had managed to pick the right size and a shade of blue that looked marvellous with her hair. Then she looked at the price tag and almost had a heart attack.

'Poppy…?' Santino prompted from the shop floor.

Poppy emerged. Santino had Florenza draped over one shoulder and looked for all the world like a male who had been dandling babies from childhood. Impervious to the sales woman oozing appreciation over him, he studied Poppy with shimmering dark golden eyes that made her cheeks fire with colour and her heart pound like a manic road drill.

'We'll take the dress,' Santino pronounced without hesitation. 'What about shoes?'

Before Poppy could part her lips Santino was requesting her opinion on the display, and within minutes she was trying a pair on. When she reappeared in her jeans, two women were clustered round Santino admiring Florenza and his deft touch with her. By the sound of the dialogue she could hear, he was showing off like mad. Both shoes and dress were removed from her grasp and paid for with Santino's credit card without her having any opportunity to speak to him in private.

'Do you have any idea how much that little lot cost?' Poppy whispered in total shock as they settled back into the limo.

Santino gave her an enquiring glance. 'No.' Poppy told him.

Santino looked surprised. 'A real steal…'

'It's a fortune!' Poppy gasped.

'Allow me to let you into a secret,' Santino teased in the best of good humour. 'I'm not a poor man.'

Back at the priory, it was a further shock to discover that her possessions and Florenza's had been moved from the nursery wing to a magnificent guest suite on the first floor. 'Are you sure I'm supposed to be here?' she asked the butler, Jenkins.

'Of course,' he wheezed.

Poppy urged him to sit down. He looked shifty and muttered, 'You won't mention this to Mr Santino, will you?'

'Well, I...' Poppy felt the old man really ought not to be working in such a condition.

And then Jenkins explained. He lived alone and he had been in retirement for five years, but he'd missed the priory and his old profession terribly. At his own request, Santino had allowed the old man to come back to the priory and relive what he termed the good old days on occasional weekends and he very much enjoyed that break. Touched by that explanation and by Santino's understanding, Poppy said no more.

Dinner was not at all the ordeal she had imagined it might be. But then she had always enjoyed meeting new people, and from the instant she entered the drawing room and Santino's dark and appreciative gaze fell on her she also felt confident that she looked her best. Late evening, Santino came upstairs with her and went into the dressing room off her bedroom to look in on his sleeping baby daughter. His lean, dark face softened, his sensual mouth curving. 'It's extraordinary how much I feel for her already,' he confided.

A discomfiting little pang assailed Poppy and she rammed it down fast. How could she possibly be envious of the hold Florenza already had on her father's heart? After all, he was marrying her for their daughter's sake. Keen not to dwell on that painful truth, she said awkwardly, 'You know, I really can't see how we can possibly get married this coming week. It takes ages to organise even the smallest wedding.'

'The arrangements are already well in hand, *cara*,' Santino delivered with a slashing grin that made her mouth run dry. 'Early Monday morning we fly over to Venice where a selection of wedding dresses will await your choice. There is nothing that you need do or worry about. I just want you to relax and enjoy yourself.'

'It sounds like total bliss,' Poppy admitted, thinking of the weighty responsibilities and decisions that had burdened her throughout the previous year when she had had nobody to rely on but herself.

'I have a question I meant to ask you earlier,' Santino declared then. 'Exactly when last year did you write to me to tell me that you had conceived our child?'

Her brow furrowing in puzzlement, Poppy told him. His eyes flared gold and then veiled.

'What?' she prodded, unable to see the relevance of that information so long after the event.

Santino shrugged, lean, strong face uninformative. 'It's not important.'

Ultra-sensitive on that issue, Poppy was taut, and in receipt of that casual dismissal she flushed. She was convinced that he had to believe that there had never been a letter in the first place and that she was merely trying to ease her conscience and fend off his annoyance by lying and pretending that there had been. And how could she prove otherwise?

'I'm tired,' she muttered, turning away.

Lost in his own suspicions of what might have happened to that letter and determined to check out that angle as soon as he could, Santino frowned. He could not imagine what he had said to provoke the distinct chill in the air, but caution prevented him probing deeper. Once they were married, caution could take a hike, but he was determined not to risk a misstep in advance of the wedding. Saying goodnight, much as if he had only been seeing an elderly grandparent up to bed, he departed.

Disconcerted, Poppy surveyed the space where he had been and her dismayed and hurt eyes stung with hot tears. The very passionate male, who had sworn she was an irresistible temptation earlier in the day, had not even kissed her. Had that plea just been a judicious piece of flattery aimed at persuading her to marry him so that he could gain total access to Florenza? Or was he just annoyed at the idea that she might be fibbing about that wretched letter? And if that was the problem, how was she ever to convince him that she *had* written to him?

Made restive by her anxious thoughts, Poppy got little sleep and, after feeding Florenza first thing the following morning, fell back into bed and slept late. Finally awakening again, she went downstairs to find Santino surrounded by his guests. A convivial lunch followed and then the visitors began to make their departures. Only then appreciating that she still had to pack up her possessions at the Brewetts' home, Poppy slipped away to speak to her former employer and decided that it would be simplest for her to return home with them and see to the matter for herself.

'I'm catching a lift with the Brewetts to go and collect my stuff,' Poppy informed Santino at the last minute.

'I can drive you over there,' Santino offered in surprise. 'No, I thought it would be easier if I left Florenza here with you,' Poppy confided with a challenging sparkle in her gaze, although she rather suspected the female domestic staff would soon help him out with the task.

Santino was merely delighted that he would retain a hostage as it were to Poppy returning again and proud that she felt that he could be trusted. In fact, his keen mind returning to a concern that had been nagging at him all morning since he had called his secretary at her home and spoken to her, he knew exactly what he intended to do during Poppy's absence.

Three hours later, in a triumphal mode, Santino hauled his office drinks cabinet out from the wall and swept up the still-sealed and dusty envelope that lay on the carpet. He resisted the temptation to tear Poppy's lost letter open then and there. He would surprise her with it. They would open it together. Maybe that way, he would feel less bitter at the high cost of Craig Belston's mean and petty act of malice.

'If it hadn't been for you being there, I'd have hammered that little jerk,' Santino informed Florenza, where she sat strapped in her baby carrier watching him with bright, uncritical eyes. 'Then maybe not,' he acknowledged for himself in reflective continuance. 'He was so scared he *was*... I suppose I have to watch my language around you. But then you don't know any Italian curse words, do you?'

Florenza was asleep by the time he got her slotted back into the limo. Santino was really pleased with himself. He was naturally good father material, he was convinced of it. She hadn't cried once, not even when it had taken four attempts to change her and his chauffeur, a long-time parent, had mercifully intervened with a little man-to-man advice on the most effective method. They had tea at the Ritz where she was very much admired. She glugged down her bottle of milk like a trooper and concluded with a very small ladylike burp that he didn't think anyone but him heard.

'We're a real team,' Santino told Florenza on the drive home, and around then it occurred to him to wonder how Poppy planned to get herself back to the priory. With a muttered curse, he rang the Brewetts only to discover that she had already gone.

Right up until Poppy had left the Brewetts' with her cases in a taxi, she had expected Santino to call and say that he would come and pick her up. Instead she'd had to catch the train. But when she saw him waiting on the station platform to greet her at the other end of her journey, a bright, forgiving smile formed on her lips.

'I ought to grovel, *amore*,' Santino groaned in apology, looking so gorgeous that there was little that she would not have forgiven. 'It didn't even cross my mind that you don't have your own transport.'

'I expect you were too taken up with Florenza.'

'We did have quite a busy afternoon,' Santino admitted with masculine understatement. 'And when we get back to the priory, I have a surprise for you.'

The very last thing, Poppy expected was to have her own letter set before her like a prize. She was gobsmacked. 'Where on *earth* did that come from?'

'I phoned my secretary this morning. She actually remembered your letter arriving the day before she went off on holiday last year because she noticed your name on the back of the envelope. That week, *I* was in Italy mending fences with my mother.' Santino's strong jawline hardened. 'And Belston was working his last day at Aragone Systems—'

'Craig?' Poppy was still transfixed by the sight of that dusty, *unopened* letter, and her fingers were twitching to snatch it up and bury it deep somewhere Santino could never find it. At one level, she was at a total loss as to what Craig Belston could have to do with the miraculous recovery of a letter that had gone missing almost a year earlier, but on another level she was already recalling with shrinking, squeamish regret the horribly emotional outpourings of her own heart within that letter. It was wonderful how what could seem right and appropriate in the heat of the moment could then threaten utter humiliation eleven months on...

'Yes, Belston. The minute I worked out that time frame, I was suspicious. So, I called at his apartment this afternoon and was fortunate enough to find him home—'

Poppy blinked in growing disconcertion, but Santino was far too caught up in his recital to notice her taut pallor. She was cringing at that very idea of him reading that letter while she still lived and breathed. Here they were on the brink of a marriage of very practical and unemotional convenience and pride demanded that she strive to match that challenge. But he would undoubtedly die of embarrassment *for* her if he was now confronted by those impassioned pages that declared how instantly, utterly and irrevocably she had once fallen in love with him.

'I really don't know why you would've thought Craig might remember anything about one stupid letter,' Poppy muttered abstractedly, regarding the item with all the aghast intensity of a woman faced with a man-eating shark.

'He had a grudge against you and he's a coward,' Santino informed her with expressive disgust. 'I had the advantage of surprise today. He was so taken aback by the sight of Florenza and I—'

'You took Florenza with you to call on Craig?' Poppy squeaked, her expectations of Santino taking yet another beating. 'I wasn't going to leave her behind when I'd promised to take care of her,' Santino pointed out with paternal piety. 'The minute I mentioned the letter and got tough, Belston spilled the beans about what he had done with it. He threw it behind a piece of office furniture where it's been ever since. Mind you, it shows you how the cleaners cut corners.'

Poppy winced. 'What a nasty, low thing to do…oh, well, all's well that ends well and all that,' she added breathlessly, snatching up the envelope and endeavouring to scrunch its fat proportions in one hand. 'I'm glad the mystery's been solved but time has kind of made this letter redundant.'

'I still want to read it…' Questioning dark golden eyes pinned to her, Santino extended an expectant hand.

Poppy turned very pale and bit her lip and closed her other hand round the crumpled envelope as well. 'I really don't want you reading it now…'

'Why?'

As the taut silence stretched Poppy chewed at her lower lip in desperation. Santino tensed, a cool, shuttered look locking his darkly handsome features. What the hell had she written? A total character assassination directed at him? The news that she hated him for taking advantage of her naive trust and over-looking contraception and never, ever wanted to lay eyes on him again? His taut mouth set hard. Self-evidently, the letter she had penned was of the poisonous and destructive ilk.

'So I won't open it, but it's still mine,' Santino heard himself counter with harsh clarity, and no sooner had that foolish offer left his lips than he regretted it.

Intimidated by the tone of that announcement, Poppy handed over the envelope with a reluctance that he could feel. Santino smoothed it out between long, lean fingers. 'I believed that we could read this together, that you'd be pleased I had the faith to believe that you'd sent it,' he continued in angry bewilder-ment. 'For the first time in my life, I feel pretty damned naive!'

Most unhappy to see him in possession of what was indisputably *his* letter, Poppy lowered her head. 'It's not the sort of thing we'd want to read together,' she mumbled in considerable mortification. 'What did you say to Craig?'

'Nothing repeatable but I didn't hit him.' Santino's dark drawl was rough-edged. 'I wanted to kill him…only not in front of Florenza.'

'Oh…' Poppy was shattered by that blunt admission.

'You see, I thought he'd cost us our chance of happiness.' Santino welded his teeth back together on the rest of what he had almost said, which was that, in his volatile opinion at that instant, *she* had just done that most conclusively. There was so much he had longed to ask and learn about those months they had spent apart, and that she could not be honest about her feelings then angered him and made him feel shut out.

'We have some forms to fill out to satisfy the wedding legalities,' Santino continued grittily. 'Then I've got some calls to make.'

He didn't even laugh when she confided that her middle name was Hyacinth. Before he went off to make those phone calls, Poppy shot a glance at his grim profile and gathered all her strength to ask, 'Are you still sure about this…sure you want to go ahead and marry me?'

'Of course, I am sure.' Having fallen still at that sudden question, Santino shook her by tossing the letter back on the table in front of her. 'Keep it. As you said, the passage of time has made it redundant.'

Poppy went up to her imposing bed and cried. What had gone wrong? Where had the wonderful warmth and intimacy gone? Surely a silly, outdated letter should not create such tension between them? And she knew that she had said and done the wrong thing. Even though it would have mortified them both beyond bearing, she should have let him have that letter…

CHAPTER TEN

AT FIVE THE following afternoon after an incredibly busy day, Poppy stood out on a Venetian hotel balcony entranced by the magical scenes taking place on the quays and the canal below.

A group of masked men and women in superb medieval costumes were boarding a launch outside the imposing *palazzo* opposite. A Harlequin and a Pierrot passed by in a gliding gondola, their outfits blessing them with total anonymity. On the quay, a trio of children, dressed up as a clown, a milkmaid and a comic spotty dog were whooping with delight over the firework display streaking through the heavens above the rooftops. Venice at carnival time: noisy, colourful and so full of bustling, vivid life that the very air seemed to pulse with mystery and the promise of excitement.

'You are pleased to be here with us?' A designer-clad little dynamo of a lady of around sixty, Santino's mother, Dulcetta Caramanico, emanated vivacity and natural warmth.

'I have had the most wonderful day...' Poppy admitted with sincerity. 'And I can't thank you enough for the fantastic welcome you have given us.'

Poppy had not expected to meet her future in-laws alone, but urgent business had forced Santino at the eleventh hour to accept the necessity of his coming out on a later flight. Greeted at the airport by Santino's mother and Arminio, his charming step-father, Poppy and Florenza had been wafted on to their motor launch and across the lagoon into the city of Venice. They had brought her to their hotel but it had taken her most of the day to work out that the older couple indeed owned an entire chain of international hotels, famed for their opulence, legendary customer service and exclusivity.

From the instant Dulcetta and Arminio had laid eyes on them, Poppy and Florenza had been treated as though they were already a much-loved part of the family circle. Florenza had been the star of the party. The luxurious suite of rooms allotted to them would have been at home in a palace. That morning, the Caramanicos had taken them to St Mark's Square to see the Flight of the Little Doves that officially opened the carnival, and after lunch Dulcetta had escorted Poppy to a fantastic bridal salon where a huge array of glorious gowns and accessories had awaited her inspection.

Dulcetta was delighted by Poppy's freely expressed gratitude, and her fine dark eyes shone with happy tears. 'It is a joy to please you, Poppy. You brought my son home to me and now you are even making him smile again. When Santino first visited me last year, he didn't confide in me but I sensed how very unhappy he was at heart.'

Poppy hung her bright head, wondering how low she would sink in the popularity stakes when Santino arrived in Venice looking as grim and detached as he had the night before at the priory.

'Santino may have inherited Maximo's looks and business acumen,' his loving mother continued. 'But inside, Santino is much more emotional and caring than ever his father was. So will you wear the dress for me this evening and surprise my son?'

Poppy focused on the utterly over-the-top eighteenth-century-style silk, brocade and lace gown on the dress form that awaited her and a rueful grin tilted her generous mouth. 'Just you try and stop me getting into the carnival spirit!' She laughed in spite of her aching heart. 'It's such a fantastic outfit…'

Maybe, even if Santino believed that she looked ridiculous, he would at least smile at the effort she was making, Poppy thought when Dulcetta had left her. Tears prickled her eyes as she removed her make-up and freshened up with a bath. Only a few days before her wedding, she ought to be the happiest woman alive. After all, she was about to marry the man she loved…but a man who would not be marrying her had it not been for their daughter's birth. Santino adored Florenza though, and he would make a wonderful father. It was just selfish of her to want the moon into the bargain.

Santino had already been alienated by her foolishness over the letter and it had finally occurred to her that he might even have got the impression that what she had written was unpleasant in some way. His unashamed anger with Craig, his belief that the other man had cost them the chance of happiness the previous year, had shaken Poppy when he'd voiced it, but at the time she had been too enervated to appreciate what Santino had *really* been telling her. Too busy conserving her pride and protecting herself from embarrassment, she had neglected to note that Santino had been making no such pretences. It shamed her that he should be so much more open and unafraid than she was. He had told her how attracted he was to her, shown her in his anger what he believed Craig Belston had stolen from them, for without his spiteful interference they might have been together much sooner…

And what had she done? Let Santino continue thinking that the valentine card had been a joke. She had saved face at every turn and given not an inch because the memory of her own adoring generosity the night of the party still mortified her. Yet it had been a wonderful night of love and sharing and wasn't it time that she acknowledged that? It didn't matter that he didn't love her. He cared, he certainly *cared*. From now on, she swore that would be enough for her.

While Poppy was anxiously owning up to her sins of omission, Santino, who had just arrived in his own suite next door, was confronting *his* as well. He needed to squash the conviction that he deserved a woman who saw him in terms of being the sun around which her world resolved. Poppy was not in love with him but that was only the beginning of the story, *not* the end. Ego might urge him to play it cool, but playing it cool was not advancing his own cause in any way, was it? For a start, he had been downright childish about that letter, he conceded with gritted teeth. Her determination to prevent him from accessing material that would damage their present relationship had been sensible. Just as Santino *still* recalled every word Poppy had affixed to that valentine card almost twelve months earlier, so he knew that he would have been haunted for ever more by the accusations he imagined had to be contained in that letter.

Anchoring the glorious feathered head-dress to her upswept Titian hair took Poppy some time. Dulcetta and Arminio had invited her to dine with them and a maid was to come upstairs to sit with Florenza. Poppy attached the glittering diamanté-studded mask to her eyes and surveyed herself. The emerald-green gown had theatrical splendour and the neat low-cut bodice flattered her lush curves in a way that made her blush. Yet she felt her own mother would not have recognised her, a stray thought that hurt just a little for she had decided not to tell her family about her wedding until after the event. At such short notice and with flights from Australia and accommodation in Venice during the carnival being so expensive, it would have been impossible for her parents to attend their daughter's special day. But in her heart of hearts, Poppy had also feared to put what she deemed to be already strained affections to the test.

When the knock on the door sounded, Poppy hurried to answer it before Florenza, who had just gone to sleep, could awaken again.

Disconcerted that it was Santino, whom she had believed might not arrive much before midnight, she fell back an uncertain step. Intent golden eyes pinning to her, he murmured something in husky Italian and his heartbreaking smile slowly curved his handsome mouth. As ever, he looked devastatingly dark, vibrant and attractive.

Her breath caught in her throat, for she had truly wondered if Santino would ever smile at her again. Her heartbeat picked up tempo and a flock of butterflies flew free in her tummy, but she held her head high, firmly convinced he would not recognise her at first glance.

'Poppy...' Santino said without a second of hesitation.

'I thought you wouldn't know it was me!' Poppy wailed in helpless disappointment.

As he closed the door his wonderful smile deepened. 'I would know you anywhere. In any light and any disguise.'

'You'll be able to dine with your mother and stepfather, after all.' Feeling foolish, Poppy reached up and unfastened the diamanté mask to set it aside.

'No. I called them from the airport and expressed our mutual regrets.' Santino's expression was now very serious. 'We need to be alone so that we can talk.'

Poppy tensed in sudden apprehension. It was as if he had pushed a panic button. Suddenly she feared he was as keen to cancel the wedding as he had been to cancel the family dinner. 'Santino...'

'No, let me have the floor first...' Santino dealt her a taut look from his beautiful eyes, his raw tension palpable. 'I haven't been straight with you. I haven't been fair either—'

'You're stealing my lines...' Poppy sped past him to snatch up her handbag and withdraw the much-abused letter, which she thrust at him in near desperation. 'I didn't think how it must've looked when I wouldn't let you read it, but it is *your* letter—'

'Stuff the letter,' Santino groaned, not best pleased to have been interrupted just when he had got into his verbal stride and setting it straight back into her unwilling hand. 'It's unimportant. What matters is that I tell you how I feel...but you're not likely to be impressed by the news that you had blown me away in Wales before it dawned on me that I was in love with you.'

In the act of ripping in frustration into the envelope for herself to produce a thick wad of notepaper, Poppy stopped dead and viewed Santino with huge, incredulous blue eyes. She couldn't possibly have heard *that*, she told herself. In fact she must have been dreaming…

'*Porca miseria*…in advance of that day, strange as it may seem,' Santino disclaimed with touching discomfiture and a look that was a positive plea for understanding in his strained dark eyes. 'I just had no idea why I was always coming down personally to the marketing department, why the day seemed a little brighter when I saw you, why I just *liked* you, why I started finding fault with every other woman I met…have you anything to say?'

In shock, Poppy shook her head.

'Your very first day when I took you to hospital after you hurt your finger,' Santino reminded her doggedly, lean, strong features taut, 'I demonstrated how macho I was by passing out at the sight of the needle coming your way. Yet even though you were a real chatterbox and all my staff would have fallen about in stitches had you told them about that episode, you kept quiet. That was remarkably restrained of you…'

'I wouldn't have d-dreamt of embarrassing you at work.' A great rush of answering love was surging up inside Poppy and playing havoc with her speech.

'I know, *amore*…' But his shapely mouth only semi-curved. 'I was furious when my marketing head overreacted to that stupid cup of coffee. I was so protective of you, and then at the party, when Belston was scoring points off you, I could've ripped him apart! And when we were together in my office and I finally had you all to myself, it was more temptation than I was capable of withstanding—'

'I felt like I'd thrown myself at you…' Poppy shared painfully.

'Who stopped you from leaving? Who kissed you? Who made all the *real* moves?'

Only then did Poppy appreciate that the prime mover had been him. 'But you had been drinking—'

Santino groaned out loud. 'I was just making excuses for myself. That night nothing had ever felt so right to me and I knew exactly what I was doing, but the next day I felt appallingly guilty for seducing you—'

'I sneaked off because I thought it was all my fault—'

'And I was furious about that. I called round at your bedsit that afternoon—'

Poppy winced. 'Oh, no…you just missed me…'

'I suspected you were home and just not answering the door because you didn't want to see me—'

'I wouldn't have done that.'

'Then I had to phone round half of Australia to track down your sister-in-law, Karrie, to find out where you were. Didn't she tell you about my call?'

Even though her heart was singing, Poppy had paled. 'Yes, but I just assumed it was because you were really worried I might be pregnant 'cos at that stage I still believed you were engaged to Jenna. Santino… I think you ought to take a look at this letter of mine before I get so mad with myself that I scream!'

But Santino had other ideas. She was still listening and her lovely eyes were soft and warm and it had been a day and a half since he had last touched her. Tugging her into connection with his lean, powerful length, he brought his mouth swooping down with unashamed hunger and urgency on hers, and for timeless minutes she clung, every fibre of her being alive with joyful excitement and the wondrous relief of knowing herself loved.

Pausing to snatch in a ragged breath, gazing down into her shining eyes, Santino muttered, 'Sooner or later, I'll find the magic combination of making you love me back…if only you hadn't hated me when you were in Wales—'

'I didn't—'

'I was devastated for weeks after that. I tore up the belated valentine card I had searched high and low for—'

'You bought me a card?' Poppy was touched to the brink of tears.

'Signed it with an unadventurous question mark...the guy with few words. All I could think about was getting you back to London. I didn't understand I loved you until that day...'

Her throat thickened. Stepping back, she handed him the letter. 'Well, I always knew how I felt about you, but I'll forgive you for that.'

With perceptible reluctance he accepted the letter, and then as he scanned the first few lines with a frown such a stunned look began to form on his lean, strong face that she had to suppress a giggle. Suddenly he was glued to every page with total, focused concentration.

'It's a...it's a love letter...a wonderful, fantastic love letter,' Santino finally vocalised with a roughened edge to his deep voice.

'It wasn't meant to be, but when I learned I was expecting your child I wanted you to know that my card hadn't been a cheap joke—'

'I should skin you alive for having lied to me, *amore*.' But as at that point Santino was looking at her with wondering, loving intensity, she was in no danger of taking offence. 'I *still* have that card you sent me locked in my office safe. I pretended it wasn't there so that I didn't have to dump it!'

He followed that confession up with a beautiful sapphire engagement ring that took her breath away. Then he looked in on their infant daughter and smiled at her peaceful little face before he strode into his own suite next door to don the very rakish matching eighteenth-century outfit his romantic mother had laid on for his use that evening. The burgundy velvet surcoat, lace cravat and tight-fitting breeches and boots gave him an exotic and dangerous appeal that thrilled Poppy no end. For a while, all he wanted to talk about was what it had been like for her to carry their daughter during those months apart from him. Then they ended up in each other's arms again and Santino pulled back and announced that they were dining out.

'Oh...' Poppy mumbled in surprise.

'We're not going to share a bedroom until we're married, *amore mio*,' Santino swore. 'It's the only way I can *ever* hope to live down that sofa.'

So he took her out into the city where he had been born and they dined in an intimate restaurant by candlelight, both of them so busy talking, both of them so incredibly happy that they had a glow about them that drew understanding and envious eyes.

On Poppy's wedding day, the early morning mist was lifted by sunlight.

She had actually forgotten that it was Valentine's Day, but then a giant basket of beautiful flowers and a glorious card covered with roses and containing a tender verse arrived. Inside, Santino had written those three little words that meant so much to her, 'I love you', and even *signed* it. So, it started out a fantastic day that just went on getting better and better.

She had only just finished her breakfast and was feeding Florenza when someone knocked on the door and her whole family—her mother and father and Peter and Karrie and her little nephew, Sam—trooped in. She couldn't believe her eyes. Santino had flown them out at his expense and they were staying in the same hotel. He had arranged that in secrecy for her benefit and she loved him even more for that sensitivity. All the awkwardness she might have felt in other circumstances with her family evaporated straight away and, watching her mother's eyes glisten over Florenza and enveloped in a hug by her father and her brother, Poppy was content.

Her mother and her sister-in-law helped her dress, enthusing over her exquisite ivory gown with its hand-painted hem of delicate pastel roses. A magnificent tiara and drop earrings arrived with a card signed by Santino. Tucked into a velvet-lined gondola for her passage to her wedding, Poppy felt like a princess. But when she saw Santino turn from the altar in the wonderful old church, that was when her heart truly overflowed with happiness.

The reception was staged in a superb ballroom and there were masses of guests. The bridegroom and the bride were so absorbed in each other that their guests smiled and shook their heads in wonderment. They watched them dance every dance in a world of their own and then depart for their honeymoon.

Late that night in Santino's hideaway home in the wooded hills of Tuscany, Poppy lay in their incredible medieval bed draped with crewelwork drapes and surveyed her new husband with an excusable degree of satisfaction.

'Just to think you were falling in love with me all those weeks I worked for you…and I hadn't the foggiest idea.' Poppy sighed blissfully and reckoned that low self-esteem was likely to be a very rare sensation in her future.

'Neither had I,' Santino quipped, dark golden eyes resting on her with adoring intensity as he gathered her close again. 'But I missed you so much when you weren't there. I love you, *amore.*'

'I love you, too. But just to think of *me* almost breaking *your* heart, it's heady stuff—'

'You are revelling in your power,' Santino groaned in teasing reproach.

Wearing an ear-to-ear grin, Poppy nodded in agreement, for finding out that he had never, ever been in love before, no, not once, made her feel that providence had kept him safe for her. They chatted about whether or not they would return to Venice for a night or two, checked on Florenza and congratulated each other on having created such a truly wonderful baby. All too soon they melted back into each other's arms and kissed and hugged, both of them feeling as though they were the very first couple ever to discover that amount of love and revelling in their happiness.

* * * * *

Rafael's Proposal

Kim Lawrence

MODERN

Power and passion

KIM LAWRENCE lives on a farm in rural Wales. She runs two miles daily and finds this an excellent opportunity to unwind and seek inspiration for her writing. It also helps her keep up with her husband, two active sons and the various stray animals that have adopted them. Always a fanatical reader of books, she is now equally enthusiastic about writing. She loves a happy ending!

CHAPTER ONE

THE DOOR OF the lift was just closing when Maggie Coe slipped in.

'I've been trying to catch you all day, Rafe!' she cried breathlessly. 'I want to run something by you.'

Rafael Ransome didn't consider a lift a suitable place to conduct business conversations, especially when he was on his way home after working twelve hours straight to persuade the intransigent CEO of an ailing electronics company that awarding himself and the senior management team a fifty-per-cent pay rise while simultaneously laying off production staff wasn't the best strategy to ensure the long-term future of the firm!

Ninety-nine out of a hundred people would have been able to deduce his feelings from the discouraging expression on his striking dark features, but Maggie Coe was not one of the ninety-nine.

Rafe ran a hand over the dark stubble on his normally clean-shaven jaw and grimaced. Her tunnel vision made Maggie an asset professionally, but it was a real pain in the rear when all you wanted was a hot shower and a cold drink.

'It looks like you have me for the next sixty seconds.' Coincidentally the same time, according to his disapproving mother, of his longest *relationship* to date.

Despite the shaky start, about thirty seconds into her pitch Maggie had his full attention.

'So effectively all she'd be doing is sorting mail.' Typically Rafe cut to the chase. 'Is that right—?'

Maggie Coe nodded, too pleased with herself to note the steely tone of disapproval that had entered his deep voice. 'And licking the odd stamp,' she added with a smile of satisfaction.

She looked up with every expectation of seeing her boss looking dumbstruck with admiration that she'd come up with the perfect solution to a troublesome problem—the problem in question being Natalie Warner, a young woman who couldn't seem to get her priorities right.

They didn't need an employee who was going to turn up late if her child had a snuffle, even if she did always scrupulously make up that lost time and more. The fact that moreover she didn't complain when she was regularly allocated an unfair proportion of the tedious, boring tasks didn't cut any ice with Maggie. As far as she was concerned, if they tolerated such a *laissez-faire* attitude they were at risk of setting a dangerous precedent, and, as she had told Mr Ransome, before long everyone would be strolling in when it suited them.

In short, anarchy.

Even though she couldn't see his expression Maggie had no doubts that a man who valued efficiency as much as Rafael Ransome, and who furthermore was capable of being as ruthless as he deemed necessary to achieve it, shared her view.

The silent lift came to a halt at the required floor, but Rafe pressed a button to prevent the door opening and turned back to the woman beside him.

'Do you not feel that opening envelopes is a waste of someone with her qualifications?' he questioned his zealous subordinate mildly. Those who knew him best would not have been fooled by the casual tone, but Maggie was blissfully blind to any signs of danger in the cold eyes or in the nerve pulsating in his lean cheek.

'Well, I'm hoping she'll think so,' came the smart reply.

Rafael's eyes narrowed thoughtfully. Maggie was prone to seeing things in terms of black and white, but she was a normally fair-minded person. Her hostility for this young woman seemed almost personal, which wasn't like her.

Natalie Warner, he reflected grimly, seemed to have a knack for aggravating people. She had certainly got under his skin... not in a personal way, of course—he made it a rule never to mix business with pleasure. It was just he hated to see talent wasted and Natalie Warner had buckets of the stuff, even though she seemed determined not to use it.

'So you're hoping that she'll be humiliated and resign...?' A child could have seen exactly what Maggie's tactics were.

'That's her choice, but let's just say I wouldn't try and stop her.'

She sounded so complacent that it took Rafe several seconds to control the sharp flare of fury that washed over him. It was ironic that the person on whose behalf he felt so angry wouldn't have felt even slightly grateful if she'd known she had aroused his dormant protective instincts.

An image of a heart-shaped face floated in the air before his eyes, a rare distracted expression entered the densely blue—some said cold—eyes of the man who was famed for his single-minded focus. Natalie Warner barely reached his shoulder and looked as fragile as delicate china, but the likeness was highly deceptive. Any man whose chivalrous instincts were aroused by her appearance would be well advised to repress them unless he fancied an earful of abuse for his efforts—he'd seen her in action and had felt sympathy for the man foolish enough to imagine she needed any special favours.

Rafe admired independent, spunky females—*admired* but avoided involvement with. At this point in his life he wasn't into high-maintenance relationships. But Natalie Warner wasn't just self-reliant, she was the sort of prickly, pigheaded female who wouldn't have asked for a glass of water if she were on fire just to make a point.

'Have you considered that she could have a good case of constructive dismissal if she wanted to take it farther?'

Maggie quickly assured him she had covered this. 'Her job title will be the same, and there will be no drop in her salary. The content of her job would even be the same on paper.' The older woman shrugged. 'So she can't claim she's been demoted.'

'This is in fact a sideways move,' Rafael mused drily. 'Exactly.'

So much for the sisterhood he was always hearing about. 'It doesn't bother you that she's a single parent with a child?'

This time even Maggie couldn't miss the steel in his voice. She blanched as his long lashes lifted from the sharp angles of his razor-sharp slanting cheekbones to reveal disapproval glittering in his deep-set eyes.

'Bother me?' she echoed, evincing confusion while she did some fast thinking. It was becoming clear that, far from being pleased with her ingenuity, Rafe was inexplicably furious—in that quiet but devastating way he had. 'In what way?' she questioned, desperately trying to retain her composure in the face of the displeasure of a man she deeply admired and whose approval she craved.

'Don't play the innocent with me, Maggie,' he drawled, an expression of simmering impatience stamped on his classically handsome features.

'You say yourself that there's no room for sentimentality in the workplace,' she reminded him with a hint of desperation.

'I rather think you might be taking that quote out of context,' he returned drily.

Maggie flushed. 'So you want her to stay where she is?'

Do I...?

Ironically his life would be a lot more comfortable if he let Maggie install the distracting thorn in his side in some dark cupboard. He sighed; as tempting as it was, he couldn't let her do it. God, sometimes he wished he weren't a good guy.

'You will not hide Natalie Warner away in some Godforsaken back room, Maggie.' Firmly he spelt out his instructions so there would be no convenient misunderstandings. 'Neither will you move her anywhere without my *personal* say-so.' He saw the alert expression appear on Maggie's face and wished he had omitted the *'personal'*. The last thing he wanted was that sort of rumour starting up again.

A while after Natalie had started at Ransome it had come to his attention that there had been whispers that he'd been taking a particular interest in their smart new recruit. He blamed himself for not having foreseen his actions could have been interpreted that way—he knew all too well how people's minds worked.

He could still remember the hurt look of surprise on her face when she'd come to him excited by an idea she'd had, and he had cut her dead—he had made sure there had been plenty of people to witness the snub. It had been a case of being cruel to be kind. Even if the affair had been fictitious, the rumour that she had made it, not on talent, but because she was sleeping with the boss, would haunt a woman through her career.

'You will carry on treating her exactly the same way you do all the other trainees,' he elaborated quietly. 'Do I make myself clear—?' He lifted one brow questioningly and the woman beside him gulped and nodded.

Having made his point, he allowed the door to open and stood aside to let her pass. 'Incidentally,' he called after her, 'there's a meeting scheduled next month to discuss flexible working hours.' Or at least there would be once he'd asked his PA to organise it. 'You might like to ask around to see what the level of interest would be in a crèche.'

The last of Natalie's co-workers had left an hour earlier, laughingly predicting how many valentine's cards they would receive. 'Are you doing anything special, Nat?' asked the young

woman who had just boasted that her boyfriend had booked
them a table at a really swish restaurant—and was pretty sure
he was going to propose.

'I'm going to a wedding,' Natalie explained.

'How romantic, getting married on Valentine's Day!' someone exclaimed enviously.

Then someone else asked the question Natalie had hoped
they wouldn't.

'Anyone we know, Nat?'

'Mike, my ex-husband, is getting married to his girlfriend,
Gabrielle Latimer...the actress.'

'Your *ex*!'

'Oh, God, she's *gorgeous*!' someone else breathed, only to
be elbowed by the guy standing beside her.

'Personally,' someone else remarked, 'I don't think she'll
age well—now, if she had *your* cheekbones, Nat...' Everyone
looked at Natalie and nodded. 'And I read the other day she's
had a boob job.'

Natalie smiled. She appreciated the loyal attempt to make
her feel better but, like the others, she knew that when it came
to looks she couldn't even compete in the same league as the
younger girl.

Natalie would have actually preferred to spend Valentine's
Day having root-canal work than attending the wedding of the
century, but her daughter, Rose, who was to be a bridesmaid,
had flatly refused to attend if Mummy wasn't there, too.

At least Luke would be there for moral support.

With a sigh she set about reducing the pile of paper on the
desk. When half an hour later Luke Oliver put his good-looking blond head around the partition that separated her from
the rest of the large office she had made good inroads into the
backlog. 'You're working late, Luke,' she observed as the rest
of his body followed suit.

'I'm not the only one—after Brownie points?' he teased
lightly.

'There wouldn't be any point, would there?' Natalie felt guilty when Luke looked embarrassed by her dry observation. 'I'm making up for a late start,' she admitted hurriedly. 'Rose had another asthma attack last night.' Natalie pinned an upbeat smile on her face as Luke's good-looking face creased with sympathy. 'Fortunately I managed to get her an early appointment at the doctor's this morning, but they were running late and by the time I'd finally got her settled with Ruth it was almost eleven.'

'How is she?'

'She's loads better this morning, thanks.' Even so it had torn Natalie apart to leave her fragile-looking daughter. It was a guilt thing, of course. Rose had been more than happy to stay with Ruth, who doted on her and was more than capable to cope with any crisis.

'So now you're working twice as hard as everyone else to prove you don't expect any special favours just because you're a single mum,' Luke suggested perceptively.

Natalie gave a rueful smile and rotated her head to relieve the tension in her neck and shoulders. 'You know me so well, Luke.'

Luke's glance dropped to the delicate, clear-cut features lifted to him—features made nonetheless attractive by dark smudges of fatigue under the wide-spaced, darkly lashed hazel eyes and lines of strain around the wide, softly curving lips.

'Not as well as I'd like…' he sighed huskily.

Natalie's smile morphed into a wary frown as she registered the suggestive warmth in his expression; she'd thought they'd got past all that stuff. 'You know that I'm not…' she began wearily.

Luke sighed and held up his hand. 'Sorry, I know I said I wouldn't go there, Nat, but…' his attractive smile flashed out '…you might change your mind?'

'No, I won't change my mind.' Natalie hardened her heart against Luke's hurt puppy-dog look. 'And anyway, you know as well as I do that office romances never work.' She smiled to lessen her rejection. 'Besides, there's no room in my life for a man.' Or for that matter much for anything but work and sleep, and not too much of the latter when Rose wasn't well!

'Have you told little Rose yet about Mike moving to the States?'

Natalie rubbed the faint worried indentation between her feathery eyebrows and shook her head. 'Nope. I suppose I should before the wedding?' *What am I doing asking a child-less bachelor advice on child-rearing when I already know the answer?* she thought begrudgingly. 'But I just don't know how she's going to react.' *Liar!* She knew Rose would react like any other five-year-old when she learnt the dad who spoilt her rot-ten every other weekend—when he turned up—was moving halfway around the world—*badly!*

Luke shifted uncomfortably. 'Actually it's about the wedding I wanted to have a word, Nat.'

His next words confirmed that the shiver of apprehension snaking down her spine was justified.

'I hate to do this to you, but Rafe has put me on the Ellis account; he's sending me to New York for a couple of weeks.' He tried to sound casual about this amazing opportunity and failed miserably.

'Congratulations.'

'Thanks, Nat. It should be you that's going, though.'

Natalie shook her head and pinned on a smile. Only a real cow would begrudge someone as nice and genuinely talented as Luke a break like this. 'You deserve it, Luke,' she assured him warmly.

'I'm afraid it means...'

'You won't be able to come to the wedding with me,' she completed, unable to totally disguise her dismay behind a sunny smile. 'That's fine, don't worry,' she added stoically.

She wasn't surprised that Luke had said yes; when Rafe *asked* hungry young executives like Luke they never said no. In fact, she brooded, people in general don't say no to him...*except me*. These days she didn't rate cosy chats with His Lordship, as the blue-blooded heir to a baronetcy was called—sometimes affectionately, sometimes not!—behind his back. Which just proves, she told herself wryly, that there is a bright side to having a career that's going nowhere.

On paper she and Luke had the same qualifications, they had even begun working at the top-notch management consulting firm within weeks of one another, but ten months on Luke had his own office and she was still sitting at the same desk doing routine stuff that she could have done asleep.

Things weren't likely to get better either. You didn't get offered a chance at Ransome twice and Natalie had, after much soul-searching, refused hers. Luke, who hadn't had to weigh his desire for promotion against the problems of child care, had not said no to his.

The rest, as they said, was history. She'd made her choice; she didn't consider herself a victim—lots of women managed to have high-flying careers and babies. Clearly she didn't have what it took.

'God, Nat, I'm really sorry.'

'It's not your fault,' Natalie soothed a guilty-looking Luke. 'It's *that* man,' she breathed, venom hardening her soft voice as she contemplated the grim prospect of attending the marriage of her ex to the glamorous Gabby without the support of a passable male to give the ego-bolstering illusion she had a well-rounded life. 'I don't suppose it even occurs to Rafael Ransome that some people actually have a life outside this place!'

'*Nat*, he's not that bad.'

'*Bad!* The man's a cold-blooded tyrant! I'm surprised he doesn't make us sign our contracts in blood,' she retorted with a resolute lack of objectivity. 'Forget all that stuff you read about him in the glossy supplements,' she advised Luke, imaginatively expanding her theme. 'He might have turned this place into one of the top management consulting firms in Europe virtually overnight—the success of the nineties...'

To Luke's amusement she proceeded to dismiss one of the

most spectacular financial successes of the decade with a disdainful sniff.

'And have every top company beating a path to his door, but I've always reckoned he was born in the wrong century.'

Luke looked amused. 'Sounds like you've given the subject some thought?'

'Not especially,' Natalie responded hurriedly. 'It's just obvious that underneath the designer suits—'

'You've not given that much thought either, I suppose.'

'Most certainly not!' Natalie denied, insulted by the suggestion she was in the habit of mentally undressing her boss. '*Sure* you haven't. So what *do* you think goes on under his designer suits, Nat?'

'I think there lurks the soul of a feudal, your-fate-is-in-his-hands type of despot. I can just see him now grinding the odd handful of peasants into the ground.'

Her voice lost some of its crisp edge as an intrusive mental image to match her words flashed into her head. In her defence, Rafe Ransome, his well-developed muscular thighs covered by a pair of tight and most likely historically inaccurate breeches, was enough to put the odd weak quiver into the most objective of females' voices.

Unlike Natalie, most women were not normally objective about her employer's looks; his mingled genes—Italian on his mother's side and Scottish on his aristocratic father's side—had given the man an entirely unfair advantage in the looks stakes.

'Nat!'

Natalie was too caught up in her historical re-enactment to hear the note of warning. 'On his way to burn down his neighbours' castle and ravish the local maidens...'

Like the modern-day equivalent, his victims probably wouldn't have put up much of a fight, she thought, contemplating with disapproval the inability of her own sex to see beyond a darkly perfect face of fallen angel and an in-your-face sensuality.

It struck her as ironic, when you considered he was set to inherit a centuries-old title and the castle that went with it from his Scottish father, that Rafael Ransome, all six feet three of him—and most of it solid muscle—looked Latin from the top of his perfectly groomed glossy head to the tips of his expressive tapering fingers.

Even she, who wasn't into dark, dynamic, brooding types, had to admit that if you discounted his disconcertingly bright electric-blue eyes Rafael looked like most women's idealised image of a classic Mediterranean male. Dark luxuriant hair that gleamed blue-black in some lights, golden skin stretched tautly over high chiselled cheekbones, and a wide, sensually moulded mobile mouth…just thinking about the cruel contours caused a shudder to ripple through her body and she hadn't even got to his lean, athletic body!

'Natalie!'

It was Luke's strangled whisper that finally made her lift her unfocused angry eyes from the computer screen, filled by now with row after row of angry exclamation marks.

Oh, God!

Even before Natalie heard the inimical deep mocking drawl the back of her neck started to prickle and her stomach gave a sickly lurch. Why, she wondered despairingly, hadn't her selective internal radar, selective as in it only spookily zapped into life when His Lordship was in the vicinity, kicked in a few moments earlier?

Her wide eyes sent an agonised question to Luke, who almost imperceptibly nodded.

I must have done something really terrible in a previous life, she thought.

CHAPTER TWO

'EMPLOYMENT LAW BEING what it is these days, I generally have to satisfy myself with the odd formal written warning, Ms Warner.'

As an alternative to ravishment?

The unbidden image that accompanied her maverick and fortunately silent response made Natalie's skin prickle with heat. She shook her head slightly as if to physically dislodge the breathless, tight feeling that made her head buzz. Being ravished, even hypothetically, by the owner of the most blatantly sensual lips she was ever likely to see was somewhere Natalie was not going.

'See you, Nat! And good luck,' Luke hissed.

And I'll need it, she thought wistfully, watching Luke making one of the fastest exits she'd ever seen—discretion obviously being the better part of valour as far as he was concerned, and who could blame him?

Still, at least there would be nobody to see her grovel, she thought dully. She took a deep breath and, squaring her slender shoulders, resolutely pushed aside a tide of self-pity that threatened to engulf her—she only had herself to blame. If you were going to bad-mouth your boss a sensible person took a few basic precautions first, such as checking he wasn't within hearing distance!

I can do humble... I *can* do humble, she silently mouthed. Even, she mentally added, if it chokes me! If I feel myself getting bolshy all I have to do, she told herself, is think about that enormous electricity bill I found sitting on the doormat yesterday.

Maybe she was worrying over nothing—for all she knew he might see the funny side to this. Did dynamic workaholics have a sense of humour?

Gripping the arm rests of her chair so hard her knuckles turned white, she slowly swivelled her chair and raised a weak smile. Underneath she felt the same prickly feeling of antagonism she always did when in his vicinity.

'Oops! You weren't meant to hear that.' She heard with dismay a high-pitched giggle emerge from her lips. You're meant to be upbeat, not manic, she berated herself silently. God, why do I always act like a total idiot when he's around? Perhaps it was a case of doing what he expected? His attitude said he expected her to do something stupid, and she generally obliged—even if it was only tripping over her own feet!

Rafe, his beautiful mouth set in a stern straight line, raised one dark, slanted brow; beneath his heavy, half-closed lids his eyes glittered like cold blue steel. He was looking down his aristocratic nose at her because, along with the fearfully smart brain and the incredible film-star looks, Rafael Ransome was also arrogant and élitist. With his pedigree, she reflected sourly, it was not to be wondered at.

The silence was shredding her nerve endings. If he didn't say something soon she might start confessing to stuff she hadn't done! Say something even if it is sneery and sarky, she quietly muttered to herself.

Her wish was almost immediately granted.

'Such flights of fantasy, Ms Warner...' he drawled in a voice that was both sneery and sarky enough to satisfy the most demanding consumer. 'Should you ever decide to commit them to paper I have a publisher friend who would be happy to cast a professional eye over them.'

Was that his way of saying she was in the wrong job? No, a brutal 'you're not up to it' was more his style.

'I really don't think they'd be that interesting,' she replied, quieting a fresh spasm of panic... *Fantasy*, he said—he couldn't possibly know about the dreams. She broke out in a cold sweat just thinking about him being privy to her nocturnal fantasies. Not that she was going to start feeling guilty—a girl couldn't be responsible for her subconscious.

'Though if I'm going to be cast in the role of villain, litigation-wise it might be a sensible precaution if you changed a few details. Change of eye colour, make me a blond...'

Giving his character a hint of human warmth would definitely work, she thought grimly—then *nobody* would recognise him! 'It was a joke,' she insisted hoarsely.

Though if anyone had been born to fulfil the role of a ruthless criminal, she decided, sneaking a covert look through her lashes at his cold, classic profile, this was the man—it didn't require much imagination to picture him in the role of the cold-eyed assassin who aimed a gun at his victim's heart without any sign of emotion. Her own heart, perhaps in sympathy for the phantom victim, began to behave in an erratic manner, which made her feel breathless and a little light-headed.

'If you find me such an oppressive monster,' he mused, ignoring her hoarse interjection, 'I'm surprised you're still with us.'

Appealing to his sense of humour had always been a long shot.

'And at such a late hour, too...' He glanced pointedly at the metal watch on his wrist. Natalie was almost as conscious of the light dusting of dark hair on his sinewed forearm as she was of the sarcasm in his voice. Her stomach did a slow backward flip. 'Such dedication...'

She felt the colour deepen in her already pink cheeks, the

sarcastic implication that she did what she had to and nothing more had enough truth in it to make her angry and defensive.

'I do what you pay me for,' she returned, successfully keeping her growing antipathy from her voice. Her control didn't stretch as far as her eyes but her antagonism did—it shone brightly in the clear depths.

This fact was not lost on Rafe, who was not displeased by the results of his calculated baiting. He reasoned that she'd eventually have to defend herself and then he might finally learn the real reason that she'd knocked back his promotion offer. He hadn't swallowed the lame 'I don't feel I'm ready' for a second.

'And not a jot more,' he completed smoothly.

Natalie's bosom swelled; smug, hateful pig! It was becoming increasingly difficult to recall her resolve to take what he threw at her and smile. I'd like to see him cope with the demands of a child and work for just twenty-four hours, she challenged mentally, allowing her gaze to sweep with simmering resentment over his tall, immaculate figure.

She exhaled noisily and tried to take control of her erratic breathing.

'Have you had any complaints about my work?' she demanded, quietly confident on this point at least. Sure, she was frequently frustrated by her inability to put more hours in at the workplace, but she also knew that she actually contributed as much and more than other people doing the same job as herself—she earned her salary.

Something that looked like amusement appeared in his eyes but it was gone so quickly and it seemed so unlikely that Natalie assumed she'd been imagining it.

'On the contrary.' One corner of his mobile mouth dropped as his eyes moved over her tense figure. 'Everyone goes out of their way to cover for you.'

In reality the simple fact was that if Natalie Warner's work hadn't been adequate she wouldn't still be at Ransome. Margaret had been right about one thing: Rafe was not sentimental about such things—when such a lot had been riding on his making a success of Ransome, he couldn't afford to be.

Quite a few people had known his own father had been behind the damaging rumours that had circulated just after the launch of Ransome, but he was the only one who knew the reason behind the old man's actions.

'If you're so damned confident how about a wager?' James Ransome had suggested when his only son had remained unmoved by the direst of his threats. 'Put your money where your mouth is, boy. If you don't make a go of it within twelve months you'll quit this nonsense and come home to run the estate.'

'Twelve months!'

'Well, if you don't think you're up to it, boy?' Failure had not been an option.

When he looked at Natalie Warner, he saw potential going to waste—actually it wasn't the only thing he saw, but it was the only thing that had any relevance in the workplace.

'I don't need anyone to cover for me,' she gritted.

'Don't get me wrong, you're to be congratulated.' Natalie's teeth clenched at the patronising drawl, which it seemed to her he kept just for her and bad weather. 'Overplaying the single-parent card could have caused resentment amongst your childless colleagues, but you seem to have the balance just right... plucky, but fragile.'

Not so fragile that she couldn't land a pretty good punch if you stepped out of line—she sure as hell looked as if that was what she wanted to do right now. At least that would be some sort of reaction, and preferable to the meek and mild, fade-into-the-background, yes-sir—no-sir attitude she had adopted even before she'd refused the promotion offer.

The line between his dark brows deepened as he compared this Natalie with the one who had arrived bubbling with enthusiasm and raw talent, displaying a fresh and exciting approach and causing ripples with her willingness to speak out of turn.

The sheer injustice of his accusation stunned Natalie into

silence. Chin up, she met his scornful scrutiny head-on and refused to respond to the provocation. To her surprise it was Rafe who dropped his gaze first.

'For God's sake, woman,' he snapped irritably. 'You look terrible. Do you even own a mirror?'

Aware that her automatic female response to his criticism had been to lift a hand to her hair, Natalie frowned and pulled it angrily back to her lap. Rafe Ransome thinks I'm a dog... This should come as no great surprise—she'd seen the type he dated. A man who could probably emerge from a hurricane without a hair out of place was never going to feel anything but disgust for someone who looked messy as soon as she walked out of the door.

The unexpected urge she felt to burst into tears just went to prove she had more vanity left than she had thought.

'Well, you've no room to talk!' Rafe looked so astounded by her sharp retort that Natalie almost laughed. It was probably the first time in his life anyone had implied there was any fault in his appearance. He might be a nicer person if they had, *and* he might be a little more tolerant of those who didn't possess his physical perfection—like her!

'When did you last shave?' she demanded with a disdainful nod towards the dark, incriminating shadow. Actually the look of dangerous dissipation it lent him was not unattractive.

Rafe lifted a hand to his jaw and looked amused. 'I had an early start,' he admitted.

'That's fine, because *I* don't judge people on appearances,' she informed him piously. 'And, just for the record, I hardly think my looks or lack of them are relevant to my ability to do my job.' And until you drew attention to it I hadn't even thought about the way I looked, she thought, angling a look of seething dislike up at his face.

Not true, the irritating voice of honesty in her head piped up—you started thinking about the way you looked the moment you saw him. It was at times like this, she thought with a sigh, that self-deception was infinitely preferable to the truth. Not that there was any sinister significance in her bizarre reactions to his presence, neither was it unique she'd seen the way other women in the building acted when he was around—God, but it must be awful to be married to someone all other women regarded with lust.

Oh, sure, Nat, a fate worse than death!

Just because you caught yourself wondering what undies you'd put on that morning when you saw a man didn't mean you were contemplating him or anyone else seeing them. Rafe was the sort of man who would be pretty knowledgeable when it came to women's underwear, she mused…or at least removing them. He was just the sort of man that made women conscious that they were…well…women! Possibly because he was so obviously and in-your-face *male*!

'Granted, but your ability to do your job is compromised if you're too tired and run-down to work and an ill-kempt appearance is hardly professional.' Neither was it professional for him to want to unfasten the piece of velvet ribbon that held the hair she'd scraped back from her face in an unattractive ponytail.

Natalie, teeth clenched and head bent over her desk, was unaware that her boss was finding the exposed nape of her neck strangely attractive. Calling her physically repulsive was one thing, but calling her unprofessional really hurt, especially when his accusation had some foundation. Uncomfortably she glanced down at her crumpled skirt and the run in her tights; he was right, she was a complete mess!

'Linen is meant to look crumpled.'

'If crumpled was the look you were after, congratulations, you've succeeded.'

Though she looked as though she'd been dragged through a hedge backwards, her nut-brown hair looked smooth and glossy. Rafe felt confident that it would feel like silk if he let it fall through his fingers.

'Are you wearing *any* make-up…?' he rasped suddenly, exhibiting what seemed to her to be a peculiar preoccupation with her appearance.

'I'm not sure,' she responded without thinking. She found this conversation, like his critical scrutiny, was getting far too personal for her taste.

'You're not sure!' he ejaculated, looking at her with the sort of expression she suspected he reserved for females without lipstick and Martians.

'Did someone die and make you the style police? Or is it now office policy not to appear without lip gloss?' she grunted with a belligerent frown.

He shook his head. 'Don't be ridiculous!' he snapped impatiently.

She wasn't even beautiful, he thought, examining the too-sharp contours of her pale, pinched face. Actually, though her features lacked symmetry they did have a certain charm and her smooth skin, though as pale as milk, was amazingly blemishless. So she was attractive, he conceded, but beautiful—no, and either she had no fashion sense at all or for perverse reasons known to her alone she went out of her way to wear things that didn't suit her. Take today's offering, for instance…he looked and barely repressed a shudder.

Natalie hunched her shoulders and lifted her chin as she registered the pained expression on his dark, saturnine features. She could have explained that she'd had things other than colour coordinating her outfit on her mind that morning. Things such as hoping Rose wouldn't end up being hospitalised *again*, but that explanation would no doubt elicit another accusation of her using her daughter to get special treatment—and no way was she going to give the smug ratbag the satisfaction.

Is it against your precious principles to say something that might make him *not* want to dispense with your services? Or is an apology too much like good sense? the exasperated voice in her head pondered.

'I'm sorry you heard what I said. I was upset…'

'Sorry I heard, or sorry you said it?'

Rafe, it seemed, was not in the mood to be placated.

She eyed him with escalating irritation. 'Well, if you're going to be pedantic...' She closed her eyes as she heard the snippy words slip from her lips. God, I'm doing it again! She opened her eyes and pinned a bland smile on her face. 'I wasn't being serious, it's just Luke had just told me something a bit upsetting.'

'I'm so sorry that work interferes with your social life.' Natalie's bewildered eyes locked with his; the depth of smouldering anger in the deep, drowning blue only deepened her confusion. She couldn't imagine what had put it there. 'You weren't happy Luke was going to New York...' he reminded her in a terse, clipped voice. 'Couldn't you bear to be parted from him that long?'

'You were standing there all that time!' she gasped without thinking. 'Well, I call that plain sneaky not letting on,' she told him indignantly.

She was actually more indignant than she might have been because there was a grain of truth in what he'd said. Of course she was pleased for Luke's good fortune, but she could still guiltily recall the wave of shameful envy that she'd felt for a split second when Luke had told her his news.

For a moment he looked taken aback by her indignant cry, then she saw his electric-blue eyes fill with laughter. His mobile lips twitched, and Natalie, who normally had no problem laughing at herself, especially when she said something spectacularly stupid—and that little gem *definitely* qualified—felt more inclined to lie on the floor and scream.

'I wasn't actually trying to hide and if you hadn't been so absorbed by pulling my character to shreds you would have seen me...or at least seen the message Luke was desperately trying to signal.'

The mention of Luke reminded Natalie of his original accusation. 'I was not upset because you gave Luke a great job!' At least the notion that she had a social life at all was funny. 'And I'm happy for him,' she insisted sturdily.

Even as she spoke she saw herself, not Luke, striding confidently into the New York office. Even Rafael would have found no fault with this glossily groomed other her, she thought, releasing the image. A realist, she was impatient with herself for indulging in this romanticised daydream.

'If you don't mind a little bit of advice?' Rafe suggested, watching the revealing expressions flit across her face with narrowed eyes.

'Do I have any choice?'

She instantly regretted her childish retort as his perfect profile hardened with displeasure. Do you actually want to lose your job, Natalie? The problem with men like Rafe, she told herself, was they could dish it out, but, surrounded by people who constantly told them how marvellous they were, they bleated foul if anyone gave it back.

'I think that it's possible you might find that your relationship with Luke would stand a better chance in the long term if you actually support his efforts to promote his career rather than trying demotivate him.' The condescension in his voice made her teeth ache and her fingers furl into combative fists. 'Some people are not happy to drift along without any real challenge.' No need for him to add that he considered her one of this breed he evidently despised when the scornful expression on his dark features said all too clearly he thought she was.

'How dare you?' His smug, sanctimonious attitude made her long to beat her hands against his broad chest, though he'd probably emerge from the attack without a hair out of place and she'd have bruised fists and no job!

Quivering, she rose to her feet; even then she barely reached Rafael's broad shoulder. As their eyes locked a wave of dizziness hit her, making the room tilt and everything but his dark, devastating features shift out of focus... They seemed to sharpen until they filled her vision; similarly the subtle male scent of his body filled her nostrils...

'Are you ill?'

Only in the head. Natalie closed her eyes and took a deep, fortifying breath. Actually this close it wasn't possible to pretend even to herself that the damage was restricted to her mental capacity, not when her body started responding in some very embarrassing ways to the man.

She had no illusions, she could have dressed up the effect he had on her in all sorts of painless ways, but what would be the point? It wouldn't change anything. He was an outrageously attractive, sexy guy—in a dark, predatory way that wasn't to her taste, at least not on an intellectual level. Problem was it wasn't her intellect that was in action here, it was her indiscriminate hormones that were responding to his raw animal magnetism.

She could be a victim of her hormones or she could rise above them.

Her knees were trembling—in fact her entire body was quivering as she tried to shake off the last remnants of the red blur before her eyes.

'If I did have a relationship with Luke, which I don't—*I don't!*—' she enunciated grimly from between gritted teeth in response to his blatantly sceptical smile '—the last person I'd take advice from would be someone with the emotional depth of a puddle! Luke is my friend.'

'But he'd like to be more?' He scanned her face as if he suspected to find a guilty secret written there.

CHAPTER THREE

NATALIE'S JAW TIGHTENED as she glared at Rafe belligerently. 'Would that be so amazing?' She was too angry to wonder at the personal comments coming from someone who was not exactly a touchy-feely boss. You did your job and didn't bring your personal problems to work at Ransome. 'Well, maybe he doesn't have *your* high standards!' she snarled waspishly.

The faces and figures of the women in Rafe's life could have been neatly superimposed by a computer on top of one another with no overlapping edges. Long, leggy and decorative, even the ones who weren't looked like models. Thinking about them made Natalie feel unaccountably angry.

'Or maybe he doesn't know a lost cause when he sees one,' Rafael suggested provocatively.

Natalie's nostrils flared as she took a wrathful breath. 'As for me being happy with a job that I could do in my sleep...*you think I like that*?' she quavered incredulously.

His wide shoulders lifted as he leaned towards her and his compelling eyes collided with hers before dropping to her quivering lips. He swallowed, working the muscles in his brown throat. 'Tell me what you would like,' he instructed tersely.

Tell me what you would like?

In her mind Natalie heard those words spoken in a way that

changed their meaning dramatically. Her soft lips parted as a sigh snagged in her dry throat. Mike had never asked her what she'd wanted, and even if he had—an unimaginable scenario!—she doubted she could have told him. There had always been a restricting self-consciousness in the physical side of their relationship.

Natalie had sometimes wondered a little wistfully if the mind-blowing sex of legend, the sort where you forgot where you ended and your lover began, actually existed. She had come to the conclusion that if it did she was not likely to experience it.

Self-awareness was a good thing, but it was still dreadfully depressing to acknowledge that you were just too inhibited to ever experience the pleasures of head-banging, no-holds-barred sex.

Though he hadn't come right out and said so, Mike had managed to reinforce this belief with the few things he'd casually let slip about his vastly improved love life with the sexually insatiable Gabby. It was impossible to avoid coming to the inevitable conclusion that the fault must lie with her.

I'm just not a sexy, throw-caution-to-the-wind woman, which is probably why I married the first man I slept with who was my childhood sweetheart to boot!

She sighed, a dreamy expression drifting into her eyes as they dwelt speculatively on the strong features of the man who had spoken...the sensual curve of his mouth did not suggest he was overly encumbered with inhibitions. Looking at it made her breathing quicken and her tummy muscles quiver in a painfully pleasurable way.

Would Rafael be the sort of lover who would...?

With a horrified gasp Natalie pulled a veil across that dangerous line of speculation. Her neatly trimmed nails pressed half-moons into the soft flesh of her palms when, despite her best efforts, tantalising little glimpses of what lay behind that veil kept intruding in a deeply distracting manner.

In an angry gesture she flicked her head, sending her ponytail whooshing silkily backwards. 'So that's what *this* is about!' she cried contemptuously.

Rafe watched, his blue eyes unwillingly held captive as her explosive action dislodged several more silky strands of hair from her pony-tail. If he had his way she'd never tie her hair back but wear it loose. In his mind he saw it lying straight and fine down her narrow, naked back almost reaching a waist he could span with his hands—though to know this for sure he'd have to put the theory to the test...

He cleared his throat and reached up to loosen the tie at his throat. 'Define "this".'

As if he didn't know! Maybe it was time they got this out in the open even if it did mean she lost her job.

'I turned down that stupid offer of fast-track promotion...' she continued carelessly, brushing a stray section of hair off her face with the back of her hand. She could see a vee of brown skin where he'd undone the top button of his shirt. She ran her tongue over the dry outline of her lips as she watched his long brown fingers release the second button.

She released her baited breath in a gusty sigh as the fabric parted.

And I'm the one who always wondered what women get from watching men strip...hell, I'm getting hot and bothered over an innocent extra square centimetre of bare flesh! I've clearly lost it.

'*Stupid...?*' Rafael shrugged. 'I suppose,' he conceded wryly, 'in retrospect it was stupid, but at the time I actually thought I was giving you an opportunity most people in your situation dream about.'

His scornful tone made her flush angrily. 'Out of the goodness of your heart, no doubt,' she sneered irrationally—since when had business been about kindness? 'What was I meant to do with a young child when I got the word to hotfoot it to New York like Luke...shove her in my hand luggage?'

Rafe looked taken aback by her aggressive question. The

line between his dark brows deepened as he shook his head. 'If *that* was the only problem why didn't you say so at the time?'

Only problem? That he could imply she was making a fuss about nothing added insult to injury.

'Why? So you could tell me you're not a social worker.' That had been Maggie's response when she had attempted to explain her dilemma to the other woman. She had gone on to warn Natalie that Mr Ransome would not be interested in her lame excuses either.

You girls these days expect it all ways. Natalie had been deeply humiliated by the contemptuous criticism; she had vowed never to give anyone the opportunity to level that accusation at her again.

His dark brows knitted. 'Social worker?' he repeated, looking genuinely perplexed. 'Being a single parent is hardly so unusual these days, is it? In fact,' he added drily, 'it's almost the norm. Half the people I know are on their second or third marriage.'

But not him. Rafe seemed one of those men who were allergic to marriage. 'More fool them.'

'You sound bitter,' he observed.

'I'm not bitter, just cautious,' she countered.

'Cautious about what?' he persisted. 'Men or marriage?'

'One is a nice idea, the other...well, just look at yourself.'

The righteously indignant expression faded from her face as she followed her own advice. She stifled an appreciative sigh; he really was the *most* stunningly perfect male imaginable.

'Me...?'

'Well everyone knows you have the staying power of a two-year-old when it comes to women. Yet I suppose one day you'll meet the *right* woman and get married,' she predicted sourly. 'It's just not logical to suppose that your personality will change overnight...' Her voice faded as she encountered the blankly astonished expression on his face. It occurred to her that her evangelical enthusiasm for the subject had made her go too far. 'Well, it seems that way to me anyhow...' she added with a touch of husky defiance.

Rafe inhaled deeply and rocked back on his heels. 'So it *seems* to you I am a shallow womaniser, who will sleep with the maid of honour at my own wedding.' Cold ice scanned her dismayed face. 'Have I got that right...?' he enquired in a cuttingly satirical drawl.

'Oh, dear, I've upset you.' An understatement, she thought, regarding his taut expression with growing dismay. Well, at least there was no need to watch what she said any more—she had obviously talked herself out of a job.

Rafe brought his teeth together in a wolf-like smile. 'How long did you say you were married for?'

'I didn't, but it was two years.'

'*That* long?' he drawled insultingly.

'There's no need to be personal.' He released an incredulous laugh and she blushed. 'I'm just trying to say that a lot of men are...'

'Congenitally incapable of fidelity,' he finished smoothly. 'Whereas women never stray.'

'Of course they do.'

'Did you?'

'Chance would be a fine thing!' she snorted. 'When Mike walked out Rose was three months old.' As far as *straying* went, any idiot could figure out that this ruled out the twelve months prior to their separation. And afterwards, well... 'Would *you* want an affair with a woman who had a baby or young child?' she added cynically.

'Some people seem to be able to combine being a mother and lover...'

The fact he had avoided the question was not lost on Natalie. 'Whereas I can't even combine it with a career.'

Rafe released an exasperated sigh from between his clenched teeth. 'Self-pity doesn't suit you,' he observed drily. His brow creased. 'Wouldn't a nanny solve your problem? Or an au pair?'

Natalie gave an incredulous snort of laughter; nobody was that näıve, surely! She searched his face—he was serious! What world did this guy live in? Not one where you juggled half a dozen tasks simultaneously and did your supermarket shopping with a fretful child dragging along at your side.

No, Rafe lived in the glamorous world of the élite, flash cars, and flashier women, film premières and weekend skiing trips. It was hardly surprising that it was his world that sold newspapers and magazines to people whose own lives, like her own, were humdrum by comparison.

'Oh!' she cried, lifting a hand to her brow. 'Why didn't *I* think of that?' Her eyes narrowed. 'Maybe,' she added crisply, 'because I couldn't afford to pay for a full-time live-in nanny or even half a full-time nanny,' she added thoughtfully. 'The fact is you have it in for me,' she spelt out before he had a chance to respond, 'because I had the temerity to turn down that job offer!'

'Have it in for you?' he echoed incredulously. His narrowed eyes homed in on the accusing finger she was waving in front of his nose and with a grunt of sheer exasperation he caught the offending digit and, folding it into her palm, covered her small fist firmly with his own. Her hand was lost within his.

His grasp was firm but not constricting; Natalie could have pulled away, but she didn't. The blood drained from her face as, almost fearfully, she stared at the long, elegant fingers that looked very dark curled against her fair skin. Illogically the contrast excited her...a furtive excitement that she dared not admit even to herself.

His thumb began to move against the blue-veined inner aspect of her wrist and she let out a sharp gasp. A heat that began low in her belly suddenly flared hot and spread through her body invading every cell with a strange, enervating weakness. She raised her shocked eyes and Rafe smiled, a smile that held a terrifying mixture of sexual speculation and understanding as if he knew exactly how she was feeling. Well, at least one of us does.

'I was meant to be overcome with gratitude—' Natalie could barely hear her own hoarse whisper above the heavy throbbing beat of her heart.

'Gratitude...? You...?' he interjected with a wry laugh. 'I'm not *that* unrealistic.'

She continued as though he hadn't spoken. 'And I said no.' His skin was cool against her overheated flesh and there was controlled strength in his light touch that she found deeply exciting. 'You took it as a personal insult, that's why I've been given every crummy job going!' The moment the words were out of her mouth she wished them unsaid.

Determined not to lay herself open to an accusation of asking for preferential treatment, Natalie had consistently refused to complain...until now.

With an angry cry she wrenched her fingers away from his grasp and, covering them with her uncontaminated hand, nursed them against her chest.

'Personal...!' A feral smile illuminated the darkness of his face. He could have told her about personal—personal was wanting to take her face between his hands before kissing her senseless, the kind of kiss that might go some way to relieve a little of the frustration being around her filled him with. The errant nerve in his lean cheek began to pulse erratically as he visualised the pleasure of her willingly opening her lips to offer his tongue access to the soft sweetness of her mouth. His body reacted to the erotic imagery that filled his mind with all the subtlety and control of an adolescent boy.

Natalie was almost relieved when he frowned and suddenly barked, 'And what do you mean every crummy job going?' For a moment there the way he was looking at her had been almost frightening—not that she could ever have been *physically* scared of him, but there had been a combustible quality to his fixed stare that had been deeply unsettling.

By way of reply Natalie picked up a pile of documents from

her desk and held them out to him. 'The perfect cure for insomnia,' she promised him.

'I don't suffer from it,' Rafael replied as he took them from her. He didn't look at them or—much to her relief—appear to notice when she snatched her hand away as if scalded when their fingertips accidentally brushed. 'I'm sorry if you feel your talents are being underused,' he replied, replacing the stack on her desk. He was detecting Maggie's handiwork here.

'Do you think I have any?' she exclaimed in mock amazement.

'You have a remarkable talent for making me lose my temper,' he told her drily. 'As for personal, you underestimate my ego... I have it on excellent authority that it is Teflon-coated.' The memory was one that seemed to entertain him—at least his expression had lost some of the edginess of a few moments ago that had made her feel uneasy. 'Apparently nothing short of a nuclear explosion could dent it.'

Natalie would have liked to meet the person who was daring and perceptive enough to tell him this to his face.

'My mother.'

Natalie's eyelashes swept down as she averted her gaze from his face; either she was awfully obvious or he was scarily perceptive. With my luck probably both, she concluded wryly.

'I hate to disappoint you, Natalie, but my job is to look at the big picture. I have neither the time or the inclination to exact revenge upon some junior members of staff with a lack of ambition.'

Well, that puts me firmly in my place, she thought bleakly. This seemed as good a time as any to remind herself that her position in the scheme of things at least at Ransome was a small and insignificant cog.

'I have ambition,' pride made her insist stubbornly. She lowered her eyes. 'But I also have other responsibilities,' she admitted with a rush. Her head came up. 'But that doesn't mean I'm asking for any special favours.'

'Why not?'

Natalie was perplexed by his unexpected response. 'Oh, sure, you're really geared up to parents...'

Rafe inhaled sharply and his hard-boned face darkened with annoyance. 'I don't think it's unreasonable to expect the people I employ to be capable of sorting out their personal lives without my unwanted interference, but that doesn't mean I'm unsympathetic when there's a problem.'

'I don't think anyone would want to invite you home to tea...' If they were talking beds she might be on shaky ground. The thought of the female staff who lusted after their good-looking boss brought a disgruntled frown to her smooth brow. 'But something as basic as a crèche and more flexible working hours might be appreciated.'

If she ever heard Mandy, his PA's scheme for a back-to-work package for new mums that included a voucher for a health spa he was in serious trouble! 'And you, I suppose, have been nominated to speak on behalf of this dissatisfied section of the workforce?' he interrupted smoothly.

'Not exactly,' she conceded, shifting her weight from one foot to the other under his ironic gaze. Not only did he make her feel like a gauche schoolgirl, now she was acting like one, too, she thought, only just stopping herself before she began to chew on a loose strand of hair—she hadn't done that since she was twelve, but at twelve she hadn't needed to distract herself from tender breasts that ached and tingled as they chafed against the fabric of her thin top.

Her chin lifted. 'A happier workforce makes for a more productive workforce...' she began defensively.

'Well, that's just fascinating. Have you any other little gems of management theory you'd like to share...any other little pearls of wisdom? You know I really ought to introduce you to the guy who drove me to the airport last week—he had some great ideas about how to run the country.'

CHAPTER FOUR

WHY AM I EVEN TRYING? Natalie wondered. The man is never going to take advice from anyone, least of all me. Hell, he made it pretty clear that I'm too low down the pecking order to even approach him directly!

Even now the memory of Rafe's bored, 'Send my PA a memo, Ms Warner,' had the power to send a flush of mortification over her skin. It had been especially hurtful because before that he had seemed perfectly happy when she'd approached him; in fact she had found herself looking forward to their conversations as the highlights of her days.

She had been deluded enough to think they'd been friends, and had even—God, she cringed to think about it now!—spun romantic little fantasies about them being more. That was why him cutting her dead publicly had hurt so much. Since then she had always been guarded and circumspect in front of him... until today!

People had been very sympathetic, assuring her they'd never seen him act like that before; the popular theory was he must have been crossed in love. This explanation didn't seem at all likely to Natalie as he seemed to change the women in his life almost as frequently as he did his shirts and, as far as she could tell, with about the same degree of emotional attachment.

'There's no need to be so damned patronising!' she exploded. 'I don't suppose it's your fault,' she added bitterly. 'It's probably genetic.' The same genes that had made him the most physically perfect specimen of manhood imaginable had also made him an élitist sod. 'God, I bet you hate children!' sheer frustration made her accuse wildly.

'Genetically impossible. My mother is Venetian and the—'

'I know your mother is Italian!' she snapped. '*Everybody* knows that,' she added quickly—the last thing she wanted was him to run away with the idea she took a personal interest in him. 'You're *famous*.'

Rafe had heard people say serial killer with the same distaste Natalie Warner managed to inject in 'famous'.

'My mother's family come from Venice. I make the distinction because she likes to—it's a regional pride thing. As I was about to say, the Italians adore children. I have a nephew and several godchildren...'

'And you think that makes you an expert?' Natalie laughed, blinking to clear her head of the image of Rafe with a golden-skinned baby in his arms...the irony was she had no doubt Rafe would be as exceptional at fatherhood as he was at everything else. In short, he'd be the sort of dad that Rose would never have. The thought brought an uneasy mixture of guilt, sadness and envy—*envy*...? Her smooth brow wrinkled as alarm shot through her. 'You'll find being a parent is quite different,' she told him with a superior sniff.

'I have no plans to find out any time soon, but you may be sure that when I do have a child I will be financially able to support a family and in a stable relationship.'

'Unlike me, you mean.'

'I have no idea of your personal circumstances.' Except that most of the unmarried men in the building would like to change them—and a number of the married ones, too, he thought grimly.

Natalie smiled. 'True, but don't let that stop you making

judgement calls, will you?' Dark colour appeared across the crest of his sharply defined cheekbones; she was pleased to see that her jibe had found its mark.

'A child needs two parents.'

Natalie released an incredulous laugh…he thinks *I* need telling this? 'Did you read that somewhere or is this original thought we are hearing?' She shook her head in disgust. 'And what will you do if the other half of this *stable* relationship decides that she isn't ready after all for parenthood…or, for that matter, marriage? What if she packs her bags and says she has to leave because living with you is stifling h…her artistic creativity? That …she doesn't love you any more and thinks maybe he never did!'

Natalie froze in horror as the lengthening silence continued to echo with the acrid bitterness of her last throbbing announcement. She was totally aghast at what she had said.

Why not just strip your soul bare, Natalie? Oh, I forgot, you already did! Her head sank to her chest as she closed her eyes. She couldn't bear to see what he was going to make of that. Her performance amounted to handing your enemy a loaded gun. *Rafe being the enemy and this being war?*

War…? The analogy struck her immediately as being on the extreme side. Why when Rafe was involved did she lose all sense of proportion—why did she go off the deep end so dramatically? Was this just a clash of personalities or was it a symptom of something much worse?

'I think I would consider myself well rid of such an idiot.'

Natalie was startled by this objective pronouncement, and her troubled gaze fluttered to his face. The bad news was he had seen through her hypothetical scenario; the good news was that nothing resembled the 'pity poor dumped wife' expression she hated so much in his face.

She gave a sigh—under the circumstances there didn't seem much point continuing the pretence. 'It wasn't really Mike's fault,' she protested. 'We were too young, and before we got married him being an artist unwilling to sacrifice his artistic integrity seemed quite romantic.' It had seemed a lot less desirable when they'd had rent to pay.

A spasm of distaste contorted Rafael's austerely handsome features—in his eyes a man who deserted a wife and young child was the lowest of the low.

'My God, I never took you for one of those pathetic females who defend the shiftless bastards who abuse and leave them!'

The lashing virulence of the anger in his voice took her aback almost as much as his accusation. It seemed she wasn't the only one in danger of going off the deep end.

'Mike wasn't abusive!' she protested. Her slender shoulders lifted. 'Just immature,' she judged generously.

Rafael raked a hand through his dark hair and gave vent to his feelings in a flood of musical Italian. It was the first time she had heard him revert to his mother's native tongue and, even though she doubted if the passionate invective translated into anything she'd like to hear, Natalie was spellbound.

Italian was not only beautiful to listen to, it was a very passionate language, she thought as his words flowed over her, smooth as warm honey. Did people who were bilingual find one language more appropriate than another for different activities…say English was good for booking theatre seats and Italian might be better for, say, making love?

'And I'm not pathetic,' she asserted, her voice rising to a panicky pitch as she tried to dispel from her head the shocking image of pale limbs entwined with dark gold. She closed her eyes in disgust and opened them with a snap when she felt the light touch of his fingers slide over the curve of her jaw. Her startled gaze collided head-on with burning blue eyes.

Natalie was too shocked by the casual physical contact to do anything but stare wide-eyed back at him like a night creature caught in the glare of headlights—and any headlights paled into insignificance beside his compelling cerulean gaze. There was no respite, no place to hide from the raking scrutiny of his lustrously lashed eyes.

Her lashes fluttered as the corners of his sternly beautiful mouth lifted; the action lessened the severity of his expression quite dramatically. His smile could have melted stone and Natalie's heart was not made of stone, and, though she liked to pretend otherwise, neither was it immune to this man's charismatic charm.

'No, not pathetic.' The half-smile reached his eyes and Natalie felt bathed in the warm glow of his approval...this was ridiculous! It's not as if I care what he thinks of me! she thought. Care or not, she was mightily relieved when his hand fell back to his side.

Are you so sure about that, Nat? Isn't there some secret part of you that wanted to prolong the contact...?

Rafe saw the tiny negative shake of her head and raised an interrogative brow.

The fight abruptly drained out of Natalie, leaving her feeling too weary to sustain her anger or resistance—Rafe was the most exhausting man to be around for any period of time. Or for that matter to be around period!

'Oh, for God's sake, if you're going to sack me or something get on with it.' She sighed, wearily sinking back into her chair.

She would have spun away from him but Rafe caught the back of her chair and turned it back towards him. Hands on the arm rests, his body curved over hers, he was an extremely big, powerful man and the action could have been intimidating, but it wasn't—it was exciting.

Natalie pressed a nervous hand to her neck. She could feel the dull vibration of her heartbeat in the hollow at the base of her throat. She was discovering that underneath his northern Celtic cool Rafe Ransome had inherited more of his mother's volatile Latin temperament than she had suspected. She might have been able to predict what Rafe would do in a given situation, but not *Rafael*, and the man who towered above her looked all Rafael.

'Or something.'

Natalie, who had forgotten what she'd said, didn't respond to the husky murmur. He was so close now that she could see the fine lines radiating from the corners of his eyes and the gold tips on the ends of his long sooty eyelashes. Through the dark concealing mesh she could see the shimmering summer-blue of his eyes. The tension in the air was so pronounced that she could almost see the invisible barrier that stood between them.

He appeared to be breathing hard; she could hear the soft, sibilant hiss of each inhalation and feel the intimate warmth of his breath whisper along her forehead and across the curve of her cheek. She found herself wondering what the texture of the dark shadow that emphasised the hollows of his cheeks and ran along his angular jaw would feel like if she ran her fingers over it... The achy, empty feeling low in her belly intensified as, unable to trust herself, she locked her fingers together tightly to prevent them doing something she'd regret.

He had angled his dark head so that the fragrant warmth now fell directly against her parted lips. The possibility he was going to kiss her no longer seemed so remote. Dizzy with anticipation, Natalie stopped breathing and closed her eyes.

It seemed like a long time later that his lips finally brushed against hers; Natalie's body stiffened, then relaxed. The pressure was light. It wasn't a lightness that could in any way have been construed as accidental; this was a leave-you-wanting-more, mind-blowingly erotic lightness.

And his technique worked. It worked like a dream. Maybe it was a dream...that was the only place she'd been kissed in a long time. She half wished it were a dream; people could behave irresponsibly in dreams and there were no consequences.

If this is a dream, don't let me wake up just yet.

'You're going to hate me in the morning,' he predicted throatily as his mouth moved with tantalising slowness down the slender curve of her throat.

'I already do,' she rebutted huskily.

'How much?' he asked, kissing her closed eyelids. 'You talk too much,' she complained.

Rafe laughed huskily, but there was nothing amused about his taut, driven expression. She looked into his smoky eyes and whimpered as his teeth gently tugged at the soft flesh of her lower lip. She bit him back and felt the purr of husky laughter in his throat.

'And there isn't going to be a night before to regret.' There wasn't; she was going to put a stop to this any minute now… any minute…

Well, what harm could another couple of minutes do? she told herself as she felt the pressure of his skilful lips subtly increase. It was just kissing.

Releasing a long, shuddering sigh, she ignored the alarmist voice of caution in her head that was insultingly suggesting she couldn't stop even if she wanted to, and instead responded to an instinct that impelled her to clutch at him to intensify and prolong the delicious experience. Weaving her fingers into his lush dark hair once she had done so seemed equally instinctual and very satisfying. If this went on for ever it wouldn't be too long, the dreamy thought drifted through her mind, before she gave herself up totally to the hedonistic pleasure of feeling his hard, rampantly male body pressed up against her.

Natalie hadn't known that kisses so addictive you couldn't walk away from them existed. Totally submerged by a tide of longing, she hooked her arms tightly around his neck. Rafe responded by encircling her narrow waist with his hands. With effortless ease he drew her upright, causing the chair he lifted her from to spin backwards until it collided noisily and unobserved into a filing cabinet.

Natalie wasn't even conscious that her shoes had slipped off as her toes lost contact with the floor.

'What if someone comes in…?'

Her agonised whisper caused him to pull back slightly. The flicker of cold reason in the passion-darkened eyes that swept over her flushed face brought the stupidity of what she was doing crashing home.

Her cheeks heated with mortification. 'This is really stupid.' She shook her head. 'We shouldn't be doing this.'

Rafe let his head fall back and she heard him exhale noisily. 'Sure,' he agreed, lifting his head and pinning her with a feverish cerulean stare. 'But think,' he advised her throatily, 'of the alternative.'

Natalie blinked in confusion. '*Not* doing it.'

'Oh!' Every cell in her body screamed in protest. 'Precisely.'

Natalie was transfixed by the dark need stamped on his hard features.

'That would be...?'

His eyes slid to her mouth, then back to her eyes. 'Unthinkable,' he completed. Still holding her eyes, he parted her lips once more and with seductive skill slid his tongue between her trembling lips.

'Yes!' she whimpered, giving herself up to the craving she could no longer pretend didn't exist. *'Oh, yes, please!'*

Her fractured sob ached with longing. It was too much for Rafe's iron self-control, self-control she naïvely hadn't been aware existed until it was no longer there. A shudder rippled through his lean, powerful body the moment before he claimed her lips. His hungry lips had barely covered hers before his tongue stabbed deep again and again into her mouth.

Natalie was swept up into a maelstrom of pure sensation.

CHAPTER FIVE

NATALIE FELT BEREFT and dizzy when Rafe abruptly put her from him.

'The phone is ringing.'

There was not a trace of the raw, driven hunger he had been exhibiting moments before in the hard planes and hollows of his face.

Natalie shivered, she suddenly felt very cold. He was going to pretend it hadn't happened... That was good, that was excellent—well, as excellent anything connected with kissing your boss with all the finesse of a sex-starved bimbo could be!

Just why had kissing him seemed a good idea? When she thought about how she had... Don't think about it, she instructed herself firmly. It didn't happen. If it works for him it works for me, she told herself angrily. It's just easier for him, she thought, sliding a resentful sideways glance at his darkly impassive face.

Rafe intercepted the look and exhaled loudly. 'This,' he grated, raking a hand through his hair in an exasperated manner, 'is *exactly* what I've been trying to avoid. Getting involved emotionally at work is a recipe for disaster.'

Wasn't that just typical of the man, acting as if he were the innocent victim of her shameless lust when he was the one who had started it? And that in itself was confusing. Why would a man who had spent the previous few minutes pulling all aspects of her appearance and character to shreds want to kiss her? Well, whatever the reason she wasn't going to accept all the blame.

'Afraid it wouldn't be good for your reputation if it got around you'd kissed someone with an inside-leg measurement of less than thirty-four?'

Initially Rafe looked startled by her caustic taunt, but within a matter of seconds an amused glint she didn't like appeared in his eyes.

'Or are you worried I'll play the sexual harassment card? Don't be!' she advised, determined he would not be left with the impression she envied in any way those blonde clones. Her small bosom heaved as she sought to control her strong feelings. 'Do you think I *want* people to know you kissed me?' She gave a very expressive little shudder.

'It's not *my* reputation I'm concerned about.'

'What are you talking about?'

'Have you any idea what people think about ambitious young women who sleep with their bosses?' He paused to let his point sink in. 'It doesn't matter how talented you happen to be, people will always assume that you slept your way to the top.'

Natalie flushed. 'Some place I'm not likely to get!' she gritted.

'If you stop bleating and start actually being positive, it's not totally impossible,' he declared callously.

Natalie glared at him with loathing.

'The phone is ringing again.'

'I know the phone is ringing, I don't need you to tell me,' she snapped back childishly. 'Hello!' she snarled down the line.

'Is that you, Nat?' a puzzled voice the other end asked tentatively.

It was hardly surprising, Natalie reflected grimly, that she didn't sound like herself—she certainly didn't feel like herself! And as for the way she'd been acting! How could you loathe someone and want to rip their clothes off at the same time? She turned her back on the tall, silent figure but it didn't stop her being painfully aware of him in every cell of her body.

'Natalie?'

'Yes, it's me,' Natalie replied, recognising the familiar voice of Ruth the child-minder. Alarm bells began to ring in her head—Ruth never rang her at work unless there had been a disaster of some sort. The last time Rose had been inconsolable because she had lost her favourite teddy.

'Don't panic, Nat.'

Nothing, in Natalie's experience, was *less* likely to soothe than a telephone conversation that began with these words, but this was especially true if they were closely followed by a horrifying, 'I'm ringing from the hospital.'

Not a lost teddy this time.

This was the sort of phone call that every parent dreaded getting. An icy fist of frozen fear closed around Natalie's heart as a dozen scenarios, each one more catastrophic than the one preceding it, chased rapidly through her head. The panic racing through her veins made it hard for her to think straight. Her lips felt stiff and reluctant to form the question she knew she had to ask, but desperately didn't want to.

'Is she...?'

There was a gasp the other end. 'Oh, God, no, Rose is fine!' The child-minder sounded horrified. 'Well, not *fine*, obviously, or we wouldn't be here, but she will be, they say.'

Natalie's shoulders sagged. *'Oh, my God!'* She was not conscious of Rafe retrieving her chair and sliding it behind her knees at the crucial moment they gave way.

A strange numbness spread through her body while in her head she could feel the dull throb of her own heartbeat.

'After you left Rose seemed a bit feverish,' Ruth relayed hurriedly. 'And later when she started wheezing the inhaler didn't work. I thought the best thing was to get her here first and then ring you.'

'You did the right thing, Ruth.' Natalie caught her trembling lower lip in her teeth. 'I should have listened to my instincts,' she gulped. 'Oh, God, I knew, I just *knew* I shouldn't have left her...but the doctor said she was fine this morning, just a cold...' She stopped, her expression one of grim self-condemnation. She couldn't pass the buck. Nobody had forced her to come into work; that had been her own decision. Because I have a point to prove—namely that a single parent can be just as good...no, *better* than everyone else.

And while I was busy proving my point my daughter was... She shook her head in disgust. What sort of parent does that make me?

Ruth's sensible voice injected a note of practicality into the endless flow of bitter self-recriminations.

'Natalie, dear, if you listened to your instincts you'd never leave Rose at all.'

'Maybe that isn't such a bad idea,' Natalie replied heavily. 'Listen, tell her Mummy will be there soon...yes...all right, Ruth, and thank you,' she said, placing the receiver down and rising urgently to her feet.

Her eyes drifted over him, but from the vague, unfocused expression in them Rafe doubted she had even registered his presence.

He watched as she opened her handbag and, extracting a wallet from the depths, began flicking through the contents with an expression of fierce concentration on her pale features. Her hands were trembling but he doubted she was aware of it; she was displaying all the classic symptoms of shock.

'Where are you going, Natalie?'

Natalie swung back and as she saw him standing there Rafe saw a flicker of shock replace for a moment the fretful expression in her wide, darkly lashed eyes—clearly she had forgotten he was there. This female, he thought wryly, seemed to be determined to single-handedly supply the dose of humility his mother—not a person exactly renown for modesty herself— liked to say he needed so badly.

'You called me Natalie,' she heard herself say stupidly. 'It's your name,' he reminded her gently.

'It sounds…different when you say it,' she observed in a distracted voice. 'My daughter is in hospital.' She looked around the familiar room as if she was surprised to find herself still there. 'I have to go…' She glanced briefly towards the mess on her desk and then back at him. *'Now,'* she added, dealing him a ferocious frown.

Clearly she thought he was an inconsiderate louse who would demand she cleared her desk before she went to her sick child, which was a great basis for a relationship. *Relationship…?* First you break the 'mixing business with pleasure' rule, which is bad, but not as bad as wanting to break it some more. Now you're thinking *relationships*! he derided himself. What next…?

'Which hospital is she in?'

Natalie told him because it was easier than telling him to mind his own business and because he was blocking her way. Actually his calm voice helped her focus her thoughts. Rafe was the sort of man that women less able than herself to take care of themselves would have automatically leaned on in a situation like this.

Natalie was fully awake to the pitfalls of leaning on a man… when they walked away you either fell flat on your face or learnt how to do things for yourself. Of course, Mike had never exactly been a pillar of strength to begin with, so it hadn't been so difficult for her. In fact the gap he'd left in her life had been pretty insignificant all things considered… Rafe Ransome, on the other hand—her wary glance flickered to his tall, vital person—well, nothing about him was insignificant!

'Give me a minute and I'll take you.' Natalie stared at him incredulously. *'You?'*

'It's on my way.'

She looked up at him, a sceptical line between her dark, feathery brows, clearly trying to figure out his ulterior motive. He couldn't help her out; he still wasn't sure if he had one himself.

'On your way where?'

'I can give you a detailed run-down of my itinerary or I can take you to the hospital.' He gave a very Latin take-it-or-leave-it shrug. 'Unless you prefer to take your chance with public transport?'

Natalie's thoughts turned to the empty condition of her wallet. If anyone had asked her earlier that day she'd have stated with total confidence that nothing on earth would have persuaded her to accept a lift from Rafe Ransome...the man who had just kissed her—*and you kissed him back*!

If her lips hadn't still felt bruised and swollen she would have imagined it had been another of those erotic dreams that woke her up more nights than she cared to admit.

Impatiently she shook her head; she couldn't think about that now.

Swallowing her pride, she lifted her eyes to his. 'Thank you.' It wasn't, she told herself, as if she were sleeping with the enemy, just riding with him. 'Don't be long!' Her anxiety and impatience made the request emerge as an imperious command.

Rafe turned, looking about as surprised as it was possible for someone like him to look. It occurred to Natalie that he wasn't used to being on the receiving end of yelled orders. Not, she acknowledged, that he did any yelling—he didn't need to. He could silence any would-be dissident with a look.

'You did say you'd only be a minute,' she reminded him, moderating her tone. 'You might forget I'm here...' she added defensively.

For a brief moment his narrowed eyes scanned her face. 'I've already tried to do that...and failed,' he revealed cryptically. A rather grim smile lifted the corners of his mouth as she looked back at him warily. 'Don't worry, Natalie, I'm renowned for my attention to detail and timing.'

This time his grin was frankly wicked.

True to his word, he was back within the minute. He walked towards her, shrugging on a dark, loose-fitting suit jacket, and the expensive fabric fell smoothly into place across his broad back. That never happens to me, she thought as she fell in step beside him. She quickly got breathless trying to keep up with his long-legged pace.

'Is there anyone you want to contact...to meet you at the hospital...?' he probed when they reached the underground parking area.

'No.'

'A friend, relation...your daughter's father, perhaps?'

Natalie, her mind on more urgent matters, was exasperated by his persistence. 'My grandmother is my only relation and she lives in Yorkshire. Hospitals freak Mike out.'

And she couldn't cope with a man who went catatonic when he saw a white coat as well as a sick and almost certainly fretful child. Mike would appear when Rose was back home, bearing expensive and often inappropriate gifts. He meant well, she thought indulgently, now she didn't have to contend with her ex-husband's foibles on a daily basis.

Rafe was not inclined to be so generous. It seemed pretty obvious to him that there had been two children in her marriage. He found it inexplicable that women were frequently attracted to the inadequate types who traded on their boyish charm.

'And is your daughter...?'

Natalie's expression softened. 'Rose.'

'Is Rose ill often?'

'No more than a lot of children,' Natalie replied defensively. 'Well,' she conceded, her eyes falling self-consciously from his, 'I suppose she is. She's asthmatic. She's fine normally with the medication. Only winter's not a good time...a cold or virus can trigger a nasty attack in some sensitive people.'

'I've heard that pollution from exhaust fumes and so forth can make matters worse.'

His depth of knowledge surprised her. 'It doesn't help,' she agreed, nodding her thanks stiffly as he opened the passenger door of a black Jag. She slid inside the luxurious interior, her tense back remaining a good two inches clear of the backrest as Rafe belted himself into the driver's seat.

'Haven't you considered moving out of the city—if it would improve your daughter's health?'

Natalie tucked a strand of hair behind her ear and threw him an impatient look. 'Some of us have to live where the work is.' She gave a dry laugh. 'Always supposing I still have work. Does it feel good to hold my fate in your hands?'

Dark colour scored the slashing angles of his high cheek-bones as he turned the key in the ignition. The powerful engine came to life. 'You've got me—we egomaniacs just love wielding power.' He turned his head and his dark lashes dipped as his glance moved with deliberation over the length of slender body. 'Only actually in this instance it felt even better to hold your body in my hands.' A firm, supple and surprisingly strong body that had proved amazingly responsive to his lightest touch.

For the briefest of moments their eyes collided. The anger in his made her recoil, but it wasn't the anger that made her look away, her heart thudding hard against her ribcage. The message in his smoky eyes had been explicitly sexual in nature…and worse was the fact her entire body responded to what she had seen.

God, she despaired, I am obviously a desperately shallow person and a terrible mother to boot to be feeling this way when my daughter is lying sick in hospital.

'I think we should discuss what happened back there…'

Natalie shook her head. 'As far as I'm concerned it didn't happen.' If she told herself this often enough, maybe she would even start believing it herself. She thought for a moment he was going to contest her statement, but after a brief nod in her direction he returned his attention to the road.

It had taken Rafe several frustrating minutes to find a parking space, so when he walked into the busy casualty department he had no expectation of finding Natalie still there.

She was.

He summed up the situation at one glance. Natalie was standing at the back of a queue several people deep that had built up behind an aggressively awkward drunk who was giving the young woman at the reception desk in the busy casualty department a hard time.

'I know my rights!' the dishevelled figure slurred loudly enough for Rafe and everyone around to hear.

Natalie, who was struggling to contain her impatience, heard the subdued murmurs of complaint as someone shouldered through the people who were waiting ahead of her, but didn't pay much attention. It wasn't until a few moments later when she glanced up that she recognised the tall, broad-shouldered figure. She cringed with embarrassment when she saw what he was doing!

Typical, she thought angrily. Rafael Ransome thinks he's too damned special to wait his turn. As she watched he began to speak in a low voice to the befuddled guy who had been holding everyone up. There was nothing threatening about his body language and the conversation, considering the older man's loud hostility, seemed to be perfectly amicable. Possibly too amicable for Rafe, she thought as the drunk suddenly threw his arms about the younger man's neck and announced to everyone that this was a good guy!

Natalie watched in disbelief as the man let Rafe lead him back to a seat in the waiting area and bring him a drink from the vending machine. It would seem that *nobody* was immune to Rafe's charm and persuasiveness.

By the time the overtaxed security team arrived the queue was moving smoothly and Rafe had, much to Natalie's discomfort, joined her.

'Did you have to interfere? What if he'd got nasty? You could have made things worse.' She heard her voice rise to an unattractive, shrill accusing note. 'You should have left it for the people who are paid to deal with that sort of thing,' she gritted. 'The ones who know what they're doing.'

One of that number chose that precise moment to approach them. 'Cheers, mate,' he said, slapping Rafe on the shoulder. 'Understand we owe you one. Old Charlie's a regular,' he explained, nodding in the direction of the old man who was now snoring happily away. 'But he can get nasty. Last time he took a swing at a nurse.'

'See, you shouldn't have interfered,' Natalie insisted, glaring up at the modest hero. 'Have-a-go heroes usually get themselves or someone else hurt.'

'Well, I didn't.'

Natalie, who was feeling physically ill visualising a scenario where he had got injured, didn't reply.

'I just need to find out which ward they've taken Rose to,' she explained hoarsely. 'You don't need to hang around,' she added pointedly.

Rafe smiled down into her face but didn't budge.

To Natalie's intense annoyance, when it was her turn and she enquired about Rose from the pretty girl behind the desk it was to Rafe the young woman replied.

'Your little girl has been taken up to Ward Six. If you and your wife—'

'She's not *his* little girl and *I* am not his wife!' Natalie snarled before she stamped away. 'That should make you happy,' she added under her breath. It just made her sick that some women were so *obvious*, and some men just lapped it up.

'You think I'm in with a chance there, then?'

He must have incredibly acute hearing. 'Listen, I'm grateful you got me here,' she said, sounding anything but, 'but, like I said, there's absolutely no need for you to stay.' As she spoke they came to another intersection; Natalie took the right turn without looking at the direction sign overhead.

'I take it you've been here before,' Rafe observed drily.

'Why *are* you still here?' she puffed, genuinely puzzled by his continued presence.

'It would be like walking out before the end of a film if I left now... I'd be wondering all night what happened.'

They had reached the door to the ward. Natalie pressed the buzzer and waited. Still slightly breathless from the brisk jogging pace he'd set, she tilted up her head to the man beside her—it went without saying that he wasn't out of breath. Just looking at him standing there in his designer suit with not a hair out of place made her bristle with antagonism. How had she ever imagined they could be friends...?

'I'm so glad we are providing some entertainment for you!' she exclaimed bitterly. 'Better than interactive telly.'

A muscle clenched in his lean cheek. 'For God's sake, woman, it was a joke. I know you think I'm some sort of heartless creep...' It was pretty hard to miss the fact—she didn't fall over herself to deny this estimation. 'What is it with you? Why can't you accept people want to help? Why do you throw their concern back in their faces?'

The anger faded from his face as he looked into her pale, upturned features—too-bright eyes looked back at him. He judged that she was keeping going on nervous tension alone. Take that away and she would shatter like a piece of the fragile porcelain she reminded him of.

Natalie blinked. '*You* want to help...?'

'I'd like to stay until you find out how your daughter is.' Rafe's frustrated urge to protect her from dead-beat ex-husbands and her own stubborn independence found release in a fresh burst of anger. 'You'll drive yourself into the ground with this I-don't-need-anyone stuff,' he predicted grimly. 'Who's going to look after your daughter then?' Natalie winced at this brutal observation. 'Your loser ex...?'

Her eyes filled with tears. Nice one, you always have to go too far, don't you, Rafe...?

'If you want me to go, just say so and I will,' he grunted.

Gold-shot green locked with electric-blue and Natalie's mind went a blank, then from out of nowhere she heard herself say, 'No! No, I don't want you to go.'

Natalie saw some emotion, strong but unidentifiable, flicker in the back of his eyes and she went pink. Her no hadn't been a laid-back, if-you-like sort of no, more a raw, you'll-leave-over-my-dead-body sort of no. Another of those silences filled with dangerous currents began to stretch between them. It was broken when a crackly voice emerged from the speaker on the wall.

With a sigh of relief Natalie identified herself and the door clicked open.

She turned to Rafe and gave an offhand shrug. 'I didn't mean to be rude but I'm used to doing this alone.'

'And do you like it that way?'

'I haven't had much choice. Someone has to make the decisions and I'm the one on the spot,' she explained matter-of-factly. 'You can stay if you like, but you'll have to wait here.' She nodded towards some seats and left him. She had no expectation that he would still be there when she returned.

He was.

CHAPTER SIX

NATALIE STOPPED MID-YAWN AND STARED. 'You're still here!' The clock on the wall behind him read half-past midnight.

Rafe languidly uncurled his long, lean length from the uncomfortable-looking chair that was far too small to accommodate him and stretched. The action caused his shirt to pull tight, revealing the definition of his well-developed chest muscles shadowed by dark body hair and his washboard-flat belly.

She knew she was staring but tiredness made Natalie less able to adequately disguise the effect this disturbing spectacle was having on her—if not from him, certainly from herself. Finally in a position where she couldn't hide from the truth, she could hardly believe that she'd been walking around for weeks acting as if the facts her blood pressure went rocketing and she couldn't think straight when he was around were simply a coincidence.

Talk about fooling yourself!

'Why...?' she asked, closing her eyes briefly while she regained a degree of composure. Now she had accepted how attracted to him she was, she could guard against it. If she'd been more honest sooner that kiss might not have happened.

When she opened her eyes again Rafe had fastened a button on his loose-fitting jacket. She watched, her expression carefully neutral, as he smoothed back his thick hair, which to her eyes seemed perfectly ordered. She found herself considering how it might feel to mess it up again...to run her fingers deep into that lush *Stop that, Natalie!*

'I had nowhere else to be.'

Natalie could not allow a lie this blatant to pass unchallenged. 'I find that difficult to believe.'

'So now you're wondering what my ulterior motives are. Actually, Natalie... I fell asleep,' he ruefully revealed in the manner of someone making a clean breast of it. 'I had a long session with Magnus Macfaden today...the usual battle of attrition.'

He seemed genuine enough and she supposed the explanation was just about plausible.

'No wonder you're tired, then.' Natalie had never met the head of the famous electronics firm but she had heard about him. 'I'm just surprised you managed to sleep through the noise.' Everyone entering and leaving the ward would have passed by him and it had been a busy evening.

'Oh, I can sleep anywhere, any time.'

'And with whoever you want, but then you already know that. Everyone who reads a tabloid knows that.' *Please tell me I didn't just say that out loud.*

'Are your objections moral or personal?' he enquired with interest.

'Neither!' she squeaked. 'Your personal life is your own business.'

'It's not nearly as...*active*, as the papers would have you believe.'

'Whatever,' she said, evincing disinterest. 'How is your daughter?'

'Rose is much better, thanks. She's finally asleep and off the nebuliser. I just thought I'd stretch my legs; if you fall asleep in one of those chairs you can't move in the morning.'

Rafe let his head fall back and flexed his shoulders. 'That I can believe,' he grimaced.

'What you need is a massage,' she observed without thinking—at least, she was thinking, but of things she had no business to be thinking about.

A half-smile played around his lips. 'Are you offering…?'

Natalie went as red as it was possible to go without spontaneously combusting. *'Most certainly not!'*

His suggestive sigh of pity combined with the lingering image in her head of her hands sliding over oiled golden flesh made her stomach muscles flutter madly. Their eyes touched and the liquid heat pooled shockingly between her thighs.

'Have you done many all-night stints in the chairs?' Natalie couldn't look at him.

'One or two. You know, about that kiss earlier… I don't want you to get the wrong idea…' she said awkwardly.

'What idea would that be?'

'I don't…well, I don't have casual relationships. It wouldn't be fair to Rose for her to get fond of a man only to have him disappear from her life. She's already had that happen once. I'm not saying this because I think you want to…'

'Yes, you do, and you're right.'

'You w…want me…?' Her cheeks burned. 'I mean you…'

'Right first time.' Natalie's jaw dropped. 'Listen, I hear what you're saying about your daughter, but what are you going to do, remain celibate?'

'It's worked for me so far.' She saw the flicker of shock in his eyes and hurried on. 'People put far too great an emphasis on sex.'

'It's a very basic need. Sex is like any other appetite…'

'For men maybe.'

'For women, too, trust me…' he drawled.

'Do I look that stupid?'

'A lot of women don't want a deep and meaningful relationship. A hotel room and a long lunch hour,' he elaborated crudely. 'Functional sex is more to their taste. Maybe you should try and develop a taste for that if you don't want any involvement.'

Was he trying to insult her? She found the idea of the sort of cold-blooded clinical encounter he described appalling. 'Is that what you're offering me?'

'I thought it was the other way around.' He didn't have the faintest idea why the idea of sex without the complications should outrage him so much.

'How do you figure that one?'

'Well, you do want to keep your home a male-free zone...'

'How does that put me in a hotel room with you?' Natalie tried to sound amused and failed.

'You don't *seriously* expect the attraction between us to simply go away, do you? Pretending it's not there doesn't work—we've tried that! It's inevitable that we'll end up in bed at some point.'

'How dare you talk to me like that?' she gasped.

'I dare because I'm the man who wants to go home with you,' he reminded her softly.

Natalie's eyes widened; this was news to her and, maybe from his expression, Rafe, too.

She bit her lip. 'We can't talk about this here.'

'Then I hope for the sake of my sanity that you're not going to be here long?'

'I think they're going to let us out in the morning this time,' she revealed, half of her wishing it were longer if it meant she didn't have to confront the issues he had raised. 'Which is a big relief. If Rose hadn't got to go to the wedding I don't like to think what sort of fuss she'd have kicked up.'

'*Wedding?*'

'Yes, the one that Luke was going to come to with me. Rose is going to be bridesmaid at her dad's wedding—on Valentine's Day,' she explained with a wry smile. Mike had not been such a romantic when he'd been married to her.

'You're going to your ex's wedding?'

Natalie grimaced at the incredulity in his voice; she'd seen that response before. 'Before you ask, I'm not actually a masochist, or that forgiving, it's just Rose wants me to come and see her in her bridesmaid dress, and Mike might not be my husband any more but he'll always be her father,' she explained gravely.

The last thing she wanted to become was one of those mothers who bad-mouthed their ex-partners to the kid caught in the middle.

Despite her apparent composure when she mentioned her ex, Rafael couldn't help but wonder if she had come to terms with the situation quite as well as she liked people to think. Inexplicably any number of women nurtured passions for men who treated them appallingly. He frowned as he scanned her face for signs of the secret passion he had half convinced himself she was nursing. It was quite possible Natalie still carried a torch for the pathetic jerk.

'And Luke was going with you?'

'He was,' she confided with a sleepy yawn.

'Then you two are...?'

'Just good friends. This is so strange...' she mused. 'What's so strange, Natalie?'

'Talking to a real person...as in one who is over ten,' she elaborated, 'here.' Her gesture took in the walls, which were covered in brightly coloured childish paintings. 'The nurses are lovely but they're always so busy.' She was totally unaware of the wistful note in her voice. 'And sometimes you just want to talk to someone who doesn't consider tomato ketchup on chips the height of sophistication.'

'I will try and do my best to supply some adult conversation.'

'So long as you remember that's *all* I want.'

'How could I forget? Why was Luke going with you?'

'If you must know, I didn't want to turn up alone looking like a sad loser.'

'Why would you look like a sad loser?'

Natalie threw him a pitying look—this man knew nothing about being a single female approaching thirty or, for that matter, looking like a sad loser. She was dimly aware that a combination of exhaustion and relief was making her not just light-headed, but dangerously garrulous, too.

'Think about it,' she suggested. 'I'm a woman whose husband left her for a gorgeous blonde and *everyone* knows a female is unfulfilled unless she is half of a partnership.'

'I hesitate as a mere man to disagree, but isn't that a slightly old-fashioned attitude?'

'It's the way it is. I suppose I should have the guts to be single and proud; asking Luke to pretend to be my lover is even more pathetic than being dumped. *Poor Luke.*'

'And I sent Luke away.'

Natalie nodded and took the cup of coffee he handed her from the vending machine. Nursing it, she sat down on one of the nasty, shiny fake leather seats. 'You could say you owe me a pretend lover.' She took a sip and winced as the scalding liquid burnt her tongue.

'Then I suppose I'm obligated to provide you with a substitute.'

'Know a good escort agency, do you? Mind you, even if you did I doubt if I could afford the rates of the sort of place you would use.' She chuckled weakly at her joke.

Rafe blinked. 'I can't say anyone has ever accused me of being au fait with high-class escort services before.'

'Gracious, I didn't mean... I don't think that you...' She gave a gusty sigh of relief. 'You were winding me up? I thought you were about to sack me for sure, or have you already done that? I forget,' she admitted with a yawn.

'No, and I have a suggestion to put to you. I have this idea about starting up a facility to offer advice to small businesses...' He stopped. 'Well, like you said, this isn't the place and you are dead on your feet.'

'I'm fine.'

'Sure you are,' Rafe murmured as he took the seat beside hers.

'I'll just rest my eyes for a minute.'

'Good idea.'

The periods her lashes lay against her waxily pale cheek before she forced her eyes open got gradually longer. For some time after her head had fallen against his shoulder Rafe stayed still, afraid to wake her. When it became obvious nothing was going to do that he shifted so that he could look at her sleeping face. It was the sort of face a man could look at for a long time without growing tired—maybe never!

Natalie woke in a strange bed. It took a few panicky moments before she recognised her spartan surroundings. She wished she weren't so familiar with the small room reserved for parents who wanted to stay overnight with their children.

Yawning, she threw back the covers. She was still fully dressed. Her frown deepened as she saw her shoes neatly placed at the bedside. She couldn't recall putting them there or, for that matter, taking them off. In fact she had no recollection of getting into bed at all—the last thing she remembered was in fact… *Good God!*

She hadn't forgotten because she hadn't done any of those things, which meant that someone had done them for her. That meant…

The nurse at the desk looked up as Natalie approached.

'Oh, you're awake.' She smiled. 'I was just going to take your boyfriend a cup of tea. Would you like one?'

'My boyfriend?' Natalie echoed warily.

'He's in with Rose. He's got quite a way with her, hasn't he?' she observed. 'Until he turned up I thought we were going to have to wake you. She was really cranky when she woke.'

'Why didn't you wake me?'

'Your boyfriend said to let you sleep.'

'He did?'

'You must have been tired,' the nurse reflected, oblivious to the grim note in Natalie's voice. 'You didn't stir when he put you to bed,' she recalled.

Natalie gulped. 'Rafe put me to bed?' Rafe, it seemed, had been busy. Not content with deciding what was best for her, he was usurping her authority with her child as well! The man just couldn't help taking charge. Well, he was about to learn that she didn't need anyone to make her decisions. She chose to forget all the occasions when the burden of making all the decisions concerning Rose's welfare had lain heavily upon her shoulders.

'Carried you like a baby,' the youthful health professional confirmed with a very unprofessional gleam of envy in her eyes.

Natalie decided it was high time she put the record straight. 'He's not my boyfriend, he's my boss.'

'Boss?'

'Yes, boss,' Natalie declared defiantly as she stomped off.

Rose's bed was in a bay of four but at that moment she was the only occupant. Natalie's impetuous stride halted as she entered. The main lights in the ward were dimmed but the night light above Rose's bed illuminated the area beneath. And the people.

Rose was seated cross-legged on top of the duvet and Rafe sat in an easy chair, leaning on the bed with his dark head resting on his crossed arms. She could not see his face but she could hear the deep rumble of his voice in the quiet of the room. Rose too was listening to what he was saying, her little face rapt.

An emotional lump formed in Natalie's throat as she stared at the tableau. She'd never been more aware of the things that, even with the best will in the world, she couldn't provide in Rose's life.

Suddenly Rose's childish laughter rang out and, brushing the back of her hand across the dampness on her cheeks, Natalie moved forward to reveal herself.

'Mummy, Rafe's been telling me a story about a boy who had a pet dragon but nobody else can see him.'

'Mr Ransome has been very kind, but he's got to go now and you must get some sleep, so snuggle down.'

Reluctantly the child complied. 'Kiss,' she commanded imperiously to Rafe, who complied.

'Well what have I done now?'

Natalie pulled a concealing curtain around them. 'Where to start?' she hissed. 'How about with taking unilateral decisions?'

'You needed the sleep, Natalie.'

'I need to stay in control. Listen, you've been very kind, but—'

'Butt out and clear off. Right, am I allowed to say goodbye to Rose?'

'Of course.' His swift surrender had deflated her.

'I'll see you on the fourteenth?' The curtain rattled as he pulled it aside.

Natalie frowned. *'Fourteenth?'*

The wedding.

'We agreed it was the least I could do as I had robbed you of Luke.'

'I didn't agree to anything...' Natalie's brow furrowed as she tried to think back, but her recollections were frustratingly hazy. *'Did I...?'*

Rafe smiled. 'Morning dress, right? Oh—' he turned back '—don't even *think* about coming into work tomorrow or Friday. No buts, *I'm* the one in control there.' Or so goes the rumour, he added drily to himself as he walked away.

CHAPTER SEVEN

'OH, YES, VERY NICE,' Mike said vaguely as his daughter waved her new patent leather shoes in his face for his approval. Deliberately not looking at his ex-wife's angry white face, he bent down awkwardly to his daughter's level. 'How would you like to come with me and Gabby to America, Rosie?' he asked the excited child in a coaxing voice.

'Will I see dolphins?'

Mike, who didn't have the faintest idea that his little daughter was fascinated by dolphins, looked momentarily nonplussed by this response. 'Sure we'll see dolphins.'

'Will Mummy be coming?'

'No.'

The child's face fell. 'Well, thank you very much,' she said politely, 'but I think I'll stay at home.'

Mike's smile grew fixed. 'In America we'll have a swimming pool in the garden.'

Rose's eyes grew round. *'In the garden!'* she gasped in awe. 'We don't have a garden here, but we have a window-box.'

Natalie gritted her teeth as Mike shot her a triumphant look and hissed, 'Out of the mouth of babes.'

'Rose, go and put on those pretty socks we bought to go with

your dress and then you can go with Daddy to have the man
put flowers in your hair.'

'Why can't you do that?'

'Because Aunt Gabby's friend is much better at fixing flowers in your hair than I am.' He'd have to be, she reflected grimly,
to justify the expense of Gabby flying him along with a makeup
artist across the Atlantic to fix the bridal parties' hair and faces.

Ironically, when Mike had turned up in person to take his
daughter to the hotel suite where Gabby and the other brides-
maids had spent the night she had actually felt touched by the
gesture. *How naïve does that make me?*

She waited until the little girl had danced away before turning furiously to her ex-husband. Without preamble she grabbed
him by the lapel of his morning suit—that got his attention.

'Good God, Natalie, there's no need to get physical!'

'That just about sums up our marriage.'

Mike coloured. 'What's got into you, Natalie?'

'You can ask that? You come here on the *morning* of your
wedding,' she began in a quivering voice of disbelief, 'to tell
me you're going to apply for full custody of Rose. What do you
think has *got into me*? You must be insane if you think I'm going
to allow you and Gabby to take Rose out of the country!' she
hissed. 'Besides, no court in the country would give you custody just because Gabby doesn't want to risk stretch marks,' she
mocked, releasing him and pressing a hand to her trembling lips.
Was there...?

Mike looked shaken but stubbornly determined as he
smoothed the fabric she had released. 'Our lawyer doesn't agree
with you, Nat. He says we have a very good chance. What can
you offer Rose compared with us?' He looked around the neat
little room with distaste.

'*Love...?*' Natalie suggested ironically.

'Sure, sure, we all love Rosie, she's a cute kid.'

'And she's house-trained.'

'It's the quality of life we can give her,' Mike insisted piously. 'She needs a proper family life.'

'Pity, you didn't seem to think so when you walked out on us.'

Mike flushed angrily. 'You're a single parent, Nat, living in a poky little flat. You're always saying how you struggle to make ends meet.'

'That could have something to do with the twelve months you didn't pay me child support.'

'Yes, well, things have changed. Since the exhibition I'm doing very well and, besides, I'd have thought you'd have been grateful to have someone else take the burden off your shoulders.'

'Rose is not a burden and if you ever say that in front of her I'll make sure you regret it.'

'For God's sake, Nat, what do you take me for?'

'A selfish, insensitive prat…shall I go on?'

'There's no need to get abusive. With us Rosie would have all the advantages and opportunities money can buy.'

'Money can't buy everything.' It could buy lawyers, though; lawyers who could twist the facts to suit their clients.

'*And* we're a married couple.'

Natalie felt a fresh flurry of uncertainty. He might be bluffing, but then again perhaps such things did still weigh heavily? 'Nobody cares about that sort of thing…?'

Mike heard the uncertainty in her voice and smiled. 'I know this is hard for you—' he placed a hand on her shoulder '—but you have to think about what is best for Rosie, Nat.'

Eyes flashing fire, Natalie angrily shrugged off his hand.

'Am I early?'

The couple, who had been too engrossed in their argument to hear the approach of the new arrival, turned towards the figure in the open doorway.

'And who the hell are you?' Mike demanded.

Rafe unhurriedly transferred his attention from Natalie's tense face. He did not feel very well disposed towards the man who had put that shadowed look of distress in her eyes and he saw no reason to disguise the fact.

'I'm Rafael Ransome,' Rafe announced, giving himself his full title. 'And you,' he observed, managing without changing expression to convey that he wasn't overly impressed with what he was seeing, 'must be the bridegroom.'

Natalie, who had never seen Rafe conduct himself with this particular brand of chilling hauteur before, wasn't surprised that Mike looked uncomfortable and angry to be on the receiving end of such studied insolence.

Identification established, Rafe seemed to lose interest in the other man almost immediately. He turned to Natalie, the warmth in his eyes a stark contrast to the dismissive contempt of moments before. He opened his hand and revealed a bunch of keys before placing them beside a colourful pot plant on a leather-banded ship's chest that had been a junk-shop find.

'I thought I'd lost them!'

Before Rafe had arrived she'd thought that Mike looked pretty impressive in his expensive morning suit and handmade shoes. Now that he stood beside Rafe she could see that she had been mistaken. Even if they had been dressed by the same tailor Mike would always have looked like a pale imitation standing next to this extraordinary man.

It wasn't just the fact that Rafe had a body that was better than incredible—anyone with enough discipline could achieve a six pack, she thought, eyeing his flat belly and feeling her own stomach muscles tighten. No, what made Rafe was that extra special ingredient that separated the leader of the pack from the common herd. He didn't have to try, he just had... well...*presence*.

Worriedly, she examined her reaction when she'd seen him standing there. Casting herself on her boss's broad chest every time he appeared was not the best way to hide the fact you were having an affair with him—or were about to. She wondered what Rafe would say if he knew that she had decided to...to...

sleep with him. Hell, I can hardly think it, let alone say it. Do I have a problem!

Of course you have a problem—you're in love with the man. You could only ignore something that was staring you in the face for just so long.

'You should be more careful with your keys,' he chided.

Natalie gulped and nodded. Oh, God, you don't know the half of it! Sure, he wanted an affair, he'd made that plain, but a clingy woman who wanted to offer him her heart—that really wasn't Rafe's style.

Mike, who had been watching this interchange with a sour expression, cleared his throat.

'Listen, if you don't mind, Nat and I were having a *private* conversation.' His hostility was still there, but it was not so overt now he had had the opportunity to fully take in the size and quality of the new arrival.

Rafe didn't even look at the other man; his steady gaze remained fixed on Natalie's face. 'Do you want me to go, Natalie?' In contrast to the intense expression in his eyes, his tone was light.

Natalie took a deep breath and turned to face her ex-husband. 'I don't have any secrets from Rafe,' she claimed.

Mike frowned. 'Since when?'

Probably something Rafe himself was wondering, too. Natalie didn't dare check out his reaction, sure that if she did her resolve would fail. She took a deep breath and plunged recklessly onwards.

'Since we decided to get married,' she announced casually.

A stunned silence followed her words.

'Well, now, isn't that convenient?' Mike drawled, quite obviously, despite his amused tone, thrown by her declaration.

Natalie was excruciatingly aware of the still, silent presence of the man beside her; she could only imagine how shocked Rafe had been to hear he was going to get married. She turned warily to look at him; with one word he could blow her out of the water. She had no way of knowing from his expression if the silent message she was desperately trying to telegraph him had been received.

'Not had time to buy a ring yet, then?'

Natalie flushed and tucked her bare left hand under her right. Observing her action, Mike regained his confidence. 'You don't really expect me to believe it?' he asked, shaking his head.

'I mean, *you*, married...?'

His incredulity stung. 'Why not *me* married?' she demanded dangerously.

'Well, you're just not the type, Nat.'

Something inside Natalie snapped. 'Not the type to what? Need a hug occasionally, need someone to laugh at my jokes... need sex...?'

'Natalie!' Mike exclaimed in a shocked tone.

She gritted her teeth and planted her hands on her hips. 'Sex, sex, sex!' she parroted defiantly. 'Just because you don't fancy me, doesn't mean other men mightn't!'

'Well, you haven't had a boyfriend for the past five years— I'd say that speaks for itself.'

Natalie's shoulders slumped in defeat as the fight drained out of her. Of course he didn't believe it, who would? Sheer desperation had driven her to attempt a rash bluff and all she had done was make a total fool of herself. Rafe was never going to back her up—and why should he? If she was going to claim a fiancé it would have been wiser to chose a more plausible candidate.

'Well, she's got one now.'

The air rushed out of Natalie's lungs in one startled gasp. Her eyes flew to Rafe's dark, autocratic face. Even though she knew the possessive warmth in his eyes was for Mike's benefit, her responsive stomach muscles quivered.

'I don't believe it. You're just saying this to stop me getting Rosie,' Mike accused, sounding like a truculent child. 'It won't work.'

'Get Rosie?' Rafe frowned.

Natalie cleared her throat. 'Gabby and Mike want to take Rose to the States...' her face crumpled '...and I'll never see her again.' The disastrous wobble in her voice made her words barely intelligible but Rafe appeared to get the gist.

'Is that some sort of joke?'

Natalie blinked back the tears. '*He* says that they—'

'*He's* talking through his...' Rafe cast the other man a look that caused the shorter man to blanch and withdraw behind a chair '...armpit,' he finished acidly. 'And I suspect he knows it.' He lifted a strand of hair from Natalie's cheek and brushed away a tear with his thumb. 'He's trying it on, sweetheart,' he promised her.

'Now, you listen here...whoever you are...'

An ebony brow quirked. 'Natalie has told you who I am. I am the man she is going to marry.'

If it weren't for the possessive arm that snaked around her waist Natalie would have fallen in a heap. Instead she turned her face into the broad chest at her disposal. There was something very soothing about the steady thud of his heartbeat, as there was about the hand that came to rest on the back of her head.

'*You can't!*'

'I think you'll find I can.' While continuing to stroke the back of Natalie's head, Rafe lifted his eyes to meet the indignant face of the other man. His lips curled contemptuously. 'I appreciate that it must be hard for you to see the woman you lost with another man. I suppose,' he added thoughtfully, 'that it's at times like this we realise what we have lost—or in your case thrown away. There really is no mystery here. We've kept our relationship under wraps because it's a bit difficult as I'm Natalie's boss. We're off to visit my parents this weekend so if you don't mind we'd like to keep it quiet until then.'

Natalie admired his ability to improvise but she wished he'd keep things simple—Mike wasn't stupid.

'Then that makes you...?'

'Quite disgustingly rich,' Natalie supplied helpfully. She

knew how Mike's mind worked. Despite his avowed contempt for money, he was always in awe of people who had it. A really horrid part of her was beginning to enjoy the sick expression on Mike's face.

'You've been sleeping with your boss?'

His tone of shocked disgust made Natalie flush.

'Well, actually, we haven't been getting a whole lot of sleep.' Rafe cupped her chin in his hand and tilted her flushed face up to him. 'Have we, angel?'

She was grateful that he'd decided to play along, but she wished he weren't doing so with quite this much relish. Already pretty messed up by the contact of his hard thigh against her own, her nervous system went haywire when he looked at her like that.

'I love it when you blush and, darling, happy Valentine's Day,' he told her in the manner of a man who found her totally fascinating and completely irresistible.

Natalie knew it was a lie but she was still mesmerised by the caressing light in his eyes.

Rose entered the room at that moment and her face lit up when she identified the tall figure standing there. 'Rafe... Rafe!' she cried, bounding across the room towards him.

'Rose... Rose!' Rafe echoed, releasing Natalie.

Well, if nothing else had convinced Mike their daughter's rapturous greeting would have swung it. Natalie was concerned by the child's enthusiasm; now with Mike about to leave it was even more important that Rose didn't grow attached to a man who wouldn't be around for long. Natalie had no illusions—she didn't have anything that could keep a man like Rafe interested for long. It was something she'd have to deal with when the time came.

'Have you brought me a present?' the little girl demanded with innocent avarice.

'*Rose!*' Natalie cried in a scandalised tone.

Rafe didn't seem bothered. 'Next time,' he promised with a grin. 'Wow, cool shoes!'

'I look pretty.' Rose preened complacently. 'Beautiful,' Rafe agreed.

'You look beautiful, too,' she observed. 'Doesn't he, Mummy?'

A choking sound emerged from Natalie's throat. As hard as she tried to avoid looking at Rafe, like a compass needle finding north her eyes seemed irresistibly drawn to his.

'Men are handsome, Rose, ladies are beautiful.'

Rose shook her head. 'No,' she persisted stubbornly, 'Rafe is beautiful.'

Natalie could only agree with her daughter's assessment of the man whose startling blue gaze was melded with her own. Her voice thickened emotionally. 'Extremely beautiful,' she agreed huskily.

'Well, I think it's time that we were going,' Mike interrupted stiffly.

It was difficult to persuade Rose it was time to go, but eventually the time Natalie had been dreading arrived—she and Rafe were alone. There seemed no point delaying the inevitable; she took a deep breath and got straight to the point.

She shot a wary glance at the tall figure who was examining the books in her bookcase. He didn't *look*, but it was reasonable to suppose, despite his performance, that he wasn't too happy with her.

'I think Mike's in a bit of a huff.'

Rafe slid a copy of a paperback thriller back; he ran a finger slowly down its spine before turning. There was a hard light in his eyes. 'I don't think I'll be losing any sleep over your Mike.'

'He isn't my Mike,' she replied irritably.

Rafe's eyes narrowed as he looked searchingly at her. *'No...?'*

'He's getting married today.'

'Most people would consider him pretty good-looking,' Rafe remarked casually.

'Fortunately Rose took after him in the looks department...'

'So you *do* think he's good-looking...?'

Natalie gave a bewildered frown. 'Look, just how are Mike's looks important to anything?' she demanded.

'If he decided not to get married, if he asked you to take him back—would you?'

Natalie coloured angrily. 'What do you take me for?' His smile was cynical. 'A woman in love?'

Natalie's eyes slid from his. 'I am not in love with Mike,' she replied guardedly. Now that she knew what being in love actually felt like she knew she had never loved Mike in that way.

Rafael gave one of his inimical shrugs. Natalie studied his face. 'You didn't like him, did you?'

His jaw tightened. 'I didn't like the number he was trying to do on you,' he revealed grimly. 'Give him custody? No lawyer, no matter how well paid, could persuade a court in the country to take Rose away from you.'

'You don't know all the facts.'

'I know you're a good mother.'

The conviction in his tone brought an emotional lump to her throat. 'But I'm stony-broke. It's ironic, really Mike has never been able to pay child support. Now he's marrying a rich woman, his uncle has died and left him a property worth over two million and the critics have decided he's the next Warhol! I, on the other hand, expend more than I earn.'

'What I said still stands—you're a good mother and that's all any judge would be interested in.'

'You're sure?' Natalie said wistfully; she really wanted to believe him.

'Totally,' Rafe confirmed.

Normally Natalie found his immutable confidence irritating, but this was one occasion when she welcomed it. 'Did you go along with...?'

'Go along with...?'

Cheeks burning, she lifted her head. 'Me saying we were engaged. Was it because you didn't like Mike?'

'I expect that had something to do with it,' he confirmed. 'I suppose you expect me to apologise for...'

'Well, going on your track record I'm not expecting it any time soon.'

Natalie's head came up, she set her hands on her hips and glared up at him. '*I* don't have a problem apologising when I know I'm in the wrong—even to you!'

One dark brow lifted. 'Meaning I do?'

'You made me feel about so high,' she said, holding her forefinger and thumb a whisper away from one another. 'And,' she added bitterly, 'if you wanted to put me in my place you didn't have to do it in front of everyone! You didn't have to...' She broke off, dismayed to feel her eyes fill with tears. 'You probably don't even know when I'm talking about.' Why would he?

'I know.'

'I was stupid enough at the time to think that we were friends,' she added in a small voice.

'Yes, you were stupid,' he agreed. 'We could never be friends,' he added harshly.

To hear him spell it so brutally hurt more than she would have thought possible. 'What's wrong, Rafe—is my hair the wrong colour?' Rafe's eyes followed the movement of her fingers as they slid through the silky strands of her long brown hair. 'Or am I from the wrong social background?' she suggested scornfully.

'Your hair...' He cleared his throat and removed his gaze from her hair. 'Your hair is beautiful.' The forceful nature of this raw declaration made Natalie look at him sharply. 'And who our parents were has nothing to do with it.'

'Pooh...says you!' She sniffed.

His nostrils flared as she turned away from him. 'Yes, I do,' he rebutted in a driven undertone. 'And I say we couldn't be friends because there's too much chemistry between us and there has been from day one.'

Natalie spun back, her face flushed, her mouth slightly ajar.

She could feel her fragile grip on reality slipping as she focused
on his lean dark face. 'You're my b...boss.'

'I don't need reminding of that,' he promised her.

'Day one!' she breathed in a stunned undertone. 'You liked
me...?'

'I don't think *like* is the correct term. Changing the subject slightly, which believe me I don't do out of choice... I was
wondering...?'

'Yes...?'

'Are you going to the wedding like that?'

'Like...?' Frowning, she followed the direction of Rafe's gaze
and gave a cry. 'Oh, God, what time is it?' she cried, drawing
the gaping lapels of her thin, loose-fitting robe in her fist.

'Relax, it's early yet.'

'You wake up looking drop-dead gorgeous; for me it requires
a little more time.'

'I think you look gorgeous like that.'

'If you're going to lie, try for something a little more be-
lievable.'

Rafe shook his head. 'My God, I've never met a woman as
hard to be nice to as you.'

CHAPTER EIGHT

NATALIE SMUDGED A little soft brown shadow on her eyelids and smeared some clear gloss on her lips. A quick flick of blusher completed her hastily applied make-up. It was ironic that the one time she had planned to really go to town with the war-paint she was in even more of a hurry than usual.

'Well, they do say the natural look is in this season,' she reflected, eyeing the result in the mirror as she fought her way into the simple soft apricot shift dress she'd decided to wear. It bore the label of a chain-store brand; Natalie had decided it would be foolish to try and compete on her budget.

She slipped her feet into a pair of high-heeled sandals that emphasised the shapely length of her slender calves and smoothed out a wrinkle in her fine lace-topped hold-ups she wore underneath. She glanced at her watch; it was the only jewellery, besides a pair of antique drop pearl earrings, she wore.

All I have to do now is something with this hair, she thought, frowning as she slid her fingers through the silky mass that fell river-straight almost to her waist. That was always supposing she *ever* got this darned zip up! She grunted softly and grimaced as she twisted around in an effort to see what the recalcitrant fastener had snagged on.

While in a position that would only be considered comfortable by a contortionist she lost her balance and stumbled against a lamp. She lunged for it, but her reflexes were not sharp enough to stop it falling off her bedside table, taking with it her alarm clock, which hit the metal bed frame and catapulted like a thing possessed across the room where it hit dead centre the cheval mirror, which shattered before her disbelieving eyes.

The noise as the glass showered onto the bare wood of the stripped floorboards was so loud that she wasn't aware of the door opening until Rafe was actually inside the room.

'I heard a noise.'

'I think they heard a noise half a mile away.' The wry smile that invited him to share the humorous side to this situation faded as her eyes encountered no reciprocal amusement in his— on the contrary Rafe's expression was unexpectedly severe, his entire manner off-puttingly grim as he stood there not reacting to the disorder around him.

Perhaps it was the thought of acting as her fiancé at the wedding that was making him look so bleak—now he'd had a little while to reflect he could be questioning if his acting ability was up to carrying it off.

Natalie was wondering if she ought to do the decent thing and give him the opportunity to back out gracefully when she caught sight of the neat stack of freshly laundered undies that were waiting to be put away on the bottom of her bed. Instinctively she reached across and drew the chenille throw that was folded across the bed over them. She realised immediately that all her prim action had done was draw his attention to them. He probably thought it hilarious that she imagined the sight of her white cotton knickers would inspire uncontrollable lust.

In your dreams! Maybe his too—*he* was the one who had mentioned chemistry. Lust at first sight, no less.

'Well, I suppose this means seven years' bad luck.'

'Are you superstitious?'

'Not especially—I have my fingers crossed.' So the joke had been pathetic, but a polite smile wouldn't have killed him!

A frown deepened the line between her arched brows as she studied his enigmatic dark face. She was beginning to get the distinct impression that he hadn't heard a word she had said.

'My zip jammed,' she began to explain. When she was nervous she babbled and his silence and the growing tension she sensed in him made her *very* nervous. Also this whole bedroom thing was something she wasn't comfortable with. 'I guess it's a classic case of more haste, less speed. I was trying to unstick it and I knocked the lamp off.' She gestured to the lamp lying on the floor. 'It was sort of a chain reaction after that—you should have seen it.'

'Is it still stuck?'

His abrupt question made her start. 'What? Oh, yes, you have to be a contort—'

'Turn around,' he instructed brusquely.

'Oh, I'll manage.' She forced her lips into a smile.

'Turn around,' he repeated in a tone that suggested he was getting bored with the subject—and, for that matter, her.

Natalie bit her lip. If she persisted in resisting his perfectly unexceptional offer it might give rise to awkward questions, such as for instance why did the idea of him touching her skin have her in such a blind panic? After all, she planned on letting him do so as much as he liked.

'Thank you.' Taking a deep breath, she turned around to give him access to the zip.

Nothing happened; nothing happened for so long that she almost turned around.

Just as she was deciding enough was enough she felt cool air touch her skin as he lifted the mesh of her loose hair off her neck. A shiver slithered softly down her spine as she felt his fingertips lightly graze her skin. At that point Natalie realised this was going to be every bit as bad as she had imagined and more...*pure torture*!

Rafe eventually managed to gather all her hair in his fist. 'There's a lot of it,' he murmured, laying the heavy swathe over her shoulder. Displaying a meticulous attention to detail, he brushed the few stray strands that clung to her neck to join them.

'Did you say something?'

Natalie closed her eyes tight shut. 'Not a thing,' she assured him brightly.

There was another agonising pause before he reapplied himself to the task in hand. The zip was jammed just below her bra strap, and Rafe's fingers slid under the lacy hem to give himself better access to the problem.

'Stop fidgeting!' he snapped tersely as she shifted restively in a frantic effort to lessen the contact that was sending ripple after ripple of hot sensation through her body. Her skin was so hot and sticky he had to have noticed.

'Then hurry up,' she retorted thickly.

'I'm going as fast as I can.' He gave a grunt of pent-up frustration. 'Damned…stupid…!'

His touch had a frightening addictive quality. 'For pity's sake, it's not brain surgery!' she gasped, desperation in her voice. 'I have a wedding to get to.' And if she did or said what she actually wanted to she was pretty sure they wouldn't!

She heard him mutter darkly under his breath and felt his warm breath stir the fine hairs on her nape as he bent closer to his task. A faint whimper escaped from between her clenched teeth.

'You all right…?'

If she hadn't been so far from all right Natalie might have noticed that Rafe's normally assured voice held an unfamiliar strained note. 'Absolutely fine!' she heard herself lie breezily.

'I'm getting there.'

So am I—she was at that very moment hovering on the brink of a precipice; one little shove would have her turning around and begging him to take her. Exhaling gustily, she dabbed her tongue to the film of moisture above her upper lip. The debilitating weakness that was already severely affecting her limbs had obviously begun to cloud her mental judgement as well.

Her suspicion was validated by the next uncensored idiot observation that spilled from her big mouth!

'Dear God, if you take this long to undress a woman the poor thing is probably asleep by the time you actually get started.'

'So far that hasn't happened; slow but thorough, that's me.'

The fiery blush travelled all over her skin, but underneath the embarrassment she was getting even more excited thinking about Rafe being thorough and slow with her.

Not now, there's a wedding to go to and all sorts of ground rules to figure out.

'Got it, I think…?' Holding the fabric taut, Rafe forced the zip upwards, it gave, and when he pulled it down again this time it slid smoothly—very smoothly all the way down.

All the way!

With a silken rush the peach-coloured fabric of the dress parted from her neck to the top of her tight buttocks and revealed the entire length of her satiny slim back, plus the interesting little dimple just above the soft curve of her peachy skinned bottom.

'Oh, *my God*!' The pressure inside Rafe's head was now so intense he knew something had to give. 'Oh, my God,' he repeated in a fainter but no less impressed tone. 'You're absolutely perfect.' He ran a fascinated finger down her straight spine, feeling the evenly spaced bony projections, letting his exploration widen to take in the elegant definition of her elegant shoulder blades.

With a mumbled imprecation that concerned his sanity, Rafe spun her around.

She stood there, visible tremors running through her slim body, eyes wide, lips parted. In the front the dress was hanging onto her slender shoulders—*barely*. One judicious tug and it would… Her wide eyes looked up at him; she was scared stiff he'd take the next step and scared stiff he wouldn't. Having suffered a similar ambivalence for weeks and months, he could readily identify with what she was feeling.

The dress fell with a sexy, silken slither to pool around her feet and Natalie stood there clad only in her minuscule lacy bra and matching pants; the stockings and high heels that completed the outfit she wore couldn't really be classed as clothing—more provocation!

Less is quite definitely more, Rafe decided, unable to stop staring like a kid at a sweet-shop window. No window...no door—in fact there was nothing keeping him away from her except his disintegrating will-power—an overrated virtue if ever there was one.

Natalie wanted to tell him that he really shouldn't have done that, but her vocal cords were paralysed—as she was—with lust. She waited for her protective reflexes to kick in, but they didn't. But then no man had ever looked at her the way Rafe was, and she felt her legs tremble.

'I've wanted you for weeks,' he confided, laying his hands heavily on her shoulders. 'I've fantasised about what you had on under those hideous, baggy clothes you wear.' He wasn't sure she was ready to hear what he had fantasised about doing once he had removed those clothes...fantasised about doing right there in his office.

Desire was like a fist clutching low in her belly. 'I dress for comfort.' She was surprised to hear an unfamiliar breathy voice emerge from her lips. 'Well, thank you for fixing my zip.' And blowing my mind into some lustful other dimension. 'But I really should be getting ready now.'

Rafe heard her out politely before he laughed scornfully and closed his hand possessively over her right breast. From the expression in his eyes it seemed to Natalie that he found the sight of her small breast covered by his big hand as stimulating as she did.

'I know a short cut to the church, we have at least forty minutes to spare.' He appeared to consider the problem. 'What do you suppose we do with that time?'

As he spoke he was scooping her straining breast out of the

flimsy bra cup with practised ease. A sibilant hiss escaped through his clenched teeth as he watched the already engorged pink bud swell and harden. Natalie cried out and grabbed him by the front of his shirt.

'You are probably the smuggest, most conceited man that ever lived,' she accused shakily.

Rafe swallowed hard and dragged his reverent gaze to her face; there was not a trace of the smugness she accused him of in his raw, driven expression. Her stomach flipped.

He gave a strained, crooked grin. 'But sexy with it, *right...?*' he croaked hoarsely.

A laugh was wrenched from Natalie's dry throat—laughter and sex had never seemed compatible until now. 'It isn't your sex appeal that's in question here, it's my sanity—' She broke off mid-complaint as she felt the catch on her bra unclick.

With a smile Rafe chucked her bra over his shoulder. 'In the interests of symmetry,' he explained, admiring the perfect symmetry of her unfettered breasts. The thought of taking those straining peaks into his mouth aroused him unbearably.

Natalie could smell the warm male scent of his body. She wanted to touch him, wanted to so badly it blocked out every other thought. Feeling bold and reckless, she laid a hand flat against his chest; through his shirt she could feel the heavy thud of his heartbeat. His body was solid muscle and bone, a long, lean and lovely body. She gave a shudder of sheer heady anticipation and let her hand slide boldly to his flat belly. She felt the sharp contraction of his stomach muscles as he sucked in his breath.

'Sorry, I'm messing up your lovely clothes.'

She went to lift her hand but he caught it hard and held it there. His shimmering blue eyes scanned her flushed face. 'To hell with my lovely clothes!' he declared, releasing her, but only to tear the tie from around his neck. This followed the same path as her bra.

'There's glass everywhere—this is dangerous. You could cut yourself.'

No, you're the dangerous one, she thought, looking at his stern, predatory profile. Desire kicked hard in her molten belly, she shivered and her eyes darkened dramatically.

Without saying a word and correctly taking her compliance as written, Rafe swept her up in his arms, and picked his way through the shattered mirror towards the bed. Before he placed her down he removed the top cover, which was covered in tiny fragments of glass, and flung it to one side.

'Where are you going?' she asked plaintively when he didn't join her.

'I'll be right there,' he promised. His bright-burning eyes didn't leave her face for an instant as he stripped off his clothes with flattering urgency.

Natalie stared. She couldn't help herself—he was beautiful in a way that made her throat ache. His skin was an even dark gold dusted lightly in significant areas by erotic drifts of dark hair. The impressive strength of his upper body and magnificent, tightly muscled shoulders was perfectly balanced by a hard, washboard belly and long, long legs. Greyhound lean, he moved with the perfect co-ordination and fluid grace of a natural athlete. He certainly had a turn for speed—in a matter of seconds he was standing there in just his boxers. As he stepped out of them Natalie caught her breath. She looked away, feeling like a guilty schoolgirl caught peeking.

Rafe gave a wolfish grin of predatory satisfaction. 'Don't mind me, I like you looking,' he confided with shameless candour.

The bed springs creaked as he landed beside her. There was no trace of laughter in his face as their eyes locked. Without saying anything he fixed his mouth to hers; it fitted perfectly. He continued to kiss her, deep, drugged kisses that sent her spiralling out of control and kept her there.

Natalie clutched at him, revelling in the smoothness of his skin and the hardness of his muscle. She didn't connect the soft guttural sounds that she could hear with herself.

Hands cupping her buttocks, Rafe drew her body into his. 'You can feel how much I want you…?'

Her body reacted as much to the sound of his voice as the erotic pressure of his arousal against her soft belly. Giving a fractured little sigh, she opened her eyes and tried to focus on his face…the outline was blurry.

'Are you crying?' Concern roughened his voice.

Natalie blinked and shook her head. The combination of lust and love was something she had never been exposed to before; she had no defences against the heady cocktail. 'I want you, too,' she whispered, touching him because she quite simply had to—*not* touching his silken length was no more an option than not breathing!

He groaned greedily and pulsed against the confines of her trembling hand. His uninhibited pleasure encouraged her to continue her erotic explorations.

It was Rafe who eventually stopped her teasing caresses.

'My turn, I think,' he announced throatily as he flipped her over onto her back.

Still ahead every step of the way, still anticipating what she wanted before she knew it herself, he slid down her body, caressing her with his hands, tasting her with his lips.

Her swollen, tingling breasts felt as if they were on fire after he had applied his clever tongue and hands to each quivering, pink-tipped mound in turn. She closed her eyes as he licked his way lower and when he reached the hot, drenched, sensitised region between her pale thighs her back arched, lifting her hips clear of the mattress.

Natalie hooked her fingers in his hair.

Rafe lifted his head. There were dark bands of colour high across his cheekbones. He took one look at her face and groaned. 'When you look at me like that I just want to…'

'So do I,' she moaned. 'So do, Rafe. Do it right now, you beautiful man!' she cried brokenly.

He kissed her neck as he settled over her. 'Oh, my God!' she moaned as he slid up into her, hard and hot. 'Oh, this is…is…' he rocked higher into her and she bit into the damp skin of his neck sobbing softly '…good…very, very good.'

'It will be…' he promised, thrusting hard. 'Just let go, let it happen,' he instructed, continuing to build a smooth, fluid rhythm.

Natalie didn't know what he was talking about, but she did know that she wouldn't mind if he carried on doing what he was for ever. A little while later she found out this wasn't true—in fact she couldn't bear it any longer. Just about that moment she discovered, in the most earth-shattering way, what he had meant—*it* happened!

In the aftermath of a climax that had involved her entire body from her toes to—well, she couldn't discount the possibility her hair follicles had been involved—she lay there in a dazed glow, curled up like a sleepy, sexy kitten in his arms. The only sound was her occasional murmur of, *'Wow!'* which made Rafe, who had his chin propped on top of her head, grin.

'I think I'm going to fall asleep,' she confided.

'Nice idea, but we might miss the wedding photos.'

With a horrified cry Natalie leapt out of bed, ignoring his warning cry of, 'Watch the glass!'

'Oh, God, we'll be late. Why didn't you remind me?' she remonstrated severely as she struggled into her clothes.

'I had other things on my mind.'

They weren't late and Natalie got to cry a little, seeing Rose looking sweet walking up the aisle behind the bride.

There was a certain novelty value attached to being the centre of attention. It aggravated the bride, too, which was a definite plus, but Natalie knew it wasn't her stunning good looks or sparkling personality that were the draw. No, it was the man beside her. That Rafe would inevitably know and be known by people on this sort of celebrity guest-list had not even crossed her mind.

She had reached the point, after two glasses of champagne, where she was actually enjoying herself when Mike introduced her as Rafe's fiancée. He did so in front of half a dozen people Rafe knew, one of whom, an opera singer of international fame, turned out to be one of his mother's best friends.

'Oh, Luisa didn't tell me and I only spoke to her on Thursday!' she exclaimed, kissing first Rafe and then Natalie on both cheeks.

'Actually, Sophia, we haven't told the families yet so I'd be grateful if you could keep it to yourself for a couple of days,' Rafe requested smoothly.

'But of course,' she promised immediately. 'And do your family know yet, Natalie?'

Natalie got the impression those bright, curious eyes were missing not a detail of her outfit.

'There's only my grandmother.'

'Oh, how sad, but you have a little girl, I believe…? A ready-made family—how nice for you, Rafe…but you have such a big family. Have you been to the *palazzo* in Venice yet?'

Natalie shook her head. *Palazzo!* That figured—blue blood on both sides.

'We'd planned to spend our honeymoon there,' Rafe slotted in smoothly.

'Oh, you will love it. Come along and tell me all about yourself, my dear,' she urged, drawing a reluctant Natalie away.

'I have never been so glad for Valentine's Day to end.' Natalie sighed later as she kicked off her shoes in the comfort of the car. Rose was already fast asleep in the back. 'I am so sorry!'

'About what?'

'About the fiancée stuff in front of your mum's friend. What'll you say to them?' she asked worriedly.

Rafe dismissed them with a shrug. 'Oh, I'll deal with them, don't worry.'

'You're being awful nice about this…?'

'I'm a nice guy,' he revealed modestly. 'Once you get to know me.'

Natalie lowered her eyes to her hands, which lay primly in her lap. 'I was wondering…' Was she making a terrible mistake?

'You were wondering what?' he prompted.

'I was wondering if you'd like to stay the night with me…if you've no plans, that is…'

There was a charged silence.

'If I had any I'd change them,' he told her with a grin that revealed his even white teeth. 'You have absolutely no idea how happy I am to hear you say that.'

'Well, I'm pretty happy to hear you say yes,' she admitted. 'The only problem is… I mean, I know that it's inevitable this thing between us has a relatively short shelf-life…'

'Is that so?'

His weird tone made her glance across at him sharply, but his profile was unrevealing.

'Well, of course,' she confirmed, determined to show him she didn't have any unrealistic expectations. 'I'm afraid…' she cast a worried glance at the child asleep in the back seat '…that Rose will get too fond of you. Perhaps you should keep your distance,' she suggested doubtfully.

'And how do you propose I do that?' he grated, not looking amused by her suggestion.

'I see what you mean. It's a pity you get on so well…'

'I can see how it might be more convenient if your child and boyfriend hated the sight of one another,' he drawled. 'For the record, I don't think it's a helpful thing to decide a relationship is doomed to failure before it's even started.'

Natalie blinked. Surely he wasn't suggesting they could have something long term!

He took his eyes briefly from the road. 'Why not see how things develop?' he suggested in a more moderate tone.

'That's fine by me,' she replied, trying to keep the jubilation and hope from her voice.

CHAPTER NINE

THE FOLLOWING FRIDAY a week later Natalie was outside Rafe's office. They had arranged at breakfast to have lunch together. They had *done* lunch together twice already that week, and breakfast every day! A smile appeared in her eyes as her thoughts dwelt on an unshaved Rafe sitting at her kitchen table with tousled dark hair falling in his eyes... Sometimes she had to pinch herself, it seemed so unreal. But there was nothing imaginary about the growing selection of male toiletries crammed on the shelves in her dinky bathroom or the pair of black men's socks that had turned her white delicate wash a dirty grey.

The changes weren't restricted to her flat. Natalie felt a different person from the one she had a mere week earlier: happier, more carefree—simply more alive!

She had her moments of doubt. It wasn't just that Rafe had quickly become part of her life—he had become part of Rose's, too.

'Things are moving a bit fast,' she suggested tentatively to Rafe after the sock incident.

His deep blue eyes lifted from the journal he was reading. 'Do you mind?'

Natalie thought about it. 'No, actually, I don't,' she revealed with a silly grin.

Rafe responded with a grin of his own—one that was not at all silly. His grin made her heart race and her knees turn to cotton wool. He didn't raise any objections when she took the magazine from his hands and climbed onto his lap—none at all!

When she had asked Rafe what she ought to tell people at work, he had shrugged in the way only a Latin male could and said, 'Whatever you like,'—which was no help at all. On reflection Natalie had decided not to volunteer anything, but if anyone asked she would tell them the truth, though sometimes she wasn't sure what that was, or where they were going.

She was totally, deeply, deliriously in love with Rafe, but how did he feel? Though expressive in many ways, shockingly so on occasions, he never once said 'love'. He told her how beautiful and sexy she was, but never once did he say he loved her. His restraint on the subject made her shy of expressing her own feelings, even though sometimes she *ached* to do so.

She was about to knock when she saw the door was ajar. She had pushed it open a little when she heard Rafe's voice inside; as she paused he switched seamlessly from Italian to English.

'Hold on, Mother, I'll put you on the speaker.'

His mother! Natalie, who had been about to move away, couldn't resist the opportunity of listening a little longer.

'Rafael, you don't call, you are never at home when I call and I've been so concerned ever since Sophia contacted me.'

The husky voice the other end was attractively accented.

'I asked her not to, so I was fairly sure she would. Why are you concerned, Mother?' Natalie could hear the sound of Rafe moving about the office—a drawer opening, paper rustling. She really ought to go—if he found her standing there eavesdropping it might be a little embarrassing.

'Do not be so obtuse, Rafael! Why do you think I am concerned? I know you were a little annoyed with your father...'

'Annoyed!' Natalie heard the sound of Rafe's harsh laugh.

'Why should I be annoyed? My father thinks he can arrange a marriage to suitable breeding stock, he puts me in an impossibly embarrassing situation…what is there to be annoyed about?'

'You know your father, he means well, but he—'

'Is a snobbish, manipulative, unprincipled… Do you suppose he's *ever* going to learn he can't run my life?'

'I know you're angry, I know you want to punish him, but really this isn't the way to do it!'

'What are you talking about, Mother?'

'I'm not stupid, Rafael,' came the impatient maternal reply. 'Remember what you said when I asked you about marriage—you told me then what the girl you married would be like. From what Sophia tells me this girl is the exact opposite.'

There was a short pause, during which Natalie held her breath; any desire to leave had vanished. 'You know, I haven't actually thought about it, but I suppose she is.'

'Add that to the fact this girl you so suddenly get engaged to just happens to be everything your father would dislike—divorced…with a child…from a totally different social background to your own… Am I supposed to think this is a coincidence? I know you want to teach your father a lesson, Rafael, but you have involved another person,' the husky voice remonstrated worriedly. 'Have you thought how this young woman is going to feel when she realises you are using her? I am assuming you are going to call a halt to this thing before you get as far as a church…?'

Natalie could have told her how *this girl* would feel—how this girl *was* feeling: numb. There was a total absence of feeling; she felt dead inside.

She turned and began to walk away, slowly at first and then quicker until she was running full pelt, oblivious to the startled glances she attracted. It all made sense, of course. That was why Rafe hadn't been angry when she had claimed he was her fiancé. He had seen it as the perfect opportunity to teach his interfering father a lesson—and the sex had been good, too.

My God, he must have thought it was his lucky day! She felt used and grubby and very, *very* stupid. She dashed a hand across her face as the tears started in her eyes. The numbness was beginning to fade, leaving a knot of pain that was lodged like a fist behind her breastbone.

'And all the while I was dreaming my silly dreams like the besotted idiot I am!'

'Ms Warner... Natalie...?'

'Yes, Maggie,' Natalie replied as she continued to empty the contents of her drawers into a bag.

'I just wanted to say... I'm sorry if...'

God, is this Maggie trying to be friends because she thinks I'm the boss's girlfriend? Ironic under the circumstances. 'Honestly, Maggie, you don't have to bother.'

'Oh, but I do, I *want* to! I think I might have treated you unfairly,' she began awkwardly. 'No, I *know* I did.'

'It's not nec—' Natalie began tiredly.

'I need to say this,' came the taut response. 'You made me feel guilty.'

Natalie straightened up. *'Guilty...?'* she echoed with a frown.

The older woman nodded. 'I had a baby, you see. I wasn't married and I gave him away...'

The simple statement hid half a lifetime of pain. Natalie's eyes filled with tears as her tender heart ached with empathy for the pain etched on the other woman's face.

'Oh, I'm so sorry, I didn't know.'

'Nobody did,' Maggie told her thickly. 'I made a choice, I chose my career over my baby. You didn't and, seeing you doing both so well, it made me ashamed that I had never even tried. Every time I looked at you I...' She shook her head and when she continued her voice was thick with emotion. 'I'm sorry I gave you a hard time.'

Natalie shook her head. 'It doesn't matter,' she told the other woman wearily. Nothing mattered any more, but Maggie's poignant tale had reminded her of something she still had—

her daughter—and for that reason if no other she had to carry on. It didn't matter how bleak her personal future seemed, the luxury of falling apart was not an option.

'What are you doing?' Maggie seemed to notice for the first time that Natalie was removing her belongings.

With her forearm Natalie brushed the entire contents from her desktop into an open bag. She fastened the bag and straightened up. 'I'm leaving.'

Staying after what had happened was clearly out of the question. The idea of seeing Rafe on a daily basis made her blood run cold. She would take Rose for a holiday to her grandmother's, and when she was there she could sort out her options, such as they were. Maybe she would stay in Yorkshire? It had a lot to recommend it, the biggest selling point being the number of miles that separated it from Rafe Ransome. It was cheaper to live in the country. Grimly determined to be positive even if her world was falling apart, she told herself the country air would be good for Rose.

'Leaving! But I thought that you and...' Maggie stopped, colouring under Natalie's wry gaze.

'I thought we were, too, but I was wrong.' Natalie clamped her trembling lips together and, brushing past the other woman with her head downbent, fled.

Natalie found herself back at the flat; scarily she had no memory of how she'd got there. Once inside she began to put her plan—such as it was—into action. It was unlikely that Rafe would follow her, but if she was wrong, however, she had no intention of being here when he arrived. She gritted her teeth and blinked back the hot tears that filled her eyes as she haphazardly piled some of Rose's clothes and toys into a suitcase. She would pick Rose up from the child-minder and go straight to the railway station—yes, that was the best thing to do.

She was struggling as she lugged the second overfull case into the living room, when she hit her shin a painful glancing blow on a low table. If anything the pain was a useful distraction from the other pain... Sniffing defiantly, she placed her burden by the front door and looked around, trying to focus her thoughts. Had she forgotten anything vital? Mentally she ticked off items on her list of necessities. Her gaze fell upon an open book. It lay where Rafe had left it after Rose had climbed off his knee the previous evening.

'Tomorrow,' he had promised when she had begged him to continue. 'You heard what Mummy said—it's bedtime for you, young lady.'

An overwhelming sense of loss washed over Natalie, followed by a violent wave of anger. Rafe could have argued he had never lied to her—never told her he loved her—and it would have been true. She was willing to take a proportion of the blame herself, blame for falling in love with him. As far as Rose was concerned *nothing* could excuse his behaviour. That little girl adored him and she was going to be desperately confused and hurt to have him vanish from her life.

For that Natalie would never forgive him!

The sound of the key turning in the lock was very loud in the quiet room. Natalie mastered her panic and lifted her chin as she turned to face the door.

Rafe stepped into the room. Tall, devastatingly handsome and very, *very* angry. Anyone with normal co-ordination and reflexes would have fallen in a graceful heap over the pile of cases that lay there, but not Rafe. Without pausing, he sidestepped the obstacle without removing his burning gaze off the slim, rigid figure who stood in the middle of the room.

Lips compressed, nostrils flared, his powerful chest rising and falling as if he'd been running, he scanned her pale, hostile face with his brilliantly compelling gaze.

'Going somewhere, Natalie?'

Natalie gave a contemptuous little laugh. 'Anywhere you are not.' Her antagonistic reply was rewarded by his sharp inhalation. 'How did you know I was gone? No, don't tell me—the loyal Maggie. You really do seem to inspire selfless devotion in women, Rafe, but consider yourself with one less devoted slave.' She placed her splayed fingers flat on her heaving bosom just in case he was in any doubt of whom she referred to. 'You can leave the key on the table when you leave.' She spoilt her dignified dismissal by adding childishly, 'I suppose you'll be relieved not to be slumming it any longer!'

Rafe shook his head impatiently. '*Slumming it?* What the hell are you talking about?'

'I did wonder that you never invited me to your place, but it all makes perfect sense now. How would you explain me to your friends?' With curious objectivity she observed the effect of her words on his composure as the nerve beside his mouth jerked.

'How could I suggest you spend the night with me when you kept telling me how you wanted to keep the disruption to Rose's routine to a minimum? Dear God, woman, you acted as if I was trying to move in when I left a toothbrush in the bathroom!'

His ability to come up with a plausible excuse and then turn the tables so that *she* was the one at fault was staggering and probably, she thought angrily, the secret of his success.

'Sure, you're Mr Considerate!'

'Stop this, Natalie,' he pleaded in a low, impassioned voice.

'Stop what?'

The calculated obtuseness of her comment drew a harsh Italian curse from him. Swearing fluently, he crossed the room. As he reached her side Natalie was extremely conscious of his sheer physical power, of his tall, tightly muscled frame—he was a man in the peak of physical condition. In the past awareness of this strength had excited her; even now her stomach lurched as he approached. Contemplating the thrill it had given her to surrender to that strength increased her sense of self-loathing. With provocative deliberation she turned her head and looked away.

'What's going on here, Nat?' Rafe took her chin in his hand and tilted her head up to him. 'This morning things were fine, lunchtime you clean out your desk and walk out without a word…now I find you about to leave. Were you planning to give me any sort of explanation?' The screaming tension on his taut features brought his cheekbones into sharp prominence.

'No.'

Her monosyllabic response had much the same effect on him as a red rag did to a bull. 'Good God!' he thundered. 'You are—' He bit off the words he was about say and inhaled, breathing deeply as if he didn't trust himself to respond. When he did speak his low tone was flat and expressionless. 'Do you not think that I deserve to know what the hell I'm supposed to have done?'

Natalie gave an enraged yelp and tore her face from his grasp. 'You deserve—you deserve!' she yelled, her voice rising to a shrill, accusing shriek. 'You deserve to rot in hell, Rafael Ransome!'

He recoiled as if she'd physically struck him. If she hadn't known better she'd have bought that look of bewildered confusion on his dark face—if, that was, she hadn't heard that incriminating conversation and if she hadn't subsequently had her heart ripped out.

'I know, Rafe. I know.' She waited for him to at least acknowledge he had been caught out, but he didn't even have the decency to do that! 'So you can imagine why I find it a bit laughable you acting like the injured party here. I'm an adult, I should have known better,' she acknowledged, 'but I'll never forgive you for Rose. It was cruel, Rafe—you made her love you!' She pressed a hand over her mouth as a sob escaped.

'And I love her.'

Natalie gasped wrathfully. 'Why, you callous bas—!'

Rafe caught her hand mid-swing and brought it firmly down to her side. 'Now you will tell me what I am supposed to have done.'

Breathing hard as if she had been running Natalie raised her bitter eyes to his. They shimmered with unshed tears. 'There's no need to pretend, Rafe. *I know.*'

As if he could compel her to speak by sheer force of will, his piercing blue eyes narrowed on her face. '*You know...?* I'm glad one of us does, because I haven't the faintest idea what you're talking about. You know what exactly? Speak to me, Natalie, because you're killing me here.'

For a moment she hesitated; surely nobody could fake the raw emotional intensity and anguish she heard echoed in his voice. Then she remembered that damning conversation she had overheard and her face hardened.

'I know that you had your own reasons for pretending we were an item.'

Natalie hadn't known that she was secretly harbouring a crazy hope that this would all prove to be some horrible mistake until she felt it die. It died when he couldn't meet her eyes.

'And you think you know what those are?' he hedged.

'I know why you weren't bothered if your parents got to know about our fake engagement—you wanted them to.'

He shook his head, his brows drawing together in a puzzled line. 'Wanted them to what?'

Natalie gave an exasperated sigh. 'I heard you on the phone with your mother.'

A flicker of comprehension appeared in his strained eyes. As she watched his head fell back and he exhaled noisily. Bizarrely his attitude seemed one almost of relief.

'I took the call on the speaker phone...' He ran a hand across his jaw.

Natalie knew that by this time of day he would be able to feel a faint stubble. Only yesterday she had complained about it when he'd kissed her in the office lift and he had laughed. Actually she enjoyed the abrasive roughness against her soft skin. The flood of heat that washed through her body was mingled with anger and shame.

'Don't bother trying to remember what you said,' she advised dully. 'I heard enough to make me realise I've been a total fool to fall in love with you.'

Rafe's head jerked up sharply; his iridescent blue eyes scanned her face. Whatever he saw there made the blood drain from his face, his normally healthily golden-toned skin looking greyish.

'*You fell in love...?*'

Clearly this was news to him and not welcome news. Maybe he had a conscience after all? Well, that was good, because if she felt this wretched it only seemed fair that he should feel a little bit bad, too.

'So sorry if you didn't bargain for that, but don't worry, I've woken up, I won't be proclaiming my feelings from any high buildings.' The way I've been acting, I probably don't need to. 'I know that this has all been about you wanting to teach your father a lesson. Everything falls in your lap, doesn't it, Rafe?' she reflected bitterly. 'You needed an unsuitable sort of girlfriend and who comes along but the definitive version—*me*? The sort of girl your father would cross the street to avoid being contaminated by!'

'So *that's* it. You think...!' He shook his head and drew an unsteady hand through his dark hair. Then unforgivably he laughed—he actually *laughed*. This fresh proof of his heartless callousness made Natalie feel physically sick. 'You were eavesdropping! Actually, Natalie, my father has been known to cross the street to get a closer look at a beautiful girl but never the other way around.'

'That only works if the girl is beautiful and I'm not.'

Her statement brought a stern, disapproving frown to his wide brow. 'If I say you're beautiful, you are,' Rafe pronounced with breathtaking arrogance.

'I have to be beautiful because you deigned to sleep with me, is that how it works? And don't expect me to apologise about eavesdropping—if I hadn't been I'd still be walking around thinking I was living out some sort of romantic fantasy.'

His eyes dropped to the lush curves of her full lips and then lower to the firm, uptilted outline of her small, pert breasts. He swallowed hard.

Seeing the contraction of muscles in his strong brown throat was the key that unlocked the door to forbidden memories. Memories of other muscles in his lean, firm body contracting and quivering beneath the glistening surface of his sweat-soaked skin and all in response to her touch.

She had almost succeeded in locking away the steamy memory when his heavy, darkly fringed eyelids, lifted revealing an expression so hot it could have started a forest fire. Natalie's pupils dilated until they almost obliterated the iris; similarly, the hormonal rush in her blood had a dramatic effect on her ability to think rationally—as in she couldn't! Sweat broke out over her entire body as she tried to drag herself clear of the sensual vortex that was sucking her deeper with each passing second.

'All my fantasies have you in,' he told her simply.

Goose-bumps broke out over her body as she suffered yet another dramatic shift in temperature. *If you believe this it'll hurt, Nat...don't believe...don't...!* She didn't allow herself to respond until she had regained some sort of control over her emotions.

'What is it with you?' she grated, trying to frame a reply that would make him realise he no longer had anything to gain from this pretence. '*I know*, Rafe, you don't have to keep up the act.'

'The only thing I've ever pretended with you, Natalie, is that I could control the way you made—*make* me feel,' he gritted with a self-derisive grimace. 'If you'd stayed around to hear the rest of my conversation with my mother you'd have heard me say as much to her. I left her in no doubt that she'd read things wrong.'

His hard jaw clenched as his brooding glance paused hungrily on the outline of her soft, quivering lips.

'The reason I didn't object when you introduced me as your lover was I liked the way it sounded.' Natalie's fractured gasp was clearly audible in the short pause that followed his words. 'As for playing your future husband, I had this idea that if I played the part really well you might decide to keep me on permanently.'

The blood drained from Natalie's face. *'Permanently?'* she parroted weakly. 'As in living together!'

'No.'

God, Natalie, will you never learn? 'Right,' she said, fighting for composure.

'As in married,' he slotted in coolly.

Natalie looked at her hands. They were shaking; so was the rest of her. This was all happening too fast for her to take in. 'But you said…'

'No, Natalie, my *mother* said. Think about it,' he suggested. She did.

An arrested expression crossed Natalie's face. *Rafe* had never actually said…had he…? Could she have jumped to the wrong conclusion?

'My mother is legendary for reading situations wrong.' His brows lifted. 'Now that I think about it, you two should have a lot in common,' he mused drily. 'Of course, if she had actually met you she would never have made that mistake. One look at you and she'd have seen that I'd be the luckiest man alive if you'd have me. Will you have me, Natalie?'

Natalie's heart was trying to batter its way out of her chest; the tight feeling her racing pulse created made it hard to breathe, let alone speak.

'What are you saying exactly, Rafe?' This time she wasn't going to jump to any premature conclusions.

A spasm of raw frustration flickered across his handsome, drawn face. 'Do I need to spell it out?' he asked thickly.

'Well, yes, actually, I think you do.'

'Marry me, Natalie.' As her silence grew so did the tension in him. 'I think we make a pretty good team…'

Natalie widened her eyes innocently. 'So this is by way of being a business merger?' she queried pertly.

Their eyes touched; when Rafe saw what shone in hers the

tension seemed to drain from his body. A fierce grin spread slowly across his dark face. 'Like hell it is!' he growled, reaching for her. 'Come here, you stupid woman.'

Resistance didn't even cross Natalie's mind as she walked into his open arms—where she belonged. His muscular arms tightened around her as his mouth found hers. The masterful kiss was raw, hard and hungry. Natalie's lips parted eagerly beneath the pressure. When they finally broke apart she was dizzy and insanely happy.

'Don't you ever, *ever* do that to me again! Do you hear me? I've aged about twenty years in the last hour.'

Natalie touched the raven hair at his temple. Despite his claim there was no sign of premature greying. 'Well, I wouldn't have jumped to the wrong conclusion if you'd told me how you felt,' she chastised him reproachfully.

One dark brow lifted. 'Like you did…?'

'I was afraid if I said anything I'd scare you off,' she admitted. 'And I felt that every time I tried to get closer you pulled back.'

'I was trying to be what you wanted—a low-maintenance girlfriend who didn't make demands…' She intercepted his wry look and grinned. 'Except in the bedroom,' she admitted guiltily.

'Let's leave the bedroom out of this for a few minutes,' he pleaded throatily.

'That's a first for you!'

Her saucy jibe earned her a long, lingering kiss.

When his head finally lifted Natalie gave a languid sigh and ran her fingers down the hard curve of his cheek. Rafe's eyes darkened as he caught her fingers and brought them to his lips. Quite deliberately he kissed each individual fingertip—Natalie found it incredibly erotic. He pressed an open-mouthed kiss to her palm before returning her hand to her.

'Is this real?' The air left her lungs as his arms tightened about her ribcage before dropping to the small of her back. The firm pressure brought her up onto her tiptoes and sealed their bodies at hip level so that she could feel—as he intended her to—the very real state of his arousal. 'You've convinced me,' she admitted with a husky chuckle.

'You see why I wanted to keep the bedroom out of this. I need to say stuff and I can't think above the waist when you're like this.'

Secretly delighted at the image of herself as some sort of irresistible Jezebel, Natalie gave a sexy little sinuous wriggle that drew a deep groan from Rafe. She gave a regretful sigh and drew back.

'You're right, we should talk. How about if I sit over there—' she pointed at the sofa against the wall the opposite side of the room '—and you sit here.'

Rafe caught her arm. 'Too far.'

'And this is too close?' she asked huskily.

'It wouldn't matter to the way I feel if a thousand miles separated us,' he declared in a deep, throbbing accent. 'Oh, my love!' His blue eyes glittered down into hers as he laid his big hands on her shoulders. 'I think I loved you right from the beginning. When I told myself I was protecting you by keeping my distance, in reality I think it was more about protecting myself—I just wasn't ready to admit what I felt for you.'

'Are you ready now?' she whispered, hearing the thud of her own heartbeat in her ears.

She watched a slow, incredible smile spread across his face. 'Ready, able and very, *very* willing.'

'Oh, Rafe, I love you so much!'

The warm, sensuous impression left by his lips made her own tingle even after he had lifted his head. While she was smiling a little stupidly up at him he slid his hands down her arms until their fingertips were touching.

'I think this is about as far as I feel safe letting you go away from me...' he confessed.

'I'm not going to run away again, but...' Rafe groaned. 'No more *buts*, please!'

'I love you but I don't want to be responsible for some sort of family rift. Your mother said your father would hate me,' she added worriedly.

He took her face between his hands needily. 'My father is many things, but stupid is not one of them.' The uncomplicated love revealed in his expression made Natalie's eyes fill with tears of sheer joy. 'It'll take him about two seconds to see you're exactly what he's been telling me I need for years. Within half an hour he'll have convinced himself it was all his idea.'

Natalie laughed. His certainty went a long way to easing her concerns.

'Forget my father, forget everyone, this is about us. We're a package deal: you, me and Rose,' Rafe declared proudly. 'Is that all right by you?'

'I think I might get used to the idea.' She laughed, throwing her arms around his neck. 'Given forty years or so.'

And Natalie was looking forward to every second of those years beside the man she loved.

* * * * *

Their Reunion To Remember

Tina Beckett

MEDICAL
Pulse-racing passion

Three-times Golden Heart® Award finalist **Tina Beckett** learned to pack her suitcases almost before she learned to read. Born to a military family, she has lived in the United States, Puerto Rico, Portugal and Brazil. In addition to traveling, Tina loves to cuddle with her pug, Alex, spend time with her family and hit the trails on her horse. Learn more about Tina from her website, or friend her on Facebook.

Books by Tina Beckett

Harlequin Medical Romance

The Island Clinic collection
How to Win the Surgeon's Heart

New York Bachelor's Club
Consequences of Their New York Night
The Trouble with the Tempting Doc

A Summer in São Paulo
One Hot Night with Dr. Cardoza

A Christmas Kiss with Her Ex-Army Doc
Miracle Baby for the Midwife
Risking It All for the Children's Doc
It Started with a Winter Kiss
Starting Over with the Single Dad

Visit the Author Profile page
at millsandboon.com.au for more titles.

Dear Reader,

Have you ever met an old acquaintance and not recognized them immediately? There's that whole "Hi there, how are you?" exchange that leaves you scrambling to identify the person. What if that awkward moment was something you struggled with every single day?

For vascular surgeon Lia Costa, that is life. Due to a childhood illness, she can no longer recognize faces, a condition called prosopagnosia. It affects every aspect of her life. When she runs into a former lover on Valentine's Day, she is stumped for a few brief seconds as to who he is. But that moment proves to be a pivotal event that rocks her world.

Thank you for joining Lia and Micah as they attempt to resolve their past issues and find a way to redefine what is important...and what is not. It won't be easy, but maybe, just maybe, they will discover something they thought they'd lost.

I hope you love reading about these two special characters as much as I loved writing their story.

Love,

Tina Beckett

To my husband, who truly makes me feel seen.

**Praise for
Tina Beckett**

"Tina Beckett definitely followed through on
the premise and managed to infuse just the right
amount of angst and passion to keep me glued
to the pages of *Miracle Baby for the Midwife* from
beginning to end."

—*Harlequin Junkie*

PROLOGUE

ILIANA COSTA STARED at the lineup of fathers, her insides beginning to unravel in panic. She tried to remember what Papa had told her to do in a situation like this. But it wasn't working. From this distance, she couldn't spot the small scar at the outside corner of his left eye, and right now all the dark-haired men blurred into one indistinct subset of humans with no defining features. No way to tell them apart other than by their clothes. And she had no idea what Papa was wearing.

She glanced at her classmates, who—with a chicken egg perched on each of their spoons—were laughing and anxious to race toward one of the men on the other side of the room.

Lia was not laughing. All she felt was fear and the remembrance of being made fun of for going to the wrong person. It had happened so many times. With teachers. With friends. With her mom and dad. The worst had been at a mother/daughter tea when she'd gone up and sat with the wrong mom at one of the fancy tables. A little girl had come up to her, chest puffed out and declared that was *her* mother and that Lia couldn't have her. Every head had turned to stare at her. And then came the whispers. Her own mom, who'd arrived late, had come over and rescued her.

It was why her mother now wore a stretchy pink bracelet

around her wrist, so that Lia could spot her from a distance. She remembered fingering that bracelet when she was nervous. It was harder with her father, who'd insisted she learn to recognize him using means other than his face. So she used the scar beside his eye. It was his tell...his pink bracelet.

Why didn't other kids have this problem?

Two of the men had beards, so she mentally marked them off the list. One was much taller than the others. Not him, either.

The whistle sounded, and the girls took off, each choosing a direction with a certainty that Lia didn't understand. She ran, too, desperately searching through the rest of the dads, looking for a clue. Then one of the men locked eyes with her, his left hand slowly coming up and forming a thumbs-up sign.

Papa! Oh, Papa, thank you!

Taking a grateful breath, she fixed her gaze on him and changed directions, moving toward him with a sureness she didn't feel. Until she got closer and saw that familiar scar.

Then she knew. *This* man was her father. Her heart swelled with love, the fear slowly trickling away.

When she reached him, she carefully transferred her egg from her spoon to his. And as he moved away from her toward the starting line, her gaze followed his every step, memorizing the clothing he had on. Dark blue shirt. Black pants. Rubber-soled shoes.

Then and only then could she relax with the knowledge that she wouldn't lose him again.

Not until next time, when her sorting process would begin all over again. Just like it did each and every day of her life.

CHAPTER ONE

THE SINGER AT the Valentine's Day benefit concert had something combustible going on with the guitar player seated next to her. It smoldered in the dark glances she sent his way. Sizzled in how he hunched over his guitar, fingers stroking the strings of that hourglass-shaped instrument as if she were on the receiving end of his touch. And the flames they generated spread to the audience as well, who sat forward in their chairs as if they couldn't get enough. As the plaintive notes of a love song cast its spell, Micah Corday perused the space, looking for a vacant seat.

He knew all about spells. Man, did he ever. But hell, he was older and wiser and had no time for those kinds of games anymore. It had been three years and a whole lot of mileage since he'd last been in this town.

The atmosphere here in Nashville was so different from Ghana, where he'd landed after a breakup. These people were not worried about their next meal or where they'd find clean water or medicine. Instead, their attention was fixed on what was happening on that stage. And between the musicians on it.

But despite that, every one of these folks had their own problems. Their own fears. That part was not so different.

His eyes continued wandering, landing on one face after another before a tingle of remembrance forced him to retrace his steps, first mentally and then emotionally.

There. He found her.

Damn. Talk about spells. He'd known there was a possibility she'd still be in the area, that he'd eventually run into her. But he'd hoped it would come later than this. When he'd had time to frame his questions about that time.

Maybe she was just revisiting her alma mater?

Her eyes were closed, and she swayed slightly to the music, but he knew exactly what color would emerge when her lids parted. Tawny tones that seemed to hold the mystery of the ages. He could remember the way that gaze had held his as she studied him in minute detail until he felt nothing was hidden from her.

It had been like that as they sat across from each other on a dinner date. As she'd straddled his hips and carried him to the very edges of sanity. It had been what had attracted him to her. The details she noticed. Details that had nothing to do what other women saw when they looked at his face. It had been... different. She saw what others missed.

At one time, he'd been so sure of everything. Of his feelings. Of hers. Of the certainty they would someday marry. Have kids.

Until graduation day, when those warm eyes had turned chilly with rejection. There'd been no explanation. No hint as to what had gone wrong.

The memory of that moment—of the strained goodbyes—made something harden in his chest. He'd had no idea what had happened. But once done, there'd been no undoing it. His pride had taken a huge hit that day. He'd evidently thought things were more serious between them than she had. He'd made certain he never made that mistake again. With anyone. His few encounters while on medical mission had been short and sweet. No unrealistic expectations. Then again, he hadn't felt the pull that he had with Lia.

Was she married now?

It didn't matter. What did matter was whether or not she was practicing medicine here at the hospital or just visiting. If it was the former, he would be working under the same roof as her, if not on the same floor.

So, best to get his facts straight now, before they met by chance in a crowded elevator. Or, worse, over a patient.

With that in mind, he moved toward her.

Lia sensed a presence.

Her eyes opened and she took in the stage, where Avery was still singing, both hands wrapped around her microphone as if needing the support. She knew how hard it had been for her friend to get up on that stage. But wow, it had been so worth it. Lia was proud of her.

The hairs on her nape sent an alert, reminding her why she'd opened her eyes in the first place. Her gaze swung to the right and saw a man staring at her from a couple of rows ahead. He was actually walking in her direction. She blinked, quickly tracking across his face, although she wasn't sure why. That never did any good. A vague sense of panic washed over her when he didn't break eye contact and continued coming toward her.

Maybe he was heading for someone else.

No. He stopped. Right in front of where she sat at the end of her row.

Her thoughts gathered around her in quick snatches, and she finally grabbed hold of the one that held her in good stead most of the time. "Hi. How *are* you?" She infused an enthusiasm into the greeting that fooled most people into thinking she'd recognized them.

His head cocked, a frown appearing between his brows.

Uh-oh. It evidently hadn't fooled him.

"Lia? It's Micah. Micah Corday?"

The second his voice sounded, a sick vibration shuddered through her stomach. *Dio.* Of course it was. How could she *not* have recognized him, of all people? He'd been her lover through most of medical school. And at one time she'd thought, maybe just this once, she would finally be able to...

But of course she couldn't. If anything, this moment in time told her her decision back then had been the right one. The instant flash of hurt in his eyes when he'd had to identify himself had provided proof of that.

She'd almost told him her secret back then. But fear had her putting off that moment time and time again. And then graduation had come, snatching up all her hopes and dreams and crushing them into dust.

She jumped to her feet and grabbed him in a quick hug, realizing immediately the imprudence of that move when his scent wrapped her in bittersweet memories. The stubble on his cheek scraped across her skin in a way that rekindled a forgotten spark in her heart and set it alight. Her breath caught on a half sob when he stiffened under the close contact.

Of course he wouldn't welcome her embrace. Why would he?

Swallowing down the ball of emotion, she took a step back. "I—I thought you were in Ghana."

"I was. I'm back."

Her tongue ran across her parched lower lip, trying to think of a response to that shocking statement. "You're back? As in for good?"

His lips curved in a smile that contained not a hint of humor, and Lia could have cried at how hard he seemed. How unlike the Micah she'd once known and loved.

No wonder she hadn't recognized him.

Her heart branded her a liar. That wasn't the reason, and she knew it. It was the same reason she sometimes needed help recognizing her parents. Her friends. Her coworkers.

Faces didn't register with her. Ever. And although medical science had a fancy-sounding name for it, the reality of it was pretty brutal on relationships. Which was why she'd had so few of them in her lifetime.

Her dad's coaching her about how to blend in—done out of love and having had a brother who was bullied in school for a disability—had backfired in some ways. She'd learned with great success how to hide her own challenges, but in doing so had ended up isolating herself. Like choosing a profession where people were in and out of her life in a matter of hours. No need to go to the trouble of remembering details about them. Relationships hovered on a superficial level.

Except with Avery, who had been the only person in her life who could actually joke about her condition. In fact, her closest friend had a scrap of commentary for every person they met: *Ear stud, right ear. Mr. Fancy Pants. Abs galore.* They were funny quips, but they also provided clues for later recognition.

"Yes. As in for good." Micah's voice brought her back to the matter at hand.

She swallowed, her throat aching. *Dio*, she didn't know if she could handle him being back in Nashville. It had taken forever to get used to life without him. Maybe it was better to know exactly what he meant by being back for good.

"Let's go to the back where we can talk." She glanced up at the stage, where Avery continued to sing. For Lia, Avery's hair was her tell. That glorious mane of curls seemed as untamable as her friend. Avery had pulled her safely from some pretty gnarly situations, like when the hospital's chief of staff had ditched his signature pompadour hairstyle in favor of a simple side part and appeared in front of her in shirtsleeves instead of his regular suit and tie. She'd had no idea who he was at first. As if sensing her struggle, her friend had deftly stepped in and greeted him just before he asked Lia about a patient of hers. She'd been grateful beyond words.

But there was no saving her from her current predicament.

She walked to the back of the venue and found a quiet corner. "When did you get back?"

"Yesterday, actually." His smile revealed his tell—the deep, craggy line that appeared in his left cheek whenever his lips curved. That…and that heady masculine scent that no one—in all her years of interacting with men—had been able to match. He used to chuckle at the way she'd press her nose to his skin and breathe deeply, letting the air flow back out on a sigh.

Dio. So many memories. So many moments lost since…

No. She steeled her resolve. She'd been doing him a favor by breaking things off. Although there was no way that he could know that. And that had been the idea. All his talk in the year leading up to graduation about doing a stint with Doctors Without Borders had made her nervous. Leave Nashville? Where it had taken forever to learn to separate the people in her own little bubble of acquaintances? Not likely. But she'd gone along with it, hoping he would change his mind. But he hadn't, as evidenced by his work in Ghana.

But he was back? In Nashville, of all places.

He'd only gotten back yesterday, so maybe that meant he was back for good, as in the United States. Maybe this was a stopping place before he continued on to somewhere else, like…say, Omaha.

"So where are you headed from here?"

"Headed?"

"I just meant…"

Dread filled her heart and permeated the ensuing silence.

"You seriously didn't recognize me?"

The dread grew into something that threatened to burst through the confines of her skin as she scrabbled for an excuse. "You didn't have a beard back then. Or that deep tan. Besides, there's a lot going on, and the last time I saw you…"

"Yes." His smile had disappeared. "The last time you saw me was…well, the last time you saw me."

At graduation.

She remembered that day like it was yesterday. The fear. The horror. As she'd stood in front of that crowd of gowned graduates, she'd been transported back in time to the day when she couldn't pick her father out of a crowd.

She'd flat-out panicked. The orange-and-white robed figures all looked the same, although if she hadn't freaked out and had given herself a minute or two she might have been able to deduce which one of them was Micah. *Might* being the operative word.

The thought of going to a country where she recognized no one—with a man she couldn't even pick out of a crowd—sent her into a tailspin. That, and the growing fear that she one day wouldn't be able to recognize her own child, suddenly morphed into a unscalable wall. What about high school graduation? Ballet class? Baseball games? Any event in which a uniform could disguise identities and steal them from her. Yes. She'd broken things off for all those reasons. And she'd never seen Micah again.

Until today.

She owed him an explanation. But where even to begin…

"I'm sorry. For everything."

His enigmatic eyes searched her features. Seeing what? How had he picked her out from hundreds of other people in the crowd? She would never understand it. "Yeah, well what's done is done. But if we're going to be working at the same hospital… *this* hospital…" His brows went up in question.

"Yes, I work here. As a vascular surgeon."

"Well, then. I guess we'd better figure out what we're going to do about the elephant now standing in the room."

She blinked, thinking maybe he'd figured it out, although her prosopagnosia was something very few people knew about. In fact, Avery was the only person at the hospital who actually knew her little secret. She'd become pretty adept at figuring out who was who. Except when she was caught off guard.

Like by the hospital administrator.

And today, by Micah.

She stood a little taller, her chin tipping up a bit. "And what elephant, exactly, is that?" The word *elephant* slipped out with an accent that belied her Italian heritage. Another quirk brought on by nerves.

"That we were once close. Very, very close."

A sense of relief should have washed over her. Instead, her mouth went dry as a few of those moments of closeness flickered across a screen in her head. The most outrageous being the time they'd had a quickie under a stairwell of this very hospital. They'd been fully clothed, and it had taken just a few minutes, but she'd been left with legs that were shaking and molten memories of the urgency of the act for the rest of the day. *Mio Dio*, if they'd been caught...

She swallowed. "Why does anyone have to know?"

The left side of his mouth cocked, carving out his cheek again. "You don't think anyone knew we were sleeping together back then?"

Okay, so probably a lot of the people they'd known had guessed. And Avery definitely knew, because she'd told her. But once she broke things off with Micah, she'd firmly told her friend she didn't want to hear Micah's name come out of her mouth. Her friend had honored her request over the past three years, never mentioning Micah or what had transpired between them. It had made getting over him a little easier. At least that's what she'd told herself back then.

"I vote we say nothing, other than that we already know each other. And if someone asks, we'll simply say that was in the past and that we've both moved on."

"Moved on. Yes, that's one way of putting it."

Wow, this broody Micah, whose syllables could cut like a scalpel, was going to take some getting used to. But *this* iteration she could handle. If he'd been the mellow, playful guy from her past, she might have had trouble keeping her distance. Might have even repeated mistakes of her past. But this man? Yes. He was a relief. Him she could resist. Could even avoid with ease.

With that thought, she sent him a smile of her own. "Yes. It is one way of putting it. But the terminology doesn't matter.

What does is that we're both adults who can work together as professionals." She realized Avery had finished singing and, as a result, her words had come out a lot louder than they might have if the music had still been playing. A couple of people looked in their direction, and she cringed, much like she'd done at that tea party so long ago.

Okay, time to make a quick getaway and find her friend. "There's someone I need to meet, so I'll say goodbye. Enjoy the rest of the benefit."

With that she turned and walked away from him, hoping her steps looked more even than they felt, and vowing she would do everything in her power to make sure they worked together as little as possible.

CHAPTER TWO

AVERY FLAGGED HER down in the hallway first thing Monday morning, making Lia smile. She'd looked for her friend after the Valentine's Day benefit, but both she and her sexy guitar player had vanished. Lia had a feeling she knew why.

"Hey, girlie, sorry I cut out on you at the benefit. But I… uh…had someplace I needed to be."

Her friend's burgeoning relationship with trauma surgeon Carter Booth had been fun to watch unfold, although she knew it had been touch and go for a while.

"You had someplace you needed to be? Or someone you needed to be with?"

"Well…both. And I have some news."

"News? So everything worked out okay?" Lia had a feeling she already knew the answer to that question.

"More than okay. I just never dreamed I would ever…" She grabbed Lia's hand. "Carter asked me to marry him."

She'd had a feeling this was coming. Things had been heating up between the pair for a while now.

"Oh, honey, I am so, so happy for you!"

Avery deserved to find happiness after everything she'd been through. One good part about Lia's inability to separate one face from another was that she had a knack for reading emotions in others without needing to have them spelled out. And Avery's emotion was there in spades. It was in the grip of her friend's hand on hers. In the tremble to her voice as she'd said that last sentence, as if unable to believe her luck.

That ability to read people made Lia hyperaware of how noticeable her own feelings could be and gave her the tools to stow them out of sight.

Although that ability had ended up causing friction between her and Micah, especially over that last year. Whenever she'd submerged her true feelings about signing up with Doctors Without Borders, he'd seemed to sense something was wrong and pushed until she snapped at him that everything was fine. Even when it wasn't. The look he used to give her when she did that stayed with her even now. As if he was so disappointed in her. It had ripped at her heart.

Another good reason to have broken it off. And seeing him again had brought up a lot of emotions she'd thought were long dead.

"I have some news of my own." She looked her friend in the eye. "Remember that name I asked you never to mention?"

Avery's eyes widened. "You mean Slash and Burn?"

Her friend's nickname for Micah made her roll her eyes. Avery had once said that every time that slash appeared in Micah's left cheek, Lia would turn beet red. And she had.

But unlike Avery, who looked like she'd gotten everything she ever dreamed of—her return to singing, finding a man who understood her and loved her for who she was—Lia didn't expect Micah's sudden appearance to cause anything but renewed heartache.

"Yes. Micah." She bit her lip. "He's back in Nashville."

"No! For real?"

"Unfortunately."

"Couldn't this be a good thing? Sometimes things happen for a reason."

Her friend's optimism probably sprang from cloud nine, the

place where Avery was currently perched. She was happy, therefore everyone she loved deserved happiness, too. Unfortunately it didn't always work out that way.

"Don't get any ideas. We're not getting back together. That's not what I want." She ignored the little voice inside her that warned her pants were now on fire. "I just wanted you to know, in case you see him around the hospital."

"He's going to be *working* here?" Avery let go of her hand. "How do you feel about that?"

"It's awkward. He came up to me at the benefit and said he had come back to work."

"Did he say why?"

"I was so shocked, I didn't even think to ask. Just got away from him as fast as I could." She swallowed. "Ave, I didn't even recognize him when he came up to me."

"I'm so sorry. But you had no idea he was here—was probably the last person you expected to see at the benefit."

Yes, that was true. But any other person would have known immediately if an ex-lover came and stood in front of them.

"At least we won't cross each other's paths all that often. I'm in ER for the most part, and he'll be…well, I'm not exactly sure, but probably up in the lab area." She forced a smile. "Anyway, enough about Micah. I'm really am happy for you. You deserve all that and more."

"Thanks. I love Carter to pieces." She seemed to hop down off her cloud. "But that's actually not why I came down to find you. Has a woman named Bonnie Chisholm been in contact with you this morning to make an appointment?"

"The name doesn't sound familiar. Why?"

She sighed. "She's had some problems going on, and I'm worried she's a stroke risk. I asked her a couple of weeks ago to call you, but she evidently didn't, since she called me again last night with a new symptom." There was a pause. "She was my sister's and my singing teacher. She's…special to me."

"Can you give me some details?"

Avery quickly ran down the list of symptoms Bonnie had been having, saying she was now having abdominal pains on top of the leg swelling and shortness of breath she'd had two weeks ago.

"She promised me she'd call you today."

"I haven't heard from her. She does need to see a specialist. If not me, then another vascular surgeon. Maybe she's worried. Any chance you could come in with her?"

"I offered to. I'll go talk to her again. I'll admit, I'm the one who's worried. She's one of the main reasons I got up on that stage at the benefit."

Lia smiled. "And here I thought that was due to my nagging. Or maybe due to that handsome cowboy who was up there with you."

"It was definitely a group effort." She glanced at her phone, which had just buzzed. "Damn. Sorry, I need to run. One of my patients needs my help."

"Go, I'll catch up with you later. Thursday night for guac and talks? If you can pull yourself away from Carter, that is." Their weekly meet up had become a tradition neither of them wanted to break. It was a time when they could vent, laugh and just generally unload about their week while enjoying the noisy, saloon-like atmosphere of Gantry's Margarita Den.

"Carter knows I need my weekly dose of the best guac east of the Mississippi, so yes, Thursday is great."

Her friend was positively glowing. Maybe someday she would find what Avery seemed to have found. But for now, she would live vicariously through her friend's romance. "See you then."

Avery gave a wave as she hurried back toward the ER.

Her friend knew about Micah and Lia's reasons for breaking things off three years ago, although Avery had pooh-poohed her fears about going on medical mission and about not recognizing her own child. She'd assured her that when the right guy came along, those fears would slide away.

But would they really? Lia had been so sure that Micah was that person. And she'd half wondered if she'd let the one get away. Until Micah had shown up at the gala after his long absence and Lia hadn't recognized him. As much as she tried to blame that on shock or the unexpectedness of his face coming back across her radar, it simply reaffirmed all her reasons for breaking off the relationship.

How fitting that she worked at Saint Dolores, who was the patron saint of sorrows. In Italian, *doloroso* meant sorrowful or painful. Both of those terms aptly described her feelings about ending things with Micah. There was still some *grande dolore* involved when she thought about him.

And now that he was here?

She was going to concentrate on seeing him as a colleague. Someone who meant nothing to her anymore. No pain. No sadness. No longing. If her dad's job as a molecular biologist had taught her one thing, it was that things could be broken down to a scientific set of molecules. Those molecules could then be manipulated to change the way they came together. So if she could change one of the building blocks that had made her want to be with Micah, she could change the entirety of their relationship and make it into something else—something that worked on a professional level but not a deeper emotional level. She just needed to find which of those blocks she needed to change to make that happen.

And if she couldn't? Then the name Saint Dolores was going to be a daily reminder of the hurt she had gone through when Micah had turned and walked away from her, head held high, strong shoulders braced to face life without her.

And from all appearances, he'd done a very good job of doing just that.

She only hoped she'd done just as good a job. Because if not, *dolore* was going to be a hard word to shake. And an even harder emotion to outrun.

* * *

"There's someone I need to meet."

Those words had echoed again and again in Micah's subconscious over the weekend. And they were making his first day on the job pretty damned rough.

He thought his pride had taken a hit at their breakup? Well, it was going to take an even bigger hit if Lia had found someone who could give her what he evidently lacked. Every time he thought of her with another man, the crunching blow of a sledgehammer seemed to knock against his ribs.

Hell, the woman had barely even known who he was at the Valentine's benefit, despite their steamy past. So it was ridiculous to even care one way or the other.

Except he was rethinking coming back to the States. Lia's reaction was a stark reminder of his childhood, when he'd felt completely invisible to two busy parents who'd handed him over to a series of nannies. He used to wonder as a kid if they would even recognize him in a crowd.

Ha! Well, he'd seen firsthand that it truly was possible to forget what someone you used to love looked like. It wasn't a fun feeling.

Unless Lia had been faking it, trying to appear nonchalant as she processed the shock of seeing him again.

No. The shock when she realized who he was hadn't been feigned. Neither had the dismay that followed right on its heels, despite her wiping both emotions from her face a second later. Something else she'd been good at when they'd been together, and another thing she had in common with his folks: hiding her true feelings.

A knock sounded on the door to his office just as he reached into a box of books he'd been unpacking onto a shelf. "Come in."

The door opened and a face that he would never forget as long as he lived peered in at him, eyes wary and unsure. She edged inside the door and shut it behind her, leaning against it as if she was ready to rip it open and disappear at the first sign of trouble. Her eyes tracked over his face, seeming to study it before moving on to his body. He remembered how her gaze used to feel like a physical touch and how strangely it had affected him the first time they met.

It was no different this time. But Micah was different. He'd been inoculated against that intense stare. At least he thought he had. "Hello, Lia. Can I help you?" He made his voice as cool and indifferent as he could.

She nodded at the book in his hand. "Well, that seems apropos."

Glancing down, he took in the title. *Preventing Recurrence: It's Up to You.*

"I'm not sure I follow."

"Oh, well, I…um, wanted to talk to you about working together. I know it's going to be weird, but I hope we can somehow figure it out."

He still didn't see how the book… Oh. She wanted to make sure he knew there wouldn't be a recurrence of what had happened between them. No worries there. Because he had no intention of allowing what had happened before to happen again. And she was right. The title was apropos. Because it was up to him—up to them—to make sure that it didn't. "I'm sure we can. Our relationship ended years ago. If you're worried I might be interested in rekindling things, you needn't bother. You made it quite clear that it was a mistake. And I came to realize you were right. We both dodged a bullet."

Her eyes widened before she nodded. "Yes, I think we did. Both of us. I think there's only one person at the hospital who knows we were once an item. And I'd prefer to keep it that way."

"There's not much chance of me broadcasting it over Saint Dolores's loudspeakers."

She seemed to cringe away from that. "I didn't think you would. I just didn't want you to worry about any gossip I might spread."

His smile was hard. "There wouldn't be much to spread. Not anymore."

"No. I guess not."

When that hammer swung against his ribs again, he quickly turned to put the book on the shelf behind his desk. "I agree that we are the key to making this work. So let's just keep our past where it belongs—in the past. There's no reason for anyone to know that we once dated each other."

"And if they ask?"

He turned back to her. "Why would they? I'm new to the hospital, as far as most people know. Would you wonder if I used to date any of Saint Dolores's other employees?"

"Saint Dolly's."

"Sorry?"

"This is Nashville. Surely you remember the nickname we've given the place?"

He'd forgotten about the hospital's second name. "Is that what you call it in front of patients?"

"No, I just…well, Saint Dolly's sounds a little more cheerful than Dolores." She looked down at her clasped hands. "And you might wonder if you heard a bunch of people use the other moniker."

"Okay, Saint Dolly's. Check. Keeping our past a secret. Check." He motioned to the box on his desk. "Anything else?"

"I, um…" Her head came up. "Actually, yes. Why here?"

Was she really asking him that?

"Why did I decide to come here? Why not? It's where I grew up. Where my—" his jaw tightened "—parents live."

"Of course. Sorry. I'm not sure why I asked that."

Did she think he'd come here to restart their romance? Not hardly. If anything, it was the opposite of that. His dad wasn't well, but that wasn't the only reason he was here. He'd come back to the place where his folks lived as a reminder of what it felt like to be invisible. A reminder to be on his guard against getting involved with someone who made him feel like they'd made him feel. Like Lia had when she'd ended their relationship.

And like when she hadn't recognized him at the benefit. Lia was a much more vivid and present image of what he'd gone through in his childhood. And now he wasn't sure he needed a daily reminder of that to keep him on his toes. Actually, he was sure of it.

"Not a problem." He was hoping those words would prove to be prophetic. "If it helps, I had no idea you were working here when I applied for the job."

"It doesn't help. Not really. But it is what it is. Like you said, we'll find a way to make it work." Her brows went up. "And my parents still live here, too. That's why I've stuck around. Besides, I love it here. I can't imagine practicing medicine anywhere else."

"I think you made that pretty obvious." Part of her little speech the night of graduation had revolved around the idea that they both wanted different things out of life. Except he hadn't realized that. Not until that night.

Right now he was wishing he hadn't been quite so quick to leave Africa. He'd done some real good there, but his mom's phone call saying that his dad's health was beginning to fail had prompted him to come home. Although he still hadn't gone to see them. This week, though, he would make it a point to stop in and see if they needed anything.

"And I have no intention of trying to convince you to go anywhere else. Not anymore."

She stepped away from the door, and for a second he thought she was going to move toward him. Instead, she half turned and twisted the doorknob. "Well, now that we've established some ground rules, I'll let you get back to unpacking."

Had they established that? Or had they just agreed that they could be grown-ups and work together? Well, he wasn't going to say anything that might encourage her to hang around his office any longer than necessary.

"Thanks for coming by."

She gave a half-hearted smile and nodded. "Thanks for understanding." With that, she was through the door, quietly closing it behind her. Micah was left with an office that looked exactly like it had before she'd put in an appearance. The space inside his chest was a different story, however. There were traces of her visit painted on almost every internal surface. His gut. His chest wall. His heart.

And like with most infections, sometimes all it took was a minute amount to put someone's life in jeopardy. So he needed to eradicate every stray cell that she'd implanted in him. He thought he'd done that.

The problem was, now that he was back, he wasn't quite sure he had.

CHAPTER THREE

LIA PUSHED THROUGH the doors of the ER on her way to the parking lot where her car was located. She'd had three difficult surgeries in a row and was worn out. Just as she was about to step off the curb, a car pulled up and a woman leaped out. "Are you a doctor?"

She blinked, then realized her lanyard was still hanging around her neck. "I am. What's going on?"

"It's my baby." She threw open the back door, where a chilling sound reached Lia. Coughing. But not the normal cough of bronchitis or a respiratory infection. This was a strangled gasping sound she would never in her life forget. "She just had a cold. It was just a cold." Her words were filled with fear and dread.

An infant who couldn't have been older than two months lay propped in a car seat.

"Let's get her inside. But I want to use the side door." She glanced at the mom. "Were you vaccinated against whooping cough while carrying her?"

The woman's face went deadly pale. "No. My doctor mentioned it, but I wasn't vaccinated with my others, and they were fine."

Vaccination during each pregnancy was a fairly new recommendation. The thought was that when the mother passed her antibodies to her fetus, she would pass them along for pertussis as well and hopefully curb the numbers that were slowly creeping up, even in this day and age.

Dio. If she was right?

Lia unbuckled the child, taking in the red, fevered face just as another bout of coughing racked the infant's tiny body. It was followed by the struggle to draw in breath afterward. With the mom racing beside her, they circumvented the double doors and the crowded waiting room and found one of the isolation rooms. "Sit with her for a minute while I do an exam. What's your name?"

"Molly. And this is Sassy."

The mom climbed onto the exam table, her own cough barking out. Damn. Lia donned a mask, not just for her protection but for her patient's. "Are any of your other children sick?"

"All three of them are, but none of them are coughing as much as Sassy."

All of them. "Who's with them?"

"My mom. My husband went to park the car. I've had a cold and just assumed…"

"It's okay." She quickly called down to Admitting to let them know that a man would be coming in and where to direct him. She also asked them to call Micah and a pediatric pulmonologist. So much for not working with her ex. But as an infectious disease expert, Micah needed to know that there might be a possible outbreak of pertussis in one of the local communities.

She listened to the baby's lungs, ignoring her phone when it started buzzing in her pocket. Whoever it was could wait.

Just as she thought—the baby's airways were clogged. "I need to get a swab. If it's whooping cough, we'll need to check your other children, and you'll need to alert any kids you've been in contact with."

"Oh, God. My sister came over with her kids three days ago. Her newest is even younger than Sass."

"Were any of them sick?"

"No." The poor woman's voice was miserable.

Within a minute, a man poked his head in. "Are you the dad?"

"Yes, I'm Roger Armour. Is she okay?"

Molly held her hand out, her husband going over to grasp it. Okay, Molly had straight dark hair and her husband had blondish hair that was cropped close. The dad also had a tattoo of some kind of fish on his forearm. She submitted those facts to memory in case she needed to recognize them later. "She might have whooping cough."

His head tilted sideways. "Isn't that extinct?"

"I'm afraid it hasn't been eradicated. Not yet."

It was amazing how many people thought the disease had gone the way of smallpox, when it was still here. Still threatening the lives of young children.

A nurse came in, and Lia handed her the swabs that she'd put in protective cases, which she'd labeled with the baby's name. "Could you run those to the lab and ask them to put a rush on it? Possible pertussis."

"Right away."

She'd just left the room when another man poked his head in. Short blond hair, although the mask obscured his lower face. "Hey, I tried to call."

The voice immediately identified him as Micah. Motioning him in, she said, "Possible case of pertussis." She glanced at Molly. "I think you may have it as well. We need to start you both on a course of erythromycin."

"Did I give it to Sass?"

She understood the mother's angst, but sending her down the path of self-blame would help no one. "It could have come from anywhere. Let's just concentrate on helping you both feel better." She glanced at Roger. "We'll want to treat you as well, just in case, since you've been exposed."

Micah came over and did his own examination. He nodded. "The signs are there. Labs?"

"Just sent them off."

"Great. We'll need to try to do a contact trace."

Some of Lia's neighbors had gotten whooping cough when she was a teen, and the sound of a coughing baby being strolled down the building's hallways had haunted her for years. One day, the baby left and never returned, and she'd been told by her mom that the infant had died at the hospital later that day. She needed to do something besides just sit here and wait for more patients to be brought in.

"I'd like to make up some flyers to alert folks of a possible outbreak."

"Flyers. Good idea."

There was something in his voice that made her look at him. "You don't think so?"

His glace met hers. "I do. Just wishing we'd had the luxury of those when I was in Ghana."

"Right." She couldn't imagine what he'd seen in his years in Africa. But she was pretty sure whooping cough was right up there. Had she been wrong not to go with him? She shrugged off the thought. There was no going back. Not that she wanted to. She'd made the right decision. Both for her and for him.

The baby coughed again, only this time when she tried to breathe back in, there was only a thin whistle of air. "She's not getting enough oxygen. We need to intubate."

Micah lifted the child from the mother, who sobbed and clutched her husband's hand. He moved the baby over to one of the nearby counters while Lia found an intubation kit designed for infants.

Things were tense for a few minutes while they got the tube into place. Attaching an Ambu bag, he glanced at the mom. "I'm sorry, but we'll need to use that bed to transport her."

"Oh, of course!" Molly scrambled down and sank into her husband's waiting arms. "Can we go with her?"

"Sit tight for just a few minutes while we stabilize her." Placing the infant's still form onto the exam table, they unlocked the wheels and rolled her out. "We'll send someone for you as soon as we can."

Once outside the room, Lia directed him the back way to a set of service elevators, where there was the least amount of foot traffic. "We'll get her up in one of the PICU rooms and institute droplet isolation."

Once in the elevator, the only sound was the squeeze of the Ambu bag as Lia checked the baby's vitals for the third time. "She's hanging in there."

"This is kind of outside your specialty, isn't it?"

Lia couldn't tell from his tone if he was ticked that she had called him in or not. "It is, but I was there when the car pulled up, and all the other ER docs were busy with patients. Sorry for calling you, but—"

"You did the right thing."

She relaxed, glancing at him and reading nothing but concern in his demeanor. He hadn't changed much, outside of his hair and beard, and she again was shocked that she hadn't recognized him right off. But it had happened before, and she was pretty sure it wouldn't be the last time she'd be confused by someone's identity. Especially if it had been a while since she'd seen them. And three years was definitely a while.

Checking the baby's color as the elevator stopped on the third floor, they found Newell Jensen, one of the pediatric specialists, waiting for them. Micah nodded at Lia to fill him in on what had happened so far. She did so with a calmness in her voice that belied the shakiness of her limbs. Whether that was from being in close proximity to Micah or from the immediateness of the emergency, she had no idea. But she had to admit she was glad to hand the baby over to someone whose specialty this actually was. "Her mom and dad are waiting down in ER. They're pretty worried."

"So am I, from the looks of her. Let's get her into a room."

Almost immediately there was a flurry of activity as Sassy was hooked up to a ventilator and her vitals were taken yet again. "We're still waiting on her labs, but from the way she sounded in the ER, I'm pretty sure it's pertussis. Two families have been exposed so far. And I suspect there are more."

"Not good. Let's start her on a course of erythromycin while we wait for confirmation from the lab." Newell glanced at them. "I'll have someone update her parents. Can you notify administration? I'll call the CDC."

"Yes."

The specialist was dismissing them, not because he was being a jerk, but because he had work to do and didn't have time to stand around and talk. Lia could appreciate that.

She and Micah walked back to the elevators, stripping their masks and gloves as they did so and dropping them into a waste receptacle. "Did you see a lot of this when you were in Africa?"

"I was actually there helping with the trachoma outbreaks."

She turned to face him. "Trachoma? As in from chlamydia?"

"One and the same."

She'd had no idea that's what he'd been doing there. Once they broke up, there'd been no need to keep in contact with each other. And for the first time, she wished they had, or that she'd at least kept track of his career. Then maybe that whole embarrassing scene at the Valentine's Day benefit wouldn't have happened.

"Why did you come back to the States?"

His lips twisted to the side in a way that was heartbreakingly familiar.

"Two reasons. My dad and politics."

"Okay, those are two things I never would have put together. Is your dad running for office?"

"No." He sighed. "He hasn't been well for the last year or so. He has cancer, and I wasn't sure how much longer he was going to be around. If I was going to visit, now was the time."

"I'm sorry. I didn't know."

"It's okay. We haven't exactly been close."

She nodded. "I remember you saying that. Did they even come to your graduation?"

One brow went up. "No. But they sent a representative. With a very expensive gift."

Reaching out to touch his hand, she murmured, "I'm so sorry, Micah." She hadn't done a very good job of timing her little breakup speech, had she?

"It's okay. You didn't know."

Fortunately he didn't add that she hadn't bothered to stick around to find out, although he must have thought it at the time. He'd been hurt by everyone he cared about that day. And it made something inside her cramp. If she'd known his mom and dad hadn't come to see him graduate from medical school, would she have broken up with him when she did? She didn't know. And it was too late to go back and change it now that she did. "I'm still sorry. Is there any hope for your dad?"

"I think my dad thinks that cancer is beneath him. That he'll somehow buy his way out from under it, like he's done with most things in his life." He sighed. "And no. According to my mom, he's been given little hope, although he's slated to start an experimental treatment sometime soon."

"Have you talked to him?"

"Not yet. But I'm planning to this weekend."

She could understand his reluctance, but if it had been one of her parents, she would have rushed home as soon as her plane landed. When she and Micah had been together, she'd known that things between him and his parents had been strained, but she'd had no idea it was as bad as it evidently was. He'd never taken her home to meet them, which she hadn't thought was odd at the time, but now that a few years had passed… Had she not noticed out of selfishness? Out of not wanting to know anything about Micah other than how he made her feel?

Dio, she hoped not.

"I'm sure that will be hard." The elevator stopped and she stepped off, waiting for him to exit as well.

"A lot of things in life are hard. But you somehow get through them and move on."

For some reason she didn't think he was still talking about his parents, and a trickle of remembered pain went through her. She knew he'd been hurt when she'd broken things off, but how much more hurt would he have been when he realized why she had such trouble putting names to faces—including his? She'd been able to laugh it off at the time, saying she was terrible with names. But it wasn't the names that stumped her. It was the faces that went with them.

Even his.

She remembered how hurt she'd been when her dad insisted time and time again that she learn a way to get around her prosopagnosia. He'd never let her take the easy way out…except for during that egg and spoon race. But once she hit high school, she finally understood why. He was protecting her from what his younger brother—her uncle—had gone through. Her uncle had been born with a speech impediment that got him ridiculed again and again, and her dad had made sure he was always there to protect his younger brother from bullies. And when he'd had a daughter who couldn't recognize faces, he'd stepped back into the role of protector. It had changed her life for the better and had been a turning point in their relationship. But it had also made her very aware of what could happen if she let people see behind her curtain.

Evidently things were still strained between Micah and his parents, but maybe they would have their own turning point someday. Only if his dad was as ill as he'd indicated, there might not be much time to make things right.

Micah had been right to come back.

They made their way to the administrative office, and she spoke in hushed tones to the hospital administrator's assistant.

"We had an infant come in with a suspected case of pertussis. Can we get in to see Arnie?"

Arnold Goff headed up the hospital much like the boxer he'd once been—deftly feinting away from any opponent before coming back with a hard right hook. Other hospital administrators treated him with respect. But the man was also fiercely loyal to his staff.

Arnie's assistant picked up his phone and let him know they were here to see him. "He said to go on in."

They went through the door, and the administrator stood to shake their hands. "You must be Dr. Corday. Nice to finally meet you in person."

"A pleasure."

Arnie hadn't been at the hospital while they had attended medical school there, which was kind of a relief. "So what brings you in?"

"We have a case of suspected whooping cough—an infant—although the labs aren't in yet." Lia paused. "The mom is coughing as well and said her other three kids are sick."

"Hell." He motioned them to the two chairs in front of his desk while he sat back down as well. "What do we know?"

She continued. "Not much. Not yet. Not sure where the family was exposed, but they've been with relatives while displaying symptoms."

He dragged a hand through his hair. "Anyone at the hospital exposed?"

"Minimal. I met the couple just as the mom and baby were getting out of the car. We went in through back doors, and I notified anyone who was going into her room that they needed to don PPE."

"Good thinking. What do you need from me?"

This time Micah spoke up. "Dr. Costa had the idea of putting up flyers around the community alerting the public to the need of reviewing their vaccination records and see if they're up-to-date. The last thing we want in Nashville is a major outbreak of pertussis."

"Agreed. And good thinking. Are you two okay with heading up the push?"

"Us?" Lia's voice came out as a kind of squeak that made Arnie look at her.

"Is there a problem with that?"

"No," she hurried to clarify. "None at all."

The man's gaze moved from one to the other. "I know you both have your own patients, but this is a good opportunity for educating the public, and I can think of no better faces to represent the hospital."

She knew he hadn't meant that comment on faces in the way of grading someone's looks, but it still made her shift in her seat. Because Lia had no idea what made for a more or less attractive set of facial characteristics.

"I'm okay with that as long as Micah has the time."

Too late she realized she'd used his first name rather than his title. But if he noticed, Arnie didn't say anything.

"I don't have anything major scheduled yet. Except this." Micah frowned. "But I'd like to go beyond putting up flyers and see if I can get a handle on where this area stands in the way of vaccinations and contact tracing."

"COVID has given us a little hand up in that area. So hopefully some of those databases can be put to good use."

"That's what I was thinking as well. I can work with the CDC on feeding them whatever info we find out."

Still with the *we*. But then again, she'd have been hurt if Micah had tried to cut her out of the loop, although if he pushed he could have. He was an infectious disease doc, and she was vascular. They weren't quite in the same specialty.

"Can you meet together and come up with a plan and get back to me tomorrow?"

Tomorrow? She'd just been on her way out of work. If she hadn't stopped to assist that cry for help, she'd be home already, soaking in a hot tub. But despite how uncomfortable it might be to pair up with Micah, they'd done fine while treating Sassy. Surely they could handle a couple of hours of planning.

Micah's eyes swung around to meet hers. "Do you have time to discuss it tonight?"

"Sure."

Arnie sighed as if in relief. "Make sure you keep me in the loop."

"Of course." She and Micah said the words in unison.

Lia gave a nervous laugh. That was something they'd always done. And they used to chuckle about it back then. But despite her laugh just now, she didn't find much that was humorous about their current situation.

"I'll leave you to it, then."

She and Micah stood and headed back through the door.

As soon as they were out of earshot, he turned to her. "Sorry about that. I didn't mean to drag you into anything."

"You didn't. The flyers were my idea, remember?"

"Of course I remember. I wasn't trying to take credit for it."

She smiled. "I didn't think you were. Besides, we both want the same thing—to protect the people of Nashville."

"So where do we do this planning?"

"How about over dinner? I'm starved."

He nodded. "Me, too. Any good guacamole joints around here? I seem to remember you having a penchant for the stuff."

And Micah, who hadn't been a fan, had turned into a believer while they were together. And she knew of a very good spot. But it was the place she and Avery frequented for their guac and talks, and she didn't really relish going there. She didn't want his memories sliding around her every time she and Avery walked into the place. Not like a lot of other things in Nashville after they'd broken things off. She'd even thought about leaving town for that very reason, despite the horror of being pushed out of her comfort zone. And now, just when she thought she'd banished all his ghosts, here he came to add new ones. It had made it easier not to go running to him and take back everything she'd said to push him away. And now that he'd returned?

She needed to stand her ground and remember why she'd ended things.

Was she really destined to be alone? Her whole life? She shook off her thoughts. Avery seemingly finding the love of her life made her feel even more alone.

"Guacamole is still the nectar of the gods, but I'm in the mood for something different. How about wings?"

Although Gantry's Margarita Den also had great wings, there were several other places that sold passable chicken other than her go-to place. And most of them already had…ghosts. Well, she didn't want his ghost inhabiting Gantry's as well. Better for him to roam the kitchen of somewhere that didn't matter to her.

"Sounds good. Is Maurio's still open here in town?"

Maurio's. She hadn't been there since the day before graduation. It was her last wonderful memory of him. Yes. That would be the perfect place, since she purposely didn't go there anymore. And wouldn't go there again after tonight.

"It is. Where are you staying? Or did you already buy something?"

He looked at her. "I haven't bought anything. I'm at a hotel at the moment. They have a shuttle that runs back and forth to the hospital." He shrugged with what looked like an apology. "I haven't gotten a vehicle yet, either."

"It's okay, I can drive and drop you off afterward. Which hotel?"

"Tremont Inn, about three blocks from the hospital. I figured I could walk to work on days I didn't want to take the shuttle."

"I know where that is. It's right on the way back toward my place."

So with that settled, they headed toward the exit before Micah stopped. "Can I check in and see how Sassy is doing first?"

"I'd thought about doing the same thing, so sure."

With that, they both headed toward the nurses' desk and asked the person behind the desk to page Dr. Jensen.

CHAPTER FOUR

MAURIO'S WAS CROWDED. And loud. Louder than he remembered. The sign at the front of the restaurant told them to "chicken dance to a table of their choice." It had seemed cute back when they were dating. And one time, Lia had actually chicken danced to one of the tables, making him laugh.

They'd been young and in the throes of medical school. Laughing had not been high on the agenda, except when he was with her.

Only the Lia of today didn't look like she'd chicken dance anywhere. She seemed more serious now. Sadder.

Because of him?

She'd broken things off, so maybe. The whys had never been all that clear, though. Looking back, she hadn't seemed all that enthused by the prospect of going on a medical mission with him. But Lia had also been a master at covering up her emotions, withdrawing or pretending to agree instead of sitting down and having a hard conversation. It had irked him and brought back unpleasant childhood memories. Like his parents' glossing over the fact that they really didn't have a relationship with their son. All Lia would have had to do was say no, she didn't want to go overseas, and he would have thought long and hard about going.

But she hadn't.

And she hadn't mentioned it in her breakup speech, which had been short and sweet. In his mind, going after her would have done no good. Instead, it had solidified his decision to follow through with his plans of going with Doctors Without Borders.

Ghana had been an eye-opener on what it was like to practice medicine where supplies were hard to come by. He thought he might go back someday, but right now he wasn't making those decisions. He just needed to get through this time with his parents, then he could look toward the future. Whatever it held.

They found a booth at the very back of the restaurant. Immediately memories danced around him—and they weren't doing anything as humorous as a chicken dance. Instead, they were memories of him and Lia crowded together on the same side of the booth, her foot sliding along his leg and her laughing when his face turned red.

Damn. This was a mistake. And he'd only suggested it because it was first restaurant that had popped into his mind.

Lia didn't sit next to him this time, though. She sat on one side of the table, and he sat on the other. Then again, they were no longer a couple, so it made sense. But it also highlighted the distance between them. One of the waitstaff came over with two menus and put them down in front of them, taking their drink orders. He ordered a beer. It was rare that he drank nowadays, especially after the night of their breakup, when he'd gotten so drunk he couldn't see straight. Literally. He'd used alcohol to try to drown his shock and dismay, but the next day it had come roaring back with a vengeance, along with a hangover that wouldn't quit. He was never going that route again.

But one beer wasn't the same as getting drunk.

She leaned on the table with her elbows rather than sitting way back in her seat, something he remembered from the past. And her hair was up in a ponytail, but the end slid over her shoulder and curled near the swell of her breast. And, hell, if he didn't acutely remember how those same breasts had felt in his hands. He did his best not to follow that train of thought, but it was damned hard.

"You said you haven't seen your folks yet. I'm kind of surprised. Wasn't that why you came back?"

The question came out of nowhere, taking him by surprise. It took him a minute or two to think of a response. Mainly because he wasn't sure why he hadn't gone to see them. His mom knew he was planning on coming home, but he hadn't given her a firm date, preferring to do things on his own terms. His dad had cancer, but it wasn't at the critical point yet. But who knew when that could change? Maybe the experimental treatment his mom had told him about during their phone call wouldn't work.

"It is, but it's been crazy trying to get things set up with work and housing, etc. Once I get a car, it should be easier."

She didn't say anything, just looked at him. And he realized he'd been home for almost a week. Maybe because he knew once he did that seeing his parents would have to take a regular spot on his agenda. And he wasn't quite sure he was ready for that yet.

"My parents and I still don't have the best relationship." The words were out before he could stop them. He knew they sounded weak, but it was the truth, and somehow he'd always had trouble admitting just how bad thing were in his household. Back then he'd told Lia they didn't see eye to eye, but he had never shared what it was that bothered him so much. Maybe because it had seemed selfish of him to want his parents' attention. As if he'd been the only thing on their plates. They were both wildly successful in their careers. They were in demand by myriad people. He was probably just one more person clamoring for their time. He himself had experienced that in Ghana when there were more sick people than there were medical personnel. It had been dizzying, and sometimes he'd just wanted to withdraw from all of it. Had his mom and dad felt that way?

"Yeah, I remember you saying that. I just thought with your dad being sick that things might have gotten better."

The strange thing was, in a way they had. At least from a distance. His mom had emailed him more while he was in Africa than she'd communicated with him the whole time he'd been in medical school. Maybe because it didn't take as much of an emotional investment to type words onto an electronic device as it did when you stood face-to-face with someone.

Like sitting across from Lia again?

Except there was no emotional investment here at all. Not anymore.

"It's complicated."

A good term for it. And for the mixed bag of feelings generated by being at Maurio's again.

Their drinks came, and they gave their meal order to the waiter. Which, strangely, was like being transported back in time. He got the spicy and she got the honey barbecue sauce. It appeared nothing had changed.

Except for them.

Micah took a swig of his beer, his first drink since being back in Nashville. It was smooth going down, the sensation helping to ground him and sweep away some of his misgivings about being here with her.

"And your folks? How are they? Your sister?"

"They're good. My dad is still working for the same medical lab, and my mom is still teaching music. Only she does it from home now. My sister is in Abilene with her husband and kids. When we all get together, it's a mixture of crazy and fun. I adore my nieces."

Her face showed the truth of that statement. The soft smile seemed to come from a place deep inside her.

"And yet you said you weren't sure about having kids of your own."

Her family was so different from his. And when they'd been dating, it was what he'd aspired to. It had given him hope that he could be the kind of dad her father seemed to be. And that he and Lia could have a relationship based on mutual respect and trust, and that they could love their kids—be hands-on parents. And yet she'd been hesitant in her response to his question about how many kids she wanted. It had taken him by surprise. She'd simply said that if practicing medicine was as busy as medical school, she wasn't sure she could give them the attention they deserved. He hadn't pushed. And she hadn't volunteered anything more on that subject.

"My work is pretty fulfilling."

Said as if having a family would make it less so?

He swallowed. That's probably exactly what his parents had felt.

How had he even thought he and Lia had had the makings of a good relationship? Maybe growing up with apathetic parents had made any kind of emotional attachment seem larger and more meaningful than it actually was. Lia had evidently agreed, since she made it seem like their relationship had been just a phase. Just part of the whole medical school experience.

The aftermath of their breakup had left him reeling. He hadn't had, nor wanted, a relationship since then. He'd trusted Lia with his heart, and she'd handed it back to him without a second thought.

So he'd headed to Ghana rather than face her again. Staying would have been hard. And the last thing he wanted was to find out he was some emotionally needy jerk who couldn't let go.

He was pretty sure he wasn't. Because when he let go, he really let go. Neither he nor Lia had contacted each other again. And although it would have been nice to have true closure, he hadn't gone looking for it. He'd just lost himself in his work.

"I get that kids are hard. I was pretty busy in Ghana, too. Anyway, I'm glad your parents are doing well."

She took a sip of her soda, glancing at him over the rim before setting it down. "Is there anything I can do to help, Micah?"

It took him a second before he realized she was talking about his parents and not about their past relationship.

"No. I plan to go car shopping after we're done here."

She set her drink down. "I could take you."

"Why?" He stared at her, trying to figure out where this was coming from. Guilt over the past? Surely not.

She shrugged, but the move seemed stiff, as if she was trying to shift some kind of weight from her shoulders, making him think he hadn't been as far off as he'd thought.

"I'm off. You're off. I have a car..." her brows went up "...you don't. Maybe we can kill two birds with one stone and look for places to put up flyers in between stops."

Ah, so that's why. It had had nothing to do with the past.

She went on. "Pertussis is a subject that makes my blood run cold. When I was a kid, a baby in the next apartment had a terrible cough. I was a teenager at the time, and I still vividly remember the sound of it. And the way my parents tried to keep us away from her. But my sister got sick anyway. Not as badly as the baby, but enough to warrant treatment." She fiddled with her napkin. "Anyway, one day I realized the cough in the hallway was gone. Along with the baby. So when Sassy coughed... that sound... It brought up memories I thought were long gone."

He could relate. Not to the pertussis angle, but to the bringing up memories that he thought were long gone.

Every once in a while, he could almost swear he felt a bare foot sliding against his leg, but it was just a phantom ache, like when a part of your body was missing but that you could swear you felt from time to time.

"The baby died."

He didn't know why he'd said it, maybe because a part of him still wanted to understand where Lia was coming from. Despite how close they'd been in medical school, he now realized they'd actually known very little about each other. He'd withheld parts of his past. And evidently she had, too. He'd had no idea her sister had contracted whooping cough.

"Yes. There were a cluster of other cases in the area, which is why I don't want to ignore this. I don't just want to alert the CDC and let them take over. I want make sure Nashville understands the very real dangers of whooping cough."

"I agree." He felt his features soften. "I'm glad your sister pulled through."

She smiled. "Yeah. Me, too. So you see why I really want to be a part of this."

"I do."

They ate their meal, and Micah found himself relaxing, chuckling when a bit of barbecue sauce landed on her cheek. She swiped at it once and missed, and he reached across with his own napkin and rubbed it away. The gesture felt oddly intimate, forcing him to lean back in his seat to detach from it.

"Thanks," she said. "I always seem to do that."

She always had. And he'd always seemed to be the one to fix it back then.

Only he hadn't been able to fix whatever it was that had happened between them at the end. Nor had he tried. His pride had been so stung that he'd simply removed himself from the situation, preferring to lick his wounds in private. Actually, he'd traveled a long distance to make sure he could do exactly that.

He didn't regret going to Ghana. The experience had been fulfilling in a way that was different than what he was doing now at Saint Dolly's.

And right now, Lia was studying him in that crazy way she'd always had and making him feel like nothing had changed.

Except it had. So he averted his eyes and stared at the foam on his beer. "What happened between us back then, Lia?"

He wasn't sure why he'd even asked the question, but once it was out, he couldn't retract it.

There was silence for several long seconds, and when he looked back at her, it was to find she was no longer looking at him. And he found he missed the touch of her gaze. He'd forgotten how much it affected him. Until just now.

"I—I just realized I wasn't ready for a relationship. Not one that involved commitment and sacrifice. I know how much you wanted to work with Doctors Without Borders, and I couldn't…" She shook her head. "I couldn't give you what you needed. What you deserved. I love Nashville. And I didn't want to leave my family."

"You could have told me that." He'd been right about her reticence to go. "You never know, I might have chosen to stay."

"I knew that was a possibility. And I didn't want to be the reason you didn't go. I had a lot going on at the time, and it seems I made the right decision." She licked her lips. "You never met anyone over there?"

He gave her a slow smile. "I met *lots* of people over there." He kept his meaning ambiguous, although putting the emphasis where he had may have been a little over-the-top. Especially when she bit her lip as if his words had stung.

Damn. He didn't want to say things just to hurt her. He needed to put an end to this conversation, even though he was the one who'd started it. Downing the last of his beer, he waved away the waiter when he asked if he wanted another.

She glanced at him. "Are you sure? I'm driving."

"I'm sure. I was never a big drinker. It's the first beer I've had in a while."

"I remember that about you."

Man, he did not want to go any farther down that road, where they started sharing remembered stories with each other. "Are you sure you want to take me? I can just as easily rent a car."

Except thinking about it, he wasn't sure that was as easy as he'd made it sound. He didn't have auto insurance because… well, no car. Did they even let you rent one without that? He'd never been in that situation before.

"I'm positive. Like I said, we can scout out places to hang flyers." She glanced at her watch. "Most auto dealerships are probably open for another couple of hours, since it's only four. If you're ready to go, that is."

"More than ready."

When they'd checked on Sassy before leaving the hospital, the infant was still holding her own, and the mom and dad had already been started on a course of antibiotics with a stern warning not to go to the store or anywhere else until the whole family had been on them for twenty-four hours.

Micah tried to pick up the bill, but Lia shot him down by laying cash for her meal on the table. "It's okay. Today is normally the day I go out to dinner with Avery." She smiled. "She owes me since she stood me up at the Valentine's Day gala. She had a good reason, though."

"*She* was the person you needed to meet."

The huge wave of relief he felt shocked him. It shouldn't matter. At all. Unless he wasn't really over her.

He was. He'd spent the last three years doing everything he could to forget her. And while he hadn't completely banished her from his head, he'd at least trapped her in a small corner closet toward the back of his brain.

Seeing her again hadn't released her from that dark room. Had it?

Hell, he hoped not. But at least he understood her reasons for breaking up with him a little more.

"Yep, but she decided to spend time with her romantic interest instead."

"The guy with the guitar?"

"One and the same." She laughed. "Avery swore it would never happen. Swore she was immune. I told her to never say never."

Well, he was pretty sure he could say "never" to his being involved with her again. Once was more than enough.

"I definitely saw something between them when I watched them interact."

Her smile was still there. And this time it was very real. It made something heat inside him.

"Something is an understatement. Carter's the one."

The one. Was there such a thing?

If so, Micah hadn't been it. At least not for Lia.

They made their way out to her car, and his brooding thoughts vanished, a smile taking their place when he spotted her vehicle. It was a little compact model that fit her to a T.

Lia had never been a flashy person, unlike his parents. It was probably one of the things that had attracted him to her. Her dad was a pretty well-known scientist in his own right, and yet she never acted like she'd grown up in an upper-middle-class family—one that had done what a lot of families would have been afraid to do: move here from another country.

Her Italian sometimes still came out when she said certain words or when she got nervous or angry. Her breakup speech had been riddled with little language blips that he was sure came from her background, although he hadn't thought they were cute that time. But looking back, he realized those slip-ups proved that what they'd had hadn't been unimportant to her. Otherwise, she would have sailed through that "I don't think we're meant to be together" speech without a problem. It made the blow that much harder knowing that while she cared about him, it hadn't been enough to make her fight for them. Fight for their future.

Because she hadn't thought they had one.

He crunched himself back into the front seat of her car.

"Micah, seriously, push the seat back. You look ridiculous."

On the ride to the wings joint, it hadn't seemed that important, since he hadn't thought he was going to be in the car for the next couple of hours. But with his knees literally pressed against the console in front of him, every pothole was going to bang them up pretty good.

So this time, he reached down for the lever and pushed the seat back as far as it would go. There. At least if they were in an accident, his legs wouldn't be pushed through his chin.

"Less ridiculous?"

"Much." She took out her phone. "So where to? Any preferences as to car dealerships?"

"Maybe one in this area of town and one over in Metro Center?" He pulled up a map of neighborhoods on his phone. "There's also Music Row, which might be a good location for flyers. I'm trying to think of areas that would get the word out the fastest."

"Okay, how about if we do two car dealerships in the downtown area, since they're closer, and then drive out to the other two spots if it's not too dark. I'm assuming we'll have to make more than one trip. Saint Dolly's is going to call other area hospitals and alert them to what's going on here. Hopefully it's confined to just this one area."

"We can hope." Kind of like his problems with Lia had been confined to one area of his heart. Fortunately he'd contained them in time to keep it from really affecting his life.

When Lia put her turn signal on and headed toward the congested area of downtown, he turned his mind toward helping her navigate and away from everything else.

There had been something heartwarming about seeing Micah scrunched in her passenger seat on the way to the wings joint, but after the strange intimacy that had wrapped around that meal with discussions about their past, she had been loath to carry that intimacy outside the restaurant. So she was glad when he'd pushed his seat back and made the car's interior seem a little less cramped.

Or did it?

The way he'd said he'd met lots of people in Ghana had thrown her for a few seconds. Female people? Or was he just trying to get out of answering what was a rather pointed question? But hadn't his question about their breakup been just as pointed?

She forced her attention to something less personal.

"There are a couple of dealerships off I-40. Do you have a preference of car type?"

He sent her a smile. "Just something a little bigger than a lunchbox."

"A lunchbox?" She laughed, glad things seemed to be heading in a more lighthearted direction. "Are you dissing the big blueberry?"

"Isn't *big* blueberry an oxymoron? There is nothing big in this car."

She looked over at him and raised her brows. "Except maybe its passenger's—"

"Uh-uh-uh. My...er...noggin isn't that big."

She had to hand it to the man. He knew how to make her laugh. And how to leave himself open for the perfect comebacks. "Who said I was talking about your head?"

As soon as the words were out of her mouth, her face sizzled with heat. Okay, so she hadn't been specifically talking about any male parts, although she was pretty sure he was going to take it that way. And maybe her subconscious had thrown that out just to torture her.

Micah didn't reply, although out of the corner of her eye she could see a muscle pulsing in his cheek. In anger? Mirth? Disbelief?

Ha! Well, she had a mixture of all three of those reactions going on herself. But she needed to pull herself together or she was going to do something she regretted. Like wish she was kissing him?

Yes. Exactly like that. Even letting that thought go through her mind had her remembering what it had been like to have the man lock lips with her. And a whole lot more.

Fortunately, they weren't far from the first car dealership.

Five minutes later they were getting out of the car and talking to one of the salespeople. Micah told the man what he was looking for. The salesman glanced at Lia. "Will your wife be driving it a lot?"

"She is not my wife."

He punched those words out in a way that made Lia's eyes widen. It was as if that idea were so far out of the realm of possibility as to be laughable. Only he hadn't laughed. Or even chuckled.

"Sorry. I just assumed…" The man didn't finish that statement. Instead, he dived into a rundown of vehicles that fit Micah's needs.

Lia's mood took a turn for the worse. Maybe she should have let him come on his own.

It didn't take long for Micah to find what he was looking for—an SUV that looked like it would work equally well in town or in the country. "Do you want to take it for a test drive?"

"No, I drove something similar in Ghana, so I'm pretty sure I know what it feels like."

Ah, now that made sense. He would have needed something rugged if he had to travel long distances or over difficult terrain. Her blueberry wouldn't have stood a chance there.

And neither would she, probably. At least not without revealing a lot more about herself than she'd wanted to. Thankfully she'd never had to explain her reasons for not wanting to go, other than what she'd said at Maurio's.

The thought of stepping out of her known world and landing in a place where she'd have to start from scratch? Learn how to tell a whole new load of people apart? No. It would be like moving the furniture in her house around and then trying to somehow make her way through it in the dark. She might not be physically blind, but face blindness still took away one of the principal means of navigating through the world…through relationships. Not recognizing Micah at the benefit was proof of how hard it was.

Dio, she'd experienced enough angst over that to last a lifetime. Besides, her father's reflections on the difficulties her uncle had faced had struck deep…and stayed there. Would knowing about her prosopagnosia have affected her job prospects? She'd like to think not, but in the real world…

She just wasn't willing to take that chance. And right now, she was glad that she'd kept the truth to herself.

As she wandered through the lot, deep in thought about the decisions she'd made in life, Micah went in to seal the deal. Fifteen minutes later, he reemerged.

"Done already?"

"Yep. It'll be delivered to the hotel tomorrow. Unfortunately that means you're stuck with me for the rest of the day. Sorry."

"It's okay. I figured it'd be easier if we're together."

Together. But only in the most superficial of ways. She'd make sure of that.

"Speaking of which, the owner of the dealership said he's willing to put a flyer up inside the building where anyone who visits will see it."

She hadn't really thought about businesses putting them up, but it made a lot of sense. "That's great. I guess we'll have to figure out what we want on them pretty quickly." Which probably meant there were more meetings in the near future if they wanted to get out ahead of this thing. And Lia wasn't sure how she felt about them huddling over pages of ideas.

They got back into the car and started toward the main area of downtown Nashville. "What about one of the parks?"

"We'll need something a little more durable than plain paper if we put them up outside."

She'd thought of that as well. "Maybe a material like the plastic yard sale signs we see around. I'm sure the hospital would let us have some of them printed up."

A couple of miles ahead, they found a park that had a lot of foot traffic. Was it muscle memory that had brought her this way? She swallowed back that thought. Of course not. They had history in a lot of places in Nashville. She found a place to park the car and looked at the green space, her hand hovering over the key in the ignition, hesitating to turn the car off.

As if reading her thoughts, he murmured, "We used to come here to get away from things. I even remember playing hooky on our classes one day."

She remembered that well. She'd been a wreck after a particularly difficult day, and Micah had talked her into taking a walk to clear her head.

Except it hadn't been the walk that had done that. It had been his kiss. A kiss that had turned into two, and then three. And they'd had their first lovemaking session in a secluded area under the cover of trees and shrubbery. They'd both missed their next class. And she hadn't regretted it. She still didn't. She shivered at the memory.

"Yes, we did." She cleared her throat. "I remember this place being pretty busy, which is why I think it might be a good place."

"For flyers?" His smooth words made her insides quiver. What else had he thought she meant?

"Yes."

"Do you want to get out and look?"

Did she? Would it cause her to relive memories that should be left in their final resting place? But to balk now would be to confirm that she hadn't gotten over him. Or this place. "I suppose we should."

She turned off the car and tossed the keys into her purse. "Maybe we should take a few pictures of likely spots, so we can remember them later."

"Pictures. Now that's a novel idea."

Was he making a joke about their history in this park? Or was he simply taking her words the way she'd meant them? Actually, she didn't really know how she meant anything right now.

They entered the park, and as soon as they did, she saw everything through the eyes of her past. The greenery that beckoned to hikers and runners alike. The cleared areas that appealed to urbanites who liked the solid feel of concrete beneath their feet. And the small stands of trees that were crafted like mini oases. Those had appealed to Micah and Lia on a day when her stress had been decidedly relieved in his arms.

What were they doing here? This was a huge mistake. She was just about to suggest they turn around and go back to the car when she realized they were...there.

Her shaky legs were thankful for the bench that stood just across the pathway from the dense shade of bushes in front of them. She sank onto it, trying to make it seem as natural as possible. She pointed up at the lamppost. "This is one of the main footpaths through the park. We could put a flyer up there." To keep her mind on the task at hand, she aimed her phone at the area and took a picture of it.

Micah sat down next to her. "Do you know where we are?"

Pretend you don't. Act like this is the first time you've ever seen it.

Like when she'd seen him at the gala? Only that hadn't been pretense. She really hadn't known who he was. At first.

But now she did. Her eyes shut. *Dio*...now she did.

"Yes." The word came out a little shakier than she would have liked, but that couldn't be helped. She covered with her next words. "We're at Butler Park. I think it will be an ideal place to advertise. We'll have to get permission from the parks department, of course, and then we'll need to design the flyers and figure out how to mount them and protect them from the—"

"Lia." His voice stopped the manic tumble of words that she'd used to keep the pull of this place at bay. It hadn't worked. Because as soon as he said her name, voices from the past came whispering toward her, sliding past her cheek, her ears, familiar scents filling her nostrils.

She half turned toward him, her words suddenly deserting her. All she could do was look at him. Those gray eyes, that short beard that was unsuccessful in hiding a strong chin and square jaw. These were things that she recognized. That helped her differentiate him from a million other people on this planet. That and the way he made her feel.

Both in the past. And right now. Right here.

"Yes?"

"Do you know *where* we are? Do you remember this very spot in this very park?"

He wasn't going to let her sidestep his original question.

This time her "yes" was whispered, and she didn't try to add anything else to it.

Warm fingers slid down her jaw until he reached the point of her chin. He cupped it, tipping her face up to his. "This is where it really began."

Yes, it was. The place where sex among the trees had transformed from a mere release of energy into a relationship that not only released energy but gained it back as they shared with each other.

Suddenly she knew he felt it as much as she did. That the magic this park had woven back then was just as potent today as it had been when they were young medical students.

That's when she knew. Knew that she wasn't getting out of this park without getting what she came for. What she longed for.

And that was his kiss.

A small smile played at the corner of his mouth, denting his cheek and making her lean closer to him. Until at last she felt a completely different kind of magic: one where his lips finally touched hers.

CHAPTER FIVE

HE HADN'T MEANT to kiss Lia. But when she sat down on the bench in front of their spot, and he looked into the bushes and saw in his mind's eye their two bodies twined together in an impossible embrace, he hadn't been able to resist saying her name. And when she turned toward him, lips parted, he'd realized he wasn't going to be able to resist her now any more than he'd resisted her all those years ago.

His mouth covered hers, and he sensed more than felt her melt into his embrace. His arms came up and wrapped around her, pulling her closer, her breasts pressed tight against him.

Hell, it had been far too long since he'd held her or any other woman like this. And that was probably why his tongue edged forward and traced her lips with a question. One that she instantly answered by opening her mouth.

He groaned low in his throat, one hand sliding into the hair at the back of her head and holding her in place as he deepened the kiss. His senses were ignited as memories came at him in snatches, like a set of fireworks that lit the sky for a few seconds before dimming and allowing the next explosion to take its place, each burst more brilliantly colored than the last.

Her fingers gripped his shoulders, clenching and releasing

in time with the stroke of his tongue. Just like she'd done hundreds of other times when they'd…

Something between them vibrated. Something that wasn't part of his body.

It happened again, and it took him a few seconds to realize it was someone's phone. Lia's, since his ringer was on.

She jerked back from him, eyes coming up to catch his as she struggled to catch her breath. "What…?"

Damn. He had no idea why he'd just done what he had.

Maybe proving to himself that she'd been as into his touch as he'd been into hers? Had he needed…closure?

As quickly the word popped into his head, he threw it away. Because that kiss had closed nothing. Instead it had ripped wide-open a door from the past, allowing everything he'd stuffed behind it to come tumbling out.

He quickly forced a smile to his lips to cover his musings.

"Saved by a little vibrator."

Wait. That wasn't the right expression. But the burn of red in her face made the mistake worth it. And it helped him realize she'd been just as caught up in the moment as he had.

The buzzing stopped and then started back up almost immediately. Lia fished her phone out of the pocket of her light jacket and glanced at the readout before frowning. "It's Avery."

She pushed a button, then pressed the phone to her ear. "Hi, Ave, what's up?"

Listening for a second, her frown deepened. "About fifteen minutes, why? We had a pertussis case and were looking at spots to—"

She licked her lips. "Um… I'm with Micah."

Evidently she was warning her friend that she couldn't speak freely. Why? Was she planning on sharing all about that unplanned kiss later on? Would she sit there and dissect it with Avery later on?

"Who?" She listened before exclaiming, "Oh, no! Okay, I'm

on my way right now. Get her on the list for one of the OR rooms. The sooner the better. 'Bye."

She looked at him. "Sorry, but I have to cut this field trip short. I'm needed back at the hospital. Can I drop you off somewhere?"

"I can just catch the shuttle at the hospital." Field trip? Really? That kiss was more than just a damned field trip. "Anything I can help with?"

"Avery has been treating one of her patients for some vascular issues in her legs. Well, she'd also started complaining about abdominal pains and just showed up in the ER complaining of severe pain in her belly."

"Vascular issues. Could it be an aneurysm?"

"That's what I'm thinking, or aortic dissection, both of which are medical emergencies."

Micah stood and held his hand out to her. "Let's go, then."

They rushed back to the car, and when Lia's hands were shaking so hard she could barely get the key into the ignition, he took the key from her. "Trade places with me."

"Thanks." The look of relief she threw at him screwed with his insides. But he managed to get out of the car and walk around to the driver's seat. He adjusted the seat and started the vehicle.

Then he turned the car around and aimed it in the direction of the hospital.

Lia couldn't believe she'd let him kiss her. Let? *Dio*, if she remembered right, it had been her who'd leaned toward him and not the other way around. But none of that mattered right now. The fear in Avery's voice had been very real. She remembered her friend asking her if Bonnie had contacted her, and she'd said no. Avery said she was going to get her former music teacher to come in and meet her, but evidently that had all changed. It was now an emergency situation. If it was an aortic dissection—where a weakness in the aorta let blood leak between the layers of the vessel—then time was of the essence, because if it ruptured completely, death could occur within minutes. It sounded like it was down low in the abdominal section of the artery rather than up near the heart. She hoped there was a surgeon at the hospital who could scrub in before she got there, because the longer the wait… It was what killed people before they even realized they were truly sick. She could think of actors and dignitaries alike who had been affected.

"Hurry."

"I'm going as fast as I safely can."

It felt like they were crawling, although when she glanced at the speedometer, they were nearing seventy miles per hour. She was a mess, and even though she was worried about Avery's friend, Lia knew that was only part of the reason for her panic.

Her former lover had kissed her again as if nothing had gone wrong between them. And that scared the hell out of her. How could she have let this happen? Micah deserved better than this. And hell if she hadn't tried to give it to him by breaking things off. Once this was over, she was going to have to make sure he knew that nothing had changed. They were not—nor could they ever—getting back together.

He glanced at her. "You okay?"

Really? He was leading with that?

"Sure. Just fine."

"Stop it, Lia." His hands gripped her steering wheel so hard she was surprised he didn't rip it from the console. "Look, I know that kiss was a mistake. Don't read more into it than there was."

What on earth was that supposed to mean? "I'm not!"

"That's not what I'm seeing by the whole 'ready to run and run hard' vibe you've got going on. Look. It was where we had sex for the first time. It's not surprising that we kissed. Exes get caught in that kind of situation all the time."

They did? And just how did he know that?

I met lots of people there. His words from earlier whispered through her skull, pulling pieces of brain matter apart and turning them against each other.

The fact that he'd used the words *had sex* rather than *made love* somehow made what they'd had look cheap and dirty, as if it was just two people with biological urges they'd chosen not to resist.

That hurt worse than the thought of him sleeping with hundreds of other women. But she wasn't about to let him see the truth.

"Sure. Whatever. Just as long as you know it's not going to lead to us having sex again anytime soon."

If she thought she'd shot a well-aimed arrow and hit a spot it might hurt, she was wrong.

"I never thought it was." He shot her a look. "Did you?"

Actually? If he had kept kissing her like that, they might very well have wound up in that same stand of trees doing the same thing they'd done years ago. And dammit, it wouldn't have been *having sex*, either. They would have been making love. At least it would have been for her.

They made it to the hospital in record time, and when he pulled up in front of the emergency room entrance, she leaped out of the car without stopping to say anything to him and headed through the doors. She'd deal with her keys and the whole car thing later on. Once she found out what was going on with Avery's friend. She had an emergency to see to, one that provided an escape that she welcomed more than she could say.

Avery waved to her from behind the double doors that led to the exam rooms.

"Ultrasound?"

"Yes. Looks like it's an aneurysm in her abdomen. Superior mesenteric. She's trying to act like it's nothing, but it's definitely something."

"Thank God." Even as she said the words, she knew how they sounded. An aneurysm could be as big an emergency as a dissection if it burst. But depending on how large the bulge was and how weak the vessel walls were, it could buy them more time. "I thought for sure you were going to say she had an aortic dissection. How big is it?"

"Looks fairly large to me. She's had severe varicose veins in her legs, but like I said, she called me complaining of some kind of twinge in her stomach, and I was afraid something else was going on. I wish she had called you like I asked."

"Me, too. Where is she? I'll want to see the location on the ultrasound and determine the size for myself."

Avery led her toward the back, where the exam rooms were. Before she even got there, she heard singing. Two voices were crooning about falling into some kind of fire pit? No, a fiery ring. She shot a glance at Avery, who just shrugged. "I told you. She's trying to pretend nothing is wrong."

Lia could relate to that. She'd been trying to pretend nothing was wrong for most of her life. Doing her best to hide her condition from friends, family…and from the few men she'd had in her life, including Micah. In the end, her secret had cost her that relationship. So she was going to make sure this patient didn't ruin her life doing the same thing she'd done: keeping secrets.

Avery squeezed her arm. "Brace yourself. Her companion is a Johnny Cash impersonator named Levi. In case they ask if you recognize who he is."

"Seriously? Johnny Cash?"

"Yep. Right down to the scar on his chin."

She stopped outside the door where the a cappella voices originated and then pushed through it into the room. Nothing stopped—the music continued, the room's two occupants seemingly oblivious to everything around them. On the exam table was her patient, and her singing partner was…okay, Johnny Cash, just like Avery had said.

The face meant nothing, but the pompadour was there, as were the dark sideburns, craggy line in his cheek and that scar. And he was dressed all in black.

The song lyrics suddenly made sense.

She waited until they were done with the chorus before moving forward, shifting her attention away from the Johnny lookalike and focusing them on her patient.

Bonnie was in a skirt that was pushed up enough to reveal knee-high compression stockings, one of which was up and the other rolled down to her ankle. She looked again at Avery with a question. Avery shook her head to indicate she hadn't done that.

"Hi, Ms. Chisholm, I'm Iliana Costa. You were supposed to call me?"

The woman's lips compressed, and she sucked down an exasperated sigh. "You're Avery's friend."

"I am. I hear you're having stomach pains?"

"They're not bad right now. Just a twinge here and there. I think they're going away, actually." Even as she said it, her face contorted for several seconds before the pain released her.

"Can you show me where it hurts?" she asked Bonnie, not bothering with the pain scale, since it was pretty obvious she was going to underplay her symptoms and her discomfort.

Bonnie ignored the request, saying instead, "I didn't even want to come to the hospital, but Levi here insisted."

"He was right. And Levi is...?"

"He's a Johnny Cash impersonator."

A laugh bubbled up inside her that she had to disguise with a cough. "I gathered that. But who is he to you?"

"He's my...er, sidekick."

Avery shot her a look that said everything. "So it's okay that he's here, I take it."

"Definitely."

Lia nodded. "Good. So where is this twinge, exactly?"

Bonnie pressed her hand on an area in her abdomen.

She looked at her friend again. "Did you save images of the ultrasound?"

"Yep, here they are." She went through the images on the computer in the room. It looked like it was indeed in a section of the mesenteric artery, and the aneurysm had ballooned to about two centimeters. It was a pretty good size. A stent wasn't going to work here. They were going to have to bypass the damaged section, hopefully before it blew out.

She went up to the head of the bed. "Okay, Bonnie, did Avery explain that you have an aneurysm and what that means?"

"She said I probably need surgery. Is that really necessary? It's really not as bad as it was. Can't I just wear a girdle to hold it in, like I do these stocking things?"

Avery stepped forward. "No, because this is deep inside you. If it ruptures, you could very well bleed to death. This is serious, Bonnie. You can't sing it away. You need to listen to Dr. Costa and get it fixed."

The man at her side moved to the head of the bed, his cologne rolling over Lia in waves. "You're the June to my Johnny. Without you, I'm lost. I need you here."

Lia blinked. As odd as this couple might look together, the concern in the man's voice sounded genuine. He cared about her. "Avery is right. We do need to operate. But once we're finished, you should recover well, as long as you're willing to make some lifestyle changes, starting with your blood pressure."

"I'm a singer. It's a high-stress profession."

"High stress can lead to high blood pressure. But I think we can help you with that with medication, so you'll be able to keep singing."

"Ugh. What do you think Avery? Do I really need to start popping pills? I don't want to be a drug addict like some of those rock stars are."

Her friend smiled. "It isn't exactly 'popping pills.' And it's what I've already suggested. More than once."

Bonnie's lips became a sideways slash that revealed her displeasure, but it didn't completely rule out what they were saying. She reached for her companion's hand. "What do you think, Sugar Lips?"

"I think you need to do what they say. You've known Avery a long time. She won't steer you wrong."

His voice was gravelly and low, and Lia couldn't quite tell if it was his real voice or if he was still playing a part. Whichever it was, he was saying all the right things.

Bonnie closed her eyes and nodded. "When does this surgery thing need to happen?"

The next part was touchy. Avery had told her that Bonnie hated hospitals. She didn't want to scare her off when they were this close to getting her to agree to a much-needed procedure. "It should be done right away. You're experiencing symptoms, which means the aneurysm could be very close to bursting."

"Like it could burst inside me right now?"

"Yes. I'm here now, so let's get this done and behind you."

Avery touched her arm, a question on her face.

Lia motioned toward the door. "We'll be right back. We're going to discuss strategy for a moment."

When Levi nodded, the friends exited to the hallway.

Avery pulled her a little way down the hallway.

"What's going on?" Lia said.

"You look exhausted. Are you sure you're up for this? And was that Mr. Slash and Burn that I saw bringing you in?"

"Would you please stop calling him that?"

"No." Avery laughed. "Because I swear right now you're about to do a 'burn, baby, burn.'" Her friend sang those three words, drawing the last syllable out on a crazy combination of musical notes, her hips swishing in time with each change in pitch.

Her antics caused Lia to make a sound that was halfway between a laugh and a screech. "I am not!"

"You should see your face. And I know what it feels like, because I get that way every time Carter gives me a sideways look."

Lia rolled her eyes. "First of all, that is you being caught up in a love mist and wishing happy endings on everyone around you. Micah and I were over a long time ago."

"Sure, sure. We'll circle back to that. Which brings me to

the other subject I mentioned. You look exhausted. I can call someone else in."

"No. She needs the surgery, and I'm already here. There's no reason to call another surgeon. As for the circling back, please don't. I took him to look for a car and to scout out places to hang some posters for the hospital."

"And that wasn't a problem at all?" Her friend studied her face. "Being in the same vehicle with him?"

"Not a problem. At all. At least I hope not." Even as she said it, Micah appeared at the end of the hallway, giving her a quick smile.

Her face turned to lava.

"Slash. And. Burn. Right on cue." Avery bumped her with her shoulder.

Micah reached them and said, "I thought you might be back here. I brought the keys to your car. I parked it in the physicians' lot."

Lia gulped, praying Avery wasn't going to say anything else about Micah's cheek, which was still dented from his smile. "Thanks. You won't have a problem getting back to the hotel?"

"Nope. Can we meet up tomorrow to discuss the situation?"

Avery's head twisted sideways to stare at her, brows raised almost to the ceiling. "There's a situation?"

Dio, was there ever. But it wasn't one she wanted to admit to herself, much less to Avery, especially since her friend was right about her reaction to his smile. It had always been that way. Maybe she would confess to her friend at some point about what had happened in the park, but not until she'd had a chance to analyze it for herself. So she quickly broke down the only situation she wanted to talk about: Sassy and the threat of a pertussis outbreak. She ended it with, "But right now I want to focus on Ms. Chisholm's aneurysm. Any other problem can wait until later."

She said that last part with enough emphasis to hopefully convince Avery—and herself—that it was true. Although she wasn't so sure her brain registered her words. It was already taking chunks of what had happened at the park and blowing them all out of proportion.

Micah glanced at her, and the groove in his cheek kicked back up, causing her to sizzle all over again. He was on to her. Maybe she'd be telling Avery about the park incident sooner rather than later. Because her friend might come up with a worse nickname than Slash and Burn, given enough time.

"Here you go." He reached in his pocket, and the tinkle of her key ring with its little bell sounded. "What's this, by the way?" He fingered the silver jingle bell attached to the key ring.

"That's Samantha's."

His head tilted. "Samantha's?"

"Her cat," Avery said. "Named for her witchy ways."

"Witchy…"

Lia explained, "She's named after a TV show character. She can be a little temperamental. And she's been known to vanish and reappear at a moment's notice."

The indent in Micah's cheek became a full-blown grin, and she couldn't help smiling back like an idiot. "I take it the bell is to let you know where she is. If that's the case, shouldn't it be with her rather than with you?"

"She…um…somehow got it off her collar."

"Well, I guess that means she knows where you are rather than the other way around. Clever kitty."

The low words made her shiver.

"I hadn't thought about that." She'd just put the bell on her key chain so she wouldn't lose it. Although with how smart Sam was, she wouldn't put it past the cat to have turned the tables on her.

She held her hand out for the keys. "I'm planning on putting it back on her safety collar tonight." The words came out a little more waspishly than she meant them to. "And I'd better get back to my patient if I'm going to get this surgery on the road."

"Anything I can help with?"

"No. But thanks for asking."

He looked dubious but didn't argue. "All right. I'll see you later, then. And I'll be in touch with you about tomorrow."

"Sounds good." She'd worry about tomorrow when tomorrow came.

Thankfully, Avery didn't say anything else as they returned to her patient's room. Lia patted the woman on the hand. "I'm going to make sure we're set as far as an operating room goes. I'll be back in a few minutes to give you an update and explain exactly what our plan is."

Bonnie's surgery was off to a rocky start. The second Lia opened her up, the weakened vessel burst, filling the surgical site with a rush of blood. "I need suction!"

"Stats are dropping, Doctor."

She needed to find that vessel. Lia reached in with gloved fingers, feeling around as another nurse continued suctioning the area. There!

"Found it. Clamp."

A clamp magically appeared in her hand, and she somehow managed to get it around the upper portion of the injured artery. When they'd suctioned out the rest of the blood, Lia looked at the screens displaying the patient's vital signs. "Okay, she's stable for now. Let's work fast."

This was not how she'd wanted this to go. If the aneurysm was caused by an infection in the vessel, it could have just released a flood of bacteria into her abdomen. What she'd seen on the scans hadn't looked mycotic, but she would rather have clamped the vessel and bypassed it than have it rupture. She could do an intracavity lavage with antibiotics, but there were mixed reviews on whether it actually helped prevent sepsis or not. What she could do instead was start her on a course of IV antibiotics to ward off infection, just in case. "Is the graft ready?"

Another doctor had been busy retrieving a vein from Bonnie's leg to use to replace the part of the damaged artery. "Yes, although I had a heck of a time finding something decent. Just suturing the site closed."

Lia took the section of vessel and used it to resection the two cleaned-up ends of the vessel. Ten minutes later, it was attached. Looking through her loupes, she checked the suture line, making sure the stitches were close and even. "Let's take the clamp off and see what we've got."

The clamp was removed, and they waited. No leaks. Everything looked well sealed. "Send the removed portion to pathology and have them look for signs of infection. I want to make sure we cover all our bases." She gave a relieved sigh and glanced up at the viewing window, where Avery was watching, and nodded to her. Then she turned back to her team. "Let's get her closed up."

An hour later, Bonnie was in recovery, and they'd allowed Levi to join her. She met Avery in the hallway to give her an update. "I want to keep her for a day or two to give her a chance to recover and so we can monitor for signs of infection." She smiled. "And you might see about getting her a private room, in case she wants to put on another concert."

"I'll work on that."

Hopefully she would have the path results back soon and they'd be in the clear. In the meantime, she gave Avery a hug. She glanced at her phone and saw it was already after nine in the evening. "I think I'm headed home to crash, unless you need me for something else."

"No. Go. I'm going to head home to Carter in a few minutes, too, before he sends out a search party." Her friend smiled. "And thank you for saving her. She's a special lady."

"I can see that. And it was a group effort. But she is going to need to work on her blood pressure."

"I agree. We'll have another discussion about that. Thanks again."

"You're welcome. We need to set up that guac date." She

felt for her keys and found them in her pocket. Hopefully he had made it home. "And please, please don't call Micah by that name again."

"Yes, to the guac. On the other thing… I'm not sure. You'll need to convince me that it's no longer an accurate representation. I could call him Mr. Slash and you Ms. Burn, if you'd prefer."

"No. I don't prefer."

Maybe because it was a little close to the truth. She needed to figure out if anyone else could see what Avery evidently could. And, if so, what she needed to do to change it.

CHAPTER SIX

MICAH SPOTTED LIA and Avery the second they came in.

"Damn." The word slipped out before he could stop it.

The elegantly dressed woman seated across from him tilted her head and frowned. "What is it, honey?"

Honey. It was how she'd always referred to him, but he wasn't sure it meant any more now than it had in the past. In fact, the word itself grated on him whenever he heard it on television or between lovers on the street. Because it brought up a whole host of memories he'd rather forget. In fact, he wouldn't be here at all with her if she hadn't contacted him and asked if they could meet.

He shook himself from his thoughts. "Nothing. I was just thinking of something."

Lia had needed to attend to another emergency surgery two nights ago when they were supposed to meet up about the vaccination campaign. And he actually hadn't seen her since then, since he'd been busy as well. Sassy was still in the hospital. So far no other pertussis cases had come in, but it was still early, and adults tended to fend off the illness better than infants. Sassy had been touch and go, but today, for the first time, it seemed she might be improving.

Something he wasn't sure if Lia knew. He probably should tell her.

While Lia looked straight ahead as if she didn't care who was here, Avery's gaze scanned the faces in the room. Her glance collided with his, and she smiled, then jabbed Lia with her elbow. Great. He'd been hoping he wouldn't actually see anyone he knew here.

The woman leaned close to Lia and whispered something. Lia stopped in her tracks, and her eyes slowly swung in his direction. Okay, well, it looked like he wasn't getting out of here unscathed. He gave her a half smile. Lia's teeth came down on her lower lip, rubbing along it in a move he found fascinating. Why had she done that? Not that he minded.

Actually he thought it was pretty damned...

Inconvenient. That's the word he was looking for.

"Are those friends of yours?" His attention swung back to his companion.

Oh, hell. The last thing he wanted to do was to introduce her to Avery and Lia. Especially since Lia had never met her. Not even when they were dating. Although maybe it had been a sign of things to come.

He struggled to find a way to describe Lia. "They work at the same hospital as I do."

Just then, the pair's trajectory changed, and they headed toward Micah's table, Lia hanging back and looking like this was the last place she wanted to go. Her first reaction to seeing him might have been crazy sexy, but right now she looked pretty miserable. But at least she'd recognized him this time.

Then they were standing in front of them, and he had a decision to make. So he stood and forced a smile that wasn't real this time. "Hi, ladies. I didn't know you liked this place."

"Best guacamole in the state. It's where we always come," Avery said with a touch of pride in her voice.

He remembered asking Lia for a recommendation of that

very dish, and this wasn't the place she'd named. He looked at her. "Is it now?"

Her teeth slammed down on her lip again, and this time a flush leached into her cheeks. "It's only one of the places I eat guacamole."

Avery's head swung around. "*One* of them? I thought you said Gantry's guac was a cut above any other restaurant's? Not that I disagree. It's fab."

So Lia hadn't wanted to bring him here. Why? Did she consider him some kind of infectious disease that would contaminate this place and ruin it for her?

Maybe it was part of the same reason she'd broken up with him. He hadn't bought the whole "We want different things from life" crap she'd thrown at him after graduation. Something had happened. Something that had changed the way she saw him in a nanosecond. But he couldn't force her to tell him if she didn't want to. And he'd been so shocked and hurt that he'd just wheeled away from her and gotten the hell out of there. He'd wound up in a bar very much like this one.

And after all this time, he wasn't going to sit here and second-guess every single thing he'd said or done. Not like he had back then.

"And who is your companion?" Avery gave him a guarded look that he could swear harbored a gleam of disappointment. In what?

He glanced at the woman seated at his table, realizing that through the modern marvels of plastic surgery, she didn't look much older than he did.

Okay, so this was even worse than he'd thought. He did not want Lia thinking he'd kissed her and then immediately gone out and found someone else. Although she probably wouldn't care one way or the other.

"I was just telling her about you both, that we work at the same hospital."

Lia stared down at her feet as if she couldn't bear to look

at him. So she'd thought exactly that. That this was his date. That was so far from the truth that it was actually ludicrous.

So with his next words, he allowed a hint of a smile to play across his lips. "Lia and Avery, I'd like you to meet Monica Corday. My mother."

Her head whipped up as shock wheeled through her. This woman was Micah's mom and not his—?

As if summoned, the woman uncoiled herself from her chair and stood. Out came a perfectly manicured hand on which was some pretty impressive jewelry. "I'm so pleased to meet you both."

Her voice was smooth, with a perfect southern drawl that made Lia's remaining accent feel thick and clumsy. She dreaded opening her mouth.

Avery broke in and saved her the trouble, giving back a greeting gripping the other woman's hand. "Pleased, I'm sure." The cool words held just a touch of prickle that no one but Lia would have sensed. It was as if she'd sensed how unsure Lia felt and was moving in to protect her. Just like her dad always had.

A dangerous prickling occurred behind her eyes. She forced it away with a couple of hard blinks.

She appreciated Avery's efforts, but she could fight her own battles. "It's very nice to meet you, Mrs. Corday, I'm Lia Costa."

Although her condition kept her from seeing the resemblance between mother and son, it didn't stop her from noticing that when Monica Corday smiled, there were very few facial lines activated. Botox. A good deal of it, if she had to hazard a guess. Not like her son, whose smile revealed a wonderful network of lines that made her stomach wobble. And that dimple...

Slash and Burn. Hell if Avery hadn't hit the nail on the head.

The insincere curve of lips appeared again. "Would you two care to join us?"

Dio. When they'd first come in and Avery had pointed him out, she'd thought Micah was here on a date. Outrage had gathered in her chest that she'd done her best to banish. It was none of her business whom he did and didn't go out with. But on the heels of that kiss they'd shared? Really?

To find out this was actually his mom had been even more shocking, if that were possible. Micah had said he and his parents didn't see eye to eye. She was starting to see why. This clinic-crafted person was nothing like the man she used to love.

"Thank you, but no. I'm sure you two have a lot to talk about." Too late she remembered that he'd said his father was ill. So her words sounded terrible.

One of Micah's brows crooked up as he smiled.

How could he smile? His dad was sick. "I, um meant, since you've been gone for so long."

Micah was still standing, and his hand slid next to hers, pinkie finger barely grazing hers for a second as if to reassure her. "I knew what you meant."

Her throat clogged. He was giving her a pass, even though he probably shouldn't have. This man affected her thought processes in so many ways that it wasn't even funny. He'd always done so, but it was disappointing that he still had this effect on her. She should be well and truly over him by now. But she wasn't. Because she hadn't broken up with him because she'd no longer loved him. She'd broken up with him for just the opposite reason. She loved him so much that she didn't want him saddled with someone who would always have trouble recognizing people she'd known for years. It would be even worse if he'd had to drag her overseas with him.

Even if he didn't find her condition embarrassing, she did. And she didn't want him going through what her dad had had to deal with: stepping in to protect his brother from ridicule. And how many times had her parents had to explain and make excuses for her when she tripped over an identity? The thought of Micah doing that made her cringe.

She looked at Micah's mom and tried to pick out things about her that she would remember the next time she saw her.

Lack of lines. Long blond hair that was the same color as Micah's. A painted-on mole at the corner of her left eye. Except that might not always be there. Maybe she dotted it on periodically and left it off at other times. Lia's eyes went crazily from feature to feature before finding something else. Her nose was slightly crooked, taking a tiny jog to the left. She wondered if it had been broken at some time in the past. Okay. Blond hair. No lines. Crooked nose.

Avery, who hadn't said anything for a minute or two, spoke up. "Lia's right. We have some business to discuss, anyway, so maybe another time."

"Certainly." Monica's response was as smooth as ever, giving no hint that her husband, who wasn't here at the restaurant with them, was ill. Although that probably was why Micah was here—to discuss things. Although maybe not. Maybe they'd already made their amends. Maybe their family was closer than hers now. In the two days since she last saw him? Hardly likely.

And Micah's eyes held a wariness that she didn't like. She might not recognize him by the parts of his face, but she knew him in a way that no one else would. At least that's what she told herself. Who knew if that was actually true or not. Surely his mom knew him well, since she'd been a part of his life since birth.

So she decided to follow Avery's lead and forced a smile she didn't feel. "It was nice meeting you, Mrs. Corday."

"You as well, dear."

She threw one last look at Micah, who nodded. She had no idea what it meant, so she just turned and went in the other direction, following Avery toward a table on the other side of the room.

Lia dropped into her chair with a sigh, holding up two fingers when their usual waitress glanced in their direction. She would know what she meant. They always got margaritas and guacamole with chips when they came here. She turned back to Avery. "Oh, God. That was one of the most uncomfortable experiences ever."

"You mean with Slash and Burn? He didn't look any more comfortable than his dear old mama did."

Needing something to fiddle with, she grabbed a napkin from the table and worried the edge of it. "I had no idea she was his mother. She looks a little young."

"You never met her while you were dating? And the fountain of youth that particular woman drank from comes at a hefty price tag at the hands of a good surgeon."

She had to agree with her. "I'm sure. And no, I never met her. Not once."

"He was probably afraid you'd run away and never come back. I might."

She kind of had run and never come back. But not because of his mother. Because of her own fears. "He said he and his parents didn't see eye to eye. At least that's why he never introduced us, I thought. But who knows? That was a long time ago. So let's not talk about them. Let's talk about your new life with Carter."

It worked. Avery moved the conversation over to something that was near and dear to her heart. And as she talked about the progression that led to their engagement, Lia smiled. "I saw Micah at the Valentine's benefit, and he thought there was some pretty heavy chemistry going on between the two of you."

"There was. But we're not the only ones who have some wild chemistry going on."

So much for keeping things shifted away from her. "If you're talking about me and Micah, that chemistry is old news. There was some at one time, as you know, but not any longer."

"Are you really sure about that, Lia?"

She crooked one shoulder up. "It's what it needs to be." She paused, torn about whether to say anything or not. But she and the ER nurse rarely kept things from each other. Especially when they were at Gantry's for guac and talks. So she plowed forward. "Except…we kissed. And it was… Let's just say I could be in a lot of trouble."

Avery sat back in her chair. "You kissed! When did this happen?"

She did her best to angle her body so Micah couldn't see her face. Or read her lips. "The day of Bonnie's surgery. We were actually in the middle of it when your call came through." Lia had to admit it felt good to get this off her chest.

"Why on earth did you answer the phone?"

"*Dio*, what was I supposed to do? I figured it was something pretty important or you wouldn't be calling me. And actually, it was a blessing. The last thing I needed to be doing was kissing Micah Corday."

"Why?"

She was stunned. "What do you mean, why? Our relationship is over. Finished. *Terminata*. To dredge it up now would be just plain stupid, since I have no intention of getting involved with him again. It was a mistake last time. It would be a mistake this time."

"You never told me exactly what happened between you last time."

Even though her friend knew about her diagnosis, she doubted Avery would agree with her reasons for ending it with Micah.

"I just realized it was never going to work between us. He wanted to go to Africa, and I wanted to stay here. In Nashville."

She prayed Avery wouldn't keep digging.

Her friend sighed, then slid her hand over hers. "I'm sorry. I remember how hard it was for you to get over him. I can't imagine what it must be like to work with him. But that kiss…"

"It was a shock to realize he's going to be staying at the hospital, for sure. I'm hoping it gets easier as time goes on." She sighed. "As for the kiss, I think seeing him again dragged up a lot of old feelings."

"I bet." Her friend glanced over at the other table. "Don't look now, but Mr. Slash and Burn is looking in our direction."

"Avery, seriously. And I'm sure he's just looking around the room. I do hope he and his mom are getting along better, though. Especially with his dad being ill."

"Is it serious?"

"Serious enough to bring him home from Ghana."

Avery's lips twisted. "So that's why he's here. That stinks."

"Yes, it does." Her heart ached for Micah. He'd rarely talked about his parents. So there must be a huge mess of conflicting emotions involved in returning to Nashville.

The waitress set their drinks in front of them, along with two large bowls of guacamole and chips. "Anything else?"

"Not yet," Avery said, "but we may need some more drinks by the time this is all over with."

Debbie, who had waited on them more often than not, gave them a sympathetic smile. "Just send me a signal when you're ready."

"Thanks." Lia waited for the woman to leave and then blew her breath out in a rush. "Why does life have to be so complicated?"

"Tell me about it." Avery smiled. "But sometimes it works out in unexpected ways. Look at me and Carter. Maybe this is another of those times."

Lia was happy for her friend. Happy that she'd found a person to spend her life with. Happy to see her friend so relaxed and at peace. But things didn't always work out that way. At least not for her and Micah. Even if that kiss had been wildly exciting and crazy good, it was doubtful Micah would ever fully forgive her for dumping him the way she had. And really, nothing had changed. She had the same fears now that she'd had back then. It was why her dating life basically sucked. She didn't see herself settling down and getting married. Having children. Not with the way she was wired.

"It's not, but I'm okay with it." She smiled. "I do hope Bonnie and Levi-slash-Johnny have a happy ending, though."

"They are a wild pair, aren't they? But they really care about each other."

"I'm hoping she'll be released tomorrow or the next day. Did she see you sing at the Valentine's Day benefit?"

Avery nodded. "She did. It was hard getting up there without my sister, but Carter helped me get through it. So did you and Bonnie."

Avery's sister had died of cancer a couple of years ago. It was the main reason her friend had had trouble singing again.

"I think April would be very proud of you, honey."

"I hope so." With that, her friend lifted her glass and said, "Let's toast to new beginnings."

Lia hoped she was talking about her own circumstances and not about her and Micah. Because sometimes there were no new beginnings. Or at least no retreading of old paths. And in this case, she had to believe it was for the best. Even if her heart might disagree.

CHAPTER SEVEN

A KNOCK SOUNDED on the door to Micah's office Monday afternoon. He'd already had a difficult weekend between meeting with his mom and going to see his dad the next day. His dad was a shadow of the strong, commanding man he'd once been. The change had come as a shock and made him realize that though he might not have agreed with the way they'd raised him, he'd been right to come home and try to make peace with the parts of his childhood that had been difficult. That included his parents.

"Come in."

The door opened, and Lia peeked in, a look of uncertainty on her face.

He motioned her inside. "Do you know?"

"Know what?" She slid into the room and perched on one of the chairs in front of his desk, looking like she might like to get up and take flight.

"Sassy, the baby who has pertussis, is being released today."

"That's great," she started, only to stop when he held up his hand.

"It's good that she's better, but there are a couple of reports that other area hospitals have seen some cases over the weekend. One of them is a neighbor of Sassy's family."

Her eyes closed before reopening. "God. I was hoping it was going to be confined to the two families who got together."

"So did I." He picked up a pencil and tapped the eraser end on a map on his desk. "The other cases don't appear to have any ties to the families. But there are always grocery stores or any number of places where a cough can cause an outbreak."

"If this gains speed…"

"I know. Which is why I think we need to prioritize getting some of these posters up. How busy are you today and tomorrow?"

"I have a surgery and a couple of consults to do tomorrow morning, but nothing urgent. I was going to head to the ER after that and pitch in where I could."

"Do you have time to talk about the design? You always did have a flair for putting things like that onto paper."

"Me?" Her voice squeaked in a way that made him smile.

She liked to sketch, and she was good. Micah remembered sitting beside her on the couch while she doodled on a pad. Sometimes the drawings were of things they'd seen that day. Sometimes they were musculature contained within the human body. And sometimes they were things as simple as the fire in the fireplace.

"Yes. You." He hesitated, not sure he should say anything about Thursday night. "It looked like you and Avery had fun at Gantry's."

"We did. Did you and your mom have a productive talk?"

He leaned back in his chair and looked at her. "I don't know about productive. But I think we made a little bit of progress. And I saw my dad."

"How did that go?"

"I'm not quite sure. But we'll see where it leads." He glanced at her. "Let's talk about making a mockup that we can take to Arnie. Can we work on that today?"

"Surely the hospital can hire someone for that part?"

Micah lifted his brows. "I'm sure they can, but all I envision is it taking forever to get all the parties to agree on something. By that time, a few cases could turn into hundreds."

If anyone knew about that, it was him. In Ghana, there hadn't been near the amount of bureaucracy that there was here, and yet it still took forever to get anything accomplished. "If you could sketch a couple cradling a baby with worried expressions on their faces, we can put together a slogan together. The sooner we get this down on paper, the sooner we can hang them around town."

Her features seemed to blanch. "I—I'm not good at drawing faces."

"I've seen some of your drawings, remember? They're really good. We wouldn't need a lot of detail, just kind of neutral features…you could depict worry through their posture, or by how they're huddled together."

She relaxed into her chair. "So just eyes, nose and mouth that could belong to anyone. I wouldn't have to make them distinctly different from each other."

"No." Was it weird that she was hung up on this particular part of the process? Well, maybe drawing faces was harder than it looked. "Just kind of like cartoon characters."

"Cartoon characters." She nodded as if thinking about something. "Actually, that's not a bad idea. If we could make it look like a comic strip, only on a much larger scale, it might attract the attention of adults and children alike."

"I like it." He grabbed a piece of paper and came around to the other side of the desk, sitting in the empty chair and putting the paper between them. "So can we work on it now?"

"You don't have anything else to do?"

"Infectious diseases are what they hired me for, so this needs to top my to-do list."

Her warm scent, probably carried on air currents from the climate control system, drifted over to him, reminding him of that kiss they'd shared. It was heady and made him wonder if having her here in his office with the door closed was such a good idea.

Of course it was. He was an adult. And he would act like it. No mooning over her. No looking for chances to touch her, like he'd done in the past.

Like he'd done at Gantry's?

He reached across her to get to his pencil cup, grabbing two pens and handing her one. Their fingers touched, and a frisson of electricity shot through him. He hadn't tried to touch her that time. It was an accident.

Ignore it. Ask a question. Anything to shift his attention back to the job at hand. "So what are we looking to convey?"

She made a humming sound and touched the top of the pen to her lip, using the pressure to click the mechanism that caused the ball point to emerge.

Micah swallowed, remembering how her teeth had captured that very same lip.

"We want to have a sense of urgency, right? People are getting sick and we want to somehow stop it." Her light brown eyes sought his.

He nodded. "Yes. So how do we do that?"

"Maybe we have a mother with an infant in her arms just as her husband or significant other comes into the room. She's holding the baby close and is looking at the man. We could use a dialogue box to show the baby coughing."

"Would there be actual dialogue between the couple?"

"I don't think so. We have a pretty diverse population here. If we could get the idea across using just the pictures of the cartoon—minimal words—it might be better."

He nodded, trying to think of a way to do that. "So we could have this couple with a sick baby in the first cartoon slide. The next one could be a hospital scene? With multiple couples holding babies, all of whom have the same 'cough' bubble above them."

"That's good. I like it." She turned a sheet of paper so it

was horizontal and divided it into three sections. Quickly she sketched a cartoon couple in the first section, just their bodies and heads, and she actually drew them from the behind, so there were no faces at all in them, but you could clearly tell it was two adults with a baby between them. She penned a dialogue bubble above the infant with "Cough-cough" written in bold, jagged strokes. "How about this?"

It was perfect. There was an element of fear in the adults' posture, the merest hint of a nose on each, as their faces were turned slightly inward to look at each other. He'd known she could do it. "That's just how I envisioned it. Can you do the next one? The hospital scene?"

She touched the pen to her lip, tapping it a couple more times. His senses reacted all over again, remembering the slide of his lips across her mouth. How smooth it was. How warm and moist and...

Shaking himself from the memory, he forced himself to focus as her pen started scratching in the next box. Three couples were now seated, same perspective, except for one standing adult who faced them. This character wore a lab coat with what was clearly a stethoscope around his neck. The face was a simple oval, devoid of features or emotion. Three dialogue bubbles hovered over the scene this time, each with the same words in them. It was an ominous scene. Outside the hospital windows, there were dark clouds, and she used hash lines to shade the space to make it look gloomy.

"Yes. That's good, Lia. Very good."

When she looked at him this time, there was a sense of relief on her face. Surely she wasn't worried about him rejecting what she'd put on that page. And the fact that she could do it so quickly was exactly what he'd hoped for. "Are you sure?"

"I am. Absolutely." He nudged her with his shoulder. "This is why I didn't want the hospital to farm it out to a business. It would have taken forever. So the last square..."

"I have an idea. How about this?" She quickly drew the same

three chairs, empty this time. There was an empty hypodermic needle in the top left corner. The view outside the hospital showed a couple walking down the sidewalk with a stroller—the top of a tiny head peeking out. The scene was idyllic with trees and fluffy clouds. There was a sense of well-being. Peace even. And no dialogue bubbles.

Across the top of the page she wrote,

Whooping cough
A not-so-silent killer
Save a baby's life
Get vaccinated

"We can put the hospital logo and a number for information. Or even for the CDC."

"Yes." He glanced at his watch. "Fifteen minutes. That's all it took. Hell, Lia, you are amazing."

"No. I'm not, really." She turned toward him. "It's not that great."

It was. And so was she. Her beautiful eyes were looking at him in that way she had of skimming quickly over his face before moving beyond it to dwell on other places, studying them intently. It had always made him feel as if she didn't really see him the way other women did: as in his physical appearance. Being valued for such a shallow thing had made him feel almost as invisible as he'd felt as a kid, only in a different way. Lia had never commented on his face. Except for that line in his cheek, which she'd loved to trail her fingers down.

She'd made him feel seen. Really seen. In a way no one else had.

His hand lying on the desk slid closer to hers before he pulled himself up short. What was he doing? That shared kiss had reminded him of all the things that had been good about their relationship. But when it had imploded...

Yeah. That had been bad. Really bad.

Not a good idea to let himself get drawn back in. He wasn't sure if what she'd said about Ghana was the entire truth or if she had commitment issues or what, but he really didn't want to push replay on whatever had happened at the end. So he did something to drag his attention back where it should be—on the cartoon she'd sketched.

"It is great, and I'm going to prove it to you." He pulled out his cell phone and dialed.

A minute later, Arnie answered.

"Hey, do you have time to look at something? It'll only take a minute."

"Sure. Where are you? Your office?"

"Yep, do you want us to run by with it?"

"Us?"

He glanced at Lia. "Dr. Costa made a mockup for the vaccine campaign we talked about last week."

"Good. That'll save me from having to get a committee together, if it's good. I'll run by your office. I'm on my way out anyway."

"See you in a few minutes, then."

He hung up, only to note that Lia's face was strained. "Are you okay?"

"Are you sure this is good enough to show him?"

"I promise I would have told you if it wasn't."

She looked down. "There aren't any actual faces."

Cocking his head, he looked at the drawing. "You know, I think it's better this way. Those images could represent anyone. Maybe a passerby will mentally superimpose their own image or the likeness of someone they know."

She quickly added a few things to the drawing: a dog on a leash in the last image. A crowd of people outside the window of the first scene, depicting how whooping cough could spread in gatherings.

By the time she was finished, a knock sounded at the door,

followed by Arnie coming into the room. He came over to the desk and stood by Lia. "Is this it?"

"Y-yes."

She was nervous. And Lia was rarely nervous. She normally knew her own mind and was confident in her abilities.

Arnie stared down at the picture for a while. Then said, "This is excellent. From one ill child to three, and then along comes the vaccine and empties out the waiting room. I like the touch of showing a happy—and healthy—family walking outside the hospital." He picked it up and went over to the copier and made a duplicate. "I'm going to keep this one, if that's okay. Can you take these to a printer and have them printed, blowing a few into poster-size prints? We'll stamp them with the hospital logo and number and display the large ones here at home and distribute the others to various business. We'll also hang them in places where it's legal to do so."

"I'll need to clean it up a little before we do that," Lia murmured.

"No. I want it left just like this. There's no need to clean anything up. And I know the board will agree with me on this."

Micah smiled at her. "Do you believe me now?"

"I guess so."

Arnie leaned down and took one of the other sheets of paper, scribbling down a name. "This is who the hospital uses for printing materials. Do you think you can get this over there?" He glanced at his watch. "They're open for another hour or so. Order what you need."

"We'll take care of it." Micah glanced at her with raised brows, asking her the question. She answered with a nod.

With that, the hospital administrator opened the door again and thanked them before leaving as quickly as he'd arrived.

"If you can go with me, I actually have my new car, so I can drive this time."

She shrugged. "Well, I guess I don't have a choice, since

Arnie made it pretty clear he wants these done immediately. And I do agree with him, it's just..."

"Just what?"

She shook her head. "Nothing. Just wish I had more time to perfect it."

"It'll be okay. You know Arnie better than I do. Would he truly let us print something—something that represents the hospital—if he didn't think it would stand up to scrutiny? I wish I'd had one of your prints in Ghana."

That last statement had slipped out before he could stop it. He'd meant it in a generic way. Right?

Because she'd made it clear back then—and now—that she wasn't interested in him on a personal level.

And that kiss?

He had no idea what that had been about. For her or for him.

Lia glanced over at him. "Thank you." The words were spoken softly with a hint of meaning that he wasn't sure he understood. Or that he wanted to understand.

"If you're ready?" He grabbed a notebook from the back of his credenza. "Let's slide it in here to keep it from getting bent or damaged."

She handed him the drawing, and he tucked it inside the front cover. Then they moved out of the room and headed out of the hospital.

CHAPTER EIGHT

GORDY'S PRINTING WAS busier than she'd expected. There were four people ahead of them, and it was only thirty minutes until their six o'clock closing time. It must be because some folks were coming right after work.

"Did you find a place to live other than the hotel yet?"

"No. Not yet. But then again, it's been so busy I haven't really had a lot of time."

She thought for a second. "I know you and your parents aren't super close, but—"

"No. That wouldn't work."

He shut her down before she'd even finished saying what she'd been going to say. That maybe it would give him time to be with his dad. Especially since he admitted himself that life was extra busy.

As if realizing how short he'd sounded, he touched her hand. "Sorry. I know it would be a good thing, but my mom and dad... I think it would be hard on both sides. I don't want to put my mom in the middle, feeling like she needs to placate both of us. And my dad—well, let's just say he's not the man I remember, and I don't want to stress him out unnecessarily."

"Is he undergoing treatment?" One of the customers left, and the line moved forward.

"He just started. They're hoping for remission."

He'd said *they*. Surely Micah wanted remission for his dad as well.

Another customer slid out of line, going through the door. Okay, so this was moving quicker than she'd thought it would.

"How probable is that?"

"From what my mom said, there's about a thirty percent chance he'll achieve it."

She couldn't stop herself from looping her arm through his and squeezing it before forcing herself to let go. "I know I've said it before, but I'm really sorry. I can't imagine what that has to be like for your family, and since you're their only child, it makes it hard on you as well."

"Well, as their only child, it's why I came home."

Said in a way that let her know that his return had nothing to do with her. Not that she'd thought it had. She'd just been trying to sympathize with him.

It was their turn, so they moved to the front. Micah opened the notebook and pulled out her sketch. "We need some prints of these. About three poster-size and we need some flyer-size prints as well, but we need them in some kind of heavier paper that's impervious to water."

"We have weatherproof sheets that are about the thickness of cardstock. They're actually plastic, but we can print on them." The clerk was young, with straight dark hair that fell to his shoulders. He looked hip and artsy, a ring on his thumb boasting an ankh symbol. His nails were painted black. A small name tag on his dark polo shirt read Curtis.

He was definitely different from the cowboy types that Nashville was famous for.

"Weatherproof," Micah said. "Sounds like what we need."

The guy took a look at the sketch. "Who drew this?"

"I did." Her heart was in her throat, wondering if he thought it was ridiculous.

He looked up. "I can't accept it like this."

Oh, God. He did think it was ridiculous. But before she could agree with him, he turned the paper toward her and rummaged through a drawerful of different kinds of pens before finally selecting one. "You really need to sign it. There are people out there who wouldn't think twice about ripping this design off and then claiming it as their own."

"Surely not."

"Hey," said Curtis. "People steal songs and lyrics all the time in this town—you think they wouldn't steal art?"

Art? Was he kidding?

Micah moved close enough to give her hand a squeeze. "Do you believe me now?"

She hadn't. Not really. Until this moment. She looked at her sketch, trying to see what they saw in it. But she just couldn't. She'd always liked to doodle as a kid and had gotten in trouble for doing that in school lots of times.

The young man held out a pen. "Even just your initials with today's date in the bottom right corner will do, but signing your name would be better."

She took the writing instrument and scribbled *L. Costa* along with the year in small letters at the corner of the last scene. "Like this?"

"Yes, perfect." Curtis blew on the lettering for a second or two before finding a plastic sleeve and sliding the drawing inside it. "And I didn't know that whooping cough was making a comeback."

Micah spoke up. "It's always been here. We're just trying to make sure what's out there doesn't turn into an epidemic."

"Good. My wife is actually eight months pregnant." The guy grabbed a pad of paper. "So three posters and how many flyers?"

"Let's go with a hundred."

A hundred of her sketches were going to be floating around Nashville? It made her a little uncomfortable, but if it saved lives...

Curtis scribbled down their order, his ankh ring catching the light a couple of times. "If you ever need a job, we have a design team that would love to have you on it."

She laughed. Okay, well, that was unexpected. "Thank you, but I think I'm better suited to being a doctor."

"If you ever change your mind, let me know." He added up the costs. "Do you have a requisition from the hospital?"

"No," Micah said. "But if you call in the morning and ask to talk to Arnie Goff, he'll give you a number. He's the hospital administrator over at Saint Dolores."

"Ah, Saint Dolly's. I was born there. My wife and I were actually in the nursery at the same time."

Lia's eyes widened. "Well, that's a coincidence."

"We were both preemies, and the hospital has a kind of reunion every year for us. We started dating in high school. Went to prom together."

"I've heard of those reunions. That's wonderful." What a romantic way to meet your future spouse. "Are you planning to have your baby at Saint Dolly's?"

"Yes, but we'll hopefully not wind up in the preemie ward."

"Well, I hope everything goes well for all of you."

"Thanks." He touched the plastic sleeve containing her sketch. "I hope everything goes well with this. And I'll check with our doctor to make sure we don't need a booster."

"That's great." Lia fished in her purse and found one of her cards and scribbled her number on the back. "Let me know if there's anything I can do. I'm not in obstetrics, so definitely check with your doctor, but if you have any questions, please don't hesitate to call." She wasn't sure why she'd done that. It was rare that she ever gave out her personal cell phone number, but there was just something about the kid she liked. His love for his wife and future baby were obvious.

"Wow, thanks. I will. Jenny is a little nervous about things. This is our first. We got married last year."

Fortunately there was no one else waiting behind them. "Well, the best of luck to both of you."

"Thanks. To you both as well."

Did he think they were a couple? Surely not.

Micah's quick grin said otherwise, making her face heat like molten lava. He slashed, she burned. *Dio*, Avery really was right. "When do you think the printing can be done once you get Mr. Goff's approval?"

"It should be done in a couple of days. So maybe check back on Wednesday?"

"We'll be here." With that, Micah turned away from the desk and headed toward the door.

He'd said *we* as if it were a given that they'd arrive back here together. Lia wasn't so sure that was a good idea. But she'd address that later. If needed, she'd make sure she had something else scheduled. Because being with him today had really rattled her. Especially when she'd been drawing that sketch, feeling his presence next to her. Feeling his eyes on her as her pen moved over that sheet of paper. It had been unnerving.

And exhilarating. In a way she hadn't felt in a long time. Maybe even since they'd been together.

They walked over to the paid parking garage, Lia pulling her coat around her against the nippy temperatures. Micah showed the attendant their all-day pass as they walked by him. "You know there's free parking not far from here."

"I know, but this was faster, and since I wanted to make it to the shop before it closed, it seemed the best solution. And it's where I used to park when I was in this part of town."

"I remember that from when we were in school."

"Yes, we spent a little bit of time kissing in this garage."

Her face heated yet again. Yes, they had.

They moved into the building and headed toward the back. Even in the paid garage, it had been hard to find a spot, so Lia knew he was right in saying this had been the best option.

They found his car in one of the darker areas, and Micah

pressed the mechanism to unlock the vehicle. Going around to the passenger side, she got in, the scents of leather and Micah surrounding her as she sank into the comfortable seat and clicked her belt.

Dio, it was like days gone by.

Micah got into the driver's seat and started the car, waiting for it to warm up for a minute or so before turning the heat on. She turned her vents toward her.

"Cold?"

"It's a little chilly out there." She glanced at him. "You probably should have worn something heavier."

"I actually enjoy the cold after spending some hot days in Ghana."

"What was it like?" She'd been afraid to go, but that didn't mean she wasn't curious.

"The people were wonderful, but it had its challenges, just like every place." He sat back in his seat and turned his torso to look at her. "Seasons of the year were measured more by dry or rainy rather than temperatures, but it was rare for it to drop below the mid-seventies, and hundred-degree days were not unusual."

A shiver went through her, whether from the thirty-degree weather and wind outside today or from being in a warm car with Micah's low voice washing over her. She could listen to the man forever.

"Wow. Nashville gets hot, but we always know there are cooler days coming. Not sure how I would have handled the constant heat."

"Your body actually adjusts after a while. And when there's so much need around you, it's easier to focus on what's important."

Which made her reasons for not going seem purely selfish.

"I can imagine. How hard was it coming back?"

He gave a half shrug. "I needed to. So I did."

The vehicle was warming up, so Lia allowed herself to relax into the seat. "I hope your father's doctors are able to help him."

"It feels kind of weird to say this, but so do I."

"Weird?"

He frowned. "Weird isn't really the right word. Maybe hypocritical would be better. My mom wrote while I was in Ghana, but…well, there are still some problems between us. So I don't feel I have the right to wish one way or the other."

"What was it you disagreed on?"

"Disagreed?"

Maybe that wasn't the right word. "You said you didn't see eye to eye with them, so I just thought…"

"Ah, I see. It wasn't anything specific. We were just never close."

"Maybe now's the time to change some of that?" Lia had felt awful about not being honest with Micah back then. But she'd honestly believed it was the right thing to do at the time. And she couldn't go back and undo anything that had happened. She couldn't undo the hurt. For either of them.

Maybe that's how Micah felt. Like it wasn't possible to undo anything that had happened with his parents. So why bother trying?

Except Lia did want to make things right with him. Not to have a relationship again—she had killed her chances of that. But maybe she could at least let him know that she was sorry. Sorry for hurting him. Sorry for letting things between them go as far as they had before breaking it off.

She took a deep breath. "Hey. I really am sorry for the way things ended between us. I should have stuck around and talked things through a little more instead of taking off like I did. I just realized at that moment that I couldn't be in a relationship. Not with you. Not with anyone else. It had nothing to do with you personally. I really did care about you."

"Really?" His eyes hardened. "It was kind of hard to tell that day."

"I know. I thought it was better to make the break quickly, that it would hurt less. And I knew how much you wanted to work with Doctors Without Borders."

"It didn't. Hurt less." A muscle worked in his jaw, and there was no sign of that sexy crease he sported. "I went out and got drunk that night."

A swift pain went through her heart. She'd known she'd hurt him, but to picture him alone in a bar hunched over drink after drink... She reached for his arm, her fingers curling around it, willing him to feel how sincere her apology was. "I didn't know, Micah. I'm so, so sorry."

He gave a rough laugh. "The funniest thing was to get back here and find out that I'd somehow landed in the same hospital as my ex. Now that was kind of a kick in the teeth from the universe."

"Maybe this is *our* chance to make things right."

"Make things right?"

"Yes. To start off fresh. Not as a couple. But maybe as friends."

He stared at her. "You think it's possible for you and me to ever be friends?"

His words struck a nerve in her. She'd been trying to reach out to him, and to have him bat her words away like they meant nothing... A spike of anger went through her, and she found her fingers tightening on his arm in response. "Are you saying it's not possible?"

His palm cupped her nape, the heat from his skin going through her like an inferno. "Are you saying it is?"

She swallowed, her teeth grabbing at her bottom lip to stop it from trembling. "I—I want to try."

His fingers tunneled into her hair, and a shiver went through her. Maybe he was right. Maybe it wasn't possible, because what she felt right now wasn't remotely close to anything she would define as friendship.

"Yeah?" The gray of his eyes was flecked with much darker

colors that shifted with his every mood. How could she ever have not recognized this man when he reappeared in her life? He was like no one else she'd ever met. He wasn't defined by the size of his nose or the conformation of his cheeks, the slope of his forehead or anything that supposedly distinguished one face from another. The difference was there, in his very being.

Suddenly, friendship or no, she wanted him to kiss her. Wanted to feel again the press of his mouth to hers. Maybe that's what all this talk about making things right was really about. Maybe it had nothing to do with righting past wrongs and was solely about what Micah made her feel. Made her want.

So she tipped her chin up with an air of defiance. "Yeah. I do."

One corner of his mouth tilted, and there went that glorious crease. She realized she'd been waiting to see it aimed at her for the last couple of hours. And here it was.

"Well, in that case." He slowly reeled her in, his gaze fastened on her lips.

Dio nei cieli. It was going to happen.

Her body flared to life as that first touch came. And come it did. This was no hesitant, questioning press. No waiting to see how she was going to react. This was war—a mind-blowing battle of one mouth against another. And she was up to the challenge, turning her head so that she could kiss him back, her hands going to his shoulders and dragging herself against him. If she could have climbed in his lap in that moment, she would have, but there was the gearshift and the whole two-separate-seats thing going on.

She opened her mouth as if anticipating exactly what he wanted and wasn't disappointed when his tongue swept in and took her by storm. A shivery need began thrumming through her, her nipples coming to hard peaks that cried out for his touch.

Her palms slid up and curled around his nape, the strands

of his hair tickling across the backs of her hands as his head moved in time with what was happening inside her mouth.

A whimper erupted from her throat. She needed more. So much more.

Somehow she dragged her mouth from his and whispered his name.

"Yeah. I know."

She toyed with his hair, fingertips dragging across his skin, and he drew in several deep breaths. "If we don't stop now…"

This was the moment of truth. Did she venture down this path? Or did she retreat and head back to her own corner?

But, *Dio*, she wanted him. So, so badly. And suddenly she knew what she was going to say.

"Come back to my place."

He didn't pull away from her, but he did lean back a little to look into her face. "Are you sure?"

"No. But I know it's what I want right now."

"Hell, Lia." His eyes closed as if thinking it through. And when they opened again, there was a dark intensity in them that gave her her answer. Without a word, he untangled her arms from his neck, put the car in Reverse and pulled out of the parking spot.

He sent her a hard grin that said he was feeling the same thing she was. "In that case, you need to tell me where you live."

CHAPTER NINE

MICAH MADE THE trip to her apartment by darting through the streets and finding the paths with the fewest traffic lights. He hadn't forgotten how to navigate through this city.

Would he remember how to navigate her body with just as much ease?

Somehow she knew he would. Her hands wound together in her lap, gripping each other for support as she waited for him to make his way to the other side of town.

Why hadn't she suggested his hotel? It was closer.

Maybe because she needed to be on her own turf. To be able to keep herself rooted to reality and not go flitting off into some kind of fantasyland.

Wasn't that where she was already? A fantasyland that she'd never dreamed she could visit again.

His hand came off the gearshift and covered hers. "You okay?"

No, she wasn't, but there was no way he could know it was because she was frantic to arrive at their destination. So she wove her fingers of her left hand through his. "Yes. I just never realized how long this drive was before."

His teeth flashed. "I agree."

Then they were less than a mile away. "Turn left at this corner. The complex is about three blocks down on the right. You can park in my space. Three oh one."

Micah swung into the apartment building and followed her directions to the parking garage. It took her eyes a moment to adjust from the sun outside to the lights inside the structure, but her space was just around the corner. He carried her hand to the gear lever and sat it there for a minute, making her shiver as together they shifted the car into first. His thumb trailed across the side of her hand as he looked at her again. "Are you sure, Lia? Very, very sure?"

"Yes." She hoped he was asking about the sex and not just about parking in her space before realizing what a ridiculous thought that was. Of course it was about the sex.

He leaned over and kissed her again, and this time his mouth was softer, exploring her on a level that made her insides knot and her heart pound. She didn't want to leave this car, but she was pretty sure her building had cameras inside the parking area, so she reached over and clicked the door release, the sound cracking through the intimate space.

When he looked at her, she attempted a smile. "Cameras."

"Ah. I thought for a second you might be running away."

Was that a reference to the way she'd left at graduation? But when she glanced at his face, she found it relaxed and sexy. There were no lines of tension that she could see.

"No. I just don't want the security people to get an eyeful." She gave a nervous laugh.

He got out of his door and made it to her side before she'd had a chance to swing her legs out. He reached for her hand and tugged her up and out of the car, one side of her jacket sliding down her arm. He reached for it, pulling it back into place. "Still cold?"

"No, not anymore."

She realized it was true. And although the parking garage was protected, she was pretty sure the warmth was left over from their earlier kisses more than from her coat.

He kept her hand, using his fob to lock the doors of his car. "There's an elevator?"

The way he said it made her swallow. "Cameras," she murmured.

That made him laugh, a sound that rumbled through her belly and drew a smile to her own lips.

"Oh, sorry! You weren't thinking in those terms."

He leaned down close to her ear. "You know I was. Remind me to get a place with no cameras. I'll take my chances."

He didn't elaborate, but she could pretty well imagine what he was willing to take his chances with. And right now, she agreed with him. Sex in an elevator with him would be better than any mile-high club ever invented.

They made it up the elevator without any incidents other than one very hot kiss, his body crowding hers against the wall and leaving her breathless. Then they were on her floor. She led him around the corner of the octagonal building and found her door. She unlocked both the locks and pushed it open. Then she heard a sound. *Oh, no.*

She put her hand against Micah's hip and attempted to push at him. "Wait behind me for a second."

He didn't budge. "Excuse me?"

"I don't want you getting hurt."

She thought she spied a blur of movement out of the corner of her eye. She quickly stepped in front of Micah, reaching for the hallway light.

"What the hell…?" His voice didn't sound any too pleased. But, dammit, she wasn't about to let anything spoil his mood. Or hers.

The light came on, and Lia spied her cat standing just to the side of them. Her tail was fluffed up in alarm. She took a step forward. "It's just me, girl."

"A cat? You're saving me from a cat?"

Samantha spotted him just about the time he asked his question. She stalked toward him, legs stiff, head pushed forward in a way that said she was nervous. It wasn't that Sam was mean. But she was scared of men and had been known to scratch first and ask questions later. The story from the shelter was that she'd been abused by some teenaged boys when she was a kitten. It had made her wary and untrusting.

Lia hadn't been abused, but her prosopagnosia had made her wary as well, so when she'd met the cat—soon after her breakup with Micah—they'd hit it off. Anytime she tried to leave the shelter's cat enclosure, Sam had clung to her leg, looking up at her with huge green eyes, her mouth opening and closing in a silent meow that was more like a plea. She hadn't been able to leave the young feline behind.

"She's not too sure about men."

He laughed, his warm breath washing over Lia's neck and sending Sam scurrying back a couple of paces. "And you suggested we come back to your place? Were we supposed to wind up in your bedroom or were you more interested in sending me to my doom?"

Rather than changing his mind or suggesting they go elsewhere, though, he stepped out from behind Lia and squatted down on his haunches. He held his hand out and murmured to the cat.

"No, don't—"

"Shh." He kept his arm where it was, and Sam inched forward, her long white fur standing up. "Come here, girl. I promise I'm good."

Yes, he was. And right now, all she wanted to do was grab him, sneak past her temperamental cat and close themselves in a bedroom to remind herself of just how good the man was. Although she remembered just about every minute of the time they'd spent together in the past.

Sam came forward another step as Micah continued to croon to her. His voice was as sweet as any country tune.

The cat came within clawing distance, and Lia tensed. But she didn't scratch. Instead, her neck stretched as far as nature would allow, and she sniffed Micah's fingers, then took another step forward. And another. And then the most remarkable thing happened. Samantha—man hater that she was—put her cheek against Micah's palm and purred.

"*Dio mio*, she never does this. Not with men."

He glanced up. "Had lots of men over here?"

"No, no of course not. That's not what I meant. It's more that the shelter told me she was hurt by guys in the past."

Micah slid his palm over Sam's head and stroked along her back. "Maybe she's checking out her competition."

"Competition?"

"For your affections." He turned to look at the cat. "Looks like she doesn't feel too threatened in that regard."

And she shouldn't be. Micah wasn't here to win back her affections. He was here because things had gotten hot and steamy in his car. And she'd gotten enough of her senses back to be able to back out of anything happening. But she found she didn't want to. She wanted this night with Micah. She wasn't sure why. Maybe for the closure they hadn't gotten or maybe just to spend the night with someone who knew how to please her physically. She wasn't sure. But in the end, it didn't matter. She wasn't changing her mind.

"Micah…"

He glanced up, hand stopping midstroke. "Hmm?"

She licked her lips, ending it with her teeth pushing down on the corner of the lower one. "I'd like a little of what she's getting."

"Would you now?" He climbed to his feet, now ignoring the cat, who was winding herself around his legs and asking for more. "And is that all you want? A little petting?"

She wrapped her arms around his waist and pressed up against him. "No. And she might not be jealous, but maybe I am."

His hands pressed against her upper back, flattening her breasts against his chest before sliding down to just below her hips. His legs were slightly splayed, and when he applied just a bit of pressure, she felt everything. A hardness against her belly. A heat that couldn't be hidden even through layers of clothing.

He leaned down. "I kind of like you being jealous. Even if the other female involved is a cat." The words were said against her cheek, the syllables warming her skin and causing all kinds of yummy sensations to begin flashing in the lower part of her abdomen.

If her being jealous caused that kind of reaction from him, then she kind of liked it, too. "I'm just glad Sam didn't leave you with a present of another kind."

"Me, too. But sometimes old hurts fade and leave you able to trust again."

Something about the way he said that made a little niggle of worry appear in her stomach. Nothing major, just the flutter of butterfly wings. But then again, maybe those butterflies were signaling something entirely different. Maybe it was due to how he was making her feel with his nose sliding along the line of her jaw, the nibble of his teeth as he came up and touched those pearly whites to her lower lip. It was heavenly and soon pushed everything else to the side as she kissed him.

"Let's not talk about Sam anymore."

His hands slid into the hair on either side of her face, thumbs brushing the bones of her cheeks. "Kind of hard when she's down there reminding me of her presence."

His hips nudged her again, sending her thoughts somewhere else entirely.

"I'd like to be down there reminding you of my presence."

His thumbs stopped all movement. Then in a rush, he swept her up in his arms, managing to somehow maneuver past Sam, who thankfully hadn't taken issue with his sudden movement. "Bedroom?"

"There's only one. Straight ahead."

He strode past her living room and into the tiny hallway,

moving into the bedroom and using his foot to close the door and exclude Samantha.

"She's not going to like that," Lia said with a laugh.

"Maybe not, but I kind of want you all to myself." He grinned. "And believe me, I need no reminders of your presence."

She reached up to touch that crease in his cheek as he moved over toward the bed.

His brows were up. "Should I play nice? Or naughty?"

"I think I'll need more information." Although she didn't, really. Naughty had always involved some kind of sexy play. And nice...well, that had been all about touch. And caring. And showing her exactly how much he loved her.

Loved her...

No. She didn't want that. Wasn't sure she could bear the way they'd made love during those times. So before he could answer, she blurted out, "I'll choose naughty."

Naughty she could handle. Naughty involved catching her up in a web of sensuality that was normally fast and hot and flamed her until she was sure she'd turn to a pile of ash.

He leaned down and caught her mouth in a hard kiss. "You may be sorry you asked for that."

"Never." She'd never been sorry for anything that they'd done together. She just wasn't sure she could rewind the clock to some of those days.

He kept kissing her until suddenly the bottom fell out. Or rather, she fell, hitting the bed with a soft *oomph* that left her dazed for a second or two before she gathered her senses and scrambled to her knees. "Hey!"

"Change your mind on naughty?"

"No." She could take whatever he dished out.

He leaned down and planted his hands on either side of her hips, his lips within inches of her own. "Good. I need a scarf. Where do you keep them now?"

She swallowed, memories coming back in a flood that almost overwhelmed her. *Dio*, they'd had so much fun back then.

This is not the past, Lia. Just enjoy the present for what it is.

She swung her feet over the edge of the bed and scooted forward, forcing him to stand up straight. "No scarves. Not just yet." With that she hooked her legs around the backs of his knees and crossed her ankles to keep him from moving away. "I think you need a little reminder of my presence."

"Lia…" His voice held an edge of warning that made her laugh.

Her bed was a four-poster monstrosity that she'd regretted getting because of how high the mattresses sat on it. Until right at this moment.

"If it's okay for you to restrain me, then I think turnabout should be fair play, don't you agree?"

She reached for his belt and unbuckled it, sliding it out of the loops with a hiss. "Should your hands be behind your back for this?" She murmured the words aloud, as if talking to herself, while coiling the belt and laying it beside her on the bed. She tightened her legs as if getting his attention. "What do you think, Micah. How still can you be?"

His Adam's apple dipped as he swallowed. "Pretty damned still."

"Good to know." She plucked at the button of his trousers, sliding her hand along the front of his closed zipper. The air hissed between his teeth as she found the bulge hidden behind it. "Just trying to see if you can keep your word."

Her fingers trailed back up the way she'd come, and his eyes closed, his jaw tight. His hands fisted at his sides as if trying to hold himself together.

This time she didn't pluck. She undid the button and slid the zipper down in a smooth motion that made something at her center clench. She wasn't so sure about the sex play all of a sudden. Wasn't sure she didn't just want him to lay her down and take her.

But, *Dio*, she didn't want this to end. If he could stand the snail's pace, then so could she.

Hooking her fingers into his waistband, she slowly slid it down his hips until his slacks were perched on the muscles of his thighs. He had on black briefs, the hard ridge noticeable against the front of them. And there was a convenient opening right here. She slid her hand into the space and found warm, silky-smooth skin that was so welcome, so familiar that it made her teeth clench for a second. How many times had he used this to bring them both pleasure? How many times had she brought pleasure to him by what she was about to do?

No thinking about the past.

She freed him, glancing up to find his face was a hard, tight mask that made her frown, until she realized he really was trying to not come apart.

Same here, Micah. She wouldn't make him suffer too long, but she just couldn't resist.

"No hands, okay?"

He didn't answer but gave her a quick nod of assent, arms held rigidly at his sides.

They'd done this so many times before, but right now, everything was new with the wonder of rediscovery.

She blew warm air over him, watching as a shudder rolled through his body. Yes. She remembered this.

Giving him little warning, she engulfed him in a smooth motion, the groan coming from above her fueling her need to drive him crazy. He wasn't supposed to use his hands, but she was allowed to use hers, so she slid them around his hips until she reached his ass and hauled him closer.

"Hell, Lia…"

He pulled free, watching her as she sat up. Then before she could do or say anything else, he'd flipped her onto her back, her head on the pillows. Then he stripped the rest of his clothes and donned a condom before climbing onto the bed with her.

He undressed her, pressing his lips to her skin as he revealed each part of her. Suddenly "naughty" was forgotten as his mouth found hers and his kisses grew urgent with need. He parted her legs and held himself at her entrance for several breathtaking seconds, ignoring the squirming of her body.

"Oh, Micah…"

He drove inside her with an intensity that pushed the air from her lungs. He paused, eyes closed, before cupping her head, his lids parting as he stared into her eyes. And what she saw there…

Need. Want. And some sort of longing that made her want to weep. Because she felt all those things, too. But she couldn't. Not now. Not when it was too late to go back.

So before she could get trapped in all those feelings and emotions, she reversed their positions until she was straddling his hips, engulfing him with her body the same way she'd done with her mouth. She moved, letting herself relish how it felt to be stretched and filled again. To take from him and to give back again and again. This time it was Lia who shut her eyes, focusing on the physical joining and praying she could evade anything that involved her heart or her head.

Hands gripped her waist, supporting her rise and fall and guiding the speed to match his need and hers. Leaning forward, she kissed his shoulder, dragging her teeth along his warm skin as if she couldn't get enough of him, and in reality she couldn't. She'd never been able to get her fill of this man.

Her movements grew quicker as she reached a set of rapids that carried her along, trying to remember to breathe as the ride grew wilder.

Micah's eyes were no longer on hers; instead it was as if he was focused on moving toward a goal that he didn't quite want to reach.

His name echoed in her head as she stared at his features, trying to distinguish what it was in his face that made him Micah. But all she could see was the blond hair that fell across his forehead, the hands with those long, talented fingers. His body with its strong arms and shoulders and taut, muscular abdomen. His scent. His voice. The unique gray of his eyes.

Those were the things that made him who he was in her eyes. And she wouldn't trade that for whatever it was that people saw in someone's face that made up good looks. Because what Micah had went far beyond any of that surface adornment of a straight nose or high cheekbones.

She sat up, still moving, and linked her hands with his, carrying them to the bed beside his head as she continued to move. A wave of sensuality swept over her as she looked at their joined fingers.

Micah chose that moment to open his eyes and look at her. And that was all it took. Her hips bucked wildly as a wave of need rushed through her, propelling her to a point beyond what she could see.

"Lia…oh, hell…yes!" He tugged his hands from hers and gripped her hips, holding her hard against him as he strained up into her. It was a picture she couldn't get out of her mind, of Micah pouring himself into her. Because he had, in a way that went far beyond sex and flowed into the very parts she'd tried so hard not to involve.

Her head.

And, *Dio*, her heart.

CHAPTER TEN

MICAH CAME TO with a sense of disorientation. It was dark, and he wasn't sure where he was.

The hotel? No, this bed was different. Softer. And...

Okay, his body definitely felt spent and heavy, as if he couldn't move. Or maybe it was that he didn't want to move.

Something tickled his face, like someone drawing a feather duster over his cheek.

And then he heard it. A low rumble that immediately identified itself.

A cat.

Then everything came rushing back to him. This was Lia's house. And what they'd done last night...

Was beyond anything he'd ever experienced.

A cold nose pushed against his chin, and he smiled. Hated men, did she?

Not so much. He reached his hand up to pet her, his hand skimming along her back and curling around her tail. He sensed more than saw a dark figure curled up at the head of the bed.

He sat up. "Lia?" A moment of panic came over him. Had he hurt her somehow? They'd made love several times last night.

Moving over to where she sat, he tipped her chin up. "Are you okay?"

She nodded. "Just surprised it happened, is all."

Just surprised it happened. Well, hell, that pretty much mirrored his own thoughts, since he hadn't even known where he was when he sat up. "Me, too. And I'm sorry, but I can't quite bring myself to regret it, though."

"Me, either." She smiled. "And I can't get over the change in Samantha. It's amazing."

"Would you rather she woke me up in a different way?"

"No."

His smile was slow when it came, a sense of lethargic well-being that washed over him in a warm stream. "Would you rather I woke *you* up in a different way?" He glanced at the clock and saw that it was just after five. The sun hadn't come up yet, but it soon would, and it would more than likely chase away the magic of last night.

"I don't think Sam is going to let us go back to sleep. Sorry, but I had to let her in. She was meowing and sticking her feet under the door, and I was afraid she was going to wake you up. So I let her in. And she woke you up anyway."

"It's okay. And who said anything about sleep?" If he pushed in this direction, maybe his mind would stay away from some dangerous thoughts that were rolling around in it like boulders.

"But Sam…"

He climbed out of bed. "I bet we could sneak away and have a nice hot shower. And some alone time. Until one of us has to get dressed and be somewhere."

"Well, I don't have to be anywhere until eight."

"Same here. So that leaves us plenty of time."

"I can't promise Sam won't cause a ruckus outside the door."

He laughed. "I can't promise that you won't cause a ruckus *inside* the door."

"Me?" She punched his arm. "I seem to remember you making a whole lot more noise than I did."

"Did I? I don't remember it that way." He got out of bed and swung her up in his arms like he had at the beginning of the night. It seemed fitting they should end it the same way they'd started it. "So let's see who causes more commotion this time."

With that, he carried her into the bathroom and shut them inside.

Hell, he was exhausted. This was the second night after leaving Lia's apartment that he'd been kept awake by memories of what they'd done. He'd tossed and turned, trying to turn off his damned brain.

It hadn't worked. And Lia hadn't gone out of her way to bump into him at the hospital. Then again, he'd pretty much stuck to his own wing, too, which was one floor above hers. Glancing at the numbers he'd gotten from neighboring hospitals of suspected pertussis cases, he was not pleased. A fourth hospital had reported a case just this morning. A one-year-old girl was in critical condition with the illness.

He couldn't put it off any longer. He needed to call Lia and see when she could hang flyers with him. He picked up the phone. But first he'd call the print shop and see where they were on the flyers.

What was the guy's name who'd waited on them? Curtis, right?

A voice answered, but it was a woman. "Hi. This is Dr. Corday from Saint Dolores. We ordered some posters and flyers two days ago. Do you know if they're in? We ordered them from someone named Curtis, if he's there."

"Your order is in, but Curtis isn't. There was actually a family emergency with his wife, and he's just left to take her to the hospital."

Hadn't he said his wife was pregnant?

"Do you know which hospital?"

The woman's voice came back through. "Why, I think it was yours. It's the closest one to where he lives. And he had a card that one of your doctors had given to him. He called the number on it just as he was going out the door, so I don't know if he ever reached her."

"I'll check. And I'll be by to pick up that order a little later today."

"Okay. Please tell Curtis to call us if he needs anything."

"I will." When he hung up, he called Lia's number, only to have it go straight to voice mail. Damn. Had Curtis even been able to reach her?

Getting up, he headed out of his office. He would head downstairs and see if she was there. He knew he'd have to talk to her sooner or later, so maybe it would be easier if it was when other people were around. Just as he reached the door to the stairwell, his phone buzzed. Looking down at it, he saw that it was Lia. "Hey, I just tried to call you."

"I saw. I'm actually down here with Curtis Matthews from the print shop."

"Good. He did reach you, then."

There was a pause. "You knew he was trying to get a hold of me?"

"I called the shop to see if the order was ready, and the woman there said he was on the way to the hospital with his wife. I also called Douglas Memorial on the other side of town, and they've had a case of pertussis."

"Oh, God."

"What?"

"Curtis's wife. She's here, and she has a bad cough. I was hoping the illness wasn't spreading."

He rattled off a few curse words in his head. "It seems to be the case. She's not vaccinated."

"No. She's not. She and Curtis thought it was no longer a threat, remember? I was just going to ask you to come and look at her."

"I was already on my way down. I'll be there in a minute."

He hung up and took the stairs two at a time before bursting through the door at the bottom.

* * *

Lia had recognized Curtis by the ankh ring he wore and by his black nail polish, although she'd already known he was coming by his frantic phone call. For all of Curtis's gothness, his wife was the opposite. She had soft, curly blond hair and had paired white skinny jeans with a loose white top that skimmed her pregnant belly. Her nail polish, unlike her husband's, was pink. They said opposites attracted, and this was one couple that she could definitely see that in. Except they were both really nice and obviously crazy about each other. Curtis sat next to the exam table and was constantly in contact with his wife via touch. Lia remembered a time when she and Micah were the same way when they were outside their med school classes.

Two nights ago, they'd been the same. She'd woken up in a dark room and realized that Micah's arm was around her. She'd flat-out panicked, then realized she could hear Sam meowing outside the bedroom door. It was the perfect excuse to let her in and then crawl back in bed and watch him sleep.

The softness she saw as he lay there—one hand draped over his belly, his muscles loose and relaxed—was a sharp contrast to the commanding man she knew at the hospital and from med school.

She headed back into the exam room when she heard some hard coughing. Curtis looked worried. "Can she bring on contractions? She's feeling something going on in her stomach."

"It's unlikely, but I've got a call in for the obstetrician. It's just going to be a few minutes because she's in the middle of a delivery. I know you said this is your first baby, correct?"

"It is." Jenny was sitting up, blowing in and out. "I should have gotten the vaccine, but I was going to do everything natural. He wanted to come to Saint Dolly's for the delivery, but I wanted to have a home water birth with just Curtis there. We were still in discussions about it." A smile played on her face as she glanced at her husband.

A little alarm bell went off. "Have you been in touch with a midwife or a doula?"

Curtis spoke up. "We always meant to, but we're both so busy with our jobs and work different schedules, so we just haven't yet. And our families don't approve of home births, which is why I wanted to come to the hospital."

That was hard. Lia's parents had always been so supportive of her, outside of her dad really pressing her to get a system together for recognizing people. But once she hit adulthood, her dad had started wearing a bright green crocheted bracelet, a counterpart for his wife's pink one. A wave of overwhelming emotion had swamped her when he'd showed up at her graduation ceremony with it on. She'd cried. Then her mom had cried with her. Her dad had remained stoic, but she was pretty sure she saw moisture in his eyes as he'd hugged her and whispered, "Congratulations, *figlia*. I'm so proud of you."

A knock at the door sounded, and then Micah came into the room. He donned a mask and gloved up. "Hi, Curtis. It's nice to see you again, although not so much under these circumstances."

"I know. Your order is in, by the way."

His eyes crinkled above the mask. "I know. I called the shop and found that you had come to visit us here at the hospital, rather than the other way around."

"Not by choice."

Micah pulled a chair up. "So tell me what's going on?"

He didn't ask Lia, but she wouldn't have expected him to. It was good for him to hear it from Curtis and Jenny.

They gave him a quick rundown with Jenny ending the story by saying Curtis had come home talking about whooping cough going around. "I've had a bad cough for about a week and started to get worried that I could make the baby sick."

This time Micah did look at her. "Did you do a nasal swab?"

"I did it a few minutes ago and sent it down to the lab."

"Good." He turned back to Jenny. "Do you know if you were exposed to anyone with a cough?"

"I make custom cakes at a bakery for parties. There are always people milling around, so I don't know. I've never thought much of someone coughing."

He nodded. "Could you get a list together of people who came in to order cakes?"

She started to answer then stopped when a set of racking coughs went through her. She held her hand to her belly until she was done. Lia handed her a bottle of water, which the patient drank from. "I can get a list, but we don't really write on the order forms if the person called or came in in person."

"I can understand that. Any kind of list will help, because we can check it against people who have come in complaining of a cough."

"I'll call them right now and ask them to text over a list. From how far back?"

Micah frowned as if thinking. "About three weeks. It's not contagious after that period of time. We won't do anything with it until we know for sure that you have it."

"Okay."

He gave her a smile. "Thanks. It'll take a few hours to get the results back. Are you two okay hanging around at the hospital in one of the isolation rooms until then? We can make sure you get something to eat and drink. If the results come back negative for both of you, then you'll be free to go. But we recommend you both get vaccinated, since we're seeing an increase in cases all over the city. The disease isn't as bad for adults, but for babies...let's just say it's bad news."

"Can I be vaccinated this late in the pregnancy?"

"Yes, although we normally recommend it be done sooner. But you'll pass the antibodies to your baby, and it will help protect him or her for the first two months of their life. At which time they can be vaccinated. We had a close call with a baby here at the hospital. She ended up living, but it was touch and go for a while."

Jenny looked at her husband with brows lifted. "I want to get it. For the baby's sake."

"I will, too. I don't think I've had one since I was a kid."

"Great. If you could help spread the word, it would be much appreciated." Micah's glance included both of them.

Curtis nodded. "After you came in, I told my boss what had happened, and he said we can put a flyer up at the print shop."

"And I'll ask the bakery if it's okay. They're kind of stinky about anything that would make people nervous or anxious, but this is important."

"Yes, it is. Thank you both."

Watching Micah interact with the young couple made a sense of admiration swell up in her. She bet he'd done great work in Ghana with his trachoma campaign.

Lia motioned to the door. "If you'll both come with me, I'll show you to a room that's a little more comfortable with this one. And I'll run to the cafeteria and get you both something to eat while you wait on the ob-gyn to get done with her delivery."

"Thank you."

She led them down the hallway to a small private waiting room that had eight chairs. They normally used the room for family groups that were waiting for news of relatives who were in serious or critical condition. "Don't be alarmed, but I'm going to put a sign on the door stating that this is an isolation room and that it's only to be entered by people who are gowned and masked. Just until we know for sure."

Lia picked up one of the nearby red-framed signs and wrote Curtis and Jenny's names on it along with the date and time. When she was done, she put tape on it and affixed it to the outside of the door. "Now, Micah and I are going to see if we can find something for you to eat. What sounds good?"

Jenny shrugged. "Maybe just some soup and crackers. My stomach is kind of in knots."

"I totally understand. Do you want some juice to go with it?"

"Some apple if they have it."

Micah had grabbed a piece of paper and was scribbling down their order. Or at least that's what she thought he was doing.

"Curtis?"

"I don't know that I can eat."

Lia patted him on the arm. "I know, but it's best to keep your strength up for your wife and baby's sakes."

"Okay, just a sandwich and chips, then. Maybe chicken of some kind. And a cola."

"Great. We won't be long."

She and Micah went out of the room, making sure the door was all the way shut. "Thanks for coming down," she said. "What do you recommend we do?"

"Exactly what you're already doing. Did they come in a side door like Sassy and her family?"

"Yes. Thank goodness Curtis thought to call and didn't just walk into the ER with her. I'm hoping it's not pertussis."

"So am I."

Although whooping cough didn't normally cause complications during pregnancy, there was always the danger of giving birth with an active infection. And the cough could strain abdominal muscles, which were already stretched by late pregnancy, making for a very uncomfortable situation.

They went down to the first floor, where the hospital cafeteria was located, and got some chicken noodle soup and juice for Jenny and a turkey and cheese sandwich for her husband.

"I'm done for the day, so I'm going to sit up there with them and wait on their results. I can only imagine how scary this is for both of them."

"I'll run over and grab the print order and get the posters at least up in the hospital. Then I'll be back to see if we can run down that list of customers from the bakery. Since Curtis isn't coughing, I'm not as worried about the print shop."

Lia took hold of the bags with the food in it. "Sounds good."

Before she could walk away, Micah stopped her with a hand to the arm. "I haven't seen you the last couple of days. I wanted to make sure Samantha wasn't traumatized by her unexpected run-in with a man."

The question made her laugh.

For some reason, she'd expected him to ask her how she was doing, or worse, apologize for what they'd done at her apartment. It was part of the reason why she'd been avoiding him for the last two days. But only part of it. In reality, she'd had no idea what she was going to say if he did either of those things.

"Sam is just fine. No worse for wear."

"And you? No worse for wear?"

Ah, and there was the question du jour. Asking how she was.

"No worse for wear." She forced a smile. "I'm a pretty resilient girl."

"I'm glad. I just wanted to make sure we knew where the other stood."

She blinked. Did he? That wasn't exactly the question he'd asked her. And thank God he hadn't. Because right now she had no idea what her response would have been. Right now, she didn't want to examine where they stood. On a professional level or a personal one. Because if her suspicions were right, she was having an awful time keeping the past and present in their respective corners.

She'd missed him. The last several weeks had proven that beyond a shadow of a doubt. Watching him interact with patients and hold baby Sassy, watching him interact with her cat...and experiencing his touch all over again...well, it made her want to go back and change the way things had ended between them.

But she couldn't. And right now, she wasn't sure if she was going to be able to keep him from realizing that. Or what she would do if Micah somehow guessed the truth.

CHAPTER ELEVEN

JENNY'S TEST TWO days ago had come back negative, and they'd sent the relieved couple home after vaccinating both of them. The hospital had had some names of midwives that worked with the medical center, and they had promised to contact someone on the list.

That was the good news. The bad was that two more area hospitals had called in cases of whooping cough. Nashville was now up to twenty, with most of the cases congregated around Saint Dolly's hospital. Micah and Lia were scheduled to go out once she finished her last procedure of the day and hang flyers in local businesses and in areas where the public gathered. The CDC had also mounted a television campaign aimed at public awareness, and Micah was helping track cases of exposure.

Lia's artwork was also getting some media exposure, after a reporter had spied one of the framed prints hanging on the wall at the hospital. And of course Arnie hadn't been able to resist saying that a member of the hospital staff had done the design on it. Lia had been mortified. But at least they hadn't given the media her full name. But since Curtis had talked her into signing the original, it was probably only a matter of time until someone realized who the artist was.

His phone buzzed, and he glanced down to see a text from her.

I'm done. Ready whenever you are.

He smiled. She always had been short and to the point. Most of the time he'd found it amusing. Except when she'd broken things off with him. That had been a killer. It had taken going to Ghana to get over her. He knew for a fact he couldn't have done it here in Nashville. Seeing her day after day would have been impossible. Running into her after that long of an absence had been enough of a shock.

And sleeping with her?

Well, that had been a much nicer shock than the original. It seemed like they'd kind of gotten their footing again around each other. Maybe sleeping together hadn't been the huge mistake he'd originally thought it was. Maybe it really had given him some closure after all these years and would allow them to do what she'd suggested when she said they could start off fresh...as friends. At the time he'd been incredulous that she could even suggest that. Then of course that had led to them spending the night together, and definitively *not* as friends.

He wasn't yet sure what it all meant. Or how he felt about it. Or her. But maybe they could walk it back and actually become congenial. It seemed like they were on their way to doing just that. And he was looking forward to going out with her this afternoon to hang the flyers, which was worlds away from how he'd felt when he'd seen her at that Valentine's Day benefit.

He typed on his keypad to respond to her text.

I'll meet you in the lobby with the goods.

He followed the words with a laughing emoji, smiling when she responded in kind.

See? Friends.

While most of his brain accepted that as a very real possibility, there was a small portion that was standing back with its arms folded waiting for everything to implode in his face like it had three years ago. Except they weren't a couple now. She couldn't break up with him again. Actually, there wasn't much she could do other than avoid him. Or quit.

That made him frown. Surely it would never get to that point? So far they'd been able to remain on decent terms. So he'd just have to make sure he kept it that way.

He got down to the lobby with an attaché filled with weatherproof flyers. Hopefully between this and what the CDC and other hospitals were doing, they'd be able to prevent the outbreak from spreading even further. Fortunately, there were still no deaths attributed to the illness.

She grinned as she walked up to him. "Is this where I say, 'Hi, honey, I'm home'?"

Honey.

He couldn't stop himself from recoiling at the word—the empty endearment his mother had used on him from time to time. Empty because there was no true affection behind it. She used it on everyone who came across her path. And to hear Lia use it in the same flippant, meaningless way…

It's just a word. It means nothing.

He gritted his teeth and worked past the raw emotions that were swirling through him.

"Micah? What's wrong?"

He needed to just shut up and not say anything. But to do that seemed wrong. Especially since she was apt to use that word again. She used to when they were together, and he'd never complained. But maybe he should have. Should have been more open about how life with his parents had been. Instead, he'd hidden it, thinking that Lia could help him get through it. Looking back, it hadn't been fair to pile that kind of expectation onto her shoulders. Especially since she hadn't even known she was carrying that particular load. The truth was, he'd hidden the truth because he'd been embarrassed, especially after seeing how loving Lia and her parents were with each other. It made his own household seem like a farce. Like some sitcom of dysfunction that never really resolved.

And since his and Lia's connection had weighed so heavily toward the physical, he never bothered to ask himself if he could even have a healthy emotional relationship with her—or anyone. But after that breakup? Hell, he'd asked himself that question repeatedly. Because apparently something had been off that he hadn't been able to see at the time.

And now that they were supposedly "friends"? Maybe it was time to come clean. At least a little bit.

"Nothing. I'm just not overly fond of that word."

"Word? What word?"

Now he was feeling a bit ridiculous for saying anything. "*Honey.* My mom just used it whenever she was trying to talk me into doing something. Or hoping I'd go away."

She blinked. "Oh, Micah. I'm sorry, I didn't know. I'm pretty sure I used to call you that...before. Why didn't you say anything?"

"I don't know. I probably should have."

"All right. I'll try to remember." She paused a few seconds. "She really made you feel like she wanted you to go away?"

He shrugged, stepping closer to her to let someone get past them. "I'm sure all kids feel like that from time to time."

Her brows went up, as if she wasn't sure what to say to that. But she didn't try to pull any more confessions from him, for which he was thankful.

Instead, she finally just said, "I won't use that word again. Thank you for telling me."

There were a few awkward moments while they tried to figure out their footing again. But finally she smiled and pulled her keys out of her purse and held them up. "So...my place or yours?" A little bell tinkled as she shook the keys, making him forget for the moment how his body had jolted to life at her question.

Hadn't he heard that bell at Lia's house the night he'd stayed over?

"I thought you put that back on Samantha's collar."

"I did. But I found it in the bedsheets this morning. I don't know how she keeps getting it off."

Man, the image of Lia sprawled across rumpled sheets was moving through his skull at a snail's pace, refusing to be hurried off his mental screen. The jolt he'd felt a minute ago returned full force. He knew exactly what she looked like when she slept. And so did his body.

To throw his mind off track, he reached over to finger the little bell, forcing himself to look for a spot where there was a fissure or break, but there was nothing. "Has it ever fallen off your key chain the way it does her collar?"

"Nope. I don't know what its deal is."

Avery's earlier words about Samantha's witchy ways came back to him.

"Maybe the problem is with the ring on her collar."

Her teeth worked at her lip for a minute like she did whenever she was thinking. Micah had to glance away when his thoughts veered back to things that had nothing to do with cats or bells.

"I'll have to check it when I get home." She seemed to shake off a thought. "So back to the question. Are we taking my car or yours?"

It was a different question than she'd voiced a moment ago and didn't flood his brain with a rush of endorphins this time. But he'd already known she wasn't talking about homes. Just cars.

"If I remember right, your little blueberry was kind of a tight fit."

Oh, hell. That hadn't come out quite right.

The impish smile she gave him made the sides of her nose crinkle. "Yes. It was kind of a snug ride, wasn't it?"

The words hit their mark, snagging his thoughts and taking them hostage.

She did not mean it that way. But that smile was the same one she'd given him in the past. The exact. Same. Smile.

No matter how many times he tried to banish the memory of just how snug that particular ride had been, a heady, terrifying warmth began to pool in his groin. It had nowhere to go...but up.

Dammit! He needed to pull himself together.

"We'll take my car." He bit the words out with a fierceness that didn't go unnoticed.

Lia's smile faltered. "Are you sure you want me to come with you?"

"Yes, sorry. I didn't mean that to sound the way it did."

"It's okay. My words a few minutes ago didn't come out exactly right, either."

Ah...so had she not realized how her words had come across until now? But she'd had that knowing little grin. When he glanced at her, he could swear he saw a tinge of pink in her cheeks. Maybe she had meant them—as a joke—but his reaction had been so over-the-top that she'd probably had second thoughts about trying to make him laugh.

He sighed. Maybe his hopes of being friends was destined to fail.

Pushing the door, he held it open to let her go ahead of him.

The frigid blast of air hit him in the chest, the cold putting the deep freeze on some very overheated parts. He drew in a deep breath or two, letting the door swing shut behind him.

The weather had taken an unexpected turn, dropping back below freezing, which wasn't too unusual for Nashville, seeing as it was still only the end of February. A severe weather alert had pinged on his phone a while ago, warning folks to look out for slick spots on the roadways due to the rain that had fallen during the morning commute.

Pulling his coat around him as they moved through the parking lot, he unlocked the doors to the car before they got there.

Once they were inside, he realized they should have taken the blueberry. Because they'd had that spectacular kiss in this car. Right before he'd gone up to her apartment.

It was too late now. He was stuck here with her for the next couple of hours. He pulled out onto the road and headed south.

"I spent part of today calling local businesses, and I have the names of some places that are willing to put up our flyers. I mapped them in the order of our route."

"Great. If you want to hand me the map, I can help navigate."

"It's in the front pocket of the attaché."

"Which is where?"

"It's in the back seat. Let me pull over and get it."

Great. Smart work, Micah.

"No problem. I'll just unbuckle for a minute. Try not to send me flying through the windshield with any fast stops, though." She unhooked her belt and then twisted in her seat, hanging over, trying to reach the bag, which was behind his seat. Something soft pressed against his shoulder, and his jaw tightened, trying not to think about what it was. He rounded a curve and sent her bottom swinging into him instead.

"Damn. Sorry."

No choice. He hooked one arm over her derriere to anchor her in place while she reached for the bag.

"Got it."

He lifted his arm to let her slide back into her seat. "Thanks for hanging on to me."

"No problem." But it was. Because his thoughts were right back where they'd started. With her. And him. Doing very naughty things in a very snug place.

She pulled the sheet of paper from the front of the bag and glanced at it. "Oh, wait. The first one is on the next block. Papa's Pizza Parlor."

"Okay. Hold on."

He swung into the correct lane and found the place almost immediately. Parking, they took a flyer in, talking to the owner for a minute before heading back to the vehicle. Maybe they hadn't needed two people to undertake such a simple task, but it was easier and safer to have someone looking for the places he'd called.

They returned to the car, and she glanced at the sheet. "We're headed to the park on Thirty-First next. It's about a mile away."

A drop of sleet hit his windshield. Great. "Hopefully we won't get much of this."

He pulled over to the curb and started to put the vehicle in Park only to have her say, "Let me just jump out and staple it to the information board. You did get permission to hang it, didn't you?"

"I did. But I can do it. I have a staple gun in the main pocket of my bag."

"Just stay here, then you won't have to turn the car off. I'll just be a minute." She hopped out of the car with the flyer and the staple gun and headed to the large plywood structure where people hung notices for different events.

She pushed the stapler, and evidently nothing happened, because she turned it toward her and looked at it before setting the flyer down, stepping on it to keep it from blowing away and giving the gun a shake before opening the cartridge and looking inside. He was just about to get out of his car to help when she picked the flyer back up and tried again. This time she was successful. She'd just turned around to come back to the car when it started sleeting in earnest. Putting her coat over her head, she sprinted toward the car and almost made it when she slipped and went down backward.

"Hell!" In a split second, he was out of the car and jogging toward her. She was already on her feet by the time he reached her. "Are you okay?" He had to shout to be heard as the sleet gave way to torrential rain.

"I'm fine." But when she went to take a step, she grimaced

before shifting her weight back onto her other foot. "I think I just twisted my ankle. I'll be okay."

"Put your arm around my waist." The rain was still coming down, and by the time she hobbled to the car, their clothes were plastered to them.

The gutter between the car and the sidewalk had become a river, and there was no way she was going to be able to step across it with her ankle like it was, so, still holding on to her, he reached over and opened the door, then before she could protest, he lifted her, stepping into the rushing water and setting her on the seat. He closed the door, then slogged his way to the other side of the car and got in, turning the heat on high. Then he looked over at her, and they both burst out laughing.

The rain was pounding the top of the car and sluicing down the windshield. He turned his wipers on high. "Well, that didn't quite go as planned, and I don't think anyone is going to let us in looking like this."

She glanced over at him. "*Dio*, your pants are so... I'm sorry you had to get in that water."

"I'll be fine. But I should probably get you home before you freeze and that ankle swells."

Despite the heat pouring from the vents, Lia's jaw was quivering as her teeth chattered. From the cold? Or had she really done something to her ankle?

"Maybe we should get that foot X-rayed."

"No, it'll be fine. I'm just freezing."

And that settled it. He pulled slowly from his spot, trying to watch the traffic as his tires sprayed water in all directions.

"Aim those vents toward you."

She reached forward and did it before widening her eyes. "Oh, no!"

"What?"

Lia held up his stapler. "It may be ruined after hitting the ground and getting rained on."

His stapler. His *stapler*. She was something else. "That's the last thing I'm worried about. We're about three minutes away from your complex."

"Just park in my spot again."

A feeling of déjà vu settled over him, along with a sense of doom. To be in that apartment again... But what was he going to do? Drop her off at the front door to the building and drive away? The least he could do was make sure she was okay. Get her settled in with a hot cup of coffee and check her ankle.

They made it to the parking garage, which, thank heavens, was covered and led directly into the building through a covered corridor. He parked and came around to her side of the door. As she stepped out, she grimaced as she tried to put weight on her ankle again.

"This is so stupid. I can't believe I was that clumsy."

"You weren't clumsy. I almost slipped, too." He smiled. "So, do you want to be carried in—which is my preferred method— or are we going back to the arm around the waist?"

"Definitely arm around the waist. Cameras, remember?"

"I seem to remember it didn't stop us from putting on quite a preshow as we went up the elevator last time."

"Ugh. Don't remind me. Every time I go by the security guard, I picture him watching that scene. Or worse, taping it and playing it for his friends."

"He's probably seen it all before. Keys?"

She handed him her keys and her purse before hesitating and then finally putting her arm around his waist. Was it that hard to touch him? Or was she really just embarrassed about the cameras?

He supported her with his other arm as they slowly made their way to the elevator. She gasped when they had to step up onto a different level once they got inside. Dammit. It would have been less painful to have let him carry her. Not to mention faster. They must look quite the sight. His shoes were literally squelching with each step, and though he didn't look behind him, he was pretty sure he was leaving wet tracks across the pristine surface of the lobby floor. Lia's long ponytail, which had been neat and tidy when they'd left the hospital, was now canted toward the left, and she had a big patch of mud on her left cheek.

A guard came running from somewhere, his hand on his hip—where he kept what looked like a Taser. "Dr. Costa, are you okay?"

"I'm fine. It's okay." Lia frowned as if realizing what a sight they must be, then shut her eyes for a few seconds. Micah could picture exactly what she was thinking—the preshow was nothing compared to this. "I just sprained my ankle. Dr. Corday was kind enough to help me get home."

"Do you want me to get the wheelchair we keep in the lobby?"

She gave a short laugh. "At this point, I'm afraid of somehow destroying that, too."

"You won't," the guard assured her, his tone worried.

"I'm fine, but thank you for offering."

What had she destroyed? The stapler? That was nothing. Maybe she was worried about his car.

"Hey, my leather seats are pretty tough, if that's what's bothering you. They'll dry as good as new."

"As good as new."

Was she sure she hadn't somehow hit her head? He needed to get her up to her apartment so he could check her over.

They got onto the elevator, and the trip to the third floor seemed to take forever, unlike the last trip, when it had sailed up at the speed of light. Finally the door opened, and he splayed out her keys, searching for the right one, the little bell from Samantha's collar jingling. That's right. Hopefully the cat liked him as well today as she had the last time. The last thing he needed was her adding to the confusion.

He inserted the key into the lock, and the mechanism released, allowing the door to swing in. Helping her inside, he toed off his wet shoes and reached over to turn on the light.

He closed the door again, latching it. "Where do you want me to take you?"

"To the bedroom." As if realizing how that sounded, she said, "I want to get out of these clothes. Why don't you go into the bathroom and do the same?"

As if she could feel his grin, she looked up, and for the first time since her sad little comment to the guard, she smiled. "You know what I mean."

He laughed. "Then maybe you should *say* what you mean. But I get it. The only problem is I don't have a change of clothes here, and I doubt you want me parading around wearing..." He purposely allowed the words to trail away.

"There's a terry robe in there that you can use. If it doesn't fit front ways, you could always pretend it's a hospital gown where the opening goes to the back."

Perfect. "Do you need help changing?"

"I think I'm good. If I need help, I'll yell."

She wouldn't. Of that he was sure. He helped her to her room and left her standing in the middle of the bedroom while he went over to her dresser.

"What are you doing?"

"Getting you some clothes."

"You don't have to—"

"I do," he muttered. "Unless you want to stand here while we argue about it."

"Okay. But don't look."

"At...?"

"The stuff in my drawers."

Did she realize how ludicrous that sounded? "Do you want me to promise to go by feel rather than by sight?" He let one side of his mouth quirk, and her face immediately turned colors.

What was that all about?

He opened one drawer and found socks. The next one had what he was looking for. Hmm...what color? The array before him was dazzling; his fingers ventured in to touch and—

"You're looking."

Yes, he was. But what did she expect a man to do? He grabbed the first pair his fingers had trailed across and started to close the drawer when he heard a screech. "No, not that pair!"

Hmm? He looked at what he was holding in his hand. Okay, there was barely anything there, except for...strings. What exactly what this used for?

He tried again, taking another pair out, a bit more gingerly this time. Okay, these looked like normal, albeit frilly underwear. He held them up for her approval.

"Yes, they're fine."

He found her a bra and jeans and a comfy-looking shirt with the words *Nashville Chick* splashed across it.

"Avery bought that for me." Said as if he expected an explanation. He didn't. But it had given him a little too much pleasure to pick out things for her to wear. He remembered doing that on some of their "naughty" nights when the sky had been the limit. Those string-a-ling undies would have been perfect for one of those sessions.

Stop it, Micah.

"Are you sure you can tackle putting them on?"

"I am positive."

Something in her face made him dubious, but she pointed her finger toward the bathroom before letting her arm fall back to her side. He doubted she'd call for help even if she landed in a heap on the floor. Giving her a final glance, he made his way to the bathroom, only to find his way blocked by Samantha, who'd—sans warning bell—sneaked up on him. "Hey, girl. I wondered where you were. Remember me?"

As if answering, she moved in, her purr box starting up immediately as she sniffed the bottom of his sodden trousers and his bare feet. "You don't want me petting you right now. I'm pretty wet."

He tried to go into the bathroom, only to have her follow him inside. Hmm... From what Lia had said, he wasn't sure about reaching down and trying to set her outside, so he let her stay. "Just so you know, scratching at anything you see in here is forbidden, got it?"

As the cat wandered around the small area, he shed his clothes, finding the bathrobe hanging where she said it would be. It was terry cloth all right. But it was pink and had a huge hummingbird on one side of the chest. Well, there was no way he was pulling his soaked clothes back on. So he took the robe from its hook and slid his arms into the sleeves, the shiny ruffled edging coming to the middle of his forearm. Thankfully when he went to wrap it around his waist it was big enough to cover him, although there wasn't much fabric to spare, and the bottom edge hung above his knees.

Hell. This would have been a winner for comedy night if they'd had one when they'd been together.

When he cinched the pink belt and exited the bathroom, Samantha followed him into the bedroom. Except he was shocked to find Lia standing exactly where he'd left her. In her wet things with the dry ones lying across the bed. Her face was paler than he'd ever seen it.

"Lia? What's wrong?"

She heard Micah's voice through a fog and looked at his face. She realized she'd been standing there, lost in thought about him. About their past. About what they'd done in this room not that long ago.

She was so tired. Tired of everything. Of the scramble for recognition that seemed to go on every time she turned around. Of how other people seemed to sail effortlessly through life, recognizing their friends and family immediately. Not having to pretend until you could finally work out who the person was.

She'd only known who Curtis was because of his ankh ring... the security guard because of his uniform.

Even Micah, who was someone she'd once loved.

Samantha rubbed against his legs as she stared at him. At

the hair plastered against his head. At the strong shoulders hidden beneath her robe.

Someone she still loved.

Oh, God. How could she let herself do this all over again? She'd only end up disappointing him when he finally discovered the truth about why she hadn't wanted to go to Ghana, about why she'd really broken things off with him.

"I—I can't. I just can't."

"You can't what? Get dressed?"

She just shook her head, unable to say any of the things that were spinning out of control in her head.

He took hold of her shoulders and studied her face.

Her damned face! The face that she didn't even recognize when she looked in the mirror. She only knew it was her in the reflection because she was standing there in front of it. She could see the features. Knew what a nose, eyes and mouth were, but put them all together on a person, and they all looked the same, with no identifiable differences.

As if he'd seen something that she couldn't begin to vocalize, he folded her in his arms and held her close. Rubbed her back, skimmed a lock of hair off her face.

"I'm going to undress you, okay?"

She forced herself to nod, even though he probably had no idea what was really going through her head. Hell, she didn't know, either. Only knew that she still loved Micah.

And that she shouldn't.

Gentle fingers were on her skin as he pulled her blouse up and over her head, undid her bra and slid it off her shoulders. She felt another shirt come down over her, covering her chest. He did the same with her shoes, pants and underwear. The old came off and new things replaced them. Things that weren't embedded with cold. A cold that had moved to envelop her soul.

"Do you want some coffee?"

Her head wagged back and forth as if it had a mind of its own.

"You're shivering. Let me get your hair down and get you

into bed." He gently removed the elastic from her hair and slid his fingers through it to loosen any tangles.

She sighed and closed her eyes. It felt good. So good.

Arms scooped her up as if she were a precious piece of china and walked with her across the room. This time he didn't drop her onto the surface of the bed. He gently pulled down the covers and placed her on it. When he went to let her go, though, she gripped the lapels of the robe. "Don't leave, Micah. Please."

"I won't." He kissed her forehead. "Slide over and I'll get in with you."

She scooted over, and Micah crawled in beside her. Her ankle throbbed in time with the beating of her heart, but having him next to her was better than any pain reliever known to man. He'd always been a balm to whatever hurt. And right now, everything hurt. Everything…except him.

Wrapping her arms around him to keep him close, the shivering gradually faded away, and she allowed herself to relax fully into him. Closed her eyes and trusted he'd still be there when they reopened.

Then she let all her thoughts and fears float toward the ceiling as she focused on the one constant in her life at this moment in time.

Micah.

CHAPTER TWELVE

LIA OPENED HER eyes with a start. It was still dark, and the apartment was silent. Micah hadn't left. He was lying facing her, one leg thrown over hers, his hand clasping her arm as if afraid she was going to disappear into the night.

She loved him. The realization from earlier this evening sweeping back over her.

Dio. How could she let this happen again?

She hadn't *let* it happen again. It was the same love she'd had for him before. It was why she'd never dated after he'd left.

Her hand trailed down his arm. And Micah. Did he still feel something for her? He wasn't married. Had traveled an awful long distance to get away from her.

Had anything really changed, though? She was the same fearful person she'd been the last time they met. Even if he still cared about her—

He stirred in his sleep and pulled her closer.

Maybe she could put those thoughts on hold for a little while.

She leaned forward and kissed his jaw. The stubble tickled her lips in a way that was more delicious than words. But it was a deliciousness she remembered. A hunger that only he'd been able to satisfy. He murmured something, and then his eyes came open with a speed that made her blink. They zeroed in on her, pupils constricting.

"What are you doing?"

"Kissing you."

He leaned back, a frown pulling his brows together. "I can see that. Are you okay? You were kind of a mess last night."

"Yes, and I'm really sorry about that. I think I was cold and then just got overwhelmed. Nothing that day had gone right, and I—I suddenly realized how much my prosopag..." She stopped. *Dio*, she'd almost blurted out the truth. But maybe he should know. He deserved to know. She'd kept it from people all her life, except for a select few who knew her daily battle. Her parents. Her sister. Avery had guessed the truth and made her spill, but no one else ever had. And no one in her professional realm seemed to notice, thanks to the lanyards they all wore at work and the tells she'd worked out on those she saw on a daily basis. She'd become adept at living a lie.

Her dad would be proud of her.

But she wasn't her uncle, and she was no longer sure her father's solution had been the best one for her.

She would tell Micah and see what happened. Just not this moment. If he rejected her, then she would at least be able to look back on this memory and hold it close.

And if he didn't push her away? If he still cared about her once he knew?

She took a deep breath and picked up her sentence again, changing it slightly. "I suddenly realized how very alone I feel."

His hands cupped her face, throat working for a second. "Oh, Lia. I am sorry. God's honest truth, I know what that feeling is like." He leaned down to kiss her. "But you're not alone right now."

"No, you're right. I'm not."

One kiss turned to two, and a shuddery laugh erupted when Samantha decided to insert herself between them, purring and rubbing her head on his shoulder.

"Is it safe for me to pick her up and set her outside? I don't want to leave your place tonight missing an eye. I'm going to need all my senses for what I plan to do next."

Anticipation whispered up her spine, and she smiled. "Somehow I think my cat has fallen in love with you."

"Just your cat?" The lightness of his smile took any heaviness from his words.

But what if she wanted heavy?

Her breath hissed in. *Don't ruin this. Let him tell you first.* So she gave a laugh that she hoped was equally light and said, "That's for me to know."

He leaned down by her ear. "And for me to find out."

Climbing out of bed, he scooped the cat up. She curled next to his chest and just ate it all up.

Lia smiled and whispered, "I can't blame you, Sam."

He set her gently outside the door and shut it.

Then he came back to bed and started to slide back under the covers before thumbing the terry cloth collar of the robe he still wore. "I have to tell you, this is the most uncomfortable contraption I have ever worn to bed."

"You never used to wear anything."

One brow went up. "I still don't. But last night, there were extenuating circumstances."

"Those are all gone. So go ahead."

"Are you sure?"

When she nodded, he undid the bow in front, and as the fabric slithered down his body, she couldn't help but run her gaze over him. He was perfect. Gorgeous. And for right now, he was all hers.

And later?

She could worry about that in the morning.

This time when he slid under the covers, she reached for him, finding his mouth with hers. And unlike the last time, there was nothing playful about his kiss. There was an intensity to it that called to something inside her. She answered the challenge and matched his mood kiss for kiss, stroke for stroke, until he finally rolled her underneath him and entered her with a gentleness that made her want to weep. And when it was over, they lay still, Micah behind her, his palm stroking up and down her arm.

He kissed her neck and nibbled her ear before rolling her over to face him. "Hey, I want to tell you something, okay?"

Her heart seized in her chest. Was he going to say what she thought he was? That he loved her?

"Yes, of course."

"I told you I know how it is to feel truly alone. I want you to know I wasn't just saying that."

"Okay." She blinked. This was not what she'd expected, but she sensed something important was going to follow his words.

"I told you my parents and I had some differences, but there was a lot more to it than that." His hand came out and touched her face, stroked down her nose, his thumb trailing across her lips. "You're so beautiful, did you know that? So perfect."

She stiffened slightly before forcing herself to relax. This wasn't about her. It was about him.

"Tell me about your parents."

His fingers retreated, and he reached down to grip one of her hands. "When I was really little, the woman I thought was my mom left and another woman came and took her place. Only that woman hadn't been my mom. Nor was the next. She was one in a long succession of nannies. Each of them was the first person I saw when I got up and the last person I saw when I went to bed. I knew other people lived in the house, but I rarely saw them."

He gave a rough laugh. "Later on I realized these people who slid in and out of rooms were actually my parents. Parents who seemed to avoid me."

"Oh, Micah, how terrible. Did they never interact with you?"

"They tried periodically, but it always seemed half-hearted. I remember one time I was six or seven, a friend came and knocked on the door. My mom answered and actually thought the kid was me standing there. She asked him why he was knocking at his own house."

Lia's heart turned ice-cold even as she forced herself to continue listening. That could have been her, mistaking his friend for her own child.

"I felt totally invisible, totally alone, like they could look at me and not really *see* me. It was as if I were simply living in their house, eating their food, sleeping in a bed they'd bought for some faceless individual. Now I realize that wasn't true, that of course they knew who I was. But back then?" He sighed and squeezed her hand. "It's really hard to have a relationship with people who I felt saw me as a generic human being. Kind of like a Mr. Potato Head doll with interchangeable parts."

The sick feeling in Lia's stomach grew. So she was going to reveal to this man that to her people really were figures with interchangeable features? If she ever had a child, was this how they'd feel? If a neighbor's kid came to the door, she actually might call him or her by her own child's name. Hadn't that happened with acquaintances who'd she'd called the wrong name and then covered it up with a laugh? Only seeing it through a child's eyes, Micah's eyes, it was a terrible, scarring truth that he would never, ever forget. One that still ate at him even as an adult.

She did not want that for her child. But maybe Micah wouldn't want children. Maybe she could tell him her fears and he would wave them away, saying it wasn't a problem. They would just enjoy Lia's nieces.

And if he wanted kids?

"I can't imagine growing up like that. Why didn't you tell me this?"

"I think I was embarrassed. I eventually realized that my family wasn't like other families. And it most definitely wasn't like yours."

She sighed. "My family wasn't perfect, believe me."

"Maybe not. But at least they knew who you were."

Yes, they did. The problem was that without help, she hadn't always known who they were.

"Did you ever talk to them about how they made you feel?"

"No. But I should have. I should have been honest with them at some point."

Well, he wasn't the only person who hadn't been honest with those around him. Maybe it was time. If he realized she didn't want to be like his parents, but that in some ways she might end up acting like them without meaning to... Then what? He would just be like, *Okay, not a problem?*

Maybe she could tackle this from a different angle. "Well, you certainly know what *not* to do as a parent."

He reached out and gripped her hand. "You know, I didn't want children—had convinced myself I'd be the worst parent imaginable, with the role models I had. But now I'm not so sure."

"You're not?" She swallowed, a chill coming over her. "The subject of kids barely came up when we were together."

"I know. I was afraid my decision not to have them might scare you off. But now... Well, in the hospital that day when Sassy came in, I held her, and as I looked down into her face, something twisted inside me. A kind of emotion that I've only felt once before in my life." He carried her palm up to his mouth and kissed it, his lips warm on her cold skin. "I think with the right partner—one who knows how just how important it is to make people feel special—I might reconsider. *If* that partner is willing to take a chance on me, that is."

He was talking about her? She almost laughed aloud. It should be the other way around. She should be asking him if he was willing to take a chance on her. A sense of panic began to rise up inside her. He had no idea who he was talking to.

Her resolution to tell him the truth shattered into a million pieces as she looked at this man she loved more than life itself. A man she'd loved enough to give up once before. And now?

She didn't know. Maybe she was looking at this scene through eyes that couldn't see the whole picture. But the portion of it that she could see—that of a young child who felt so totally invisible to those who should have loved him—tore at her heart and caused a pain she wasn't sure she could withstand. Wasn't sure she could take the risk of becoming *that* parent: the one who couldn't see what was right in front of her.

Dio ti prego aiutami.

Her silent prayer for help brought no answers. And she couldn't bear to contemplate the subject anymore. So she murmured, "Tell me more about your life as a child."

Maybe Micah would somehow lead her to the answer she so desperately needed.

So as he continued to open up, she let him talk, making sympathetic noises whenever there was a lull in the conversation. But the iciness that had started in her heart slowly encased her in a prison she felt there was no escape from.

Finally Micah was all talked out, and he reached for her again. She held him. Kissed him. Loved him. Hopefully, by morning, she would have her decision and have the strength to carry it out. Once and for all.

Micah woke up in the morning feeling refreshed in a way he hadn't felt in a very long time. He'd poured out his heart to Lia. The very first person he'd ever shared that with. He sucked down a deep breath and smiled.

Hell, he loved the woman. Wanted to be with her. Wanted to have children with her.

When she looked at him, there was no feeling of invisibility.

Speaking of Lia, she wasn't in bed. Maybe she was taking a shower. He rolled out from beneath the covers, finding that ridiculous robe and pulling it on. He ventured out into the hall. The bathroom door was open, and when he went into the kitchen, she was there bent over a basket of laundry, folding it.

Her back was to him, but he recognized his slacks. A feeling of warmth went through him.

"Hi, there. You didn't have to do my laundry."

Lia whirled around, holding the pants in front of her almost as if they were some kind of shield. That was ridiculous. Of course she wasn't. He'd just startled her.

"Sorry. I didn't mean to scare you."

"You didn't." She added his trousers to a small stack of clothing. "I think they should all be dry by now."

Her words and movements were quick and flighty, like a bird peck, peck, pecking at the ground and picking up anything it could find. He went to touch her, but she moved away, making it seem like an accident, as if she didn't know what he'd been trying to do. But that initial flinch said otherwise.

What was going on? Last night she hadn't been able to get enough of him, and this morning... Well, if they'd been at his hotel room he could almost guarantee that she'd already be out of there.

He took a step closer. "Are you okay?"

"Fine. I just need to be at work in about a half hour."

"I'm sorry, you should have woken me."

She smiled, but the curve of lips didn't reach her eyes. "I figured you could let yourself out once you got up."

Ah, so it didn't matter if they were at his place or hers. She was still going to run. Just like she had at graduation, when she said they weren't meant to be together.

Maybe he was reading too much into this. It could be she was telling him the truth. Maybe she really did need to be at work and she was just trying not to be late.

"Okay, how about tonight?"

"Tonight?"

He swallowed. "Do you want to get together?"

Her teeth came down on her lip in that way that drove him crazy, only this time, it didn't. Because something strangely familiar was climbing up his chest and settling there, its spiny surface digging deep.

When she didn't answer him, he nodded, suddenly feeling just as alone as she'd said she felt the previous night. He could stand here and try to get her to open up until he was blue in the face, but something told him she wasn't going to tell him anything. Even after everything he'd told her last night.

"You don't want to, do you? Get together."

A shimmer of moisture appeared in her eyes as she slowly shook her head. "Micah, I am so, so sorry."

He hadn't been overreacting. She was taking the last page from their book and inserting it into their current chapter. And no matter what he might do or say, their story was going to end exactly the same way—with them going their separate ways.

He'd already had this particular dance with this woman, and he was damned if he was going to draw it out any longer than he had to.

"You're right. I would have seen myself out."

He pulled in a deep breath and drummed up the courage to be the one who said the goodbyes this time. "Sorry for unloading on your last night. I think we were both cold and tired and said some things we might not normally have said."

"It's okay."

It wasn't. But maybe someday in the far distant future, it would be. But this time he wasn't going to head to a bar and get flat-faced drunk. He was going to go to the hospital and do his job. He was going to see this pertussis crisis through, and then he was going to sit down and reevaluate his life. He needed to stay here for a while and sort through things with his parents. But after that?

He didn't know. But what he did know was that he wasn't going to let someone make him feel invisible ever again.

And he wasn't going to do this the way she had, simply severing ties. He was going to run this race all the way to the finish line, setting the pace for any future interactions.

His brows went up. "How's your ankle?"

"A little stiff, but it'll be fine."

"Good to hear." He took another step toward goodbye. "I'm planning on going out to hang up the rest of the signs this afternoon, but I can manage that on my own."

This time, she hesitated for a split second before saying, "Okay. Thank you."

And that, it seemed was that. So now he was going to make it very clear. He walked up to her and picked up his pile of clothes. "I know you have to be at work, so I'll make this short. We'll probably run into one another at work, but I won't make things any more uncomfortable than they have to be. I'll be staying in Nashville for a while longer for my parents."

Her teeth dug into her lower lip again, but this time there was no core meltdown inside him. Just a sad tiredness that wanted this over and done.

"I hope things work out for you in life, Lia, I really do."

Her hands gripped the counter as if needing its support to remain upright before she whispered, "Thank you."

"Okay. I'll get dressed and get out of your hair, then."

With that he took his clothes and, without another look back, headed for her bathroom. Unsurprisingly by the time he was came out again, Lia was long gone. All that was left was Sam, her cat, pacing back and forth in front of the door with a pitifully soft meow. When she saw him, she hurried over, rubbing against his legs. He squatted down in front of her. "I know, girl. But there's nothing more I can do. So it seems this is goodbye."

The last thing he wondered as he locked her door and shut it behind him was how the hell she'd gotten to the hospital without her car.

CHAPTER THIRTEEN

GUAC AND TALKS WAS A pitiful affair. Lia had put Avery off for three weeks before finally agreeing to go. But by the end, her friend hugged her and ordered her to go and deal with the thing that was bothering her. It was as if she'd known exactly what that thing was. Or who.

Micah had made it pretty clear that this time their breakup was permanent. Well, in his defense, she'd kind of beaten him to the punch, opting not to tell him the truth, just like the last time they'd been together.

But it was as if Micah had probed her deepest, darkest fears and stood them up in front of her, saying, "This was how my life was." And when he took her hand and mentioned having kids—implying she was the person he'd choose to have them with—it had been her undoing. The panic from that time long ago, when she couldn't recognize her own dad, had taken her down, paralyzing her.

Dio, the man had poured out his heart and soul to her, and the next morning she'd acted just like the people in his story. She'd barely spoken a word to him other than to say she was sorry. She'd never even told him what the hell she was sorry for.

And it wasn't fair.

Not to Micah, and not to her. But what other answer was

there? He'd grown up not feeling seen by anyone in his life. And here was someone who was incapable of seeing him. Not because she didn't want to see him. But because she *couldn't*, dammit. She couldn't!

There was a huge difference between not wanting to and not being able to. But wasn't the end result the same? The odds were that she would one day call him or someone near him by the wrong name. Just like his mom had done to him. How could she live with herself if she did that?

How could she raise a child and have any different outcome than Micah had had?

The questions rolled around and around inside her, and then the loop started all over again.

She plopped into her chair at work and opened a file, staring at it, but not seeing it.

She'd seen her artwork all over town. Micah had indeed hung the flyers by himself. And in the end, his and the CDC's strategy seemed to be working. They were having record numbers of people coming in for their vaccinations, and the new reports of pertussis were beginning to wane.

She had acted terribly when Micah came out of the bedroom. That had been wrong. So wrong. He'd deserved the truth that day, and she hadn't given it to him. He deserved to know *why* she thought their relationship was doomed.

At graduation, Micah had asked for an explanation, and she hadn't given it to him. This time he hadn't asked. He'd basically told her, "Never mind. I don't need to know. To hell with you."

The thing was, he wasn't the one who'd sent her to hell. She'd sent herself. Time after time. Relationship after relationship, whether it be girlfriends or high school boyfriends. She'd sabotaged every one of them in order to keep her secret. She had very few friends outside of Avery, because no one else could survive the freezing temperatures that came with inhabiting her world.

You owe him an explanation, Lia.

Why?

She already knew why. The man had shared his darkest moments with her, had told her things about himself that she'd never known.

Why now, when he hadn't the last time they were together? He'd said it was because he was embarrassed.

But maybe it was because he'd finally trusted someone enough to tell them. And that someone had been her. And what had she done? By being unwilling to become just as vulnerable as he'd been, she'd batted his revelation away like it was of no importance.

But it was. It was so very important.

She swallowed. She'd never trusted anyone that much. Ever.

Pushing away the chart, she realized she needed to trust or she would remain that scared woman who'd stood frozen in the middle of her kitchen, too petrified to let down her guard and live life.

Avery was right. She needed to deal with the thing that was bothering her. Or someday, when she least expected, it was going to deal with her.

What if Micah told her to get the hell out of his office without even giving her a hearing? Then she needed to find someone else to tell. And she needed to keep on trying until there was no secret left to tell.

She climbed to her feet, picking up her cell phone and scrolling until she found his number. She should probably call rather than just barging into his office, right?

What would she do if she was in his shoes and had advance notice of his arrival?

She'd make sure she was long gone by the time he got there. Kind of like she'd done when Micah had gone to get dressed that morning.

Okay, then she needed to just go. If he wasn't there, she would camp outside his office until he finally did appear.

So she took the elevator to the third floor and made her way down the hallway until the very end. Then she stood in front of his door for a very long time, her heart quaking in her chest. Then she raised her hand and knocked. Hard enough for anyone within earshot to hear.

"Come in."

Dio, could she do it?

The fact was, she had to. She went into his office and found him up to his elbows in…boxes.

Panic swept through her. "You're leaving?"

"Yep."

"I thought you said you were staying in Nashville to help with your parents."

His brows went up, and there was a coolness to his eyes that made her want to cry out. "I'm not leaving Nashville. Or the hospital. But I am changing locations. The CDC liked our campaign and asked me to come on staff as a representative of Saint Dolly's."

"Oh." The wind went out of her sails.

"Did you need something?"

Her reason for coming here skittered back through her head at his words. Whether he stayed or whether he went was immaterial at this point. But she needed to be as honest with him as he'd been with her.

"I do. I need to talk to you for a minute, if you have the time."

For a second he looked like he might refuse, then he lifted some boxes off one of the chairs and motioned for her to sit. Whew. At least she wasn't going to have to do this standing up, because she wasn't sure her legs would support her.

Micah didn't take another seat, however, he stood over her, a hip leaning on his desk. It was disconcerting, as if he were trying to subtly convey that he didn't want her here and wasn't going to do anything to make her stay more comfortable.

Well, it was working.

"So what is it?"

She'd kind of thought this would go differently. That they'd both be sitting across from each other where she could watch his body language. But where he was didn't change what she was here for.

"You remember when you told me you felt invisible to your mom and dad? That you felt like some faceless entity? A Mr. Potato Head with interchangeable parts, I think you said?"

He shrugged. "I never should have told you any of that."

"*Dio*, Micah, yes, you should have. Because you hit my deepest dilemma on the head. You nailed the reason I broke things off with you all those years ago, and why I couldn't quite face you the last time we were together."

"I don't understand."

"I know you don't. And I should have told you all this at graduation. But I was... I was too afraid. I've been afraid all my life."

"You?"

"Yes." She looked down at her hands, twining her fingers together. This was it. It was now or never. "People's...faces... they, well, they don't register with me. I see them. I look at you and can see your face as plain as day. But when I look in the mirror, I see the same thing. A face. When I look at Arnie Goff, I see...a face." Her gaze came back up. "But they're indistinguishable from each other. They're Mr. Potato Heads."

He was looking at her like he had no idea what she was talking about.

She tried a new tack. "Ever hear of a condition called prosopagnosia?"

Something in his eyes clicked, and he frowned. "Face blindness? It's extremely rare."

She pointed her thumbs back at herself. "Dr. Micah Corday, meet Extremely Rare."

He tipped the chair next to hers, dumping the contents onto the ground, then turned it so he sat across from her. "You have prosopagnosia? You've had it the whole time we've known each other?"

"I've had it since I was an infant. I had a stroke that affected that part of my brain."

"So when you didn't recognize me at the Valentine's Day benefit…" His eyes closed. "Hell, I thought you didn't remember me."

"Oh, I remembered you. There's a huge difference between recognizing and remembering."

"But how did you finally realize it was me?"

Lia looked at him. "You opened your mouth, and *you* poured out of it. And I normally recognized you." She reached out and touched his face. "Your dimple. The color of your eyes. The way your hair falls over your forehead. There are a thousand things about you that tell me it's you." And she loved every one of those things. Would always love them.

"So why did you break things off?"

This was hard. And real. And scary. She wasn't sure she could make it through the explanation without falling completely apart. "Everyone was in their caps and gowns that day. I looked over the crowd, and all I could see was a sea of orange and white. All the little indicators I used to tell people apart had suddenly been taken away. Including you. I panicked. One of my biggest fears was not being able to recognize my children, and a million moments ran through my head and I realized how many times we wear uniforms and ballet costumes and…caps and gowns."

"If you had told me…"

"It wouldn't have changed anything. That fear was…*is* still there. You described perfectly what any child born to me was going to experience. The sense of invisibility. Mistaking a neighbor's child for my own. You said you felt like a placeholder in your own home. That is the world *my* child will live in. And when you took my hand and said you wanted kids… with the right partner—" Her voice ended on a sob. One she swallowed down before it became a torrent. "I felt like absolutely the wrong person for you to do that with. You deserve so much better. You deserve to be seen. *Really* seen."

"Lia. No. That's not true. God, I had no idea how you would take any of that."

"I know. But it rang so true. It matched what I feared so perfectly."

He grabbed her hands and held them tight. "You say I deserve to be seen. Do you want to know how I felt when we were together back then? I *felt* seen for the first time in my life. Like you could peer inside me and see what no one else could. I felt like more than..." he smiled "...an indistinguishable set of parts. I felt whole and wanted."

"But you're an adult now. If I ever had a child—"

"If you ever *have* a child, he or she will be very, very lucky. Can't you see? That little person will be known in a way that very few people will ever experience. What happened with my parents was willful and hurtful, even if they didn't mean it to be. I felt unwanted. Would yours feel like that?"

"No. Never." She lifted his hand and pressed it to her cheek. "I'm sorry, Micah. I should have told you. Back then. And when you were in my apartment that last time."

"That's why you acted so strange the next morning. You felt like you would doom your child to the life I was describing?"

She nodded.

"I should have seen it. Should have guessed you were struggling with something. If I had..."

"It's not your fault. The only person who has ever guessed the truth was Avery."

He smiled. "I can see how that might be. She's a good friend."

"Yes, she is."

He pulled in a breath and released it. "So where do we go from here?"

Something twitched in her belly. She hadn't been looking for anything more than to just tell him the truth. "What do you mean?"

"Did you break up with me because you didn't love me?"

"No, of course not."

He dragged her onto his lap and planted a hard kiss on her mouth. "Said as if that's a ridiculous thought. Well, it wasn't to me. You put me through hell, Lia."

"I didn't mean to. I was trying to save you. From me."

"What a misguided, unbelievable and totally incredible woman you are. But you didn't save me. You almost destroyed me." He cupped her face and looked into her eyes. "I have a very important question. You said you didn't break up with me for lack of love. Is that still true? That there's no lack of love?"

A veil lifted from her eyes, and she could see him clearly for the first time in her life. "There's no lack. I love you. I always have."

A muscle worked in his jaw. "What can I do to help you?"

"To help me? I don't understand."

"How can I help you believe that what you see when you look at me is enough? That it's always been enough." He smiled. "I have never felt invisible in your eyes."

"I believe you." Hope raged in her chest, breaking free from the fear she'd carried with her from childhood.

"And you believe that your children...*our* children—maybe five or six?—will never feel invisible?"

She laughed. "Five or six? *Dio*, we may have to color code them. My mom always wore a pink crocheted bracelet on her wrist to help me spot her from a distance. She still does, although she probably doesn't need to anymore."

"There's your answer, then. If you're afraid, we'll have a different color bracelet for each child."

"We'll? Are you sure you want to—"

"Have children with you? Yes, and I'm hoping you feel the same way. I love you, Lia."

Love and belief swamped her heart, and she could finally envision a future where she could drop her guard and be herself.

In trusting Micah enough to tell him the truth, she'd given

herself permission to be happy. And she was happy. Happier than she'd ever been. And she had a feeling life was only going to get better from here.

His kiss held a promise that didn't need facial recognition software to become reality. Because he'd told her he loved her just as she was. And so would their children. And this time—finally—Lia believed him.

EPILOGUE

MICAH PLACED A pink crocheted bracelet around their baby's wrist, careful not to wake Lia, who was still sleeping after her difficult delivery.

Lia's mom had fashioned a tiny identification band that looked identical to the one she wore. It wouldn't have any information printed on it like you might expect on one of those kinds of bands, but it would serve as a tell, as she put it, the same way Micah's bright orange wedding band did. She'd sworn she didn't need him to wear anything more than a gold band, that she would always recognize him. But he wanted to. It was a sign that he supported his wife and would do anything he could to make things easier for her. And his band wouldn't be hidden under the sleeve of a coat the way a bracelet might.

He'd almost ruined things by not understanding why she'd withdrawn after their night together, and by not pressing her for answers. Once they figured things out, they'd sworn they would keep no more secrets from each other. Lia had gone to Arnie Goff as well and shared about her prosopagnosia, and he assured her it would have no effect on her job at the hospital.

As for his parents, he'd been surprised and pleased by their response to the news he was getting married. His mom had actually taken it upon herself to make the bridal bouquet and the one for Avery, who was Lia's matron of honor. Little inroads were being made every time he turned around, it seemed. And his dad's experimental cancer treatment was working better than expected. He hadn't gone into remission yet, but there was a very real possibility it would happen.

The only glitch had come when Lia found herself unexpectedly pregnant a month before they said their vows. It was her deepest fear and the reason she'd broken things off with him. He'd taken her in his arms and reassured her that their baby would not get lost in the shuffle. They would make it work. And with her mom and dad's help, they had.

"Hey, handsome." Lia's tired voice came from the bed behind him, and he turned toward her. "Is she okay?"

"She's more than okay." He perched on the edge of the mattress. "How are you feeling?"

"Better."

Lia had developed preeclampsia in her thirty-eighth week of pregnancy, and because of the stroke she'd had as an infant, they'd decided rather than risk her blood pressure going any higher, they would deliver the baby. Fear had crawled up Micah's spine at the thought of losing Lia so soon after they'd found each other again, and when he'd been kicked out of the surgical suite, he'd found himself sitting in the hospital's chapel. There, with clasped hands resting on the chair in front of him, he'd poured his heart out to whomever in the cosmos might be listening. That's where the surgeon had found him a half hour later. And where he'd learned that both Lia and Chelsea Day Costa-Corday had made it. He would be forever grateful. And never would he take these two precious gifts for granted.

Micah stroked her damp hair back off her forehead. "You are my world—do you know that?"

She nodded. "Ditto, honey." She frowned and then put a hand on his arm. "I'm sorry. I forgot."

Surprisingly, the word didn't send his world spinning into chaos like it had that other time. Instead, it brought a sense of peace. "It's okay. I think it's growing on me. Especially since everyone in your family calls everyone honey. Well, in Italian."

"It's part of my heritage. I could use the Italian term if you'd rather."

"No. Although there are times when I really do like hearing you speak in your heart language. Like when you're cussing." He grinned and leaned closer. "Or when you're loving me."

"Micah!"

It was a huge turn-on when his wife was so caught up in the moment that she breathed words he didn't understand across his skin. Even thinking about it caused areas that should be quiet to wake up.

It would always be this way. He wanted this woman. Only this woman.

"Sorry. I can't help it."

She slid her finger down the left side of his face. "It's okay." Her eyes shifted to the clear bassinet a short distance away. "Can I hold her?"

"Of course." Micah helped her sit up and propped a pillow across the area where her incision was. Then he turned and reached into the bassinet and gingerly lifted their child, moving with careful steps until he reached her. Laying her in Lia's arms, he moved around to the other side of the bed and slid in beside her.

This was where he belonged. And this was where he would stay.

He saw her reach for their daughter's wrist and touch the bracelet. "Where...?"

"Your mom brought it in while they were doing the C-section."

She gathered her baby close, tears filling her eyes and spilling onto her cheeks. "I just never thought I'd be this lucky."

Micah kissed the top of her head, trying to banish the burning sensation behind his own eyes. "Luck? I don't think so. I think maybe your friend Avery was right."

"What do you mean?"

He leaned his cheek against her temple. "Remember when she was talking about Samantha?"

"Samantha? As in our cat?"

"Hmm… Yes, her little bell jingled on your key chain, and then Avery said you'd named her for her witchy ways."

"Well, 'witchy' was a nice way of putting it."

He laughed. "Well, be that as it may, contrary to her fierce reputation, she didn't exactly attack me that first night I met her."

"Unlike me on that same night." She sent him a look that told him exactly what she meant.

"Don't distract me. But even that kind of proves my point."

"Proves your point?" She tilted her head until it rested against his. "So are you somehow saying that Samantha had something to do with me sleeping with you that first night? With us getting together afterward?"

"Maybe. I'm forever hearing her little bell wandering around our house at night."

"And?"

"I swear I've seen her nose twitch a time or two when she looks at us."

Lia laughed, then her free hand came up and curved around his cheek, turning his face so she could kiss him. "You know, I think I've seen that, too. So you think Sam twitched her witchy little nose and cast a spell on us?"

"Are you denying it's a possibility?"

"No, and now that I think about it, she did kind of force her way into my heart at the shelter not long after I broke up with you. She helped me grieve your loss that first time. And she helped me work up the courage to tell you about my condition."

"That cat deserves a medal for making our problems vanish, if so."

"No. That cat deserved a family. And it looks like she got one. One that isn't going to disappear."

His arm tightened around her. "Good. Because I'm not going anywhere."

"That makes two of us. I love you, Micah."

As he stared down at his little family, his heart filled with love and gratitude. And then he glanced out the window at the skies and beyond and mouthed, "Thank you."

* * * * *

A Valentine's Proposal

Kim Findlay

WESTERN

Small towns. Rugged ranchers. Big hearts.

Kim Findlay is a Canadian who fled the cold to live on a sailboat in the Caribbean and write romance novels. She shares the boat with her husband and the world's cutest spaniel. Bucket list accomplished! Her first Harlequin Heartwarming, *Crossing the Goal Line*, came about from the Heartwarming Blitz, and she's never looked back. Keep up with Kim, including sailing adventures, at kimfindlay.ca.

Books by Kim Findlay

A Hockey Romance

Crossing the Goal Line
Her Family's Defender

Visit the Author Profile page
at millsandboon.com.au for more titles.

Dear Reader,

This new series, Cupid's Crossing, was inspired by my Heartwarming editor's wish list. My brain connected a small town and holidays and added in the humor that I find makes everything go better.

Carter's Crossing is a small place a few hours' drive from large cities like New York and Boston. Abigail Carter, matriarch of the Carter family, has the idea of converting the former mill town into a destination for romantic events: proposals, weddings, weekend getaways. This three-book series follows the transformation of the town from Carter's Crossing to Cupid's Crossing.

Abigail reaches out to a former college beau, who sends his granddaughter, Mariah, a wedding planner, to spend a year launching the plan. Mariah decides that staging some events for Valentine's Day would be a great way to kick off the town's new business.

Most of the town is on board, except for Abigail's grandson Nelson, the local vet. Fortunately, Cupid has some tricks up his sleeves, including a Great Dane, some rescue horses, as well as a can't-live-with-them, can't-live-without-them group of friends.

Cupid has his own plans for his namesake town.

Happy reading!

Kim

To LeAnne, Amanda, Adrienne and Johanna,
who helped to bring this series to life.

CHAPTER ONE

THE IDEAS WERE pinging nonstop. Fizzing with excitement, Mariah pulled into an empty parking lot, grabbing the tablet beside her and opening up the map app. With the limited parking here in Carter's Crossing, they'd need to set something up with trains, or planes, to get larger parties here, or people without cars from cities like New York or Boston. Where was the closest train station? Airport? How would they convey people from there? Limo? Convertible in the summer? No, that would only be for the big budget events. Maybe a shuttle bus? They'd have to arrange for a van for luggage…

Absorbed in her thoughts, her surroundings faded until a voice near the open car window broke through her concentration.

It had an impatient edge, as if this wasn't the first attempt to reach her.

"Can I help you?"

Mariah's head snapped up, and she shrieked.

The big head, the teeth, the tongue…it took her a moment to place the unexpected image.

A Great Dane, drooling into her car. She backed farther into her seat before the big nose snuffled her ear.

"He's friendly." It was the same voice, and Mariah finally caught sight of the man attached to the dog.

He was at the other end of a leash. Tall, dark hair, wearing blue scrubs for some reason. He was also good-looking, but the smirk on his face canceled out most of the benefit of a strong chin and high cheekbones. The smirk annoyed her. She wasn't afraid of dogs; she'd just been startled.

"I'm sure he is. I'd still rather not wear his saliva."

Okay, maybe her voice was a little…curt, but this was an expensive suit and she already had some drool on her sleeve. Her pulse was racing from the shock.

The dog's head retreated as the man pulled on the leash.

"Back off, Tiny." He pushed the dog behind him and leaned toward her. "We didn't mean to startle you. Just wanted to help you find your way."

Mariah's fists clenched on the map. This man didn't know her. He didn't know her hot buttons, or the number of times she'd been offered unsolicited directions. He probably didn't even realize the assumptions behind that offer. She had literally navigated around the globe, and she could certainly make her way around a town so small it had only one stoplight.

She'd been questioned on that ability a few times too many. "I'm not lost." She set down the tablet. She wasn't lost. Planning was her forte. She knew exactly where she was and where she was going, and all she'd wanted was a few moments to work out the brainstorm she'd been hit with. This could be her best idea yet, and she wanted the chance to start working it out.

"Just taking the scenic route?" he asked, still smirking.

Oh, to be born with the confidence of those with a Y chromosome. He undoubtedly expected her to admit the map was just too much for her little ole brain and would gladly tell her where to go in that same smug tone…or maybe she was projecting, just a bit. Probably better not to leap to conclusions.

Still, it wouldn't hurt for him to learn to take a hint. If she needed help, she was perfectly capable of asking for it.

So she smiled through gritted teeth and repeated, "I'm not lost, but I wouldn't mind if you were."

She held the smile as the penny dropped and he lost his smirk.

He backed off, hands in the air, Drooly backing up with him. To his credit, he didn't call her a name, defend his niceness or tell her she was cute when she was sassy.

Maybe she'd gone too far.

"I'm gone. Good luck finding where you're going."

She could do without the sarcasm, too. Yeah, she didn't need to feel sorry for him, or his healthy ego.

He turned to the building at the back of the small parking lot where she'd pulled in. The falling penny this time was for her. He was in scrubs, with a dog, and the sign on the building read Carter's Crossing Animal Hospital.

Okay, first meeting with a local didn't go well. For a moment she considered apologizing.

She checked the time. No, she needed to get going. She didn't have time for him to explain how he hadn't meant anything by it.

Shoving the incident, and the tablet, behind her, she put the car in gear and turned left.

This was an incredible opportunity. She was going to blow the socks off everyone, and then she'd have achieved her dream, all on her own. She was at the helm, and she was kicking butt and taking names.

Fortunately, none of her plans required the assistance of the local vet.

Nelson Carter watched the car pull out of his parking lot. His empty parking lot.

It was a Sunday afternoon, and the clinic wasn't open. There were no other cars in the lot; just his clinic van. He was here because he'd been called in to help Tiny, the Great Dane.

Great Danes were known to suffer from gastric torsion, as Tiny's owner had read on the internet. Every time Tiny ate something he shouldn't, which he did frequently, Nelson got a call in case Tiny was about to bloat and torque his digestive tract. To date, Tiny's digestive tract was cast iron, but Nelson always responded.

Tiny's owner, Mavis Grisham, was a good friend of his grandmother's, and devoted to her pet, who probably out-weighed her by a good thirty pounds. Tiny was a happy, good-natured goof. After checking the dog out thoroughly, he'd taken Tiny for a walk, making sure the guy would survive his first taste of habanero sauce. Nelson was more worried about what would happen when that worked its way through Tiny than he was with what was going to happen while it was still inside the big dog, but he was due for dinner at his grandmother's. Mavis would have to handle that.

He also wondered why Mavis was using habanero sauce but was probably better off not knowing.

Nelson had been about to return Tiny to Mavis when he'd noticed the out-of-state car in the clinic parking lot.

Carter's Crossing was a small town. It wasn't on the way to anywhere else of any consequence, so few people other than locals were likely to drive through. Nelson knew all the locals. He'd grown up in Carter's Crossing. Now that he was back, his practice covered more than just the town. Almost everyone here had an animal, either for business or pleasure. He'd quickly caught up on any new arrivals since he'd left.

In Carter's Crossing there weren't any strangers.

He'd guessed the driver of the out-of-state car was lost, and the map open on her tablet confirmed that she'd gotten con-fused on the back roads.

His first impression had been good. She was pretty, with dark, shiny hair, a straight nose; her brow crinkled as she stared at the map like it was her best friend. He'd offered to help, thinking it would be a pleasant interlude to wrap up his day.

She hadn't been nice. Sure, Tiny's face could be startling up close, so the yelp she'd made had been perfectly understandable, but that was no excuse to tell him to get lost. He'd only been trying to help.

He'd learned the hard way not to push ideas or advice on anyone else, so he let her go. She'd find her way, or she'd ask someone else for assistance. As far as he was concerned, she could drive around in circles if she wanted.

In fact, that would be a kind of poetic justice.

He tugged Tiny toward the clinic van. He'd drop the drool monster off to his anxious owner, and then get himself cleaned up for dinner. His grandmother had requested his company because she had something she wished to discuss with him.

His mood improved as he thought of Abigail Carter. She took her position as head of the Carter family, the family for whom the town was named, seriously. It had been a blow to her and to the town when she'd had to close the mill. Since then, she'd been trying to find a way to inject life and money into the local economy.

Nelson had no idea how she'd accomplish that, but if anyone could, it would be his grandmother. He'd carefully avoided any involvement himself. He wasn't going to be that guy anymore, the one who made plans and moved heaven and earth to get them done.

He was happy as things were, handling the care of the animal population of Carter's Crossing and surrounds. He had his horses to fill up his spare time and energy. He had his grandmother for dinners and nagging, and friends to keep him company. He was good.

He wasn't going to hurt anyone again trying to get what he wanted. Even if all he wanted was to give someone directions to wherever they were going.

Mariah's jaw dropped. The house was beautiful.

Abigail Carter had given her careful directions to find it, and honestly, the town was small. For someone who'd grown up traveling the world on a sailboat, finding the largest house in

Carter's Crossing wasn't a challenge. She'd driven all through the town, examining it for potential. The town had charm and beauty in abundance, and she and Abigail could build on that.

She drove through the gates and up the drive before pulling to a stop in front of the immaculately maintained Victorian; its sloping yard carefully manicured. There was a huge wrap-around porch decorated with harvest touches. This place was ready for promotional photos as it was, without any additional work. She pictured it with snow and Christmas decorations. It would be gorgeous.

She was creating the publicity materials in her head already. This was the kind of thing that would make Carter's Crossing a romantic destination worth the travel. The excitement was fizzing again.

The front door opened, and a tall, elegant, silver-haired woman came out, smiling in welcome at Mariah as she exited her car. The woman was dressed in wool pants and a silk shirt with a sweater knotted over her shoulders. Her hair was pulled back, and her makeup was perfectly applied. In a town this size, she was a surprise.

Mariah was glad she'd worn her suit.

"You must be Mariah. How lovely to see you."

Even her voice was charming. Mariah had had some doubts about this partnership her grandfather had set up for her, but first impressions were positive.

"Yes, I'm Mariah Van Delton. Thank you so much for inviting me here, Mrs. Carter."

The woman shook her head. "Abigail, please. We're partners in crime now."

Abigail came down the steps and enveloped her in a scented embrace. She then stood back and cocked her head as she examined Mariah.

"How was your drive? Any problems finding your way?"

Mariah thought of the man with the dog and shook her head. "Not at all. You have a lovely town."

"Let me know, before I get myself carried away, am I crazy, or do we have a chance?"

Mariah reined in her own excitement. "I've just got here. There's still a lot to consider." Seeing Abigail's face fall, she added, "But this place has already given me ideas. Big ideas. I just won't tell Grandfather until we've worked the details out."

Abigail's face lit up. "I'm so glad. Now, do come in. Do you have a lot to carry? I can ask Nelson to bring your things in when he gets here, or tomorrow I have the staff to deal with it."

Staff made sense. This house must require a lot of upkeep. Mariah wasn't sure who Nelson was, but she was perfectly able to carry her own luggage.

"I didn't bring a lot, so I'm quite capable of handling it."

Abigail shot her a look. "Of course you are. I'm undoubtedly capable of mowing this lawn, but I would rather someone else do it. Sometimes accepting help is…strategic."

Mariah paused. At that moment it was all too clear that Abigail had been not just a beautiful woman, but a clever one, as well. Anyone who underestimated her would find themselves in trouble. Mariah made note.

Mariah hadn't brought much with her because she'd had some serious concerns about her grandfather's decree that she should stay with his old college friend. Even if she was confident she could make this plan for Carter's Crossing work, she didn't necessarily want to be sharing a home with someone she'd never met before. But the house was so large that there'd be no problem with a lack of privacy. She already felt sure that she and Abigail could work together. She should have known that her grandfather's friend would be up to this. He hadn't built his business empire by being wrong.

"Let me at least take your briefcase and I'll show you to your room." Abigail held out a hand.

Mariah passed it over and grabbed the two bags from the trunk. "Thank you again for offering me a place to stay."

Abigail, holding the door open for her, waved that aside.

"This place is much too large for one person. And I'm grateful for your help, and for Gerry sending you."

Gerry? Right, her grandfather. No one had called him anything but Gerald as far as Mariah knew.

"I'm happy to be here, and I'm excited about the project."

Abigail's eyes were sparkling. "Excellent. I expect we can accomplish great things together. I've put you on the second floor, at the other end of the house from me so that we each have our own space. I'm sure we'll soon be heartily sick of each other and need a retreat."

Abigail led her upstairs to a room overlooking the lawn at the back of the house. "I apologize. The room doesn't have an en suite, but there's only the two of us in the house, so the bathroom next door is all yours. Take a few minutes to settle in. I'll be waiting on the porch. I want to enjoy the last of the warm days before the cold keeps us all huddled indoors. We'll eat once Nelson gets here. He shouldn't be long." She glanced at the delicate gold watch on her wrist.

Mariah wasn't sure if Nelson would be serving the meal or eating with them, but she hoped his presence wouldn't interfere with talking to Abigail. The idea she'd been struck with when she drove around Carter's Crossing had inspired her. She'd wanted to blurt it out as soon as she arrived, but this was important. She had to be sure she'd thought it through first.

She weighed the pros and cons in her head again. She had a lot riding on this job. She needed it to be perfect.

The bedroom was gorgeous. Not a surprise after meeting Abigail. Mariah decided to unpack later. She didn't want to be late for dinner, and she was eager to talk to Abigail.

She found Abigail on the porch, sweater now on to fight the cool of the autumn dusk.

"Come, sit for a minute, Mariah. Did you find the room comfortable?"

Mariah sat on a wicker chair with a plump cushion on its seat.

"The room is beautiful. I'm sure I'll be more than comfortable."

"Thank you, dear. Did you want to start talking shop tonight, or wait till tomorrow? I don't want to press you, at least, not yet. Are you tired from the drive?"

Mariah tamped down her own excitement. "Not at all. I'm ready anytime, but if you'd rather wait…"

"I'm excited about it—oh, but that looks like Nelson coming now."

"Who exactly is Nelson?"

"Nelson is my grandson. He's the only family I have here in Carter's now. He lives in the carriage house, and I insist he comes over for dinner regularly. I tell him it's for his own good, but really, I'm happy to have the company.

"He was called in to work earlier, but he just texted that he was on his way home."

Mariah saw a white van heading toward the house.

"Is Nelson going to be involved in this project?" The information her grandfather had provided her about Abigail Carter had been sparse.

Abigail allowed a small smile and shook her head. "Oh, no, this isn't his kind of thing at all."

The white van turned in the drive. The lettering on the side read Carter's Crossing Animal Hospital.

Mariah's excitement took a nosedive.

"What does Nelson do?" But she knew the answer already.

"He's the town's veterinarian. He was called in this afternoon to take care of Tiny, Mavis Grisham's Great Dane."

Mariah swallowed a sigh. If she was a believer in signs, she'd be worried about now.

Nelson noticed the car parked in front of his grandmother's house as he drove around to the back. It looked familiar. Then he saw the plates.

How had Miss I'm Not Lost ended up here? He'd like to

see her explain that, but she'd probably get directions from his grandmother and be on her way before he arrived at the main house. That is, if she'd admit she was lost at all. Maybe she was stopping all over town trying to find her way again. She must be geographically challenged.

Happy he wouldn't have a second meeting with her, he pulled his van into the garage below his apartment in the former carriage house and took a moment to roll the kinks out of his neck. He didn't have time to shower, since Grandmother was big on punctuality, but he had a few minutes to change. She wouldn't let him come to dinner in scrubs. Once in his place, he threw what he was wearing in the laundry and pulled on a cashmere sweater she'd given him last Christmas and some dress pants. Grandmother would never allow jeans or sweats at her dinner table. A quick glance in the mirror assured him he'd pass muster, and he headed over to the house.

He let himself in the back door and sniffed appreciatively at the aromas drifting his way. Coq au vin. His favorite. His grandmother loved the classic French dishes. It had been a few months since he'd enjoyed her coq au vin.

His grandmother insisted he come to dinner a couple of times a week, and he was happy to oblige her. She said he needed to have a civilized meal occasionally. He knew she wanted company. He did, too.

It wasn't just that she was a good cook; he worried about her living here all alone. It was a big place, and he was the only family left in town. She had her staff who came in on weekdays, but evenings and weekends she was still alone.

She'd been left a widow with four kids at a young age, and he admired how she'd handled her family and the family business on her own. He knew she was working on something new, but she hadn't shared the details with him yet. She had a good mind for business, but he hoped her plan didn't involve him. Especially not his personal life.

There was a lot of *grande dame* about his grandmother.

He heard voices coming from the living room and paused. Did she have a guest? She hadn't mentioned it. Normally, it was just the two of them at dinner.

Surely Grandmother hadn't invited the rude stranger to stay. Better Mavis and Tiny.

He made his way to the doorway and stopped in surprise.

"Oh, Nelson. There you are. Nelson, this is Mariah Van Delton. Mariah, this is my grandson, Nelson Carter."

Abigail smiled at him as if she'd just given him a pleasant surprise.

Mariah smiled, as well. It was patently fake. "Oh, we met earlier, though we didn't exchange names."

Nelson had never worried about his grandmother being scammed before, but his Spidey senses were tingling now. Somehow, he knew this woman, with her *I'm not lost* and fake smile, was going to be trouble.

He wouldn't admit that part of that certainty was because she was also much too pretty for his own good.

Abigail raised her eyebrows delicately. "Oh?"

"I offered to give Ms. Van Delton directions." Which, he could acknowledge to himself, might not have been necessary if she was heading to see his grandmother.

But why was she?

"I thought you said you'd found your way without any problems, Mariah?" Grandmother asked, frowning.

Mariah sat a little straighter. Her eyes were flashing. "I did. I merely stopped to make some notes and your grandson *assumed* I was lost."

Nelson narrowed his own gaze. "Not many people stop in at my clinic on a Sunday afternoon to *make notes.*"

Abigail was watching them with an amused smile. Very *grande dame.* Nelson quickly changed direction.

"You didn't tell me you were expecting a guest, Grandmother."

"No, I didn't, did I? If we're going to keep each other posted

on every little thing, then let me tell you that Mariah is going
to be staying here for a while, helping me with a project I have
in mind. We'd just started discussing it."

Nelson felt the hair on the back of his neck lift. That look
Grandmother had on her face meant trouble. And he already
knew Ms. Van Delton was going to be a pain.

Abigail rose to her feet. "Let me bring in dinner, and I can
hear more about this new idea of yours, Mariah. It's time we
went public, so we can let Nelson in on it."

Mariah insisted on helping and followed Abigail out of the
room.

Nelson frowned. He shouldn't be the one feeling left out
here. It was his home, his town, and yet he was the last to know
what was going on.

Grandmother discussed things with him. At least, the major
things. She'd had to shut the mill not long after he'd returned
to Carter's Crossing, and he knew how difficult a decision that
had been for her.

He couldn't readily imagine Mariah as the savior for the
town's economic woes. She didn't look old enough to be the
CEO of any well-established business. It was undoubtedly prej-
udice on his part, mostly as a result of being told to get lost,
but he wouldn't trust any business she was touting. His grandmother had been the town leader for so long, she'd come to
believe herself a benevolent despot. But sometimes her ideas
were a little…unconventional.

He made his way to the dining room, already set for dinner
for three, and poured the wine she'd left out. Then he headed
for the kitchen. He could help carry in the food.

He didn't make a lot of noise. He'd spent enough time in
this house to avoid the squeaky boards by habit. Just before he
reached the door, he heard them talking and paused.

The phrase that eavesdroppers never heard any good about
themselves wasn't quite accurate. Eavesdroppers didn't hear
good, period.

Mariah was speaking, responding to something his grandmother had said.

"In that case, you could say that working for Sherry Anstruthers taught me everything I needed to know about wedding planning, and I've taken those lessons to heart."

After that, all Nelson heard was white noise. He made himself move back to the dining room just as quietly as he'd left, but he was on autopilot.

Sherry Anstruthers was one person he despised, almost as much as he despised himself, or at least the man he'd been three years ago. He could not believe Grandmother had invited anyone connected to that woman to her home.

Maybe she hadn't known that Mariah Van Delton had a connection with Sherry. He sat back in his chair. Right. She hadn't known. She couldn't have. And now she'd send Miss I'm Not Lost packing.

He found his fists clenched so tightly on the chair arms that his knuckles stood out, white against the oak. He relaxed them, with an effort, just as he heard footsteps in the hallway. He stood up when Grandmother and Mariah came back in, bearing hot dishes.

Mariah was here. But not for long.

Nelson had just swallowed his first mouthful when the hammer hit.

Mariah led off. "Abigail, I think you have a good idea, but you're thinking too small."

No one had ever accused his grandmother of thinking too small. If Mariah was thinking bigger than anything his grandmother could come up with, it was going to be a nightmare. Even if Mariah wasn't going to be staying here, she could do a lot of damage before she left.

He glanced at his grandmother, but she wasn't offended. Her eyes were sparkling as she waited, her fork resting on her plate.

Why wasn't she freezing out this interloper?

"Carter's Crossing would be a beautiful wedding destination, but I don't think we should stop there."

The chicken went down the wrong way in Nelson's throat, and he started choking. Mariah frowned at him, and he'd swear his grandmother was holding back a laugh. It would serve her right if he did choke. He managed to swallow his food, and grabbed his wineglass, needing to soothe his throat so he could talk.

Because no way was Carter's Crossing going to be wedding central. Not if he had anything to do with it.

"Wedding traffic would drive business mostly in the summertime. This is a beautiful four-season location, and we want to take advantage of it. We don't want Carter's Crossing to be a center for weddings."

Nelson's shoulders relaxed. He finally agreed with the woman about something. They didn't want Carter's Crossing to be a center for weddings, especially the kind of weddings that would be connected to people coming from elsewhere. Those wouldn't be the small local weddings the town was used to. The usual, ordinary, happy events. The ones couples planned for themselves, with help from friends and family.

He didn't mind those.

It was the big-production, showstopper weddings that he was opposed to. The ones that required a wedding planner, like Sherry Anstruthers. He'd had personal experience with those, and it had been a nightmare. His nightmare.

He didn't want that for his town, or the people who lived here.

But Mariah didn't finish the sentence the way Nelson would have.

"No, we want Carter's Crossing to be the Center for Romance." She said it that way, like romance had a capital R on it. Like Romance was also a big production.

Like it needed a planner.

No way.

Before Nelson could interrupt, his grandmother was asking, "What do you mean?" Nelson had a bad idea he knew what she meant.

Mariah wasn't looking at him anymore. She was focused in on Abigail. "I want Carter's Crossing to be the place people go for romantic getaways. For anniversaries. The place they come to propose, to get married, to fall in love. We find the romance in every season. Lemonade and boat rides in summer, cider and leaf season in fall, snuggling around the fireplace in winter, drinking hot chocolate…"

Nelson was distracted for a moment, trying to decide what beverage she was serving in spring.

"Oh, that's incredible," Abigail said. "I like that. You're right—if we do this well, it's business for the town year-round."

"And," Mariah added, "we can get started before you have the mill ready."

Nelson finally found his voice. "The mill?"

His grandmother gave him a big smile. A beautiful, elegant, phony smile. She knew. She knew exactly how much he was going to hate this.

"Yes, I'm converting the mill to an event venue."

An event venue? When did his grandmother start talking about things like event venues?

"We'll have a kitchen for catering, and space for indoor and outdoor events."

"Events?" he asked, his voice high and tight.

"Yes, like weddings."

Just kill him now.

CHAPTER TWO

SOMETHING WAS GOING on here. There was a current under-
scoring this conversation strong enough to tow swimmers out
to drown, and Mariah didn't know what it was. But as soon as
Abigail said *weddings*, Nelson growled. Honestly, she couldn't
think of a more accurate word to describe it.

It gave her pause. The romance destination idea was good.
More than good. This town could be perfect; it had lots of big
old houses that Abigail swore were set for bed-and-breakfast
locations. There were four lovely churches and the town gazebo for wedding and vow-renewal ceremonies, as well as the
mill that Abigail was renovating. The small river that wound
its way along one side of the town might not be big enough for
yachts, but it was pretty, and could handle canoes and kayaks.
A couple of nice restaurants, a few more activities for visitors,
and this could be stellar.

But if Nelson was opposed, she didn't know if the plan would
go ahead. She had no idea how much influence he wielded over
his grandmother or the rest of the people in the town. She had
the definite impression he didn't like her.

Well, he hadn't liked her when she told him to get lost. And
yes, that was fair. But since they'd served dinner, she'd felt his
animosity like a force field around him.

Could he torpedo this whole idea?

There was one way to find out.

Abigail and Nelson were staring at each other like tomcats considering a fight.

"Is this a problem?"

"Yes."

"No."

The answers crashed over each other.

"Nelson," Abigail said. It was the *I'm the parent, you're crossing the line* kind of voice that mothers and fathers had used since Adam and Eve.

"You know…" He was growling again.

"I do. But it's been long enough. I've been trying to find some way to save this town. This is our best opportunity. Can you get past it?"

Mariah wondered if she should have excused herself. But the clash between them had come up so suddenly… She wasn't sure what the issue was, but apparently, it was major. And whatever it was, it was going to have a big effect on her plans for this next year.

Nelson stood. "It's not up to me, is it? You've already made your decision. Just keep me out of it, please. Excuse me, Ms. Van Delton, Grandmother." He turned and left, leaving Abigail and Mariah staring at the doorway where he'd disappeared.

"I'm sorry," Abigail said. "I shouldn't have sprung that on him. You must think we're crazy."

Mariah shook her head. "I'm not the one who's upset here. But I need to ask, are you sure this is a good idea?"

Abigail nodded firmly. "Absolutely. Your idea of a romance destination is wonderful. I'll get the committee on board and you can tell us what we need to do."

Mariah's glance drifted back to the doorway.

"And your grandson?" Mariah wasn't sure Abigail had any other family. She had no desire to find herself in the middle of a family drama.

Abigail sighed. "As you can tell, he has an issue, yes. But it's time he moved on. He won't do anything to stop us."

Mariah was afraid her skepticism must be showing on her face.

Abigail smiled. "I've known Nelson all his life. He'll be fine, once he gets accustomed to the idea. And this shouldn't affect him at all, should it? I don't imagine any of your ideas for romance involve a veterinarian."

Mariah had a quick vision of Nelson, soft lighting, romantic music, and shook her head. No, she wasn't thinking of any romance involving a veterinarian. Definitely not. And not in the way Abigail meant, either. She had limited her vision of romance to people, not animals. She didn't foresee bringing any livestock into the picture.

Though they could—and she slammed the door on any thoughts about indulging people's pet wedding fantasies, Persians in veils or terriers in tuxes. Maybe later.

"Nelson's work won't be affected, so he really has nothing to be upset about. He just needs time."

Mariah had the feeling Abigail was trying to convince herself.

Abigail shook her head. "I should have known better than to make coq au vin. Please, enjoy your meal—I'll take Nelson something later, when he's cooled down a bit.

"Now, what do you need from me to make this work?"

Nelson stalked across the driveway to the carriage house. He could *not* believe his grandmother was doing this.

He veered between frustration and anger. He was angry that his grandmother ruined what would have been a spectacular dinner by bringing up the one topic guaranteed to give him heartburn. He was frustrated that she had made such a big plan without talking to him. And he could not believe that Mariah—*Mariah*—was the one still at the dining room table instead of him.

He wished Mariah had been truly lost.

He stormed into his apartment. Yes, being angry with Mariah was something he could get on board with. She'd annoyed him when she turned down his offer of help. Maybe she wasn't lost, but she could have been polite. And here she was, ready to bring the chaos and stress and havoc of elaborate weddings to Carter's Crossing.

He knew *exactly* what that was like. And the people who got hurt as a result.

He didn't want something like that here.

He growled and threw himself in a chair.

If his grandmother was determined, he had about as much chance of changing her mind as he did of stopping the seasons from turning, but he had to try. There had to be another option, some other way to make Carter's Crossing come back to life.

Ways that didn't include Mariah Van Delton.

He just had to think of them before his grandmother got her plan in motion. No problem.

Sometime later there was a knock on his door, and no idea had come. He considered ignoring it, but he knew it was his grandmother, and she had her own key.

He stood and strode over to let her in. He stepped back, arms crossed on his chest, frowning.

She ignored his frown. She was holding a dish, and he didn't need to examine the contents to know she'd brought him some of her coq au vin. But no chicken, no matter how well done, was going to make up for her bombshell.

"I know." She shoved the dish toward him. "But don't cut off your nose to spite your face. You'll want to eat this eventually."

He took the dish from her hands and set it on his kitchen countertop. When he turned, she'd sat herself down in one of his easy chairs.

"You know I didn't drop the news on you this way by accident."

He stiffened. He should have realized, but he'd been too upset to think it through.

"After tomorrow, the news will be spreading all over town. I wanted you to have a heads-up."

He opened his mouth to ask why she hadn't told him herself, when she held up a hand.

"I didn't want to tell you, and have you start an argument. You are a stubborn and determined man, Nelson, and I didn't want you to try to stonewall this. I wasn't going to change my mind, and I did not want the fatigue of endless arguments."

It wasn't much of a stretch to discover where Nelson had learned his determination. He leaned back and crossed his arms again. If his grandmother was going to take over the conversation, he wasn't going to help.

"It's a done deal. Mariah's grandfather is an old friend of your grandfather's and mine, from our college days." A pained look passed over her face. His grandfather had died long before Nelson was born, so he had no memories of him. Grandmother had never married again, so the family assumed it had been a love match, one that she'd never gotten over.

"Gerry Van Delton has a very successful event planning business in New York City. His company handles professional sports events, Hollywood premiers, political fundraisers— all much larger events than anything we could do in Carter's Crossing. When I was trying to think of something we could do here, something to keep the town alive along that line, I reached out to him.

"He thought that a wedding destination was something we could manage and offered his granddaughter as a consultant for a year to get us up and running."

"Why?" Nelson asked. "Why send someone?" It was more assistance than seemed reasonable.

His grandmother stared past him; her lips pursed. "I don't know. We were close, back at school, but I haven't seen him in years. There's more to it. He's not someone to be generous to his own detriment."

She drew her gaze back to him. "I know he had some issues with his own children. He may be wanting to test Mariah in some way. I'm not sure."

Nelson considered. Maybe Mariah couldn't pull this off, and he wouldn't have to worry about it. But she didn't look or act incompetent.

And while he'd be happy not to have big production weddings in Carter's Crossing, he didn't want his grandmother to sink money into an endeavor that wouldn't pay off. Because if she was backing this plan, he knew she'd be putting up cash.

"And, Nelson, it's time."

And that took all those kind thoughts and blew them away. "I'm fine, Grandmother."

She looked down her nose. It took talent to do that when he was standing, and she was in a chair. "If you were fine, you wouldn't have left the house in a tantrum. Without eating your dinner."

He wanted to argue that he hadn't been in a tantrum, but he had walked out without his favorite meal.

"I don't have to discuss this with you." He didn't.

"Nelson, it's been three years now. You didn't commit a crime. No one died. You were thoughtless, and you hurt someone, but I think you've served your time."

Nelson held back an angry response with effort. He knew what he'd done, and what he hadn't done. That wasn't the point. Or at least, it wasn't the only point.

Getting married was a big deal. It was a major commitment, and one that shouldn't be entered into lightly. Having a big, elaborate party simultaneously added tremendous pressure to an already stressful time. It could result in some terrible decisions. Decisions he'd made.

Made with the help of Sherry Anstruthers.

He couldn't condone that kind of thing. And that was exactly what his grandmother was wanting to rebuild the town on. She couldn't really expect him to support that, could she?

"I heard the two of you in the kitchen." He saw from his grandmother's face that he knew exactly what he was talking about.

"How could you invite someone like that, someone like Sherry Anstruthers, to wreak havoc on Carter's Crossing?"

"Oh, Nelson." She shook her head and sighed. "Mariah is not like that woman."

Nelson snorted. He'd heard the words himself. She was just like that woman. That was what she wanted to be.

"Nelson, people make mistakes. You made a mistake. But it doesn't mean you're a bad person."

Nelson wished he was more sure of that.

"You want proof that Mariah is different? Well, the last wedding she worked on, before coming up here, was Zoey's."

More white noise. Nelson tried to understand what his grandmother was saying.

"Zoey's? My Zoey's?"

She nodded.

His mouth opened, but no words came out.

Zoey was married?

It had been three years. They hadn't kept in touch. But…

But she'd moved on, found someone else and gotten married—with a wedding planner. After…after everything.

Nelson dropped into his seat.

"You didn't know?"

He hated the sympathy in Abigail's voice. He hated that it implied that she worried about him, that he wasn't strong and he wasn't over it.

Maybe he wasn't.

She shook her head at him.

"I guess you do need more time. I didn't realize. I'm sorry that Mariah has upset you. But, Nelson, this is happening. Prepare yourself. It shouldn't affect you so perhaps we just need to agree to disagree on this. I won't ask for your assistance, and you won't take Tiny and come into town stealing all the wedding paraphernalia until your heart grows three sizes, okay?"

She stood up to leave.

"That dog was named Max, and he wasn't a Great Dane."

She opened his door and headed out.

"And I'm not the Grinch!"

Mariah hung up her suit in the wardrobe in her room. She'd unpacked now and was reconsidering her wardrobe choices. Did everyone in this town dress up all the time?

She shrugged. She'd get her roommate to send her some more of her clothes if she needed.

That gave her a thought, and she went over to her phone. She added a notation to her list: clothing store. If this was going to be a destination, there should be clothes available for emergencies. Not wedding dresses, though if they got far enough along, a wedding dress store would be wonderful; bridal parties could come to shop for dresses and spend time at the spa she'd previously added to her list. But if a guest damaged their outfit, or forgot a tie…

And if people were coming for weekends together, they might like a T-shirt or hoodie with the town's name on it.

In a rare moment of doubt, she wondered if this was going to work.

The place looked like a postcard. Its days of prosperity had left a town of beautiful brick and wooden homes, but many needed attention. Abigail insisted that was being taken care of. And the less attractive homes, the poorer ones, were literally on the other side of the train tracks that used to lead to the old mill.

They needed to include this part of town in the plans somehow.

The churches and the town green were all perfect for their plan. Tomorrow they were supposed to check out the mill and see what needed to be done there to make it the event venue they needed.

There were still things the town required to make this a success, and a year wasn't enough time to get them all done. She had plans for beyond the year. A spa, definitely. And more restaurants. But also, for the wedding part, the support industries like a bakery, a florist, catering, decorating...and for other visitors, activities, things for people to do. Winter was coming, and for that they'd want hikes, cross-country ski trails and other outdoor events. Horses for riding and sleigh rides? Maybe a tour of antiques stores in the area. Were there maple syrup farms around? That would be great in the spring. It was probably too cold for wineries...

She reined in her imagination. This was beyond her brief, so that would be up to other people to realize. Part of the beauty of her idea about making Carter's Crossing a destination for all things romance related was that romantic weekends didn't require the dresses and catering that a wedding did. They didn't need to have the mill finished and ready to go. But it would require more than leaves turning color and a pretty stream.

It would require a lot of community support, and that brought her mind back to Nelson. She'd found him setting up a seat in her head more often than she wanted him to this evening.

Yes, he was attractive. That sweater he'd worn to dinner had been even more flattering than the scrubs had been. He was obviously fit, and the color made his eyes look very blue...but she didn't need to dwell on that. More important, he was not a fan of what she was doing.

Or of hers.

She couldn't help wondering why. His grandmother said it was time to get over it, so something had happened. His wife died? Something went terribly wrong at a wedding? His wedding? His wife died at their own wedding?

She shook her head. Nelson was not her problem, and they should have no issue keeping out of each other's way. She was planning for romance and setting up the support network for romantic events. Overgrown pets like Tiny shouldn't play a part, and she couldn't imagine anything that would take her to the animal clinic.

Nelson was on edge as he made his way into the clinic on Monday morning, running late. He wasn't happy about the plans his grandmother had for Carter's Crossing, he wasn't happy about the woman who was here to help with them and he wasn't happy about the talk he'd had with his grandmother last night.

If any out-of-state cars pulled into his parking lot today, he wouldn't offer assistance unless asked, and even then, the only help he'd give them would be to direct them right out of town.

Okay, that was overkill, but he was unsettled, and hadn't slept well, old dreams popping up out of the depths of his subconscious to poke at him with reminders of just how badly he'd behaved. He didn't need that, he knew, and strived every day to be a different guy.

He wasn't looking forward to the talk he'd be hearing at work today, either. Gossip flew around a small town. Now that Ms. Van Delton had arrived, he expected the news about Romance Central would be everywhere by noon.

His assistant and receptionist were already at the clinic: Judy would check on any animals they were keeping on-site, and Kailey would prepare their schedules for the day. They were chatting when he came in from the back but stopped as soon as they heard him.

The news had traveled even more quickly than he expected. He didn't want to hear it.

"Morning, Judy, Kailey. Anything I need to know?"

He hoped they knew he meant related to work only.

"The Fletchers were hoping you could come out and see one of their pigs sometime today." Kailey said. Kailey was ten years older than he was and tended to believe she needed to keep him in line. She could keep their clients in line, as well, so he endured the fact that sometimes she thought she was in charge. "You don't have anything booked after two, so I told them you probably could."

Nelson nodded. The Fletchers had a small farm and orchard. It wasn't far from his own property out there, so he could swing by his place when he was done.

"Did you two have a nice weekend?" Nelson didn't want them asking about his grandmother's plans, so he steered the conversation in a different direction. He checked the list of appointments he had till two, mentally preparing what he'd need.

"Sure," Kailey said. "You had Tiny yesterday?"

He'd left his notes on the desk for Kailey. "Habanero sauce this time. I didn't ask why she had it."

Kailey rolled her eyes. "Mavis has been watching the Food Network again."

Judy was quiet. With her slight build and fair coloring, she could vanish into the back of the clinic without anyone noticing. She was more than competent in her work, and she didn't usually talk a lot, but she was so quiet that he wondered if he'd offended or scared her somehow.

After his interaction with Ms. Van Delton, he began to wonder if he was coming across as overbearing without realizing it. Again.

"Didn't I hear you were going out with Harvey this weekend?" He was trying to be one of the gang, just chatting around the watercooler. The metaphoric watercooler.

The two women exchanged glances.

Nelson felt like he'd stepped in it somehow.

"What? What did I say? Did you break up?"

Kailey shook her head. "No." She winked at Judy. "I'd say they were the opposite of breaking up."

Nelson looked at Judy. "Should I ask?"

Judy flushed. "We— I— I mean, we didn't want to make a big deal of it."

Nelson was puzzled. "A big deal about what?"

Judy looked at the floor with a smile crossing her face. "He asked me to move in with him."

Nelson still didn't see the problem. "That's good, right?"

Judy nodded.

"And you don't want to make a big deal out of it because…?" He was out of his depth here.

Judy was still looking at the ground, grinding the toe of her shoe into the floor.

Kailey sighed. "She doesn't want to rub it in."

Nelson looked over at Kailey. "Rub what in? Where?"

Kailey rolled her eyes. "They're getting serious. Like, maybe soon walking-down-the-aisle serious."

Nelson rolled his hand, hoping Kailey would soon get to the point, since Judy must have run out of words.

"Nelson, everyone knows what happened to you. We don't want to make you uncomfortable."

Nelson stepped back. Wow, way to suddenly make him uncomfortable.

"I wasn't, not till you said that."

He paused and braced his hands on his hips.

"Judy, I'm very happy for you. And if Harvey pops the question, I'll be happier. And I hope you have a lovely wedding and live happily-ever-after. If you want to."

Kailey opened her mouth and he held up his hand to stop her.

"I'm not some fragile, broken person here. Yeah, I know my wedding didn't happen. It doesn't mean I want everyone else to be miserable, or that I'm opposed to people dating and being happy together, and I don't need my staff avoiding 'sensitive' topics when I'm around to support my fragile ego. Okay?"

Judy nodded, and headed back to prepare for their first appointments. Kailey, of course, couldn't let it go.

"If you don't want us thinking you're still heartbroken, maybe you should start dating again. Or, I don't know, stop avoiding anything related to weddings."

Nelson threw up his hands. "I missed one wedding because

my horse had colic!" He looked at her expression. "Seriously, you think I faked it? Unbelievable."

He stomped back to help Judy. He hadn't realized missing one wedding—*one!*—when his horse was sick had started rumors that he was now a bitter misanthrope.

Sometimes he hated small towns.

"Wow," Mariah said.

Abigail had brought her to the old mill. The place had been shut down for a couple of years, and the outside of the building was industrial, but the setting…incredible. Harking back to the original structure, the building sat beside the river that flowed through the town. The trees surrounding the mill and growing on the hillside behind it wore garlands of yellow, orange and vivid red, the notes of evergreens adding lowlights in contrast.

The natural surroundings were at their peak, helping to sell the mill as a romantic venue. Unfortunately, the mill itself was lacking that natural beauty.

Any of it.

Still, Mariah could look past the gray metal siding. It was a big building, and the parking lot, though untended, also had plenty of room. What could happen from there depended on how much Abigail was willing to invest.

"The location is perfect." Mariah paused.

Abigail nodded. "I couldn't have picked a better time to bring you here, but I know the building is not anywhere close to what it needs to be. Let's look inside. I had the place assessed, and structurally, it's still sound. But it will need a complete refit to make it what we need."

Mariah followed her to a door. It squeaked, but less in a "you're about to die" creepy way and more in the annoying, needing grease way. Mariah hoped the place hadn't been left to deteriorate.

It hadn't.

Dust motes were dancing in the sunlight coming through

the windows, high up. Along the far end, metal stairs led to a second level. Where they stood, the ceiling soared above them, heavy wooden beams at the near end, morphing into steel beams as the space had expanded over its lifetime.

Space. Lots of empty space.

Mariah circled around. She could picture rows of chairs with an aisle to a chuppah, or an arch, where couples could make their vows. Or remake them. Over there they could have a place for the reception with a big dance area, and a kitchen back under the second floor. Upstairs, offices or rooms for the wedding parties to prepare.

Dances, anniversaries, parties—this space could handle them all. She crossed to one of the few windows on the first-floor level and saw the river outside. If they had sliding doors to open here when the weather was warmer…maybe they could clear some space behind the building for an outdoor patio, as well.

She turned to Abigail.

"No machinery?"

Abigail shook her head. "We had everything that could be salvaged sold off. It was added to the pension fund."

Mariah looked around again. She wasn't an engineer, or an architect, but she could imagine that refitting this space would be expensive. At least, to make it fully functional and anything close to what Mariah was imagining.

"The place has enormous potential." Mariah said, carefully.

"And needs enormous work." Abigail sighed. "I'm inquiring about an architect to come and prepare plans, but I wanted your input into what we need here. What do you imagine this place like?"

Mariah's eyes swept the space again.

"You'll need an industrial kitchen—assuming this would be the place to host receptions, parties, dances, et cetera. I don't imagine there's any place with that capability in town now?"

Abigail shook her head. "We only have a diner, one 'nicer' restaurant and the pizza and sub parlor. None of those are designed for catering large events. Anyone local has to travel to Oak Hill, and it's not that impressive once you do."

Mariah considered.

"You need the space to be flexible—for services, meals, all with different numbers of guests. I wouldn't dream of guiding your architect, but I had thought it might be nice if, say, the kitchen was back there, where there's a second floor, and over it could be offices, rooms for the wedding party to get ready on-site, and then have the events in this space where we could possibly keep these high ceilings."

Abigail nodded. "That makes sense to me. I hadn't thought of all that."

"And, if we're dreaming big, imagine sliding doors on the wall facing the river. The view would be incredible, and when the weather cooperated, we could open them up, bring all that in."

Abigail smiled at her. "And we have to do something to the exterior. Would we want outdoor space, for more than parking anyway? Maybe around back?"

Mariah cocked her head. "Are you reading my mind?"

"I hope not. That would be terribly uncomfortable, I'm sure."

Biting the bullet before her imagination got away from her, Mariah decided to be frank.

"It's going to be expensive. I don't know how much you're willing to invest."

Abigail examined the space with a narrowed gaze. "I'll have to see what the architect comes up with. My pockets are undoubtedly shallower than your grandfather's, but I'm willing to do a lot."

Mariah looked around, looking at more of the details. She and Abigail had walked around the interior, but they hadn't left footprints. She could see dust motes in the air, but they weren't breathing in dust and musty smells.

"You've been maintaining this place, haven't you?"

Abigail nodded. "Yes, I have. It was the place that built Carter's Crossing. I hope it can still do that, with a bit of work."

Mariah wondered, for the first time seriously, just how much money Abigail Carter did have. Mariah's grandfather was paying her own salary for this year, while she worked to makeover Carter's Crossing. Abigail was providing room and board, so that Mariah could spend all her time working on this plan. She'd assumed they wanted to do this on a shoestring.

Mariah worked with large and small wedding budgets, so she hadn't been concerned with the idea of going more cheap and cheerful than all out.

But she could only imagine the cost for the renovations on this building. Abigail's home, and the maintenance it would require, wasn't cheap, either.

She also wondered, not for the first time, why her grandfather was doing this. He'd sold Mariah on the idea as a challenge, an apprenticeship. But what was her grandfather getting out of this? Why was he helping an old friend, one who called him Gerry?

Abigail was still a beautiful woman. Perhaps she and her grandfather—

Mariah put a brake on those thoughts. None of that had to do with her job. And she was sure her grandfather wouldn't want her speculating on his past.

Abigail turned to Mariah. "Can you write up a list of everything you think we'd need for me to give to the architect? What things we must have, what we'd like to have and what we might even dream of, if we were to go a little crazy? We can give that to him, have him come and look around and see what we can do."

Mariah nodded. "That's not a problem. I've done weddings in a lot of different spaces, and I have my own ideas of what works best. And what doesn't. Coming up with a list like that will be easy."

Abigail sighed. "It's going to take a while, though, isn't it? Now that I've decided on this, I'm anxious to get going."

"As it happens," Mariah teased her, "I have some ideas about that, as well."

Nelson pulled the van into the drive of the old farm. His old farm now. The house was boarded up, but the barn was still functional. In the paddock outside, he counted the five horses.

He parked the van by the barn and made his way into the building. He heard the hoofbeats of the animals coming in the open side door.

One brown head was already bobbing at him as he pulled out a bale of hay, setting it down in the aisle.

He rubbed the horse's forehead, and the horse butted his head against him.

"Yeah, yeah. Hay is coming. You guys behaving?"

Most of them were in the barn now. Nelson ran his gaze over them, checking that they were looking alert, moving smoothly, their hair lying flat and their eyes bright.

He pulled a pocketknife out and slit open the hay bale. Two more heads pushed over the top rail of the big pen.

When he'd decided to use this place for rescued horses, he'd wanted a space that was low maintenance, but provided the animals with shelter, as well as the freedom to enjoy their life without additional restrictions.

Half the barn had been made into a large pen, or box stall, with an open doorway to the paddock. There was a water trough, self-filling, and he augmented the grass with hay and grain as needed.

The rest of the barn included a tack room, feed room and smaller stalls in case the horses needed to be segregated. Nothing fancy, but a safe place for horses that needed it.

Nelson greeted each eager horse, and then tossed hay into the manger. He held one flake in his hands, and finally, the oldest and slowest member of his herd came forward, nudging

Nelson with his gray muzzle. Nelson gripped his halter and carefully examined the yellowed teeth, making sure he was still able to eat.

"You're holding on there, Sparky. You make sure these other guys behave."

The final member of the herd hesitated in the doorway. Nelson kept his movements slow, and his gaze away from the chestnut watching him with white-rimmed eyes.

"So, Sparky, how's the new guy doing?"

Sparky took another bite of hay.

"Yeah, we'll let him settle in a little longer. You tell him he's safe here. Maybe next week I'll be able to spend some time with him. Just don't let him talk about weddings, okay?"

Mariah entered the kitchen and found Nelson walking through with a basket of apples. She paused.

He flicked a glance her way. "Delivery for Grandmother."

Mariah narrowed her eyes. That tone—yeah, that tone was for her. She was about to respond in kind, when she pulled in a breath.

She wanted to make this plan for Carter's Crossing work. Not just for herself, though that was certainly a big reason. She wanted to do it for Abigail, who was so determined to keep the town alive. And for her grandfather, who had sent her here for his own reasons.

She didn't need to antagonize anyone. Undoubtedly, she'd step on some toes somewhere in this process, but Nelson was Abigail's grandson. He would carry influence in this community. Her plans might not directly affect a veterinary practice, but he was someone in this town. Being on good terms with him would be smart.

Plus, she had been a little…maybe not exactly rude, but a little short. Curt. Testy. And that hadn't been on him. It was a conditioned response from the behavior of other men, but she should clear the air.

However, if he responded like a jerk, she would happily put him in the group with those others and feel free to be curt in the future.

"I'm afraid I wasn't very…gracious when we first met."

He'd taken the apples into a pantry. He turned and stared at her. Yeah, he hadn't expected that.

"Tiny had got away from me, or he wouldn't have been in your face like that. I understand that not everyone likes dogs. And Tiny is big."

She rolled her eyes. Okay, he was heading straight into the holding pen where "those guys" resided in her estimation.

"I told you, I'm not afraid of dogs. I was startled. And I've had my ability to navigate questioned too often."

He cocked his head. "Do strangers need to offer direction to you frequently?"

Oh, he was in that pen now, and he was going to be the leader of the misogynistic pack.

She glared at him. "Drop me in the middle of the Pacific with only a sextant and a watch and I could tell you where I was and navigate to the nearest safe landfall. However, it seems to be a concept many men can't handle, that I can find my way around without possessing a Y chromosome."

"Wouldn't you need a boat?"

She eyed him suspiciously. He was leaning against the counter now, smirking.

"I can find my way on land, as well, without a boat."

"But if I was dropping you in the middle of the Pacific with only a sextant, you might drown before you found your way to that safe landing."

"Seriously? That's what you're taking out of this? I tell you I'm a proficient navigator, and you want to nitpick the semantics?"

"Well, I wasn't going to out-navigate you but maybe I've got a better sense of humor."

Oh, that had been a joke, had it?

"I have a great sense of humor."

"Right."

"I don't appreciate jokes about my navigational skills. They tend to be a cover for latent misogyny."

"Now you think I'm a misogynist?"

"I'm testing the hypothesis. So far all signs look good."

He stared at the ceiling, jaw tense.

"I think I have a good appreciation of women and what they are capable of. I grew up with Abigail Carter, and there's not much she can't do.

"But the other day? I find a car in my parking lot, out of state, when the clinic is closed. The driver has a map open on her tablet in front of her. I would have offered help to anyone, with or without a gender. It's how I was raised."

Mariah opened her mouth, then closed it.

When you put it that way...

"I'm sorry." She could see she'd surprised Nelson again. "I grew up on a boat."

"In the middle of the Pacific?"

She ignored him.

"My mother grew up sailing. My dad didn't. But if we came into a marina with my mother at the helm, every man within hailing distance would come to 'assist,' yelling directions and basically assuming she was incompetent. That did not happen when my dad was at the wheel, though he was the one who'd need help. And even though I spent my life on a boat and was a better navigator than either of my brothers, that bias was still there.

"It's slowly getting better in the sailing community, but I admit, I'm a little testy about that. In this case, I wasn't looking at the map to find out where to go—seriously, this is a small town. It's not that difficult to navigate. I'd just got some ideas buzzing through my brain and I was trying to find the nearest railway stations and airfields. I was caught up in that and didn't realize how it would look to someone else."

He'd been teasing her, for a moment, and she'd felt that they could maybe be friends. He'd had reason to be upset by what she'd accused him of, and he'd let it slide. But now she could see his face close off as he pushed himself to stand.

"Fine. If you see Grandmother, tell her the Fletchers sent the apples."

Right. He wasn't a fan of this wedding/romance idea.

"Why are you opposed to your grandmother's plan?" Would anything change his attitude on that?

"It doesn't matter." His voice was flat.

Sure it didn't.

"Are you going to fight it?" Mariah wasn't sure what he could do, but if he was opposed, she needed to find out. Find out and defend against it.

He paused at the kitchen door. "My grandmother knows how I feel. I would never do anything to hurt her. I'm not going to get involved in this one way or the other. I'm never going to be part of it, but I'm also not going to stand in the way."

Mariah wished that reassured her. She was afraid that his attitude would affect other people in town. And without knowing why he felt this way, there was nothing she could do to offset that reaction.

"She's investing in this, time and money," Mariah said. "I'm going to make sure it works for her."

He looked at her, something sad in his eyes.

"I'm sure you will." He turned and left.

Mariah sagged against the counter. Well, she didn't think he was going to hate her for her response to his offer of assistance in his parking lot. He was going to hate her because she was helping his grandmother make Carter's Crossing a wedding and romance venue.

Somehow, not the improvement she'd been hoping for.

CHAPTER THREE

TUESDAY NIGHTS WERE darts nights.

In a town the size of Carter's Crossing, these were important events. Unless there was a birthing emergency, or a horse with colic, Tuesday nights found Nelson at the Goat and Barley with his friends.

The Goat and Barley was halfway between Carter's and Oak Hill. It was a pub, with a halfway decent menu and an excellent selection of draft beer. It was far enough from Carter's that not everyone would know what you'd done, and anyone who came from Carter's wasn't wanting to talk about you because you might talk about them.

In theory. Nelson was pretty sure his grandmother still knew everything that went on here, but she didn't say anything, and he kept his own confidences. He wasn't doing anything beyond playing darts poorly and drinking some beer anyway.

He leaned back in his chair. He and his buddy Dave had just been soundly beaten in darts. Same old same old. While their two friends from Oak Hill were taking a turn, Nelson had his chance to tell Dave about the conversation with his staff yesterday morning.

After his talk with the wedding, sorry, romance planner, he wanted some sympathetic feedback.

He swallowed a mouthful of beer and picked up an onion ring. Dave was watching the hockey scores over the bar.

"Hey!"

Dave turned back. "Hey, yourself."

He'd known Dave since grade school. Maybe before. Long enough ago that they knew each other well.

"I gotta tell you what Kailey and Judy said yesterday."

"This doesn't have anything to do with tapeworms, does it? 'Cause that was just gross, man."

Nelson grinned. Dave was surprisingly squeamish. They'd gone through high school biology together with Nelson dissecting while Dave wrote up notes. Without looking.

"I could tell you about the Fletchers' pig, if you wanted. But no, it wasn't anything to do with work. Did you know Judy and Harvey were getting serious?"

Judy and Harvey were a few years younger than Dave and him, but that didn't matter much now that they were long out of high school.

Dave stopped with his glass halfway to his mouth. "I knew they were going out."

"He asked her to move in with him."

Dave took a careful swallow. "That's your big news?"

Nelson frowned. Dave was looking at him, not with a "hey, that's interesting" face but more like he was waiting for Nelson to start talking about tapeworms.

"No, but Judy and Kailey didn't want to tell me. They were afraid I'd be upset."

"Were you?"

Nelson threw his hands up. "Why would I be? I mean, I like Judy fine, she's a great assistant, even if she hardly talks, but it's nothing to me if she moves in with Harvey."

"That's good," Dave said. "Why are you telling me? I'm not interested in Judy, either."

"They, Kailey and Judy, thought I was too fragile or something. That if someone talks about weddings or engagements I'll freak out."

Dave was still watching him carefully. "You're okay, though?"

Nelson pointed a finger at his friend. "You think that, too. You think I still haven't gotten over it."

Dave shrugged.

Nelson ran his fingers through his hair. "What is it with people in this town? It's been three years! I'm not going to burst into tears if someone gets married! I'm not upset."

"You kind of seem like it now."

"That's just because everyone thinks I'm a romance invalid. I'm fine!"

"Okay," Dave said soothingly.

Nelson frowned at him. "If you say 'there, there, now' I'm going to hit you."

Dave grinned. "Okay, you're fine."

"Of course I'm fine! What is wrong with people here?"

Dave grabbed his own onion ring and took a bite. "You haven't dated anyone since you've been back."

"I brought Rachel to the concert last year."

Dave rolled his eyes. "You and Rachel have as much chemistry as you and I do. Less. She's been your backup date since you were kids. I mean, you each drove there separately, and your grandmother sat between you."

Nelson crossed his arms. "Still counts."

He knew he was splitting hairs. He'd known Rachel so long as a friend that he sometimes had to remind himself she was a woman. It wasn't that she wasn't pretty, because she was, in a nice, good girl way, but there'd never been a spark between them.

Dave pointed his half-eaten onion ring at him. "And you skipped out on the wedding."

"My horse had colic!"

His voice was loud enough that patrons at the bar turned around to see where the sound was coming from.

Nelson lowered his voice. "Sparky was sick. Colic is serious. I had to deal with him."

"Really?"

"Why would I lie?"

Dave shrugged. "Before the wedding, someone said they bet you'd weasel out with some excuse."

Nelson grit his teeth. "The horse was sick."

"Okay, I believe you, I promise. But that's what everyone thinks."

Nelson let out a breath. "Sometimes this town drives me nuts."

Dave finished his onion ring, looking carefully at Nelson.

"So you'd be okay if I told you something."

"I'd be okay. Fine. Ecstatic. Whatever."

"Jaycee and I are getting serious."

This time it was Nelson with the glass paused halfway to his mouth.

"You and Jaycee? Really? How did I not know this?"

Dave shrugged. "You know how I've been spending Friday nights taking cooking classes?"

Nelson narrowed his gaze. "With Jaycee?"

Dave nodded.

"And you didn't tell me because you thought I'd curl up in the corner?"

Dave shrugged. "You're not going to do that, right?"

Nelson looked away. "You really think I wouldn't be happy for you?"

"You're right. I'm sorry." Dave shoved the basket of onion rings over to him in apology. "That's what Jaycee said, too."

"Jaycee is a smart woman. Except, of course, for that whole getting serious with you part."

Dave grinned. "She is smart. And don't tell her she shouldn't be with me. I know that, but she hasn't figured it out yet."

Nelson looked around the bar. "So how many other people have been hiding their dating lives in case I couldn't handle it?"

"I'll tell Jaycee to spread the word. Are you good if she joins us next Tuesday, then?"

"Absolutely."

He didn't mind, not really. But he had enjoyed his time with just the guys. Obviously, though, that wasn't something he could share, or he'd have people running for cover any time he showed up, expecting his breakdown.

Wait till word got out about the Romance Center in Carter's. He hadn't heard anyone talking about that yet. On the other hand, apparently, no one would talk to him anyway.

The next wedding-type event this town had, he'd better be there front and center or everyone would believe he was permanently damaged.

Small towns.

Mariah looked around. This was the power center of Carter's Crossing.

It was also the parlor of Mavis Grisham's house. Mariah was reintroduced to Tiny. Tiny apparently considered the encounter at the clinic parking lot to be the beginning of a wonderful friendship. Mariah did her best to push him away while not offending Mavis.

Fortunately, Abigail was on top of this as much as everything else she did. She told Tiny to sit, and he did.

"Good afternoon. We can finally start talking about our plan for Carter's Crossing. It's happening, so let's get things going."

The room quieted as Abigail spoke.

"I think you all know by now that the new face here belongs to Mariah Van Delton. She's been loaned to us for a year to help us implement our plan to make Carter's Crossing a wedding destination."

There was a smattering of applause, and some nods in Mariah's direction.

"Mariah has just arrived, but she's already provided valuable insight, and has, in fact, expanded the original vision we came up with. So, Mariah, why don't you share your idea with us?"

All eyes turned to Mariah, including those of Tiny. His ears even perked up.

Mariah set down her cup of tea.

"Thank you for welcoming me here. As Abigail said, I came to help you develop Carter's Crossing into a wedding destination. I've been a wedding planner for five years, so I have inside knowledge of what people expect when they book a wedding."

She paused and glanced around the room. She was the center of attention. Tiny cocked his head, waiting for her to continue.

"Unfortunately, there are some major drawbacks to your plan."

Everyone froze.

"I know Abigail is going to convert the old mill, but it's not ready yet, and it's going to take a while. Months at the minimum."

Heads nodded. Tiny cocked his head in the other direction.

"As well, when people come here for a wedding, they'll have guests. This is a little far for people to drive from the city, enjoy a wedding and return in the same day. Currently, there's no hotel or other place for these guests to stay."

Now people began to talk. Abigail raised her hand. "She knows our plans, everyone. Let her finish."

Tiny lay down with a sigh.

"Thank you, Abigail. I know, you have every intention of setting up B&B's, but they also aren't ready yet.

"In any case, that will limit the size of weddings that can be put on here. And it's okay. This isn't going to be the place where the big, five-hundred-guest weddings take place. This isn't that kind of destination."

Mariah heard the rattle of a spoon on a teacup, and Tiny's eyes closed.

"So the idea I had was that instead of making Carter's Crossing a wedding destination, we make it a Center for Romance."

She paused, but the silence was complete.

"Not *just* weddings. Romantic getaways. A place to come to make the perfect proposal. Anniversaries, vow renewals… and, also, weddings. In fact, if someone came here to propose, it could naturally lead to having the wedding here."

She could feel the attention focused on her.

"The benefits of this kind of plan include taking advantage of the four seasons' worth of beauty that Carter's Crossing offers. Most weddings are summertime events, but if we're a Center for Romance, we can have people here year-round, not just in the summer for a wedding.

"Another advantage is that we don't have to wait until the mill is ready to get things underway. What I'd like to propose is that we plan some events to happen on this upcoming Valentine's Day. Probably involving local people, considering the time and hospitality limits, but if we can get some publicity for this, then people will start looking at Carter's Crossing when they think of a place to go for a romantic getaway. We'll have the initial infrastructure here to support our plans, and we'll have some photos and experience already."

Mariah stopped. She hoped that was enough to get things rolling.

Heads turned now to Abigail. Tiny sat up and looked at Abigail, as well.

Abigail was smiling. "I think this idea is genius, but it will take all of us to make it work."

Heads started nodding, and voices murmured. Then the questions started.

"What kind of events? What would they require? What do we need to do?"

Mariah explained that without the B&Bs ready, they'd need to find romance among the people already in Carter's Crossing or surroundings. Mariah didn't know the area and didn't know the people. If they could find three events to stage for Valentine's Day, the whole package would be a manageable size, while still being large enough to attract attention.

Everyone loved the opportunity to assess the dating activity in town. Mariah heard the women discuss who was together, who'd broken up, who might be getting serious. She didn't know the names yet, but she would.

Mavis spoke up. "What about Gladys and Gord?"

Conversation ceased for a moment.

"It's their fiftieth wedding anniversary on Valentine's Day."

Mariah sat up straighter. "That would be wonderful. Celebrating that milestone would work beautifully. Do you know if they'd be interested in an anniversary party?"

Faces frowned at each other. "I don't know that Gord would want to pay for a big party. Now that the mill is closed—"

Abigail's clear voice spoke through the room. "These first events, for locals, are going to be paid for by the committee. Gord and Gladys won't have to pay for anything."

Eyes widened. Mavis said, "I'll talk to Gladys. I'll tell her we want her anniversary to be the first event for our plan, and then she won't think it's charity."

"Thank you, Mavis," Abigail said. "Now we just need two more romantic events."

"That went well," Abigail said as she and Mariah walked back to the Carter home. Fallen leaves crunched under their feet.

"I think the committee's offer to pay for the events helped a lot."

Abigail smiled. "It seems only fair. We need this to launch our plan, and we need local people to do that. Things have been difficult here, financially, so I—we don't want to make this a hardship."

Mariah looked at the woman walking beside her. She was coming to a better understanding of her partner in this endeavor.

"Tell me about this committee."

Abigail's eyebrows lifted. "That was the committee you just met."

"And what is their budget, so I know what we're spending on these events?"

Abigail shot her a sideways glance.

"I'm that part of the committee."

"And the budget is…" Mariah said.

Abigail shrugged elegantly. "What it needs to be."

Mariah shook her head. "You're investing a lot in this plan."

Abigail nodded. "I was raised to believe that the benefits my family gathered from the mill meant that we also had a responsibility to the town. I want to make sure Carter's Crossing survives."

Mariah wondered how much family pride was driving Abigail. This town was the Carter family's legacy.

"I had a thought," Abigail said. "What would you think, if this plan works, if we changed the name of the town to Cupid's Crossing?"

Mariah paused. "Could you—would you do that?"

Abigail nodded. "I could make it happen. I thought, along with the romance idea, if we had the name, and people could post letters, or use that address for events, it would help with the marketing."

"That sounds like an excellent idea."

Abigail nudged Mariah with her shoulder. "Together, we're going to hit this town so hard it won't know what's happened to it."

Nelson dried his hands and wandered back out to reception. Kailey and Judy were talking again. They paused when he came up to the desk, but at least they weren't looking guilty.

"Kailey, can you let the rescue people know they can pick up those two cats tomorrow? The usual after care. They should be ready for adoption within the week, just have a little bald spot."

Kailey made a note. "The rescue agency said to tell you they might have another horse needing help."

Nelson considered. "Any more details? I'm still getting the chestnut settled in, so if this one needs a lot of work, I'll have to change some fences at the farm."

Kailey shook her head. "No details, but I'll let you know once I hear. And, speaking of letting people know, why didn't you tell us the romance woman is staying with you?"

Nelson took a step back. "Hold on, no one is staying with me. Are you talking about Mariah Van Delton? Is she what you call a romance woman?"

Here it was. Word had spread.

Kailey crossed her arms. "You did know. And if she's staying with your grandmother, that's almost as good as staying with you."

Nelson could see a lot of ways that anything going on with his grandmother and her home had nothing to do with him. He refused to stay in the house exactly for that kind of reason. He didn't want to know everything his grandmother was up to, and he certainly didn't want her to know that much about him.

If he hadn't been concerned about her, living alone in that big house and refusing anything like help, he wouldn't even be staying in the carriage house.

And Mariah Van Delton? He wanted to stay as far away from her as possible.

"Why did you call her the romance woman?" He'd been surprised not to hear about this crazy plan of Mariah and his grandmother's before this, and had half hoped that meant they'd reconsidered.

Kailey rolled her eyes and even Judy gave him a skeptical look.

"Are you really trying to tell us you don't know what's going on?"

Nelson shrugged. "I heard a bit—just a bit," he defended

himself as Kailey's mouth opened. "And I hoped it would blow over."

Judy gave him a look of pity. "But you said…" Her voice trailed off. It was as much of a personal conversation as he'd had with her since he'd tried to convince them he wasn't a wounded misanthrope.

Apparently, it hadn't been that convincing.

"I'm all for romance, and love, and marriage, and kids, and the American dream, and whatever else. But I think emotional events are best left private."

Kailey turned to Judy. "Told you."

Nelson frowned. "Told you what?"

Kailey shrugged.

"I told Judy she should get Mariah to help her propose to Harvey on Valentine's Day."

"What?" Nelson had a hard time getting his brain wrapped around that. Judy was the quietest and shyest person he knew, so he couldn't picture her proposing. Especially not in an event engineered by Mariah. Because that event would be big and public and focus all kinds of attention on Judy.

"Yeah, I knew it was a long shot. But we need something for Mariah to set up for Valentine's Day. I've been married for years, so there's no chance for me."

"The Donaldsons are doing a vow renewal," Judy interrupted.

Nelson blinked. They were?

Kailey shook her head. "That's different. It's their fiftieth wedding anniversary on February fourteenth. Bert and I got married in June, and it's been seventeen years, so not a milestone."

Nelson could see his grandmother and her crew having their fingers all over the Donaldsons' anniversary. They'd probably talked the couple into it.

"Then there's the Valentine's Day event taken care of." That wasn't too bad. In fact, celebrating that major event was kind of nice.

Kailey shook her head. "We need two more events. We've been running through any couples in town who might be ready to celebrate something, and that's why I was nudging Judy."

Nelson looked at Judy, who was staring at the ground.

"I don't think Judy wants any nudging." Judy shook her head, so this time he figured he had it right.

Kailey sighed. "Okay. How about Dave and Jaycee?"

Nelson shook his head. "What Dave and Jaycee are doing is entirely up to Dave and Jaycee. I don't think Dave wants to make a spectacle out of their relationship, so why don't we focus on the animals here in Carter's Crossing and leave my grandmother and Ms. Van Delton to worry about their—plans?" He'd almost said *nonsense*.

He wasn't sure about the looks the two women were giving him, even though Kailey had turned around to her computer and Judy was heading back to check on the two cats he'd just spayed for the animal rescue.

"And for the record, if Judy decides to propose to Harvey, I'd be happy to hear about it."

A slight exaggeration, but he didn't need to be handled with kid gloves.

"So what do you think?" Dave asked Nelson.

Dave had stopped by the carriage house before they met for darts. He'd told Nelson he had a question for him.

Nelson was still processing the backstory to the question.

"You and Jaycee are that serious."

Dave rolled his eyes. "I told you that at darts last week."

"You said you were serious. You didn't say you were shopping for a ring."

A goofy grin crossed Dave's face. "When you know, you know."

Nelson considered. Dave and Jaycee had grown up here in

Carter's, so they'd known each other since they were kids. He didn't think they'd been dating that long, but they'd been friends for years.

"Why not give her the ring some other time than Christmas?"

Dave shook his head. "We talked about it. We can't afford to spend a lot, so the ring is our Christmas present to each other."

"Then why are you asking if you need to get her something else?"

"Because I think she's going to get me something else, and then I'll look like a jerk if I didn't do the same."

Nelson wiped down his countertop. He'd just finished his dinner when Dave stopped by. The neatness he'd had to incorporate into his work spilled over into his personal life. He liked things clean and put away.

"Well, since the ring is a piece of jewelry that she wears, not you, that seems more like a present for her anyway. But if you really want to cover your bases, get her something."

Dave slapped a hand down on the freshly wiped countertop. "But if she didn't get me something, she's going to be mad. It'll make her look bad, and like I'm not listening to her."

Nelson nudged his hand away and rewiped the spot on the countertop.

"You didn't let me finish. You get her something, but don't put it under the tree. You keep it hidden away somewhere and pull it out if needed."

Dave frowned. "Okay, but what if she didn't get me anything? I return it? What if she finds out about that?"

It was a small town. News usually worked its way around.

Nelson lifted a finger. "No, you save it for the next time you're supposed to give her something. Like Valentine's Day."

Dave pumped his fist.

"Genius, man. You are a freaking genius."

Nelson thought of the work he'd done to get his veterinary degree. The animals he'd saved. And Dave was impressed with a bit of gift-giving chicanery. People were weird.

* * *

"Thanks for inviting me to join you," Mariah said, looking at Jaycee driving the vehicle, and then Rachel in the back seat of Jaycee's car.

Jaycee shot a look at Rachel. Mariah held in a smile.

She'd been pleased when the two women had invited her to join them for darts night. There were a limited number of women her age in town, and fewer were single women. She'd been working hard, but it was nice to take a break.

Not to mention that she was good at darts. Darts were a staple at so many places around the globe.

The whole town was buzzing with the plans for Valentine's Day. And Jaycee was dating someone, so Mariah suspected Jaycee had a plan she wanted the Romance Committee to assist with.

It didn't hurt that Jaycee had long dark hair offset by golden skin and would look fantastic in promotional materials.

Mariah needed a couple more good events. Her grandfather had promised to provide publicity, if she gave him something worth publicizing. So far everyone who'd approached her wanted a romantic dinner or getaway. Which was fine, but not really the kind of big thing they needed to kick-start their plan for Carter's Crossing.

The vow renewal was sweet, but they also needed to appeal to a younger age demographic. A dinner date was nice, but currently, what Carter's Crossing had to offer along that line wasn't going to bring people in from the city.

She needed something big. Something splashy.

She hoped Jaycee had something more like that in mind.

"Go on, tell her," Rachel said to Jaycee.

"Okay, I hate feeling like I'm using you, but I am glad you're coming along with us tonight because this is the first time I've joined Dave and—"

"Jaycee, cut to the chase!" Rachel shoved Jaycee's shoulder.

"Dave and I are getting engaged this Christmas."

Mariah waited. A Christmas engagement was not a Valentine's Day event.

"We know we want to get married, but we don't have a lot of cash right now. We're getting the ring for Christmas—that's all we're doing for gifts, because we're saving up for a house, and the business..."

Rachel poked her friend again. "Come on, Jaycee. Get to the point. She doesn't need to know all these details right now."

Jaycee huffed a breath as she turned into the parking lot of a brightly lit pub called the Goat and Barley. She pulled the car into an open slot, and then turned to Mariah.

"We're doing everything low-key, because of money, but I would love to have a big engagement party, so that everyone knows. Our first date was on Valentine's Day. I wondered if the Romance Committee might make an engagement party one of their events."

Okay, this was much more what Mariah needed. If she and Abigail could come up with a big enough venue, they could probably get by without professional catering, if they found a good band, and made it mostly about the entertainment. Wait, what about a skating party? Bonfires, a dance...

She realized Jaycee and Rachel were waiting to hear her response.

"Sorry, guys, my brain started firing. This might be just what we need. Do you have anything in mind? Would you want to have the proposal then, too?"

Jaycee shook her head. "Nothing in mind, just having everyone come to celebrate. I don't think Dave's mom approves, so maybe a party will get her on board. And no, I'm not waiting a minute longer than I have to for that ring. If we could afford it now, I'd be wearing it already."

Mariah could believe it. Jaycee's smile, the glow in her dark eyes, the way her fingers were tapping on the steering wheel: everything said she was happy and excited and in love.

Rachel looked just as thrilled for her friend.

Mariah wanted to throw Jaycee and her fiancé a party. She wanted to give them a chance to enjoy themselves with the support of their community, especially if his family wasn't completely on board.

She held up one gloved hand. "It's not my decision alone. And there are things to work out. But it sounds like a great idea to me."

"Yay!" Jaycee and Rachel high-fived.

"Don't say anything till I've talked to Abigail, okay?"

Jaycee pouted. "I have to tell Dave."

Mariah frowned at her. "Can he keep a secret?"

"Of course he can."

Mariah wasn't reassured by the doubtful look on Rachel's face.

Before she could suggest leaving Dave out of the loop, Jaycee squealed. "There they are!"

She flung her door open and raced to meet her Dave. Mariah watched her as she threw herself into the arms of an attractive blond man who got out of the driver's side of a pickup truck, and then stopped, halfway out of the car.

Dave wasn't alone. And she knew the guy he was with.

Rachel spoke from behind her. "That's Dave, in case you didn't guess. And you know Nelson, right? He's Abigail's grandson. You must have run into him at her place."

Mariah pasted on a smile. It became a lot more genuine when she saw Nelson spot her, and frown. Oh, this was going to be a fun night.

CHAPTER FOUR

THE FIVE OF them entered the Goat and Barley. They found a table, and Nelson avoided Mariah, sitting by Rachel. She nudged him with her shoulder.

"You playing darts?" She was holding back a grin, brown eyes sparkling.

Nelson had done complicated surgery on expensive thoroughbreds without making a wrong move, but he couldn't hit a bull's-eye to save himself. It didn't stop him from trying most nights.

Not tonight, though. He didn't need Mariah getting the best of him. Not when he was absolutely, one hundred percent certain she was a ringer. And no one else caught it.

He was certain when she shrugged and admitted she had played before, while not claiming any special skill. He was certain when Dave offered to play for the next round of drinks. He thought of warning Dave but decided to let him find out what Mariah was really like.

After this, Dave might listen to him if the time came to warn him about something more serious. He wished he'd had someone to talk to when he'd been up to his eyeballs in wedding plans. Someone other than Sherry Anstruthers.

Mariah and Rachel teamed up against Dave and Jaycee. Rachel was almost as bad as Nelson was, but Nelson still would have bet his money on that team. And he was right. Mariah was an ace.

Dave bought the next round when they returned to the table. He was laughing, and making Mariah promise to play with him against the Oak Hill guys.

Nelson was quiet, watching Mariah charm his friends.

Dave shot him glances, and Rachel poked him in the ribs, both concerned with his uncharacteristically quiet behavior. He ignored them and took a break to hit up the men's room.

He took his time, trying to work out a plan of action.

This engagement party had raised all his suspicions. Jaycee blurted out that Mariah was going to throw an engagement party for Dave and her as soon as they'd met in the parking lot.

Dave was obviously surprised by the news. Jaycee had never been much for big parties, so obviously this was Mariah's idea. She needed more events for her Valentine's Day plans, so she'd roped Jaycee into it. He didn't know how she'd done it, or what she'd promised, but he knew how bad things like that could get. He'd been through this before.

He wasn't sure what to say. He hadn't shared all the details about the disastrous end to his wedding, and he didn't want to do so now. But he'd have to explain his problem with Mariah. He could see the worry on his friends' faces.

His reticence had probably contributed to the town's belief that he was still wounded from his aborted wedding ceremony. The truth was that he hadn't wanted anyone to know what a jerk he'd been. He'd hoped to avoid that. Rachel was the only one who knew most of the details, and she still didn't understand.

Why did his grandmother have to decide to make the town a wedding destination—no, a romance destination?

He stopped at the bar to get the next round. Rachel slipped into the seat beside him, strands of her long brown hair falling from her ponytail.

"What's up, Nelson?"

He turned to her, waiting for their drinks.

"Is it the wedding planner thing? Too soon?"

He crossed his arms. He knew exactly what everyone believed the problem was. That he was upset because of Mariah's job. Well, he was, but not the way they thought.

"It's been three years, Rachel. I'm over it."

He could see she didn't believe him. "I'm over being upset about it. But what happened was the result of a bad decision I made, based on bad advice I got. And that bad advice I got was from Mariah's boss."

Rachel's mouth dropped.

"Does she, I mean, does your grandmother—"

"Grandmother thinks Mariah deserves a chance. But I'm a little…skeptical."

Rachel's brows lowered. "I'm sorry, Nelson. I had no idea. Would you rather leave now?"

Part of him did. But he couldn't tell Rachel he didn't want to leave Mariah alone with Dave and Jaycee. Even he could see that would sound a little…paranoid, at best.

But Rachel hadn't been through what he'd been through. He was the one who'd gotten too wrapped up in plans, and he was the one who'd been advised by Mariah's boss that he was right, and that Zoey just had nerves.

He hadn't understood that Sherry's primary interest wasn't in making their wedding day something they'd always look back on and remember with happiness and joy. Sherry had been interested in her fees, her reputation and impressing the next potential client.

Nelson had been stupid and had made the wrong decision. He'd made it because he'd put his goals ahead of what Zoey wanted and needed. He didn't exempt himself from that. But he'd trusted Sherry and relied on her advice, not his own instincts. He thought they both bore blame.

He didn't think every wedding planner was evil. He wasn't that stupid. But he knew, absolutely, that Sherry was selfish and greedy. He'd heard Mariah say she'd learned everything from that same Sherry.

His grandmother thought Mariah deserved a chance. Nelson wasn't sure he agreed, but he'd promised not to interfere. And he wouldn't, unless Mariah's schemes were going to hurt people he cared about.

He finally told Rachel he was happy to stay. When she looked skeptical, he explained, "I need to do this, Rach. It's come to my attention that the people in this town think I missed that last wedding because I couldn't face it, not that Sparky really had colic."

Rachel looked guilty, and he shook his head.

"You, too? My horse was sick. I swear. But if I run away every time Mariah is around, those rumors are going to continue. I don't like her, but I'm not afraid of her. I'll stay and hang out with my friends."

Rachel chewed on her lip, but she didn't get a chance to respond before their drinks were slapped down on the bar top.

Nelson led the way back to their table, happy to see that Mariah had vanished.

It was too much to hope that she'd left, but at least he could enjoy his friends' company without her. Then he saw who she was talking to.

Harvey. Judy's Harvey.

It was a small town, but couldn't she insert herself into the life of someone other than the people he hung out with and worked with? Was it too much to ask?

Mariah wasn't surprised when a stranger asked if he could talk to her. It hadn't taken long to discover that she was known to everyone, and everyone knew why she was there.

This time the young man, named Harvey, had a good idea for her. He wasn't the first to approach her, but his idea was one she could work with.

She sympathized with the many people who'd been undergoing financial hardship and wanted to take their partners out for a dinner on Valentine's Day, but that wasn't what they needed right now as a Valentine's promotion.

She let Abigail know about all these requests, and each time she could see Abigail take that responsibility on her own shoulders.

Mariah was impressed by how hard Abigail was working to keep the town alive. And Mariah wanted to help. She was learning to like these people.

She caught a glare from Nelson.

Most of these people.

She wanted this romance plan to work, and to bring life and prosperity back to Carter's Crossing. She needed something better than a dinner out to promote the town. And Harvey had something better.

He wanted to propose to his girlfriend.

These days people didn't just go down on one knee or have a ring show up in a dessert to ask someone to marry them. Proposals had become elaborate, complicated and sometimes expensive. And often went viral.

A proposal that took advantage of what Carter's Crossing had to offer, things that other places didn't, was exactly the kind of event she needed.

Mariah didn't remember hearing about a Harvey when the committee had gone over the dating prospects in town, so she wasn't sure if she'd missed it, or this was one they didn't know about. In any case, she'd happily help Harvey with his proposal.

As always, she cautioned, "It's not just my decision in this. But it sounds really promising. I'd have to get approval, but assuming I did—"

Harvey had an anxious look on his face. "I want to surprise her. I don't want her to hear about it from someone else."

Mariah nodded. It was a valid concern, from her short experience in Carter's Crossing.

"I'll just talk to Abigail for now. But I can't approve this on my own."

"It's okay if Mrs. Carter knows. She'll be careful. But a lot of people talk in this town."

That was the truth.

"Assuming this all works out, what kind of proposal were you thinking of?"

Harvey chewed on a cuticle.

"I want something special. I want her to be able to tell all her friends about it. I want to show her that she's special."

That was sweet. And perfect.

"Why don't you tell me about her, what makes her so special and what it is that's special between the two of you? What you have in common that other people don't? We want it to be something unique, but also something she loves."

"Sure." Harvey stopped chewing. "Her name is Judy, and she's beautiful. She works at the veterinary clinic."

Mariah closed her eyes. No. Way. Another chance to bump into Nelson Carter? The man made a face like he'd sucked on lemons every time he saw her.

It was annoying. And provoking. And puzzling.

She'd decided she should avoid him as much as possible. And now she had two events that were going to impinge on him. She'd noticed his reaction when Jaycee blurted out about the engagement party. It hadn't exactly been a happy face.

And now a proposal for someone who worked for Nelson. Was this town really that small?

Harvey had stopped.

"Sorry, you were saying Judy works at the vet clinic?"

He nodded. "She's wonderful with animals. Loves them all, and they love her. She can't have a pet at home, because her sister is allergic, but once we get married, we can buy a house and have as many animals as she wants."

Harvey might not be the handsomest man in Carter's Crossing, but he was in the running for sweetest, Mariah thought.

"So are animals the bond that brought you together?"

His eyes widened. "Oh, no. Not that. We're both big fans of *The Walking Dead*. We love that show. We dress up for Halloween, and go to cons together…in fact, that's what I'd like to have for the proposal. Can we do a *Walking Dead* one?"

Mariah blinked, and blinked again. A zombie proposal.

Yeah, that wasn't what she'd been expecting.

The problem with small towns was that avoiding someone was almost impossible. Well, there were other problems, but this was the one troubling him now. In theory, a wedding or romance planner and a vet shouldn't cross paths often. But the odds were not shaking out in his favor.

It didn't help that his grandmother still expected him to join her for dinners that were no longer for two, but three. He would have liked to avoid them, but as much as he didn't like spending time with Mariah, he still wanted to know what she was up to, and who might be in the path of her impending explosions.

Not that it was much of a secret.

"Nelson." His grandmother caught his attention at the next dinner. Beef bourguignonne. Another dish he liked. Another one he couldn't properly enjoy with Mariah at the table. But he was eating it anyway.

"Yes, Grandmother?" She couldn't complain about him having a tantrum. He was eating, and he wasn't staring at Mariah. At least, not once he realized he was doing it.

"I'm not asking for your assistance, or involvement, but you are aware that Dave and Jaycee have asked to have an engagement party this Valentine's Day?"

He took a moment to make sure his voice was even.

"I heard that their engagement was being considered for one of your parties, yes."

Mariah narrowed her eyes at him. "It was Jaycee's suggestion."

Nelson believed that the words had come from Jaycee, but

he had suspicions as to where the idea had come from. Since it wasn't a question, he didn't respond.

"I had no idea their first date had been on Valentine's Day," Mariah continued, glaring at him with a laser focus. Was she reading his mind? No, or she'd be throwing something at him.

Grandmother interrupted the one-sided argument.

"As Dave's friend, we need to know if you're attending, and if you have any suggestions, or comments to offer. This is obviously not an endorsement of my plans," she added, the sarcasm unmistakable, "but it would be appreciated so that we can make this event something that they will both enjoy and remember."

Nelson heard the challenge. She'd said she wouldn't involve him, but it was an empty promise. In a town this small, people he knew would be part of the *Romance Lives in Carter's* thing she and Mariah had going. He couldn't boycott everything they did without hurting people he cared about and who cared about him.

And even if he'd wanted to avoid any event they came up with, he couldn't, because the town already believed he was still scarred from his own aborted wedding. He'd promised himself he wouldn't avoid the next wedding-type get-together.

With jaw gritted, he forced a smile. "Dave is my friend, and if he invites me to his party, of course I'll be there. As far as the event itself, Dave and Jaycee are small-town people. Our events are usually small-town, as well."

Mariah rolled her eyes. Grandmother stared at him under lowered brows.

What did they expect? It's not like he and Dave had ever discussed their dream engagement parties. He was willing to bet all the money his grandmother was investing in this project that Dave didn't have a Pinterest board on the topic.

"Those kinds of events aren't going to keep this town alive, Nelson."

He understood, but he didn't believe their town was going to survive big wedding plans, either.

He wasn't going to bring that up again. He and Grandmother had agreed to disagree.

Nelson had managed to finish his plate, so he stood.

"Dave and I play baseball in the summer, watch hockey in the winter, and drink beers and play darts on Tuesday nights. He doesn't like dressing up, and he hates broccoli. That's all I've got for you, so I'll clean up after myself and let the two of you get to work."

An hour later he was at his farm. The horses had all come into the indoor pen for the night, since temperatures were dropping. He checked that the barn was warm enough and fed them some hay. He noticed that the new chestnut stayed inside while Nelson was in the building now but wouldn't come to get any of the food while he was leaning on the rail.

He stayed where he was. The new guy needed to learn. His frustration with Mariah and his grandmother melted away as he watched his horses.

Sparky was the oldest, and needed the most attention to his physical care, but the chestnut was the most vulnerable right now. Nelson wanted to give him time with a nonaggressive human nearby, letting him know that not all people were bad, and not all of them would hurt him.

He watched his horses eat, rubbed necks and muzzles as they were offered and let the calm and quiet work on his perspective.

One party was not going to destroy the town, or his friends. He'd let Dave know he should feel free to refuse anything that made him uncomfortable. That would take care of him.

Maybe it was time for him to start working on the house here at the farm. If Mariah was living with Grandmother, he didn't need to stay so close. Maybe space would be good for both of them.

He thought he'd made over his life for the better, here in Carter's Crossing. He'd pulled back on his competitive, take-charge side, and found a life beyond his practice. But ever since

Mariah Van Delton had stopped in his parking lot, things had gotten complicated.

He wished she really had been lost.

The next Tuesday night it was an all-guy dart night, and Nelson was careful not to let on how much that pleased him.

"Did the girls not like playing darts?"

He didn't know why they wouldn't. Thanks to Mariah, the girls beat every comer.

Dave shrugged. "I don't quite get it. Jaycee had wanted to come for weeks, and now all she wants to do is plan this party."

Nelson straightened up. This was his cue.

"Are you sure you want to have this party?" Okay, he'd promised his grandmother he'd stay out of it, but she'd asked him for advice on what Dave liked, so he decided that gave him wiggle room. Maybe what Dave liked was to not have a party.

Dave shrugged. "It was Jaycee's idea, but I'm happy if she is."

"Are you sure?"

Dave gave him a puzzled look. "What do you mean?"

"I wondered if Grandmother and… Mariah had the idea first."

Dave frowned. "I'm not sure. I first heard about it from Jaycee, last week, when we got here. You heard her."

Nelson swallowed some skeptical, and impolite, words. "You don't have to do this if you don't want to, you know."

Dave speared an onion ring. "I don't care, myself. But Jaycee is pretty excited about it."

"Really?" Jaycee had always been a practical, down-to-earth type of person.

Dave nodded, and swallowed. "She thinks it will help my mother come around."

Nelson paused in midreach for his own onion ring.

"Your mother? What's she got to do with it?"

"Jaycee doesn't think Mom likes her."

That surprised Nelson. Jaycee was hardworking, kind and pretty. Watching her with Dave last week had convinced him that the two truly cared for each other.

"Why wouldn't your mom like her?"

Dave's cheeks flushed. "Jaycee has a point. Mom has never gotten over when I dated your sister."

Nelson glared at his friend. "That was junior year of high school, and you swore nothing happened."

It was the single incident that almost ended their friendship. When Dave told Nelson he wanted to ask Delaney out, Nelson almost hit him. Well, once he got over the shock that anyone wanted to date his sister. That shock dealt with, he wanted to wrap her up and keep all guys away from her.

After the short dating event with Dave, Nelson had had to clue in. His sister was a lot prettier than he'd realized, and someone else had wanted to go out with her not long after Dave took her out. Then he and Dave united in trying to keep her safe. Safely single.

He thought Dave was long over that. His sister hadn't been back to Carter's for anything more than a flying visit in years.

Dave held up two fingers. "Nothing happened, scout's honor. But Mom seems to think that something might yet. Jaycee thinks Mom likes the idea of being connected to the Carters."

Nelson almost choked on the beer he'd swallowed.

"Is your mom crazy?"

Yes, Abigail was awesome, but she could focus that awesome on someone in uncomfortable ways. And the rest of them? His parents were working in—was it Azerbaijan now?—and his sister was totally a city girl. His aunts and uncles and cousins had all moved away.

Dave screwed up his lips. "Possibly. Jaycee says in Mom's eyes she's still from the wrong side of the tracks."

"That's messed up, if your mom thinks so." Nelson had friends from both sides of the literal train tracks in town, and the side of the tracks had nothing to do with the character of the resident.

Dave nodded. "I know. I think Jaycee is overreacting, but Mom does like your sister, and tells me everything she hears about her. I figure, if the party makes Jaycee happy, I'll do it. She's promised they'll do all the planning, and I just have to show up."

Those words sounded familiar to Nelson.

Dave bumped his arm. "You'll come, right?"

"Of course," Nelson agreed. "Unless I get a call—"

Dave's brows came down. "You'd better be there, or I want pictures to prove something was wrong with your horse. I don't want to go through this alone."

Nelson remembered his own engagement party. And to his shame, he remembered how little of it he'd spent with his fiancée.

"I'll be there, unless an animal is dying. And you can come with me for proof if I get a call."

Mariah sat down across from Abigail Carter. They each had a notebook, and Mariah had her laptop open. This was business.

"So, Jaycee and Rachel and I sat down and did some brainstorming last night."

Abigail nodded. "You came up with something promising, right?"

Mariah tapped a pen on her notepad, which was covered in scribbles.

"I think so. Can you assure me that the mill stream will be frozen solid by mid-February?"

Abigail stared past her. It took her a minute to respond.

"I can remember only two years where the stream didn't freeze. And I remember a long way back. I'd say there's probably a ninety-five percent certainty that the water will be frozen. It's not too deep there, so it freezes more quickly than south of town."

Mariah bit her lip. "Then we'll need a plan B, but I'm hoping a skating party will work."

Abigail sat back. "A skating party. I didn't expect that."

"We want to invite most of the town. We can't do an event for everyone who asks, but almost everyone can come to this. Jaycee and Dave know a lot of people, and since we're going to use this to promote Carter's Crossing, we need to show something big. We want the whole town to feel a part of this. Jaycee is on board for that.

"Since we don't have a big indoor facility—"

"Not yet," Abigail said.

"A skating party would be a good outdoor event. If we do it at the mill, we can stage everything there, and if needed, provide indoor space. The stream is beautiful, and we can do it up with lights and music. There's enough potential ice space to have more than one 'rink,' so different ages and skill levels can be separated."

"Lights. An evening event?"

"Afternoon-to-evening event, but days are short here in winter, and we don't want things to look dark. We don't have the facilities to provide full catering, but we could have hot chocolate and cider, fire pits to cook s'mores and hot dogs on sticks and, of course, some champagne to toast the happy couple. Then there are the practical things to think of, like heaters and Porta-Potties."

"A skating party seems very retro, kind of Norman Rockwell."

Mariah nodded. "That's something we can make the most of about the town. With the older homes, the lack of chain stores and restaurants, we need to focus on what makes this place special. I think the skating party works for that, and Jaycee assures me she and Dave can skate. She's even considering a skate/dance for the two of them to their song."

"What's their song?" Abigail asked.

Mariah bit back a grin. "Jaycee is still deciding on that."

"I thought songs were supposed to arise spontaneously from a particular moment."

"Jaycee is going to make the moment happen."

Abigail smiled. "I do like that girl. It's a wonderful idea, and we should be able to pull it off. Let me know what you need, and I'll get the committee working on it."

Mariah looked down. "I'll take the notes we made last night and work them up. Then we can discuss with the committee what we can do, and when."

Abigail ticked off a line on her own notebook.

"Now, about this proposal you mentioned."

Mariah crossed her arms. "This one is a little more difficult. Harvey wants to use a *Walking Dead* theme."

Abigail tilted her head. "Excuse me?"

"Apparently, he and Judy are big fans of the TV show. It's what brought them together, so he wants to use that in the proposal."

"I'm not familiar with this particular show. What's it about?" Abigail had a wary look on her face.

Mariah screwed up her nose. "Why don't I play the first episode for you?"

Abigail came around the table to sit beside her while Mariah moved her cursor until she found where she'd located the pilot episode.

Mariah had never dreamed that setting up Carter's Crossing as Cupid's Crossing would entail watching a zombie show with Abigail Carter.

She hit Play and waited to see how Abigail would respond.

She was quiet until the credits rolled.

"No."

Mariah had been racking her brain for ideas for a zombie proposal. Trying to make it suitable for Valentine's Day, rather than Halloween, had been a challenge. She hadn't expected Abigail to have much in the way of ideas for the proposal, but she hadn't expected a no, either.

"No, we aren't doing the proposal?" Mariah wanted it clarified. A proposal on Valentine's Day was a truly romantic event. But the zombie part was trouble.

"No, we aren't doing a zombie proposal."

Mariah opened her mouth, but Abigail continued before she could interrupt.

"I know Judy. She and Harvey may love that television show, but Judy does not want dead people proposing to her. I know a couple of young women who would enjoy something a little shocking for an event like that, but Judy is not one of them."

Mariah blinked. She'd been assuming Harvey knew what his fiancée wanted, but Abigail could be right.

"If Harvey believes this is what Judy wants, and he wants to surprise her, how do we check out what Judy really does want? Does she have a close friend we could ask who could keep the secret?"

Abigail considered, and shook her head.

"I wouldn't trust her sisters, and she doesn't have a lot of friends. She's very reserved. Harvey is a good match for her, but he is not a man of imagination."

Mariah tapped her notebook again. She had to question Abigail's statement, because a zombie proposal sounded like something that required a lot of imagination, maybe more than Mariah had.

She wanted to make this proposal work, but she didn't know how. Normally, she just asked her client. She'd never planned a proposal before where she was in the dark as to what the askee liked.

"Her mother?"

Abigail shook her head. "Kailey is our best bet."

"Kailey?"

"Kailey works with Judy at Nelson's clinic. Kailey is older and settled and can keep a secret. And most important, she has access to Judy forty hours a week. If Kailey can't get the information out of her, I don't know anyone who can."

Abigail frowned, and Mariah could imagine the planning going on in that well-coiffed head.

"It would be best if you took Kailey out for lunch. She's busy outside work with three kids and a husband to take care of. Nelson's staff gets an hour for lunch."

Abigail smiled at Mariah. Mariah smiled back, less happily.

Nelson avoided her, and barely talked to her when he couldn't. Mariah knew there was a story there, but Abigail wouldn't tell her, and Nelson never hung around long enough for her to ask him again. Even if she asked, she couldn't imagine him telling her.

She did her best to keep away from him. She didn't want to stir up any more animosity. Abigail swore he wouldn't get in the way, but Mariah was learning how impossible it was, in a town this size, to avoid someone.

He was going to flip when he found out she was spending time with one of his employees. And she could imagine no scenario in which he didn't find out.

CHAPTER FIVE

HE DIDN'T JUST find out, he was standing in the reception area, wearing those blue scrubs again, when she walked in to meet Kailey.

There were two women there. One improbable redhead with a matronly figure and an air of confidence. The other a petite blonde who appeared to want to blend into the woodwork.

Mariah knew the older of the two was her lunch date, but even if she hadn't been able to figure that out, Kailey had a coat on over her own scrubs.

The blonde must be Judy.

Doing her best to ignore Nelson while greeting Kailey and trying to study Judy was difficult. More like impossible. Mariah's eyes started to cross.

"Mariah?" Nelson asked, surprise in his voice.

"I told you I was going out to lunch, Nelson." Kailey's tone told him she was taking no flack.

"But I thought you were meeting Bert."

"You obviously thought wrong, Nelson. I'm having lunch with Mariah. I won't introduce you, since you two live together."

"We don't—" Both Mariah and Nelson reacted to that statement, but Kailey ignored them.

"And this is Judy, Mariah." Mariah smiled at the younger woman, who looked down at her feet.

"Kailey…" Nelson spoke in a warning voice.

"Nelson…" Kailey echoed.

"Are you getting involved in something you shouldn't?" Nelson looked at Judy, and back at Kailey.

Did Nelson know what was going on? Mariah expected a full-on hissy fit.

Kailey put her hands on her hips. "Nelson, I'm your receptionist, not your daughter. You can tell me what to do while I'm behind that desk, but you need to ask nicely, and you stop when I walk out those doors."

She pointed at Nelson.

"And you'd better not think I would do anything to hurt or embarrass my friends."

A confused look passed over his face.

"Then why…?" he started.

Kailey marched to the door. "I'm walking out the door, Nelson. Time's up!"

Mariah followed Kailey out the door with a glance back. Kailey had just rocketed up the list of people she liked. She understood now the confidence Abigail had in Kailey.

"Abigail said you had something to talk to me about."

Kailey had waited only till they were safely in the car and the engine on.

"Don't tell me my Bert wants to do something romantic."

Mariah choked out a laugh. "I haven't met your Bert yet."

Kailey wasn't upset. "I'd have to send him for a medical checkup if he had. Bert is a wonderful husband, but he doesn't have a romantic bone in his body."

Mariah didn't know how to respond to that.

"It's okay, though, because I don't, either. Romantic doesn't pay the mortgage or feed the kids."

"Oh." Since Mariah's whole purpose in Carter's Crossing

was to focus attention on romance, she wasn't sure that Kailey was the right person to help her.

"But I can enjoy other people being romantic, and I absolutely want this plan to work in Carter's. I love this town, and I want my kids to have the option to stay here. So how can I help you?"

Mariah pulled into a parking slot in front of the diner.

"It's about Judy."

"Please tell me she called you to ask for help proposing to Harvey." Kailey's face had lit up.

Mariah shook her head. "No, it was actually Harvey."

Kailey burst out laughing. "Let's go in and order some food. Then I'll tell you why that's funny."

Once they'd ordered and were on their own, Kailey explained how she'd suggested Judy propose as one of the events for Valentine's Day.

"Do you think she wants to marry Harvey?" Mariah asked.

"Oh, definitely. But she's too shy to ask him herself. And I think she'd like a more conventional proposal, with Harvey asking the question, not her, so this works out perfectly."

Mariah sighed. "About that. Harvey suggested a *Walking Dead* proposal."

Kailey looked shocked. "What in the—oh, you mean, the TV show?"

Mariah nodded. Kailey shook her head.

"No, I don't think that's what Judy would want. She might like that show, but she also reads a lot of romance novels."

Mariah relaxed. "Okay, that's good to hear. Abigail has already vetoed the zombie proposal. Can you tell me what she would like?"

Kailey gave a nod. "That's what this is about, then."

"I need someone who can tell me what Judy likes, what would make this a proposal she'd enjoy and remember, and it has to be a secret."

Kailey held up a hand. A moment later the waitress put their plates in front of them.

"Anything else?" the woman asked.

"We're good, thanks."

After she left, Kailey leaned forward. "I'll keep it quiet, no problem. I don't know the answers right now, but I can find out."

Mariah picked up her fork. "And she won't figure out what you're doing?"

Kailey grinned. "I can use the excitement over Jaycee and Dave's party to draw her out. The girl is not a big talker, so she's used to me asking her a lot of questions."

Mariah chewed, and then asked, "Will she be okay with something public like this? If she's that shy?" Everyone mentioned that Judy was quiet and shy, and Mariah didn't want to embarrass her. She never wanted to do that to someone, and in this case, when they were trying to get publicity for Carter's Crossing, a disastrous event would be worse than no event.

Kailey considered. "If it's romantic enough, I think she'll be fine. Nothing embarrassing, but I know she wants to marry Harvey, and I think she'll feel special knowing he went to this much trouble to make it memorable for her."

"That sounds good. But I need to ask, is Nelson going to be a problem?"

Kailey picked up a forkful of her dish. "He's got a bit of a thing about weddings, of course, but don't worry, I can handle Nelson."

Mariah wished she could say the same.

Nelson was relieved that Mariah didn't stay in town for the holidays. Grandmother asked her, while the three were dining *à trois*, what her plans were for Thanksgiving.

Nelson had closed his eyes, bracing himself to hear that she would be part of their celebration. But Mariah was returning to New York. She'd spend the holiday weekend with her own family, whatever members weren't sailing around the planet somewhere, and update her grandfather on the plans for Valentine's Day in Carter's Crossing.

Nelson didn't ask for details on those.

He spent his own holiday with Grandmother and an assortment of the town orphans; mostly elderly women who would otherwise spend the day alone. Nelson would deny it with his dying breath, but he kinda liked these get-togethers. The women fussed over him, and while he'd hate that on a constant basis, once in a long while it was nice.

And after dinner his grandmother would relax, and he'd hear the stories she'd rather he not know.

Like now.

"So have you heard any more from Gerry?" Mavis Grisham had asked. Fortunately, she'd left Tiny behind. Tiny had once embarrassed himself with the turkey, so he was no longer invited to holiday dinners.

Nelson almost asked who Gerry was, but bit his tongue. If the women forgot about him, they were much more revealing.

Grandmother shook her head. "No, Mariah usually talks to him."

Ah, right. Mariah's grandfather. He'd forgotten.

"Does she know about...you know, you and him?"

Oh, this was getting good. Grandmother had a history with Mariah's grandfather? That would explain the man's willingness to help. Or would it?

"I don't know what she knows. I haven't told her anything."

"Do you have any regrets? Wonder what would have happened if you'd made different decisions?"

Nelson didn't intend it, but surprise had him dropping the fork in his hand.

Six pairs of eyes swiveled in his direction, all with accusing looks.

That wasn't fair. It wasn't as if he'd sneaked in to eavesdrop. They'd just forgotten about him.

"Are you done with your pie, Nelson?"

From the tight-lipped expressions he saw aimed his way, he wasn't hearing any more tonight.

He nodded. "I should probably head out now. Thank you all so much for a lovely day and a wonderful dinner. Happy Thanksgiving!"

He left cheerfully, but determined to return in the morning and ask his grandmother some questions. Mariah Van Delton was stirring things up in Carter's Crossing, and it appeared that part of that was a result of a past relationship between Abigail Carter and Gerry Van Delton. He thought he had the right to know more about this thing that was causing him stress.

Plus, he was curious. Who knew his grandmother had a past?

Scratch that. Abigail Carter was exactly the kind of woman who would have a past.

He was in the kitchen making coffee when his grandmother came downstairs the next morning.

"Good morning, Nelson. You're up early."

He passed her a cup, made the way she liked it.

"I wanted to catch you before you got busy."

Her eyebrows arched. "Oh, really?" There was amusement in her voice.

"I didn't know you and Mr. Van Delton had known each other, romantically. I was curious."

Abigail stared at him for a moment. Nelson knew she would only tell him what she wanted, and he didn't have a lot of leverage to try to change her mind. He'd hoped she'd be less discreet before she had an injection of caffeine.

"Gerry and I dated in college."

"Was it serious?" he asked, intrigued by the idea of his grandmother with a slew of boyfriends. He'd seen pictures of her when she was young. She'd been beautiful. Still was.

She nodded. Her gaze drifted over his shoulder, her mind obviously in the past.

"I had two serious suitors, Gerry and your grandfather. My father wanted my husband to take the Carter name and settle here, in Carter's Crossing. Take over the management of the mill."

Nelson knew his grandfather had done just that.

"Gerry didn't want to do that?"

She shook her head.

"What did you want?"

He was intrigued by the image of a young Abigail, torn between the two men. He knew the Van Deltons had businesses in New York. They were wealthy on a big scale. He could easily picture Abigail there, attending galas and running charities.

Had she wanted that, all those years ago? Had she chosen duty?

"I wanted someone who loved me enough to put me first. Your grandfather did that. Gerry did not."

Her gaze focused again, and she looked at him.

"I don't regret the choices I made. But I do wonder if Gerry does."

"Why?"

"He's been divorced twice and is single now. Mariah's father is estranged from him, and I'm not sure how close he is to his daughters. Mariah hardly knows him."

Nelson suspected there was a tinge of satisfaction in his grandmother's voice.

His grandmother was not sweet and shy. She was strong and proud, willing to make hard choices and stand by the consequences. She would not like being someone's second choice.

Interesting. If, or when, the two of them met up again…

Nelson stopped himself.

He was not getting involved. He didn't want Mariah here. He didn't want her grandfather here, either.

"I'm going to check on the horses. Is there anything you need me to do for you?"

Abigail shook her head. "No, I've got everything under control."

He wished he could say the same.

* * *

New York was an adjustment.

It had been an adjustment when she'd first left the boat and settled in Richmond, Virginia. A home that stayed still, all the time. People, always around. More noise, pollution and people. After living in a relatively small space with five people, she was alone, in the midst of many.

New York took that to an exponential degree. Especially after months in Carter's Crossing. The crowds, the noise, the smell—it was all an assault on her senses.

Then there was her grandfather's home.

Abigail's house was large, beautiful and certainly not crowded with just the two of them living there. But her grandfather's house was larger, had more expensive furnishings and felt emptier, despite the live-in servants.

Her grandfather was very wealthy. He was also, she suspected, lonely.

He still put in long hours at work; he wasn't home when she arrived, and she didn't see him till the next day. Of his three children, none of his relationships were close.

Her father was his only son. The last she'd talked to her parents, they were in Indonesia. She wasn't sure her grandfather knew what country they were in. Her dad rarely spoke to his father.

The breach had happened before Mariah was born. Her dad had wanted to marry her mother, buy a boat and sail the world, giving up on the business life her grandfather had groomed him for. Her dad was tired of the long hours, constant phone and email demands, and had fallen in love with her mother and with the ocean.

Her grandfather had not taken it well. He told her father that the only way he could touch his trust fund was if his son promised he would never marry the woman his father considered to be scheming for a rich husband.

Her father had given his promise to never marry her mother.

He got his trust fund money, used it to buy the boat and sail away with her mother. To this day, her parents weren't married.

Over the years that heated anger had dissipated, giving way to cold hurt. Her grandfather had apologized and retracted the promise he'd forced. Her father hadn't. Her dad kept in touch with his parents, but as acquaintances, not family. He hadn't forgiven.

As she grew up, Mariah discovered how much it hurt her mother that her father wouldn't marry her. Her mother hadn't forgiven her grandfather, either.

Not a happy family. She had two paternal aunts. One had broken off all contact with Gerald. The other had married another wealthy businessman and was now divorced. She relied on her father for financial support. Her son worked for the company. He was presumably the heir apparent. Her cousin and aunt both suspected Mariah wanted to supplant him.

Mariah recognized both the strengths and flaws Gerald possessed. While she didn't want the life her parents had, she didn't want the life her grandfather had, either. She wanted something that fell between those two extremes.

She wanted a simpler life than her grandfather's, with family and friends. She wanted friends and neighbors who stayed put. She'd been lonely growing up, making friends only to have them leave, or to leave them behind as her parents continued their wandering life.

She wanted a position with her grandfather's company that she'd earned, that she could count on, and a place here in New York, where she would never feel lonely and left behind.

She knew she wasn't going to find it in her grandfather's house. But she would get her own place, settle down and grow roots that would never be dug up.

This had been her plan for the past five years. She'd spent them in Richmond, learning how to plan events, how to make sure things ran well and got done. The opportunities that opened for her had been in wedding planning, but she didn't want to be limited to that.

She'd done this on her own. She hadn't asked her grandfather for a handout. He'd respected that.

This fall he'd given her an offer. If she'd work in Carter's Crossing for a year, making it a successful wedding destination, he'd give her a partnership in his event-planning company.

As much as she knew his faults, and how he'd hurt her parents, she also understood he wanted to do better. He just didn't know how.

The family, those in the city and still on good terms with her grandfather, gathered for an elaborate Thanksgiving dinner in the formal dining room.

It was a small party. Her grandfather, her aunt Genevieve and her cousin, Pierre. Mariah had prepared herself for a long, dull dinner. With the suspicions Aunt Genevieve and Pierre harbored, she didn't want to talk about anything related to business at dinner, and there was nothing she had in common with them. Tomorrow she should be able to talk to her grandfather about Carter's, and she could wait for that.

Her grandfather hugged her, with warmth, her cousin kissed her cheek formally and her aunt gave her a languid wave. They took their seats around the table, well spaced, even though the additional leaves weren't in. A typical family gathering for the Van Deltons.

The staff brought in the first course. Aunt Genevieve opened the conversation with complaints about her housekeeper, and a problem at the last charity ball. Mariah was quiet. She didn't have a housekeeper, didn't want one, and was more interested in planning a ball than attending.

Her aunt would think she was crazy.

Pierre interrupted to bring up some issue at work.

"We can discuss that at work, Pierre. This is a holiday. I want to hear how Mariah has been enjoying small-town life."

Her grandfather smiled at her, and it was sincere. Pierre

frowned, slightly, and Aunt Genevieve didn't pretend to have any interest.

Mariah smiled back at her grandfather. "It's been interesting. It's much different than here, or even Richmond, but I've enjoyed the people I've met."

"How is Abigail?"

"Who's Abigail?" Pierre asked, his voice suspicious. It must be exhausting to be looking for competitors everywhere.

"Abigail is an old friend from college," Gerald answered, attention still focused on Mariah. Pierre relaxed and looked bored.

"Abigail is a force of nature." Mariah noticed how intently her grandfather was listening.

"She always was."

"Her husband died while her children were still young, and she took over responsibility for the mill and her family then. It's part of the town lore."

Her grandfather nodded. "I'm not surprised she finally had to close her mill. Lumber isn't the same business anymore. Cheap imports, protective tariffs—I knew she wouldn't be able to maintain it."

Mariah wondered if he'd been keeping track of Abigail.

"I'll tell you tomorrow how the wedding/romance event plan is going, but I find it hard to believe it could fail with Abigail involved."

Gerald nodded. "I wanted her to come to New York, back when we were in school together."

Pierre almost choked on his food. That brought his mother's attention back to the conversation.

"What did you want that for?" Pierre asked.

Gerald shot him a glance. "I wanted to marry her. She'd have excelled here."

Genevieve's eyes widened. "What?"

Her grandfather had a twinkle in his eye, one that Genevieve and Pierre missed. Mariah watched him warily, not sure what mischief he was up to.

"What do you think, Mariah? You know her now. Wouldn't Abigail have taken to New York?"

Mariah shook her head. Her grandfather might be playing with her aunt and cousin, but she was going to give an honest answer.

"She has an absolute loyalty to Carter's Crossing. To her, it's not an obligation, but her calling. She's determined to make the town a success, somehow, by sheer force of will if nothing else. If anyone can do it, she can. But she has control there. I'm not sure New York, with all the competition, would suit her."

Genevieve nodded. "Someone from a little town in the middle of nowhere wouldn't know what to do here. It would be a disaster."

She shot a worried glance at her father. Mariah suspected her aunt lived in dread of a third marriage.

"Abigail would play this town like a fiddle. Wouldn't she, Mariah?"

He was definitely stirring up trouble. But was that all he was doing?

"She could, I'm sure. But she wouldn't want to deal with the...the pettiness. The jostling for status. She's happy where she is, able to run things as she likes.

"At least, that's what I think. But who knows?" Mariah shrugged.

Her grandfather had his head tilted, considering her words.

"You think she's happy where she is?"

Mariah suspected he was more invested in his question than she was comfortable taking responsibility for.

"She appears to be. But I'm not sure anyone would know if she wasn't."

Her grandfather let the topic of Abigail Carter drop, but she was sure her aunt had added Abigail to her list of worries.

The next day Mariah finally had a chance to sit down and talk with her grandfather about what she was doing in Carter's Crossing.

"You're exactly right, Mariah. The lack of rooms for out-of-town guests will limit the size of any events, no matter how many B&Bs they come up with. Not everyone wants to stay in someone's home. Is there any other space that could function as a hotel? I might be willing to invest in that."

Mariah blossomed in his praise.

"Abigail's house would make a lovely small hotel, but I don't think she'd consider giving it up. It's been her home her whole life. Downtown doesn't currently have appropriate vacant space, and I don't think you'd want to locate a hotel on the literal wrong side of the railroad tracks. That's where the loss of employment has been the most obvious.

"You could buy land outside town, I suppose. I don't know the zoning rules, though."

Her grandfather shook his head. "I'll wait to see how things go. I think right now this idea of making it a 'Romance Center' takes advantage of what the town can offer and exploits its assets year-round, just as you concluded.

"Tell me about what you have planned for Valentine's Day."

Mariah straightened her notebook, though she didn't need it. "We have a fiftieth wedding anniversary and vow renewal. The couple was married on Valentine's Day and have lived in Carter's Crossing their whole lives. Abigail's committee is doing most of the legwork on that. They're tracking down the minister who officiated, to see if he's still alive, and have found most of the remaining wedding attendants. The church they married in is still in town, so they're using that space for the celebration.

"I don't expect a lot of people will necessarily want to celebrate a fiftieth going forward, not in Carter's, but it shows that romance can start and last there, so it's a feel-good story, and sets the tone."

Her grandfather leaned back in his chair. "Okay, have you got something splashier?"

"Absolutely. An engagement party. The mill isn't renovated yet, but we can use the space for staging. We're having an outdoor, old-fashioned skating party on the part of the river that goes by the mill."

"Weather?"

"It would be extremely unlikely that the river won't be frozen, and we can handle a snowfall or cold snap with lots of heaters and covers. We're still working on the indoor plan B if the weather suddenly gets unreasonably warm or rainy."

"Get lots of video—that should have a lot of appeal."

"Of course. And the final event is a proposal. You know how they've gone viral if done right."

He smiled at her. "And you'll make sure it's done right."

"Thanks to Abigail. We're going to use the gazebo in the middle of the town green. We're stealthily getting information on the woman's favorites, so the details are still being worked on."

Her grandfather tapped a finger on the desk. "The couple is reasonably attractive? They'll look good?"

"Not drop-dead gorgeous, but she's pretty, and he's totally in love with her, and it shows. They look like real people, which might be better than if they were too picture-perfect. She works for the local vet, so we could bring in animals, and he's a schoolteacher in the next town."

"I'm proud of you, Mariah. This all looks great. I look forward to having you working for me."

Mariah must have been tired, because she wasn't as excited over that affirmation as she should be.

"I'm looking forward to that, as well."

"You sure you don't want something more? You've got a good head on your shoulders. I can see a lot of myself in you."

Mariah put a hand over his. "I may not want to be just like my parents, but I do want to make sure I keep enough time to enjoy my life. I don't want to take over the world."

Her grandfather's smile was twisted. "I get it. I've made mistakes. It might be time for me to try to enjoy some of my life, as well."

CHAPTER SIX

NEW YEAR'S EVE was a bust.

Nelson had been looking forward to a night of fun with his friends. He had a rare night where he planned to not be on call. Mariah had gone to New York again not long before Christmas, and was staying through the New Year, helping with her grandfather's company and its many events.

He'd been relieved that he could enjoy the holidays without her. Somehow, he was thinking about her even when she wasn't around.

Worrying about what she might do to his friends. That was all. But for the night, he could push thoughts of her aside.

Then, just as he was heading out the door, he'd gotten a call from the answering service.

A dog, hit by a car. The family was in tears. There wasn't time to get the vet from Oak Hill.

He quickly changed to scrubs and raced to the clinic.

The damage to the golden retriever was extensive. There was massive internal bleeding. The owners insisted he do anything he could.

He called in Judy, apologizing for disturbing her New Year's. She shook her head. She loved all animals and was as determined to save this one as he was.

They tried. The surgery lasted four hours. He knew it was still touch and go. He offered to let Judy leave, but she wouldn't go till she knew if the dog would survive.

The dog didn't make it.

Nelson hated it. Hated that a beautiful animal was dead. Hated that he'd exhausted himself and Judy and hadn't been able to save him. Hated having to tell the news to the family.

It was a crappy New Year's.

By the time he'd wrapped up at the clinic, the ball had dropped in New York City, everyone had kissed whoever they were kissing and, while there was still partying going on, Nelson was heading home.

He was in no mood to party. He had a glass of whiskey on his own at home, as a salute to a lovely dog who'd no longer be a loving part of his family.

Then he went to bed and did his best to forget the whole evening.

A week later Dave told him they were having a do-over on Nelson's ruined New Year's Eve.

"A do-over," Nelson repeated, voice flat.

"Yep. You deserve a night to have a good time. Jaycee and the women are planning that party still, so we, the guys, are going out to the Goat and Barley and getting drunk and celebrating."

"What are we celebrating?" Nelson didn't have a lot to celebrate right now.

"A new year, good things coming. I know you had a crappy night, but that doesn't mean the whole year is going to suck."

Nelson managed not to promise. He didn't often let himself loose. He was the only vet in town.

When the family of the golden retriever he couldn't save reached out to ask for time to cover their bill, the one he had to send because, unfortunately, he had a business and had to pay for Judy's time and the materials he'd used, he agreed, and cut back the bill. Then he texted Dave to tell him he'd be coming.

He needed a break. He wasn't worried about the rest of the New Year. He just wanted to forget the now.

Nelson was drunk. He hadn't been this drunk in a long time. Words were coming out of his mouth before he had time to censor them.

This was a really bad idea in a small town, where he had a reputation to uphold, and where his grandmother always found out everything that was going on. Tonight, however, he just didn't care. He needed to forget about the dog and the family, and alcohol was the only weapon he had for that right now.

Yeah, he was drunk. And so was Dave. Otherwise, Dave wouldn't be telling him about his problems with his engagement party. Using large gestures.

"Hey, I like to skate. I mean, regular skate. Like, hockey skate. Ya know?"

Nelson nodded, his head feeling loose on his neck.

"Fairly nights. I mean, fairy lights. Yeah. Those things. I said no problem. Hot chocolate, good."

"You like hot cholate," Nelson agreed. He had a sense that was the wrong word, but it didn't matter, because Dave kept going.

"I know. You're a good friend, Nelz'n."

Nelson reached out to slap Dave's arm, but got his head instead.

"Sorry, man."

Dave giggled. "It's okay. It's all okay. Except for the dancin'."

Nelson pointed his finger in Dave's general direction. "You don't like dancin' now? You did in high school."

Dave grabbed at Nelson's finger. "Don't point at me. Not nice."

"Sorry, dude. I'm drunk."

Dave stared at him. "You're a genius. A frickin' genius. That's how they'll get me to dance on skates. They'll have to make me drunk. I just have to stop drinking and I'm safe." Dave was nodding and didn't stop.

It seemed like a good plan to Nelson. But one part didn't make sense.

"Why are you dancing on skates? You play hockey on skates."

"Ezactly. Zactly. Right."

"We don't dance when we play hockey. 'Less we score. Then we cel'brate. But you don't dance."

"I *know*. But Jaycee wants me to dance on skates. At the party. Like they dance at weddings. But this isn't the wedding. It's the party. The skating party. So we have to dance on skates. It's all part of the plan."

Nelson took a moment, and then figured it out. The plan. Planning. Party planning. Wedding planning. Mariah Van frickin Delton.

That was the problem. Jaycee didn't want Dave to dance on skates. Jaycee had never asked Dave to dance on skates. Right?

"Dave," Nelson said. This felt like a very important question. "Have you and Jaycee ever danced on skates?"

Dave shook his head violently and grabbed at the bar when he almost fell off his chair.

"No, skates are for hockey, not dancin'. Wait, they want us to dance on skates at the party."

"Zactly. Did Jaycee ever ask you to dance on skates before?"

"Never." Dave banged his fist on the table.

"Then the problem is Marijah."

Dave focused on his face with extreme effort. "Who?"

"Mahira… Marij… Wedding planner."

"Oh, right. Her. She's the one who wants to dance on skates?"

"She's the one that wants *you* to dance on skates."

"You sure about that? She didn't say anything."

Nelson frowned. "No, that's not how they do it. She tells Jaycee, and then Jaycee tells you."

Dave blinked owlishly. "That's sneaky, man. Really sneaky."

"I know. That's what they did to me." Nelson tried another head shake. Still loose.

Dave's jaw had dropped. "Jaycee asked you to dance on skates, too? Wha— Are you trying to take over my party?"

Nelson concentrated and managed to put a hand on Dave's leg. "No, not Jaycee. Not your party. My party. My weddin'."

"Whoa, man," Dave said. "Is that what happened? Dancing on skates? But that doesn't make sense."

"I'll tell you what happened. But ssshhh. Don't tell everyone." He meant to put his finger on his lips, but it ended up on his nose. Weird.

Nelson had a suspicion that this wasn't the discreet place he should be talking about this. But he had to save Dave. Dave shouldn't lose Jaycee because of the wedding and the wedding planner. Or party planner. Whatevs.

"So I was getting married. Right?"

"That's right," Dave agreed.

"And then Sherry and I ruined it."

Dave blinked. "I thought it was Zoey. Was this another wedding?"

"I was marrying Zoey. Sherry was the wedding planner."

"Okay." Dave nodded. "Marry Zoey, plan Sherry."

Close enough. "And we had a big plan. Big, fancy wedding. Lots of guests. Important guests. I wanted it to be perfect."

Nelson wasn't sure why he was waving his arms around, but Dave was following his argument.

"Right."

Nelson sent a message to his voice to lower. Less volume. When Dave flinched, he wondered if it didn't happen right.

"Zoey didn't like it. She said we should 'lope."

"'Lope," Dave echoed.

"But there were all these people, right? We'd spent money, right? I mean, if we 'loped, everyone would be mad.

"So I said, Sherry. Sherry. Sherry."

"Sherry, Sherry, Sherry." Dave sang it back to him.

"Sherry was my wedding planner."

"I know. But you had a problem."

"Right. Right. Sherry, we have a problem. Zoey wants to 'lope. Not get married. Wait, elope married. Not a wedding. She said it was too much. Too stressssssful."

"Just like this skating party!" Dave shouted.

"And Sherry said, not a problem. She said brides were like this. Zoey would be glad when it was over. So I said, nope." That final *p* popped with a satisfying snap of his lips. "No eloping."

"Aww."

Nelson nodded his head. It was hard to make it stop, but he had to because he couldn't see Dave when he was nodding.

"Sherry was wrong."

"No." Dave looked shocked.

Suddenly, Nelson's head cleared as memories of that black day came back, escaping the wall he normally had solidly erected against their return.

"Zoey didn't show up for the wedding."

Dave lunged to hug him. "I'm sorry, man. That's awful. I wish I coulda been there, but Austalia... Stalia...it was too far."

Nelson closed his eyes, shoving aside the moment of clarity, welcoming the numbing confusion of the alcohol back.

"Yeah. So I gotta tell ya. Eloping is better than a big wedding. I should have eloped when she asked. Don't let Mariah plan a big wedding. Just elope. Much better."

Dave nodded. And nodded and started to tip out of his seat. Suddenly, the bartender was there, saying things like they'd had enough, and it was time to go.

Even the haze of alcohol couldn't remove the gloom that settled over Nelson as he remembered that time.

He shouldn't have gotten drunk. He needed to keep control. Keep the bad memories away. He stood, and the room swirled around him.

Yet another mistake. He wondered sometimes if he'd ever learn.

* * *

Nelson's head was pounding. His mouth tasted like the bottom of a kennel, and his head pounded. And pounded.

When his head started to yell "Nelson" he realized it wasn't just his head pounding. It was his door. No, someone pounding *on* the door.

He pulled a pillow over his head to drown out the noise, and the movement made him queasy.

The pounding and yelling didn't stop.

After a struggle, he identified the yeller as Mariah.

He waited for her to go away, but she didn't. And he realized she wasn't going to.

That was some angry yelling she was doing. No one was stopping her, but the only person who could was his grandmother, and she was probably in on it.

Nelson groaned and shoved the pillow off. He pushed against the mattress and forced himself upright.

He wanted to fall back down, but the yelling was getting louder.

She probably learned to yell on a boat.

He managed to get to his feet, and finally, reluctantly, opened his eyes. He winced, even though the day was overcast, and not much light made its way into his bedroom. He reached a hand out to a wall and started to stumble to the door.

He finally got to the doorknob and twisted it. The door pushed back so quickly it hit his arm.

"Stop it," he croaked.

Miraculously, the pounding outside his head and the yelling stopped for a moment. He turned to feel his way to the kitchen. He'd just managed to turn on the tap when the door slammed, and he closed his eyes and groaned.

The water turned off, and he found a glass of water thrust in front of him. He gulped half of it down and took a breath.

"Aspirin?"

The voice was still loud with that question, but not as painful as it had been.

He furrowed his brow, thinking through the haze in his head. "Bathroom."

He swallowed the rest of the water and carefully placed the glass in the sink, as gently as possible. The noises from the bathroom as Mariah hopefully located the medication were still loud and echoing in his head.

Her footsteps clacked in the hallway, and she thrust a couple of pills at him.

He swallowed them dry. Then, feeling dizzy, he stumbled to his couch and half sat, half fell on it. He let his head rest on the back as he tried to will the aspirin to hurry through his system and provide some relief.

The footsteps clacked and stopped in front of him. He kept his eyes closed, hoping against hope that she'd vanish, in a puff of smoke.

Futile wishing. There was obviously something big bothering her. Big enough that she'd pounded on his door for what felt like hours.

"So I guess your excuse is that you were drunk?"

Sure. Make that his excuse. He had no idea what she was talking about, and he was in no condition to deal with it anyway.

"I don't care if you were drunk. I don't care if you were temporarily insane. I don't care if it was a full moon and you were about to turn into a werewolf. You made this problem, and now you need to fix it."

Nelson didn't know what the problem was.

He held up his hand. "Give me time for the aspirin to work."

She huffed, something he'd never imagined sounding so loud, and then dropped into the chair across from his seat.

What he wanted to do was crawl back into bed and sleep until his hangover was gone, but he knew enough about Mariah to know that wasn't going to happen. She'd pounded on his door, gotten him water and aspirin, and then plunked herself down on his chair.

She wasn't leaving.

He tried to take advantage of the temporary quiet to figure out what the problem was.

She considered his being drunk an excuse. He thought back, and yep, she'd said that. Which probably meant something had happened last night.

He and Dave...

Oh, no. He'd been talking to Dave. Talking a lot. Talking without a filter, in the way that one did when drunk.

What had he said to Dave?

He couldn't hold back a groan when he remembered what he'd revealed. He'd told Dave, and possibly anyone else at the Goat and Barley last night, about his own aborted wedding. About Zoey asking him to elope. He'd said something about eloping being the right option.

Had Dave eloped with Jaycee? That would create a problem for Mariah. Maybe Dave had just refused to have the engagement party. There'd been something about dancing on skates, but it didn't make a lot of sense. Why would anyone want Dave to dance...?

"What exactly did you do last night?"

Nelson opened his eyes. He took his first real look at Mariah this morning.

She was wearing jeans, hair back in a ponytail. He didn't notice any makeup. With a flicker of pain, he figured she'd rushed over here without taking time to get ready. And still managed to look good.

He glanced at his watch, realizing he was wearing the same clothes he'd had on last night. They were wrinkled and untucked. He imagined he looked bad.

That didn't explain the look on her face. She was angry. No, she was furious.

How to put this so she didn't start yelling at him? The aspirin was dulling the edges of the pounding in his head, but he'd only had a few hours of sleep. He was in no shape for a fight.

"Dave and I went out."

She interrupted, "That much I know. Why?"

"I missed New Year's." And he had that whole issue with the retriever...

"Fine. You had to catch up on a chance to get drunk."

That wasn't fair. He didn't do this regularly. Not since Zoey—but he clamped that thought down.

"So Dave and I went out—"

"To the Goat and Barley. I know."

If she knew so much, why was she here yelling at him?

Crap. Dave must have eloped, so she couldn't find him to ask. Probably couldn't find Jaycee, either, and if they were on a plane on their way to get married, they wouldn't answer their phones.

How had Dave managed to get on a plane? He'd been as drunk as Nelson, and Nelson was having a hard time staying upright on the couch.

"We had some shots, talked a bit..."

"What did you talk about?" Her voice was still dialed up to much too high a volume, but he could think, a bit.

"Dave was upset about dancing. Yeah, he didn't want to dance. It all started from that."

Honestly, if she and Jaycee hadn't tried to make him dance on skates, Nelson would never have ended up advising him to elope.

"Dave's a big boy. He could have refused the dance."

Oh. They really did want Dave to dance. He'd have to figure out why later.

"Things went from there, and I might have told him to elope."

He looked over. Mariah had her arms crossed, but she wasn't yelling at him. Why wasn't she yelling at him?

"Okay, fine, we'll deal with that later, but when did you talk to Harvey?"

Nelson felt his mouth open, and he quickly shut it. Too quickly. It hurt.

He repeated her question in his head. Still didn't make any sense.

"Did I talk to Harvey? I was pretty sure Dave and I left together after that."

"Pretty sure?" Now she was getting closer to that yelling volume. "Well, I'm 'pretty sure' that Harvey and Judy just eloped. No, not just pretty sure since Harvey left me a voice mail!"

He pressed his hands over his ears, trying to control the volume shrieking into his poor, abused brain.

"Why do you care? They love each other—do you have to corner every possible wedding within a certain radius of Carter's Crossing?"

"I care—" His hands couldn't block out that volume level. "I care because our third event for Valentine's Day was Harvey's proposal to Judy!"

"What?" This made no sense. He'd talked to Kailey. Judy hadn't wanted to propose to Harvey... Wait, Harvey was going to propose to Judy?

"I'd convinced him to do something better than the zombie thing, but he told me he'd decided to elope to Vegas instead, thanks to you."

Nelson couldn't understand. He hadn't talked to Harvey— unless Harvey had been at the bar? Would Harvey have heard them?

Yeah, they'd been a little loud. But what was the thing about zombies?

"I didn't talk to Harvey. I mean, if he was at the bar, he might have overheard us—"

"You think? Yesterday he's fine, we've got almost everything settled, and this morning he's on a plane to Vegas, and says it's because of you. Sounds like the explanation to me."

"I didn't know you were doing any proposal. Especially not with my staff."

"It was supposed to be a surprise. Have you noticed how news flies around this town?"

That, he had.

"We have five weeks till Valentine's Day. I told my grandfather we had three events lined up. Now you've cost us one. How are you going to fix that?"

He wasn't going to be able to fix anything until he'd had a lot more sleep and his brain was working better.

"How am I supposed to fix an elopement? I'm too late to fly to Vegas to object to their wedding."

There was silence, and he risked opening his eyes. He regretted it. The light had brightened and shot painfully through his aching head. And he didn't like the expression on Mariah's face.

He closed his eyes again.

"You're going to find me another proposal."

He almost laughed. He was the last person in town anyone would tell about a proposed proposal.

"Right." If Mariah wanted to talk about crazy…

The next thing he heard was the slamming of the door.

He relaxed, allowing his abused body to lie down on the couch. Thank goodness she was gone.

He'd have to talk to her about this…encounter they'd had, but first, he needed sleep. And finally, he was alone and could get that.

"We have a problem."

Mariah met with Rachel and Jaycee in the back booth of the diner. This had become their unofficial planning space. The Goat and Barley was the guys' place, and if Jaycee and Dave were in the same vicinity, Jaycee tended to be distracted by her fiancé. They were now officially engaged, and Jaycee was showing off her ring any chance she got.

At the diner, though, Jaycee was focused and intent. The news of the engagement had not gone well at Christmas. Jaycee's mother-in-law-to-be had been all politeness on the outside but managed to get in some digs. Dave hadn't noticed but they had hit Jaycee. Why the rush to get married? Was there a reason?

Dave said he couldn't wait to make Jaycee his wife. Jaycee saw her MILTB looking at her stomach, as if Jaycee had planned a pregnancy to trap her son.

Jaycee was determined to prove she was going to be a great wife to Dave and had decided that the perfect engagement party would be the first step. Mariah was happy to help her. She thought Jaycee was a wonderful person, and that Dave's mother needed to see that. But she was getting a little worried about Jaycee.

The party was supposed to be a celebration of their engagement. It was supposed to be fun. Jaycee had promised that she and Dave loved to skate. But Jaycee was getting a little lost in the details. Like this dance on skates. Mariah thought it was a fun idea, but it sounded like Dave was dragging his blades, so to speak. Jaycee was starting to clench her teeth when she talked about it.

That problem could wait for now. The anniversary party was well underway, with the committee, under Abigail's supervision, taking care of most of the details. Mariah was overseeing that one on a much bigger picture scale.

Now she needed to see if Jaycee and Rachel could help her with the aborted proposal. She wasn't sure how much she trusted Nelson to fix the mess he'd made.

"What's the problem?" Jaycee asked, looking a little frantic.

Mariah put a hand on Jaycee's. "Nothing to do with your party, so just breathe, okay?"

Jaycee took a long breath.

"Told you." Rachel shook her head at her friend. "Mariah's got it all under control."

The waitress stopped by, and they placed an order.

Once the drinks arrived, Mariah filled them in.

"There was a third event lined up for Valentine's Day—it

was a surprise, so I couldn't tell you about it. But it's not happening now, thanks to Nelson Carter, so I was hoping you two could help me out."

Jaycee and Rachel looked at each other. "Nelson? What did he do?"

Mariah carefully did not grind her teeth. "You know Harvey and Judy?"

They nodded.

"Harvey wanted to propose to Judy. A beautiful, romantic, surprise proposal."

"Aww." Rachel smiled.

Jaycee frowned. "How did Nelson mess it up?"

Mariah pursed her lips. "You know he and Dave went out last night?"

Jaycee nodded, looking worried.

"Harvey was at the bar, heard Nelson talk about weddings and something about how eloping was better, so Harvey and Judy flew to Vegas this morning."

Rachel snorted a laugh. "Seriously?"

Jaycee appreciated the seriousness. "I guess that means the proposal is off."

Mariah nodded. "I need a third event. I've told my grandfather about our plans, and he's arranged publicity. I need to show him I can pull this off."

"Could Judy and Harvey have a reception on Valentine's Day instead?"

Mariah shook her head. "That's not going to work for a few reasons. First, our other two events are already for things that happened previously, so I really wanted something that was happening on Valentine's Day.

"If Carter's Crossing is going to be a place where people come for romance, we should be able to have a romantic event happen on the actual Valentine's Day. Nothing against your party, Jaycee, but I want something that isn't a celebration where the really romantic part happened off camera, so to speak.

"Secondly, there aren't a lot of venues in Carter's right now. The engagement skating party is happening at the mill. It's not ready yet, but it does have a roof and walls. The anniversary party is at St. Christopher's reception hall. That's the only full-size space the churches have between them.

"The proposal was supposed to take place at the bandstand in the park. I can't have a wedding reception at the park in the middle of February. Everyone would freeze. The proposal was perfect for that space."

Jaycee bit her lip. Rachel nodded.

"Okay, I see why that won't work. How can we help?"

Mariah clenched her hands under the table. "Can you think of someone who might be ready to propose? It just fit so perfectly, and I've got everything ready to make the bandstand beautiful. I could adapt it with different flowers, or music, or whatever, but starting from scratch would be a problem."

Rachel looked at Jaycee. "I can't think of anyone offhand. Can you?"

Jaycee twisted up her lips. "Tanya broke up with Kevin, right?"

Rachel nodded. Jaycee shook her head. "I'll try to think of someone, but honestly, the dating pool is a little shallow here."

Rachel rolled her eyes. "Tell me about it."

Jaycee blew out a breath. "Sorry, Mariah. We'd love to help, but this is a tricky one."

Mariah sighed. "I was afraid of that. Well, I told Nelson he has to fix it, so I hope he can come up with something."

"What about a pet wedding? That Nelson would know about."

Mariah frowned. It was meant to be a joke, she knew. But this was serious business. Her job wasn't a joke. And the thought of letting her grandfather down made her anxious and tense.

The lessons she'd learned growing up—don't make a promise unless you can keep it; and if at all possible, don't promise anything, because you might have to break your word.

She'd never used the word *promise* with her grandfather,

but she thought he was taking it as a serious commitment. She needed to make this work.

She was an outsider, so she had a disadvantage. But Mr. Elopement Carter was not. He'd better step up.

CHAPTER SEVEN

"HE'LL COME CLOSE to eat but backs off right away."

Rachel stood beside him, watching the skittish chestnut.

"That's better than when you first got him, though, right?"

Nelson's gaze was focused on the horse. "It is. I need to be patient, but I don't want to take in another until he's settled."

Rachel nudged him. "You asked me out here to give advice on your horses?"

He shot a glance her way and saw the smirk on her face.

"Are you telling me you don't have any?"

"Come on, Nelson. We know each other. This is the place you come to think. If you wanted me out here, you've got something you're thinking about, and you want to talk about it in private."

This just might work, Nelson thought.

He'd had a difficult week. Getting drunk and hungover on his days off was not a great way to start. Finding out just how much he'd told Dave, and apparently everyone else at the Goat and Barley, about what had happened at his non-wedding made it worse. And then, Mariah.

Mariah's visit had been a little hazy in his memory, but she'd reminded him that he'd agreed to fix his mistake, or he'd be destroying Carter's Crossing's future and his grandmother's dream.

He didn't remember agreeing to that. Mariah didn't care.

He should have told her to run with the two events she had and leave him alone.

Except…

Except that he'd promised his grandmother he wouldn't ruin everything. He wouldn't sneak into town and steal the Christmas presents and decorations and food.

And though he hadn't done it intentionally, he had allowed, under the influence of too much to drink, his own viewpoint and history to spill over and upset their plans.

He hadn't had any intentions of influencing Harvey. But he had wanted to let Dave know that Dave had a say in his wedding and engagement, and that fancy parties might damage his relationship with Jaycee.

He should probably thank his lucky stars that Dave hadn't run off to elope with Jaycee. Nelson suspected that Jaycee wouldn't have run. She was pretty wrapped up in this party planning.

Not that Nelson was going to offer any more advice. He'd done enough already.

Instead, he'd tried to find out what dating life was like in Carter's Crossing. Not to participate, but to find out if anyone was ready to make things serious. He was restricted by the fact that no one thought he wanted to know. And no one wanted to tell him.

He'd talked to the owners of his patients, which had led to more than one awkward conversation, and two offers of blind dates, for Nelson himself. He'd asked Kailey, giving her ammunition for months when it came to keeping him in what she considered to be his place.

He'd been forced to face the same truth that Mariah and her committee had. There were not a lot of dating locals, and none were ready to get married, except for Dave and Jaycee, and Harvey and Judy, who were now already married.

Thanks to him.

The elopement had been nothing but great for Judy. She had a smile on her face, most of the time, and now volunteered comments without prompting. It didn't help Nelson in his quest, however.

He'd come to the end of his ideas. He just had one, mostly crazy, hail-Mary, last-chance idea. And he needed Rachel on board.

He tried to put the words together.

"Are you involved in any of this romance stuff?"

He felt her shoulders shrug beside him.

"I'm helping with Jaycee's party."

Yeah, it was more Jaycee's party than Dave's, but that wasn't something he could fix, as much as he might want to.

"Did you know about the proposal Mariah had planned?" She'd said it was a secret, but Rachel and Jaycee had been spending a lot of time with Mariah.

He'd apparently taken more notice of it than he'd realized.

"Harvey and Judy, yeah. We heard about it after the elopement. Mariah asked if we knew anyone else who might be interested, but we couldn't think of anyone."

Of course not. That would be just too easy.

"Mariah blames me for the two of them eloping."

"I know."

Nelson shook his head. No secrets in a small town.

"Nelson." Rachel sounded insistent. He turned to look at her.

"I know why you don't like Mariah and her plans." She did. Before he shot off his mouth at the Goat and Barley, Rachel had been the only person with whom he'd shared any details of his almost-wedding. Because they were friends, and because the town wanted to pair them up.

He'd been avoiding dating for several reasons. He needed to understand how he'd allowed himself to be so cruel to someone he loved. Someone he'd wanted to marry. He wanted to be sure he'd never do that again. He'd removed himself from situations where he could take over like that, and, as a result, possibly ignored figuring out why.

"But, Nelson, Mariah isn't like your wedding planner. I swear. She isn't like how you described that Sherry woman."

Nelson drew in a breath. He'd promised not to interfere, but Rachel was a good friend. He needed to be able to tell someone.

"Mariah not only worked for Sherry. I heard her tell Grandmother that she'd learned everything from her."

Rachel was speechless. Her mouth opened and shut, and she finally shook her head.

"Nelson, I don't know. I don't know what you heard. But seriously, she's trying to rein Jaycee in from being too crazy over this. She's being considerate, and really nice. I like her."

There it was. If there was a contest, with Nelson on one side and Mariah on the other, Mariah was going to win. Even Rachel, who knew his story, liked Mariah.

Well, until Mariah screwed them over. He didn't want that to happen, but it didn't seem like anyone would listen to him. If Rachel and Grandmother wouldn't, who would?

He might as well see if Rachel would help him with his crazy idea. At least Rachel shouldn't get hurt over this.

"Let's see how things go, okay? What I wanted to talk to you about, well, what I wanted to ask you, was about a way to help Mariah. And Grandmother."

Three guesses who he really wanted to help.

Rachel shrugged. "Okay. I'm happy to help."

She always was. Rachel was the nicest person he knew.

"Mariah wants another proposal to plan. And no one is ready to propose. So what if I propose to you?"

He watched Rachel's face. Surprise. Shock. Suspicion.

"You want to propose to me?" she asked, carefully.

He puffed a cloudy breath into the cold January air.

"I don't want to be involved in any of this at all. But I'm supposed to fix my mistake."

Rachel was still speaking precisely. "You want to marry me to fix your mistake?"

Nelson almost stepped back. "No, no, not marry you."

"Of course, how silly of me. Just propose."

He relaxed, slightly. Now she got it, and she hadn't yelled.

"Right. I'll propose, you'll say yes and then, after things die down, we'll break up."

Rachel crossed her arms. Her lips were pressed tightly together.

"Let me see if I understand this. We'll pretend to start dating."

Right. They should do that first.

"Sure." Nelson nodded. "That's not a problem."

"Well, good. I'd hate to have our fake relationship be a problem."

Okay, Rachel was not taking this well.

"Then you'll fake propose on Valentine's Day. With a fake diamond, I assume?"

"We can use a real diamond. Really, we can pick a ring, and you can keep it. I hadn't thought that far ahead because I wasn't sure you'd agree to it."

"There is that pesky agreement to get through, isn't there? But I have more questions. How long are we fake engaged?"

Nelson tried to think of an appropriate time range. It had to be long enough that no one suspected it was fake, but not so long that they had to make serious plans.

"And who's going to break it off? Are you ready to be jilted again, or am I supposed to take one for the team?"

He hadn't thought that far ahead, either. Obviously, having two women jilt him was not going to do his reputation any good. On the other hand, if Rachel did this favor, he couldn't insist that he be the jilter.

"We could make it a mutual decision."

Rachel rolled her eyes. "Right. If that's the case, then we

need to set a timeline before either of us starts dating again, because whoever dates first would be the winner."

Nelson began to understand the magnitude of stupidity his fake engagement idea entailed. He'd thought that since he and Rachel were friends, and kind of dated, whenever one of them needed a plus one, that this was something he could pull off.

But there were ramifications and subtexts behind all these decisions that he hadn't understood.

"My dad would talk for the rest of his life, or my life, whichever was longer, about how I'd blown my chance. You do understand that half this town thinks I should be trying to get you to propose to me for real, don't you?"

No, he did not. Not completely. But he did understand that he'd hurt his friend. He needed to let it drop, right now.

"Rachel."

He waited this time until her gaze returned to his.

"I'm sorry. It was a stupid idea. I thought, since we were friends, that we could pull this off, but I don't want to make your life more difficult. It's my problem, not yours."

Rachel looked away again.

"I have my own problems, Nelson. I just—really, I can't take on yours, too."

He examined Rachel, while she watched the chestnut. He'd assumed Rachel was happy, contented, living in Carter's Crossing, taking care of her dad, working for her uncle, helping everyone in town.

He'd shared his problems with her. He hadn't been a good friend, though, because he hadn't helped with hers.

"Rachel, if you need something, just ask, okay? You've been a good friend to me, but I haven't been as good to you."

Rachel let out a long breath of cold air. "It's okay. I'm just— I don't know. Having a midlife crisis or something."

"Rachel, you're not even thirty yet. I don't think you can call yourself midlife."

"I'm advanced for my age, I guess."

* * *

Mariah knocked on Nelson's door. This time she heard steps coming her way and didn't have to yell and pound.

Since she was no longer blazing angry, that was just as well. She didn't have any pounding and yelling in her today.

Just a desperate flicker of hope that somehow, Nelson had come through. He'd asked to talk to her, so she hoped he'd found someone ready to propose.

That was plan A. The next plan she had was a plan F at best.

Nelson wasn't in wrinkled clothing, and he didn't stink of whiskey, so things were looking up already. He didn't look excited, like he had a great idea, but she didn't think he'd be excited even if he did find someone for her.

He didn't like her. Or at least, he didn't like what she was doing, and he hadn't been willing to look past that.

It bothered her more than it should. Despite their rocky beginning, she had to recognize that he was a good guy. To everyone except wedding planners anyway.

He was a crappy darts player, but he cared about his friends and grandmother. He was a good vet, according to anyone she'd heard talking about him. He even rescued horses.

And yes, he was good-looking. But none of that mattered. He wanted nothing to do with her. She had less than a year here anyway, so it really shouldn't bother her.

"Come in." He stood back to let her enter.

She hadn't paid much attention to his place last time. She'd been frustrated, angry and convinced she was going to fail. She'd wanted to make him feel some of that pain.

Today she noticed that the apartment was extremely tidy and finished in a way that reflected his grandmother's house. Like he wasn't the one who'd bothered to pick out the furniture and curtains.

She was probably just trying to find things not to like about the man.

"Have a seat. Can I get you anything?"

Two people who want to get married? She shook her head. She wasn't interested in anything else.

She sat on a chair, and Nelson sat on the couch across from her. Exactly like they had a week ago.

He drew in a breath and exhaled again.

"I'm sorry. I wasn't able to find anyone."

She clenched her fists. No, no, no. He couldn't do this. She needed this, so much. She'd made a commitment. Almost a promise. She had to come through.

He shook his head. "This is a small town. Kids who grow up here often move away. There just isn't a big dating pool, and no one in it is ready to make the leap to the married pool."

"Except for Harvey and Judy." She knew she was being bitchy. She didn't care right now.

"I promise, I tried. I asked every client I saw this week. I asked Kailey, and what she doesn't know, or Grandmother, doesn't happen in this town."

She frowned at him. He said he was sorry, but he wasn't invested in this.

"I know you don't like what we're planning for Carter's Crossing. And deep down, you probably hope it fails. But the town needs this."

She saw anger on his face.

"I know the town needs outside business to survive. I might not be a big fan of this particular idea, but I didn't plan to sabotage it. I really tried to find someone who would like to take advantage of your proposal. I even asked Rachel if she'd agree to a fake engagement, just so you'd have someone to get a ring on February fourteenth. But it was a stupid idea, and she said no."

Mariah blinked at him. A fake engagement? He'd really tried to arrange a fake engagement?

That could have worked. It's not like engagements didn't get broken. The big thing for now was to show a romantic proposal, one that would entice people from out of town to come here to replicate.

Maybe she could get Rachel to change her mind?

Mind buzzing again, she made sure. "Rachel said no?"

"She had good reasons. I hadn't thought it through."

Right. Mariah wouldn't push Rachel into this. But it was a smidgeon of hope. A possibility. If there was someone else who would agree to a fake proposal with Nelson.

Someone desperate. Someone motivated.

She sighed. She knew of only one person right now that desperate and motivated. Could she make it work?

"I'm sorry, really. I tried. But there's nothing more I can do."

He stood up, waiting for her to leave, convinced he was off the hook.

No, she wasn't giving up on that hook.

"I'll do it." She almost called the words back. This was crossing lines, smudging borders.

Nelson's brow creased. "You'll do what?"

"I'll accept your fake proposal. We can get engaged for Valentine's Day."

Nelson shook his head. Then pinched himself for good measure.

She thought they were going to get engaged on Valentine's Day? Okay, now he knew. She was crazy. Certifiable.

She flipped open her notebook.

"We're going to need to set some rules and make a plan. If we suddenly act like we're madly in love, it will look suspicious."

Nelson choked.

Mariah narrowed her eyes. "There's no way we can do this otherwise. No one will believe it."

Now she was making some sense.

"No one will believe it. With Rachel, at least we've been friends since we were kids. Like Dave and Jaycee. But us…"

He didn't think he needed to clarify just how much the two of them had been anything but friendly.

"Exactly. The first rule is that we're going to need to spend most of the next few weeks before Valentine's Day together."

Strange how she could start that sentence saying "Exactly" and then take it in *exactly* the wrong direction.

"I have a practice to maintain." He hoped she didn't miss that edge he added. What, was she going to sit in on his day-to-day work? If so, he hoped the Fletchers needed more visits to their pigs. He could almost smile at the picture of Mariah hanging out at a pigsty.

"Right. And I have a lot of planning to do. But we have weekends and evenings."

Nah ah.

"I have other things to do on weekends and evenings." Things he enjoyed. Things that relaxed him.

She looked up at him. "I'm sure I can survive spending a few evenings at the Goat and Barley."

Did she think that was all he did in his free time?

"I'm working with rescue horses on my time off." Sure, Mariah grew up on a boat and could apparently find herself anywhere in the world with a sextant and who knows, a box of nails, and she was killer at darts, but he was pretty sure a life on a boat didn't give her a chance to become a horse whisperer.

"That will work!"

Oh, no, she really was a horse whisperer. Kill him now.

"We'll go out for dinner tonight. The Moonstone. I want to talk to you about using your horses in my plans for the town. We can work out the details on that. Then we'll discover that we actually 'like' each other and start dating. I can offer to teach you how to play darts, and—"

"No."

Nelson used to be like Mariah. He'd run his plans all over poor Zoey, with his wedding planner urging him on. He wasn't going to do that now, and he wasn't going to let anyone do it to him. Especially not to his horses.

Mariah had already sailed quite a distance past him. "No?"

"No, you're not using my horses."

Mariah rolled her eyes. "Tell me about that tonight, not now.

You have dated before, right? You know what you're doing? I don't have to coach you?"

"Uh, yeah. I've dated." She'd been upset that he assumed she was lost but she could assume he'd never gone on a date? He'd dated, proposed and almost got married. He knew how to woo a woman. When he wanted to.

"Okay, then. I'll leave you to make the reservation. You can pick me up just before seven. The sweater you wore that first night I was here was nice—you could wear that again."

Nelson opened his mouth to answer when her phone chimed. She glanced at it and stood up. "Sorry, I need to take this. I'll see you at seven and we can hammer out the rest of the details."

And while Nelson mentally mustered up his arguments, she was gone.

He stood, listening to the door close. Except for the whisper of perfume in the air, it was as if she'd never been there.

But she had. He could try to pretend, but she'd been there, told him they were dating and would be getting engaged in a few weeks.

She was definitely in the right career for her. Bossy, managing, planning, riding roughshod over others.

He had to follow her over to Grandmother's house and make her sit and listen to reason. Or just flat-out tell her he wasn't doing it. But when he got to the door, he saw her car pulling out.

Okay, he could go over there at seven and tell her it wasn't happening and why. With Grandmother listening in.

No, he couldn't do that. Mariah was right; he wanted to make up for his mistake. He didn't want the chaos and stresses of big weddings messing up his town and his friends, but he didn't want Grandmother to lose everything investing in a disaster. She was committed to saving Carter's Crossing.

This whole idea had been a conflict for him since Mariah arrived.

Fine, they could talk tonight at Moonstone. He'd make the reservation, but it was going to cause a lot of gossip.

He texted Jaycee, since he didn't want to talk to anyone. He told her he wanted a table for two at seven. Sure enough, she responded right away.

You've got it—best table in the house! Looking forward to seeing your date! We're all rooting for you.

Right. He'd forgotten for a while that he was a damaged husk of a man after his non-wedding.

That was when the beauty of it struck him. He'd been told he needed to date again so that people would stop feeling sorry for him. He needed to show everyone in town that he wasn't traumatized by weddings.

Okay, then. Mariah wanted her event. If he dated her, the romance planner, he'd show people he was fine. He was over the jilting of the past. They could start treating him like a grown-up again.

But he had one important rule for Ms. Van Delton. He was not going through this whole poor-baby routine again. This time he got to be the jilter. And that was nonnegotiable.

Mariah had been confident when she ordered Nelson to pick her up, but now, with the clock ticking down toward seven, she wasn't sure he'd show. If he did, she wondered whether he'd play along with her. She didn't like the idea of a fake engagement, but she also wasn't thrilled about falling short of her commitment.

And, she argued to herself, so many engagements didn't last. It wasn't a big deal if this one didn't. She could stage a fake proposal to promote Carter's Crossing without claiming it was real, just a publicity event. It would market better if everyone thought it was real, that was all.

She wasn't happy with the arguments she was using to convince herself. She wasn't going to give up on finding another proposal or similar event that would be real. But having this in her pocket, ready to go if needed, made sure things were going to work out.

She wanted Nelson to agree for that reason, but she had another reason she wasn't going to share with him. Nelson demonstrably had influence in Carter's Crossing. He'd already managed to blow up one event she'd planned. She didn't intend to let him have the chance to mess up anything else. If they spent all their free time together, then she could make sure he didn't do any more influencing.

That was why she tried on four outfits before finding one that looked good without trying too hard. And took time to curl her hair and apply extra makeup. She had a fake romance to sell, so she was working hard on selling it.

It was not to impress Nelson. They were coconspirators here, not dates.

When Nelson did pull up in front of his grandmother's house, at seven exactly, in a car that wasn't the clinic van, she was pleased to see, underneath his jacket, that he was wearing that sweater. The one she'd told him to wear. It wasn't because it made his eyes look extra blue, or that it outlined what was undoubtedly an attractive chest. No, it just meant he was going to do what she'd asked.

Suggested. No, demanded.

She had to work a little harder to explain the pleasure that sizzled down her spine when his eyes widened in appreciation when he saw her. She hadn't wasted her efforts. Right.

He followed her out to the car and opened the door for her. She thanked him. Then he walked around the hood to the driver's side and slid behind the wheel. He'd left the engine running, so the interior had warmed up.

As he put the car in gear, he shot a glance at her. "How did you get Grandmother out of the way?"

She shrugged. "I lucked out. She got a call—about the architect, I think."

She noticed Nelson's frown. Probably better not to talk about that. Renovating the mill was going to push all the buttons he had against this project. Another reason to make sure he was on board. She'd half expected him to bail, but he was here.

"We'll have to tell her the truth."

Mariah stifled a grin, as something warmed her from the inside. If he was laying down rules about telling Abigail, he was in. This was good.

"We can lay down the guidelines when we're at the restaurant."

Nelson shook his head. "Not really."

Mariah sat straighter. "No? Any good reason for that other than contradicting me?"

He pulled into a parking space, not far from the restaurant. It was a small town, and they were already here.

"If we're lost at sea, I'll be sure to do what you tell me to. But Carter's Crossing is different, and here I can navigate better than you.

"I made the reservation with Jaycee. I didn't tell her who I was bringing, but I'm willing to bet any amount you want that she's going to be there, watching every move we make. We can't be overheard making rules about dating, or no one is going to buy what we're selling."

Mariah squinched up her nose. "Fine. We can't talk about dating in there."

"I have two stipulations." Nelson moved his body over, leaning against the door, watching her face in the light from the storefront in front of them.

Mariah frowned. She didn't want to argue this. She just wanted it done. This was her job—couldn't he just let her do it?

"What are the two things you want to stipulate?" She wasn't going to accept anything blindly.

"The first is telling Grandmother."

Mariah nodded. She hadn't been looking forward to pretending to fall in love with Nelson in front of Abigail. She was a party planner, not an actress. Keeping up the front in public would be hard enough. She wasn't sure she could sell Abigail.

No, she was sure she couldn't.

"And secondly, I end it."

Mariah shifted back in her seat. She hadn't seen that one coming.

"You end it? You get to unilaterally decide when and how?"

Nelson huffed. "No, we should agree on that. But I'm the one who breaks it off, as far as everyone knows."

Her mind struggled to wrap around this stipulation. Did he have that fragile an ego? He couldn't bear to have a woman end things with him?

As she opened her mouth to tell him what he could do with that stipulation, she suddenly understood.

Mariah was leaving Carter's Crossing in the fall. Once she had everything underway, Abigail and her committee could take over. Mariah might offer some assistance from afar, but she'd be gone from Carter's.

Nelson would be here still. She could put it all behind her, but he couldn't. If he didn't want to be the jiltee it made sense, even if it wasn't the gentlemanly behavior she'd expected from him. He wouldn't have to pretend to be heartbroken once they were done and she was gone.

So instead of arguing, she agreed. Though she would have liked to argue on principle.

He sighed. "Do you have more rules to add?"

She nodded and watched his mouth quirk up. He wasn't surprised she had rules. He wasn't stupid, either.

"I plan the proposal, but you do the asking."

He rubbed his jaw, freshly shaven, she noticed.

"No problem. I don't want to *plan* anything."

He was more forceful in that comment than she'd expected. He really didn't want anything to do with the Romance Center idea.

"I'm going to keep looking for another option, and if I find one, we cool off on the 'dating.' But if we do have to roll out this proposal, it needs to be done well, and that's my forte. I'll do the planning, but ask Abigail to front for it, so we can pretend that you're behind it. I can't appear to be planning something for myself."

Nelson's gaze was centered on the dash of his car. Mariah wondered what he was thinking.

"I want to hear about it beforehand. If it's supposed to be coming from me, it needs to look like something I'd actually do."

That might limit her. This proposal had a primary purpose, which was promoting Carter's Crossing as a romantic destination.

"Will people believe you planned a truly romantic proposal? Something beyond asking if I wouldn't mind?"

Nelson's gaze drifted over her shoulder, and it didn't look like he was seeing the hardware store across the street.

"If it doesn't include me making a fool of myself, then yes, people here will believe I could pull something together. Something nice.

"We should head in now. Jaycee will be looking for us."

He'd cut off the conversation, and there was a lot behind his statement that he wasn't sharing. She remembered that first dinner and knowing that there was more going on with Nelson than she knew.

She was tempted to tell him he had to let her in on whatever it was, or she wouldn't go through with this. Because as gossipy as this town could be, no one had shared with her what had happened to Nelson. And she hadn't asked, because, well, what reason would she have beyond a personal interest in the man? Which she didn't have, obviously. Not before.

She had no leverage to make him open up. He'd agreed to this fake dating and proposal, presumably to help his grandmother, but she didn't think he wouldn't happily opt out if possible.

She was taking a risk here, and she didn't like that. Not at all.

CHAPTER EIGHT

JAYCEE'S MOUTH DROPPED as the two of them entered the front door of the restaurant together. It was a quiet night—there were only two other occupied tables, but those parties also stopped and stared.

He'd known this would happen. He was prepared. But he wasn't happy about it.

For the next several weeks he was going to have to spend all his free time with Mariah. And even after that, he understood, once they were "engaged," they'd still need to spend time together. Would they even have something to talk about?

But no one could say he hadn't gotten over his aborted wedding after this, or that he was against weddings. And once they'd broken it off, people would be off his back for a while.

Jaycee took their coats and led them to a table, right in the window. Nelson rolled his eyes mentally. This town was too involved in everyone's lives. It would serve their purpose, though. The town would talk about them dating.

Jaycee pulled out a chair for Mariah.

"I had no idea you were the person Nelson was bringing to dinner tonight."

Nelson broke in before Mariah could respond.

"Mariah wanted to talk about my horses. She thought they might be useful in her plans."

Jaycee's forehead creased. "But—"

Nelson grabbed the menus from Jaycee's limp hands. "I know. I'll tell her."

Mariah shot a glance between them.

"Ooookay, then," Jaycee said. "Can I get you something to drink?"

Nelson shook his head, while Mariah asked for white wine. Jaycee left with a puzzled look.

Mariah leaned forward. "What is it about your horses?"

He leaned forward, too. "I'll tell you after you've got your drink and we've ordered."

Mariah sat back and frowned. She flipped open the menu and scanned the contents. After making a decision, she set it down and stared at his still-closed menu.

"Aren't you going to order anything?"

He shrugged. "The menu hasn't changed for a while."

"Why aren't you drinking?"

"I'm the only vet available tonight. I limit my drinking times. I'm not a saint, but I try not to be out of commission too often."

"The other night wasn't something you do often?"

He groaned and dropped his head. "I haven't been that drunk in years."

"Did something happen?"

His chin firmed. "Bad case."

Jaycee came back then with their drinks. Nelson ordered a steak; Mariah opted for pasta.

After Jaycee left, Mariah leaned forward again.

"Okay, enough stalling. What's the story about your horses?"

"It's not anything big. I have some rescue horses."

He left it there. Mariah waited for a moment, then said, "Okay, you have rescue horses. You're giving them a home, I guess?"

Nelson nodded.

"Is this a state secret? What is it about these horses?"

"The place I provide is for them to recover, relax and live out their lives in peace. They aren't workhorses."

"No one rides them or anything like that?"

He shook his head.

"Why not?"

"Some of them are old. Very old."

"And the rest?"

If he gave points for persistence, she'd be a high scorer.

"They've been abused. I'm trying to teach them to trust people again."

"And are you successful?"

"Moderately." He was very good, but he'd made new habits, and downplaying his achievements was among those.

"But not enough that they'd be of any use to people coming to Carter's Crossing?"

Did she think he wasn't doing his job?

"What would people want from them? I'm not providing carriage rides around town or trail rides on the farm."

Mariah held up her hands. "I don't know anything about horses. I just wondered. That's part of my job. You said you're trying to get them trusting people. I'm going to bring people into town, so I wondered if there was a way to help each other."

Jaycee brought over their plates before he could tell her there was no way her plans were going to help his horses.

He took advantage of the distraction to remind himself to relax. He didn't understand why, but everything Mariah said made him want to argue.

After Jaycee left, Mariah leaned forward again. "Can you try not to look like you want to snap my head off? We're supposed to like each other enough to start dating. Serious dating."

Nelson ground his teeth together. She was right. He needed to behave.

"I'm sorry." He gritted the words out, annoyed that he needed to say that. "Why don't you come and see the horses? Then you'll understand."

Mariah narrowed her eyes. "Are they going to bite me? Knock me into the mud?"

Nelson held in a laugh. He'd found something Mariah was not an expert about. "No, you don't have to get close enough to be bitten or knocked down. They're behind fences, and you can stay outside those."

"Okay, then."

She still looked so uncharacteristically nervous that he reached over and squeezed her hand. "You'll be perfectly safe. I go there all the time just to chill."

Jaycee came over to ask how their meals were, and Nelson drew back his hand. Jaycee had been staring at their hands.

Why had he done that? He shook his head. Jaycee looked sold on their date being real, so he was getting caught up in the act. That was all. Otherwise, he was getting soft on Mariah. Not a good idea.

Nelson managed to turn the conversation to places she'd traveled while growing up. Since she'd been almost everywhere, conversation never lagged again. They did argue, once or twice, but it didn't veer into personal territory. He might have even enjoyed someone who pushed back, someone other than his grandmother.

As they got in his car for the short drive back to his grandmother's, Nelson was surprised to note that, for the most part, he'd enjoyed his evening. It had been a while since he'd spent time with anyone who hadn't grown up with him in Carter's Crossing. It had been fun. Maybe this fake dating thing wouldn't be too painful.

It was a short date. No, Mariah corrected herself. It was a short predate.

Seven wasn't a late start for a dinner in many places. New York, French islands in the Caribbean, Europe. But in Carter's

Crossing, it was a late start, and Nelson had to get to his clinic in the morning.

Mariah was back by nine. Abigail was still up.

"Was that Nelson who dropped you off? Not that I mean to pry, but yes, I'm prying."

Mariah laughed. "Yes, it was Nelson, and I'll tell you all about it. How was your call with the architect?"

"He's coming out tomorrow to look at the mill and assess if we can work together."

"That's great news. And your contractor can start soon?"

Abigail nodded. "Winter is slow for her, so she's glad to have a chance to put her crew to work. Would you like some tea?"

Mariah agreed, and after hanging up her coat, followed Abigail into the kitchen.

Abigail plugged in the kettle and brought out the teapot. Mariah, familiar by now with the routine, found the cups and tea. Then she sat at the table while Abigail fussed with napkins and spoons, milk and sugar, lemon and honey.

Once the kettle had boiled, and Abigail steeped the tea, she sat across from Mariah.

"You were out with Nelson?"

"You haven't heard already?" Mariah was sure the news had started the rounds.

Abigail merely poured tea into two cups and passed one toward her.

Mariah added some milk. "You know how upset I was when Harvey and Judy eloped."

"And you blamed Nelson."

Mariah shrugged. "The message Harvey left me said it was because of something Nelson said. I think blaming him was an obvious choice. And, to be blunt, he was drunk."

Abigail grimaced. "Nelson doesn't usually allow himself to lose control that way."

"He said he'd had a bad case."

Abigail nodded. "A beautiful family pet hit by a car. He couldn't save the dog, and the family was devastated."

Mariah learned more from Abigail about what had happened than she had from Nelson. Because he wouldn't confide in her? Or because it still upset him?

"I went to see Nelson."

Abigail smiled. Mariah suspected this wasn't news.

"I told him he needed to find a replacement proposal for the one he'd lost us." She swallowed. "I was not very nice."

"He's a big boy."

Mariah expelled a breath. She was lucky Abigail wasn't more protective of Nelson.

"He did try. He even spoke to a friend, asked her to pretend to get engaged to him."

This caught Abigail's attention. "Rachel?"

Again, Mariah wasn't surprised by Abigail's knowledge of her town and its people.

"She said no, so, I uh, I said I'd be willing to be fake engaged to him."

Mariah waited for Abigail's response. Would she think it silly? Dishonest?

"I assume he agreed, and that's why you were out tonight?"

Apparently, neither silly nor dishonest bothered the woman.

"He insisted that we tell you what was going on, but we don't plan to tell anyone else. If I can find another event, we'll forget this, but we're running out of time, and I told Grandfather…"

Abigail was staring past Mariah, a small smile on her face. Mariah had the feeling there was a joke that she was missing.

"Thank you for telling me, and I'll respect your confidence. Does this mean Nelson is now part of the proposal planning?"

Mariah shook her head, and she could have sworn Abigail was disappointed.

"I think it's best if I plan it, and let you execute it? Then we can pretend it's coming from Nelson, but make sure it comes out the way we need. We aren't hurting anyone, are we?"

Abigail smiled. "No, I can't imagine anyone being hurt. Unless of course, you or Nelson...?"

Mariah's eyes widened. "I'm not sure Nelson is going to be able to convince anyone he even likes me. And I'm not looking for anyone right now. I need to get Carter's Crossing set up and settle in with Grandfather's company. We'll be good."

"Then this should all be fine," Abigail agreed. But somehow, Mariah still felt like she was missing the punchline on a joke. One at her expense.

Nelson wasn't surprised to find that his dinner with Mariah had already become common knowledge and was now of more interest to his staff than Judy's elopement.

Judy had been considerate enough to only miss two days of work, so he hadn't had much to complain about. And while she didn't talk much more to him than previously, she was smiling most of the time.

Kailey was also smiling when he came in the door of the clinic. In theory, the three of them started work at the same time. Most days Nelson was the first in. But he swore Judy and Kailey must coordinate on days when they wanted to embarrass him, because then he'd walk in to the two of them staring at him.

"Now what?" he asked, grumpily. He hadn't slept well last night. Some instinct of self-preservation told him he'd been incredibly stupid to fall in with Mariah's fake engagement plan.

"So is it serious?" Kailey's eyes were sparkling. "How long have you two been together? Does this mean she's staying in Carter's Crossing?"

He sighed. He didn't want to feed their nosiness, but this was supposed to be the start of a relationship with Mariah. He couldn't be too grumpy, but if he didn't object to some degree, they'd get suspicious. At least, they should.

"I presume you're talking about the fact that Mariah and I had dinner together last night."

Kailey squealed. He raised his hand to stop her.

"She wanted to talk about my rescue horses. She had some crazy idea about using them in her plans for the town, so I told her no. That's all it was."

Kailey shook her head. "I don't think so. You could have talked about that at your place. Come on, boss, you can tell us."

Sure. Then he decided he could have some fun with this.

"I told Mariah that, but she wanted to go to Moonstone."

He scowled, but inside he was grinning. They hadn't decided who was going to be the initiator of this dating thing, so he'd start the ball rolling. That was as far as he was going to go for now, though.

"Don't you two have real work to do?"

Judy headed to the back, a smile on her face, though Nelson wasn't sure if it was about his having dinner with Mariah, or just the same newlywed glow she was wearing these days.

Kailey leaned over, glancing to make sure Judy was gone.

"Seriously, boss, I'm happy for you. Even if this doesn't work out, you're putting yourself out there."

Nelson headed to the back to get ready for his first appointment. He didn't respond to Kailey, but inside, he was smug. This was going to work out well. Well enough that Kailey wouldn't be the only one who'd stop worrying about his social life.

And he felt a little warm inside. Sure, small towns were nosy, but they cared.

He wondered what Dave would say at the next dart night.

CHAPTER NINE

MARIAH WANTED TO get the next event in Project Proposal underway. They had only a limited time to fall madly in love in front of the town, but she had a planning meeting tonight. She, Rachel and Jaycee now had a standing date to meet and go over the details for the engagement party on Tuesdays while Dave was at darts night with Nelson.

She was happy to be part of girls' night, even if it was work related.

Growing up on a sailboat, traveling all around the world, had obvious advantages. If she'd been given one of those world maps, the kind where you color in every place you've been, Mariah would have been kept busy for a long time and used up most of the crayons. Pretty well any place that touched water, she'd been.

She'd seen different kinds of people, and a variety of lifestyles. She'd picked up bits of many languages and lost her breath at incredible beauty.

But she'd been the only girl. Her brothers hadn't left her out maliciously, but they'd had more things in common and were closer in age to each other. She met girls her age on other boats, not that many, since full-time cruisers tended more to retirees than young families, but she had met some.

When she was younger, finding another girl to play with had been a highlight. As she grew older, it was rarer to find one who shared her interests and became a friend, not an acquaintance. But while the two families might travel to a few places together, eventually they'd part ways. Everyone promised they'd meet up again, and occasionally they would, but it was random, rare and at the mercy of weather and her parents' plans.

Rachel and Jaycee were best friends and had grown up together. Mariah envied them their long friendship. She couldn't imagine how secure it would feel to have friends who'd known her since before kindergarten. Who shared stories from her whole life. Who were there. All the time.

When the planning meetings got sidetracked into other topics, Mariah was happy to follow along. She basked in the feeling of being included. This was what she wanted. When this project was done, and she settled in New York City, she could have her own place, set down her own roots and make her own circle of friends.

In Virginia, she'd been so career focused that she hadn't made an effort to find friends. She wasn't sure she knew how. Here in Carter's Crossing, she was learning. She was looking forward to finally finding her place, and her people. She might not have someone who knew her growing up, but she could make friends who would last the rest of her life.

She'd idealized friendships. Someone to spend time with. Go shopping with, go out with, talk over things with. She hadn't considered that there were things about having good friends, involved friends, that might not be as wonderful. She'd ignored the part about talking things over that she might not want to talk about so much. Concern that headed into nosy territory.

Jaycee hadn't even said hello before she started. "What's up with you and Nelson? How long has this been going on?"

Rachel was the voice of reason. "Jaycee—don't get carried away. You don't know anything other than they had dinner together."

Mariah set down her notebook and pens. She met two pairs of eyes, zeroed in on her. They weren't going to back down; she could tell.

Huh. This was part of being a friend, as well. Good thing she wanted to talk.

"First of all, we've had dinner together before. Abigail has Nelson over a couple times a week. Last night Abigail was dealing with the architect who's coming to look at the mill, so we went out because I wanted to ask about his horses."

Jaycee wasn't convinced. "You didn't have to come to Moonstone to do that."

"Nelson didn't want to disturb Abigail, and what, was I supposed to go to his place? Like that wouldn't have got everyone talking?"

Yeah, make it sound like Nelson came up with the idea.

Rachel gave Jaycee a knowing look. "I told you so."

Jaycee pouted. "I hoped Nelson was dating again."

Since Mariah was the one who was going to be dumped, she didn't need to look like she was chasing him now. She had some pride. But she was puzzled. Why wasn't he dating? If he was, he wouldn't have asked Rachel to pretend to get engaged to him. And she wouldn't be starting a fake romance. Was there no one around he was interested in? Unrequited love?

There was a story about Nelson. She wished these gossipy people would talk about it, but they either knew already and were all talked out, or they didn't want to tell her. She almost asked. These two would know what the story was. But it felt wrong. Gossipy. Prying.

Like she wanted to know because she was interested in him. But she was supposed to be, right? But what if it got back to Nelson?

The person she should ask was Nelson. After all, if they were going to fall in love, she should know his past, especially as it related to love affairs. Was it a love affair? Some past dating thing? Would he even tell her?

Why did it feel important that he be the one to tell her?

She mentally shook her head and caught up with the conversation between Jaycee and Rachel.

"Dave's mom has been talking about her own engagement party, and how they had a sit-down dinner. Maybe we should try something like that? I mean, is this skating party too informal?"

Mariah snapped into planning mode. A sit-down dinner was not the kind of event that would promote Carter's Crossing. It was also nothing like Jaycee and Dave. They were active, fun people, and deserved a party that people would remember and talk about, not a cookie-cutter dinner.

Jaycee was a confident, outgoing woman, with a clear idea of what she liked, but Dave's mother was her weakness. Mariah was just beginning to understand the social divide the railroad tracks made in this little town.

The wrong side of the tracks was more than just an expression.

"Jaycee, I want you to have the best engagement party ever. I don't want to make it the party I want. I want it to be the party you and Dave want. You sounded excited about a skating party. Neither of you even talked about a formal dinner. Isn't that the kind of thing you said you hate?"

Jaycee played with a strand of her hair and nodded.

"Dave's mother may not have enough imagination to see this, but your party is going to be fun, unforgettable and in excellent taste. Abigail supports this. Remind Dave's mom about that if she gets to be too much.

"Now, how's the song choice going?"

Mariah kept glancing at her watch. Nelson was taking her to see his horses, and she somehow found herself ready early.

She tried to tell herself she wanted to make sure he hadn't caused any trouble last night out on his own, but if she was honest, she was looking forward to the trip just for the chance to see his place and his horses. She wanted to know why they were verboten for anything she had planned. She was curious about what his farm was like.

She wanted to understand him better.

Um…

Because of the fake proposal. They needed to set up more dates and work out the logistics for this "relationship." She had a rough plan worked out, but she didn't know if he'd agree to everything.

She'd dealt with all types of people planning events, mostly weddings. There were guys like Dave, who were easygoing and didn't care much about the details.

There were people like Jaycee, in the middle of the spectrum, who had a good idea of what they wanted, but still needed support for their ideas. They would listen to suggestions and accept guidance.

And on the other end, the bridezillas.

Mariah was good at identifying the types. Nelson wasn't an easy guy to figure out.

Nelson was easygoing at times, but not like Dave. He had more confidence than Jaycee, but while he'd certainly pushed a lot of her buttons, he hadn't gone into bridezilla territory.

Not knowing was making her a little nervous.

He'd told her to dress warmly, so she had long johns on under her jeans and sweater. In New York at Thanksgiving, she'd stocked up on warm clothing, so she had a new, warmer coat, as well. This far from the moderating effect of the ocean, things got much colder. The stream by the mill was frozen already, and she kept her fingers crossed that it would last.

Except when she was outside because her fingers got too cold to move.

Nelson pulled up in front of the house in his clinic van. Mariah didn't wait for him to get out. She scrambled to open the door as quickly as she could, grateful that the van was warm.

Nelson was grinning. He was still dressed in his work clothes, but he looked comfortable in the cold. He would.

"Blood still thin?"

She wanted to make a smart comment back, but it was obvious she wasn't comfortable in the cold. Her teeth were chattering. She rubbed her hands on her arms and leaned into the warm air coming from the vents.

"It's not this cold in Virginia, where I've been working these past few years, and on the boat, we stayed where it was warm."

Nelson leaned over and turned up the heat.

"Did you never head north, or south, when it was colder?" He glanced at her before pulling the van into gear and heading to the mysterious farm.

Mariah shook her head. "We traveled up the coast of the US and Europe, down Africa and South America, Australia— pretty well anywhere we could get on saltwater, but we went when those places were having summer. It's more difficult to keep a boat warm when the water is cold, and we can't move where there's ice. So no, I'm not used to this cold."

He took his attention off the road long enough to run his gaze over her. She felt it, moving over her skin along with the heat coming from the vents.

"Did you dress warmly? The barn is a little drafty."

Mariah glanced down at herself. "Long johns, sweater, hat, scarf and mitts. I hope that's enough."

"Let me know if it gets too cold and we can come back."

She nodded. "I will." She wouldn't. She had things to do, and a little cold wasn't going to stop her.

"Tell me about your horses. How did you start rescuing them?"

Nelson had driven them out of town, away from the mill. He pulled off onto a side road. "I worked at an equine practice when I first graduated. It was my specialty. I've always liked horses. Helping horses was natural, once I had my own place back here in Carter's."

"You didn't want to stay with Abigail?"

He shook his head. "When I came back, I didn't like the

idea of Grandmother living on her own. I know she has staff, but they're only there in the daytime. I didn't want to share the house with her, though. I mean, I love her, but..."

"I guess that makes sense." Mariah was enjoying her time with Abigail, but it was temporary. If she was going to live in Carter's she'd probably like her own space.

Whoa. Where had that thought come from?

"Believe me, it would have been a disaster. Grandmother knows everything that goes on in this town, and believes she knows what's best for people. We needed space or she'd have driven me up the wall.

"I bought a farm. The house needs to be completely redone. I should maybe just knock it down and rebuild, but I've been working on the barn."

Nelson turned onto a side road. This was the most Nelson had shared with her since she'd arrived in Carter's Crossing. It was almost like they were friends. She waited to see if he'd keep talking.

"Not long after I got here, I was called in on a case. An old man, a recluse, had died, and his horse had been tied up in the barn without food or water for days. The horse was old, and I'd been asked to put him down.

"Despite what he'd been through, he was still affectionate, and other than the malnutrition, healthy. But he was too old to be of any use to anyone. I took him to the farm. Then I started repairing the barn, making it a home for him.

"Once the rescue people heard about that, I became their contact when they come across a horse in need of a home. A couple of the horses I've had have been rehomed, but the ones that are too old, or too abused, they stay here."

Nelson turned the van into a long driveway. Mariah saw the dilapidated house, and on the other side of the drive, the barn.

The house had boarded-up windows, and the porch floor had collapsed. The barn, on the other hand, looked sturdy and warm. Mariah noticed a couple of horses in the field, watching the van pull in.

"This is it. I've got some stuff in the back to carry in. If you go in that barn door, you'll be warmer."

Mariah looked at the door. Were there horses in there? Were they loose?

Nelson must have understood her hesitation. "When you enter the barn, you're in an aisle, separated from the horses by a fence."

Mariah's breath was a white cloud as she sped to the barn door and pushed it open.

She heard a rustling as she rushed in. A couple of horses leaped to the doorway at the other end of the barn, startling her. A third stood by the partition nearest her, watching her with patient curiosity. Mariah heard Nelson approaching, and stepped back, away from the horses, looking around to make sure there weren't any others.

Nelson pushed the barn door open, carrying a bale of hay. Mariah closed the door behind him.

"Thanks. I've got a feed delivery coming, but not till tomorrow. You guys still want to eat, right, Sparky?"

The horse who'd been watching Mariah had turned his attention to Nelson and stretched his head over the wall.

Nelson dropped the hay bale and reached to scratch behind the horse's ears.

"Sparky?" Mariah asked.

Nelson looked over his shoulder at her. "Do you want to meet him?"

Mariah hesitated. She had never been around large animals. Not wanting to give Nelson fodder for mocking her, she forced herself to walk over.

"This is Sparky. He's the first horse I mentioned."

Sparky was rubbing his head on Nelson's sleeve. Mariah noticed the gray around Sparky's muzzle and eyes. The two other horses she'd startled had come back, heading to Nelson and the food he offered.

"How old is he?"

"He's almost thirty."

She took another look at the horse. Was Nelson serious?

"Really? I didn't know horses lived that long."

"Sparky's enjoying himself too much to give up."

Then the two horses who had been outdoors came around the open doorway. That made five. Was that all of them?

Nelson followed her gaze.

"The chestnut, the light, reddish-brown horse, is the newest, and he's very skittish." Nelson's voice was calm and level. "Don't make sudden moves or loud noises, if you don't mind. He's still getting used to me."

Mariah nodded slowly. She watched the horse, noticing how he hung back, ears flickering, eyes focused on the humans.

Mariah thought her own ears would be flickering if they were able. She felt as uncomfortable as the horse looked.

Nelson continued to introduce her to the horses as he opened the hay bale and dropped chunks of it in the manger.

"The gray is Juno. She injured a tendon and has a limp. She'll never be able to carry a rider or travel too far. The bay is Star. He's blind but knows this field and barn well enough to make it around on his own. Juno normally travels with him and keeps him safe.

"Toby is the chestnut, and with him is Maggie. Maggie is another senior citizen, but she calms Toby down. He'll finally let me touch him, but probably not today while you're here."

"What happened to Maggie?"

"She was another victim of neglect. Her hooves hadn't been tended to for so long they'd grown out to where she couldn't walk on them anymore. It took a while, but she's okay now. She's also developing osteoarthritis, so requires extra care."

While Mariah watched, Toby followed Maggie as she came

closer. He stayed just out of reach but finally came close enough to get his share of the food.

Mariah carefully sidestepped down the aisle in front of the partition, slightly away from Nelson, wanting to give him space to touch Toby if possible. She didn't want to disrupt his plans for the horse.

Nelson was right. None of these horses were going to be of any use in making Carter's Crossing a Romance Center. Two old horses, one blind one and one crippled. None of them provided the image that visitors would be looking for, let alone the ability to pull a sleigh or wagon. The final horse was afraid of people.

She hadn't really expected anything. It had been a means to an end, to start the love story of Mariah and Nelson.

If they wanted to promote Nelson as a romantic lead, however, this would certainly fit the bill. Watching him with his horses, talking to them, running his hands over their necks, scratching their ears—it was enough to make a woman feel a little swoony.

She shook herself. She couldn't get carried away. They were going to pretend to date and get engaged. It was good that she didn't find him repulsive, but there was no need to go overboard.

This was what Nelson had meant about his farm. It was a place of refuge for these animals. Not recreation for people.

"Don't move." She realized Nelson was talking to her. His voice had been in the background, talking to the horses, but now it was pitched toward her. It was still level and calm, but there was an underlying note of caution.

Mariah froze. "Is there a spider on me? You don't have poisonous spiders up here, right? You aren't running a black widow refuge, as well?"

Maybe she had a thing about spiders.

A corner of his mouth quirked. "No, not the season for spiders. Nothing's wrong. It's just that Toby is approaching you."

Toby? The skittish one?

"Did I upset him?" She stayed still, but her muscles were tense, ready to move. She trusted Nelson on this, but only so far.

"No." The smile was growing. "I think he likes you."

At that, Mariah looked out the corner of her eye. Toby was two feet away, on the other side of the partition, watching her.

"What should I do?"

"Just what you're doing."

Mariah didn't want to stand in place indefinitely. It was warmer in the barn than outside, but she was still cool. She turned her head, slowly, and Toby stayed in place.

She turned her body, just as slowly, and watched him back.

"I don't know what you want, horse. I don't have any food."

Toby snorted at her. He took a hesitant step closer.

"Whoa there, buddy. I'm not a horse person. Unless you want to get married, we have nothing in common."

He shook his head, and Mariah tensed. He stretched out his nose, and she leaned back.

"Toby." Nelson took a couple of steps toward her. The horse held his ground but brought his muzzle back toward his chest. Nelson stopped his advance but kept talking. Mariah was feeling it; that low, comforting tone inserting itself under her skin.

She totally got how he charmed his horses.

"You like it when a girl plays hard to get, is that it, Toby? It's okay. You can flirt with her, but I gotta warn you, I don't think you're her type."

Nelson maintained the low voice and leaned his arms on the partition. Toby flickered his ears.

"Would you step up here beside me, Mariah? Nice and easy. He won't bite, but I want to see if he'll come closer."

Mariah had some second and third thoughts about this idea, but with Toby's eyes on her, she came up beside Nelson. She kept her arms safely down at her sides and looked at Nelson for guidance.

He was watching the horse but must have been aware of what

she was doing. "That's good. Ignore him. He's taking a step toward you. Don't move—he's just curious. He won't hurt you."

With no change of tone, he talked to Toby. "You're not used to someone like Mariah, are you, Toby? Did you know she grew up on a boat? And she can find where she is, even in the middle of an ocean? That's what she told me."

Mariah felt warm air on her cheek. She almost swore she felt a velvety softness, and then it backed away.

"So that's it, Toby, is it? You're a ladies' horse? Well, if you're nice, maybe Mariah will come around again."

She heard muffled hoofbeats and turned to see Toby backing off. The air swooshed out of her lungs.

"What was that?"

"I have no idea. But I've never seen Toby approach a person before. Apparently, he likes you."

CHAPTER TEN

"I'VE NEVER SEEN anything like it." Nelson paused to finish his beer.

Dave gave him a strange look.

"Really?"

"Really. I once saw one of those horse whisperers, and it was amazing. But Mariah isn't a horse person. At least, she said she'd never been around them, and she acted like they might be dangerous. But Toby..."

Nelson was still in disbelief over the whole thing.

"Not just Toby," Dave said into his mug.

Nelson raised his fist, then set it back down, frustrated. "Don't go making something out of this. It was just...something I hadn't ever seen before. It's not like—"

He broke off, since he'd been about to say that it wasn't like he was rushing to marry Mariah. Because, in actual fact, he had a countdown to when he was going to ask the woman to marry him.

A fake proposal, but still. Everyone was supposed to believe it was real. He'd thought it would be a hard sell, and he hadn't been sure he could pull it off.

Maybe not. Maybe he had untapped acting skills. He decided to push.

"Tell me something, the truth."

Dave put his glass down. "Like what?"

"You reacted like Judy and Kailey did. Like you thought there was something going on with Mariah and me. Do you? Think that?"

Dave picked up his glass and took another swallow. Nelson suspected he was buying time. Which meant his answer wasn't no.

"I don't know if I thought there was something happening, but you're different with her."

That was not the answer he expected.

"Different?"

"Yeah. She bugs you. I get it. But it's like there's something more. You can't ignore her. So maybe it's one of those love-to-hate things." Dave shrugged. "That's what Jaycee said."

Nelson closed his eyes and took a long breath. This might make the proposal harder to sell, but he needed to be honest with his best friend.

"I didn't tell you this, but Mariah worked for the wedding planner who organized my wedding."

Dave's eyes widened. "Really? Did Mariah work on your wedding?"

Nelson shook his head. "I heard her telling Grandmother that she'd learned everything she needed to know from her boss."

"You mean the woman who did your wedding."

Nelson nodded. "I said something to Grandmother about it, and she told me she trusted Mariah. And that Mariah had planned Zoey's wedding just before coming here."

Dave's eyes nearly bugged out of his head. "Your Zoey?"

"My Zoey. So she might have some magical spell on Toby, but I have a hard time trusting her."

Dave nodded. "I get that. Why didn't you tell me before?"

"It's not my favorite topic—how I ruined my own wedding and chased off my fiancée. And, maybe Grandmother was right.

Maybe Mariah's better now. I can't imagine Zoey working with her otherwise. But…"

"Yeah. That's a big but." Dave stared down at the table.

Nelson shouldn't have brought this up. It was unfair to Mariah. He knew he was anything but impartial. And it was going to make it harder to sell a big love affair with Mariah these next few weeks.

But he'd also been concerned about Dave. Dave hadn't complained, lately, about his engagement party, but Nelson knew something wasn't quite right. When the topic came up, times when they were hanging out with the girls, Dave's expression tightened. Nelson couldn't understand why Jaycee didn't see it.

Dave and Jaycee had started to practice their dance. Jaycee had brought it up, not Dave. In fact, all Jaycee talked about these days was the party.

Nelson would have liked to talk to Jaycee, ask her if she was considering how Dave felt about all these decisions she was making, and the time and energy she was spending on it. But he'd promised not to interfere.

He'd compromised, telling Dave why he was skeptical about Mariah. He'd be there for his friend if Dave needed him. He was not going to charge in, telling people what they should do.

He'd been that guy and it cost him his fiancée, so he couldn't be that guy again. For three years it had been easy. Now he was going to need dental work from grinding his teeth.

"Another game of darts?" It was time to distract his friend. Nelson had dropped his hint, and now he'd leave it up to Dave.

Dave blinked, obviously miles away.

"Sure."

Nelson might have doubts about Mariah as a wedding planner or romance coordinator, but he wanted her help with Toby. If she could bring Toby close enough for him to touch again it would advance his rehab. Unlike the other horses, Toby had a chance at a second life with people. The right kind of people this time.

It was worth asking her.

He wasn't sure if she'd be interested in a return trip to the barn. It might not fit into her dating timeline since it wasn't someplace people would see them. When she agreed, he wasn't going to second-guess the opportunity, though, so he picked her up on his next afternoon off.

He'd brought a space heater, to keep the barn warmer. He hoped to spend some time with Toby, if Mariah's magic worked again, and it wouldn't help anything if Mariah turned into an icicle in the meantime.

Her one condition had been that he go with her to a couple of locations she needed to scout before they went to the farm.

Nelson almost bit his lip hard enough to draw blood, holding back the mocking question about whether she needed his help to navigate. She'd never admit it, he knew, and she'd probably claim this was to sell the dating story, but he liked his version better—that Mariah, the mighty navigator, needed his help to find her way around New York state.

He pulled up in front of his grandmother's house, in what was becoming a familiar move. Mariah was ready. He had to give her points for promptness—she never kept him waiting. She was wearing a red coat that made her look pretty. She was carrying a briefcase and a duffel bag.

He got out of his car to open the trunk for her.

"Thanks." She dropped the duffel bag into the trunk. "I brought a change of clothes for the barn."

"You couldn't have just worn something more casual?"

She frowned at him. "I need to look professional."

Nelson was wearing jeans and boots with a jacket. He was dressed for warmth. No one had mentioned needing to look professional. "What exactly are we doing?"

"I'm doing research, looking for activities, points of interest and other locations for out-of-town visitors."

Nelson sighed.

Mariah shot him a glance. "I'm not going to ask you to do

anything, well, anything major. But you can give me a male reaction—just 'I'd hate that' or 'I'd like to do this.' I need more feedback. If you and I are going to convince people that we're dating, I can't very well ask some other guy from town to drive me around."

He didn't want to admit it, but she had a point.

"Plus, if I'm helping you with your horse, you should be able to help me in return."

She shot him a challenging glance.

Nelson couldn't think of anyone else who'd say something like that to him, and he had no idea why he liked it. "Where do you want to go?"

Mariah opened her briefcase and pulled out a sheaf of papers and her phone.

"I've got the first location here on my phone app. In case we lose connection, I printed out directions."

Was she serious? She was angry when he offered a stranger direction, but she didn't think he could find his way around the place he lived?

"No sextant?"

"I'm keeping that as a treat for the next time."

An annoying voice on her phone instructed him to turn left as he pulled away from his grandmother's house.

Once they'd left town, Nelson was able to ask where they were going. Mariah might have her app and her printouts, but he'd grown up here. He'd be able to navigate to any place around here better than an app.

Mariah fiddled with the scarf around her neck.

"A place called Evertons?"

Nelson took his gaze from the road to check if she was serious.

"Evertons?"

She nodded.

"I was told they have a corn maze in the fall and make maple syrup."

"Yeah…did Grandmother tell you to go there?"

Mariah shook her head. "No, I found out about it from some-one else. Abigail said she couldn't help me but didn't want to tell me why. She thought I should go in unbiased."

Nelson sighed. "You should go in without me, then. The Evertons aren't fond of my family."

Mariah shook her head again. "No, I won't present myself under false pretenses. I'm working with Abigail. I won't hide that."

"Then you're not going to get very far."

Mariah looked at him. "Let me guess. Long, long ago, a Carter and an Everton wanted the same land. They flipped for it, and after the Carter won, it was revealed that it was a two-headed coin. Ever since then—"

Nelson laughed and shook his head. Mariah tried again. "The Evertons started the mill and the Carters won the deed in a poker game?"

Nelson couldn't help looking at her again. There was a teas-ing glint in those eyes. She might actually have a sense of humor under all her lists and plans. He wanted to find out. But the Everton story wasn't a funny one.

"There was an accident at the mill about fifteen years ago. Mrs. Everton was hurt and died a few years later. The Ever-tons blame the Carters."

Mariah was quiet for a moment.

"And what do the Carters say?"

Nelson took a long breath. "That Mrs. Everton was in a place she shouldn't have been. If you want to be unbiased, I'll leave it at that."

"Thanks." Mariah looked down at her notes. "I understand why Abigail didn't want to influence me, but I feel better com-ing in with an idea of what's going on."

Nelson slowed, ignoring the voice on the phone app. "We're almost there, so I hope you're ready."

Mariah gave him a worried look. "They're not going to come out with a shotgun, are they?"

Nelson toyed with the idea of saying yes, just to see her reaction, but he wasn't that mean. There didn't need to be any more bad blood between the Evertons and the Carters.

"No. I don't know of anyone around here who's likely to greet visitors with a gun. But give them time—they don't know you yet."

The worry vanished from her eyes, replaced with a spark.

"If you haven't driven them to it after all these years, I think I'll be okay."

Nelson hid his grin. He wouldn't admit it to anyone, but he liked that she pushed back at him. After the fiasco with Zoey, Mariah was a relief. No one was going to push her into anything she didn't like. He could relax and be himself.

He turned into the driveway, toward a house set back in the trees. As he pulled the car to a stop, a man his own age stepped out. He was dressed in work clothes and heavy boots, and a bushy beard covered the lower half of his face.

He had a dog on a tight lead beside him, something related to a German shepherd, and the animal was focused on them with a laser gaze.

Nelson had never seen this dog before, unsurprisingly, but he recognized it as a guard dog, undoubtedly dangerous in the right circumstances.

Jordan spoke, and the dog sat.

He wasn't carrying any other kind of weapon, but the expression on his face was so far from welcoming as to make Mariah's concern plausible.

Well, that and the dog.

Mariah was reaching for the door release, so Nelson quickly got out of the car. He didn't want her to face the wrath of the Evertons on her own. Especially not with a guard dog at the ready.

"Nelson." The bearded man's voice was cold.

Nelson nodded. "Jordan. How're things?"

Jordan ignored him to examine Mariah. Nelson had to fight an urge to stand between the two. "Mariah, this is Jordan Everton."

Mariah stepped forward, hand outstretched. "I'm Mariah Van Delton, Mr. Everton."

Jordan stood in place, ignoring her hand. The dog curled a lip.

"I've heard of you."

His tone didn't indicate that he was very happy with what he'd heard.

Mariah was unfazed. She dropped her hand with no indication of embarrassment.

"I don't know what you've heard, so let me give you an introduction. I'm here to set up a new business in Carter's Crossing. The business is intended to benefit everyone. I plan to make this place a destination for everything related to romance—weddings, anniversaries, proposals, weekend getaways. The town looks like a Norman Rockwell painting, has four seasons for variety and is located within a few hours of several large cities, so I have every confidence I can make this happen.

"I'm paid by my grandfather, who handles events in New York City, among other things. My room and board are provided by Abigail Carter, as I'm sure you're aware. However, this is *my* project. And the project is for the benefit of everyone in the area.

"I intend to take advantage of everything the town has available—bed-and-breakfasts, restaurants, activities, special locations. Currently, Carter's Crossing is almost invisible online, and there's very little promotion for what Carter's Crossing has to offer. That is going to change. I hope to get people to come here, provide business for those who live here and attract more investment and expansion in the town.

"I understand that you have a corn maze on your property in the fall and make maple syrup in the spring. I think both of those activities would work as an attraction for visitors, and I would like to work with you so that I promote your enterprise. I don't mean to tell you how to run your business, but I can advise you as to what is likely to be lucrative with the people we're bringing in."

Mariah brought her pitch to a close and waited. Jordan stood, watching her.

"If I don't cooperate, what then?"

Nelson had been impressed by Mariah's spiel, though he'd never tell her that. She had some good arguments, but he also knew how stubborn the Evertons were. Jordan's father was convinced that the mill was at fault for what had happened with his wife, and he'd passed that belief on to his son.

"Nothing will happen if you don't want to be part of what we're doing. You won't be featured on our website. I won't share with you my ideas to make your events mesh with our romance theme. I won't tell you how I think you could keep people coming in during summer and winter.

"We won't shun you. We won't discourage people from coming here or spread rumors about your place. But I need partners in this enterprise, and I'll focus my attention on them.

"If we bring in more people, I'm sure that will still benefit you, but not as much as you could if you cooperate with us. I do understand that there are things of more value than money, so I'm not going to pressure you. I would like you to work with us, but that's your call.

"One last thing I'd like to mention. I've been working closely with Abigail Carter, as the original idea was hers. She's determined to make this work and has plans to change the name of the town to Cupid's Crossing, to help with marketing. That means your business would not be connected with the name Carter."

Nelson shook his head slightly; not sure he was hearing correctly. Grandmother was going to take the Carter name away from the town?

Was Mariah serious? Or was she manipulating Jordan?

Jordan had his arms crossed, a frown on his face. "Your sidekick here doesn't seem to be aware of that."

Nelson clenched his jaw. He didn't like being called a sidekick, and he didn't like being caught unprepared. Not about something big like this, something that would affect not only him but also everyone else in town.

"I don't think Abigail has told anyone but me. She wants to be sure this idea succeeds before she changes the name."

Jordan shot a smirk at Nelson, enjoying his irritation.

"Well, Ms. Van Delton, I'll consider what you've said. Perhaps you and I could talk about this further, if I decide I'm interested."

Nelson didn't like being cut out. He almost argued the point, but then paused, unsure why he felt this way.

He'd asked to be left out of the romance idea. He had no reason to think Mariah's spending time with Jordan was a bad idea, even if Jordan did look like he was interested in more than talking business with Mariah.

He wasn't her boyfriend...or was he?

They were supposed to be pretend dating.

He moved a few steps closer to Mariah. He didn't think he could get away with wrapping an arm around her, but he reached out and tugged on her scarf.

"We should get going. You still had a couple of stops you wanted to make before we see the horses."

Jordan gave them a mocking salute. "Call me in a week or so, Mariah, and I'll let you know."

"Thanks for listening to me, Mr. Everton."

"Jordan, please."

Mariah nodded. "I hope we can find a way to work together."

"Me, too."

Nelson wanted to tug Mariah and stuff her into his car. Jordan had no intentions of working with anyone connected to a Carter. He was just messing with Nelson. And unfortunately,

Nelson was upset by that, because he'd agreed to a fake engagement because…it took him a few beats. Because he'd had
a part in Harvey and Judy's elopement and didn't want his
grandmother to lose everything in this plan she had to revital-
ize Carter's Crossing, or Cupid's Crossing, or whatever name
they came up with.

And Mariah was supposed to help with his horses.

Mariah finally sat in the car, after he'd held the door open for
her, and they left the Everton farm behind them, Jordan watching them drive away, the dog now on its feet.

He'd have to tell Dave about this. Jordan and Dave and Nelson had all been in the same grade going through school and
been friends—until the accident. Jordan's dad had pulled him
out of school. It had been the end of their friendship.

That one, at least, wasn't Nelson's fault.

Mariah was nervous about going back to Nelson's farm.

It was flattering, and a definite ego boost to be the horse
whisperer her last time here, but she didn't have any abilities
in that regard. It must have been a fluke. She was going to feel
awkward and out of place if the horse ignored her this time.

Too late to worry about that. They were at the farm, and
it was time to discover if she had equine superpowers or not.

She opened her door without waiting for Nelson. She grabbed
her bag from the trunk and changed her coat and boots, shivering in the cold.

"You could change in the barn—it would be warmer."

Mariah finished buttoning up her coat. "It's okay. I'm done
now." She wasn't sure why, but she hadn't wanted to change in
the barn, in front of the horses.

Nelson stood staring at her.

"Is something wrong?" Was she dressed wrong? She'd
brought the same clothes as last time. Maybe the horse had
just liked her coat.

"Are you okay? You don't really have to do this."

Mariah let out a breath. Was she that transparent? "I'm afraid I might not be able to do it again."

She closed her eyes. Why was she admitting this? She didn't want to appear weak in front of Nelson. So often it felt like they were opponents. And this was being...vulnerable.

His response surprised her.

"You don't have to do anything. Maybe Toby was just curious about you because you were new. If so, no harm. I still got closer to him than I've been able to when he's loose.

"If he does want to come to you, that's a bonus."

Maybe they weren't opponents. Maybe they were just people with different goals. Except for the next few weeks. Unless she found another couple ready for a proposal, they had a shared goal of appearing to fall in love.

Guess she should start with Toby.

"Okay, then, let's see if I'm irresistible to horses."

Mariah headed to the barn, but Nelson put a hand on her arm.

"If you're warm enough, let's just stand at the fence. The horses are outside, so we'll see if you're irresistible out here, as well."

Nelson rubbed his hands up and down her sleeves. It was a nice gesture. And she couldn't think of an ulterior motive for it. There was no one here to see them. He was being...nice.

The friction did help. She finally batted him away.

"Okay, I'm good now. I'll go try my magic at your fence."

She followed him to the fence, where they could see the five horses under some trees on the far side. A couple had their heads down, looking at something on the ground. Two had their heads on each other's backs, and one was staring at them.

Within a couple of minutes the herd had started their way.

"Is that me?"

Nelson rested his forearms on the top rail. "Would you be devastated to know that the four of them always come to see anybody who stops by?"

"No. I don't need to be the pied piper of the equine world. It's just if Toby comes, right?"

Nelson's eyes were glued to his horses.

"Right."

"Should I hold out my hand or wave or something?"

The corners of his mouth quirked, but he kept his eyes on the animals walking toward them.

"No, just the power of your presence should do it. Sudden noises or movements are more likely to startle them."

All five horses were heading this way. Was it working? She felt a tug of affection for Toby.

"So what will you do with Toby if he gets over his fear? Will he stay here with the others?"

"It depends on how well he does. If he could be useful, and enjoy himself, I'd try to find him a home. I have limited room here, and I can only keep so many horses. I need to be sure I have space for those who have no other options."

This was a side to Nelson she hadn't known before. She hadn't realized the horses were a key to the Nelson lock.

"There's no chance I could talk you into expanding to have regular horses, as well, to ride or do wagon rides or sleigh rides on your farm, is there?"

Nelson shook his head slowly. The horses were almost within reach. Toby was with the herd but hanging back.

"I'm not running a business out here. Having horses for those activities would require a lot of time and money. I have a job, one I'm quite happy with."

Mariah turned sideways to watch him. The first couple of horses had stretched their heads out to touch him.

"Did you always want to be a vet?"

The first nose had reached Nelson, and he ran his gloved hand up the side of the horse's face, rubbing behind the ears. The horse shoved his head against Nelson's body, obviously enjoying the attention. The next horse reached in, wanting the same.

Mariah wondered how he could handle all four if they crowded around him. She wouldn't be comfortable with that.

"As long as I can remember. I like animals."

Then she felt warm air against her cheek. She stayed still.

"Did I do it again?" She kept her voice low and calm, imitating Nelson to the best of her ability.

Nelson had a warm grin on his face, one she couldn't help responding to.

"You sure did."

Then she felt a push, gentle, but still a push, that felt very much like what she imagined Nelson had felt when the first horse rubbed up against him.

"What should I do?" she asked, uncomfortably out of her element.

Nelson had better have been telling the truth about the horses not biting.

"Hold out your glove and see what he does."

Mariah could do this. She braced herself and slowly held out her hand. A chestnut muzzle moved over it, snuffling a cloud of warm breath over her cold glove.

Mariah watched for a moment, mesmerized. Was this really her, charming a horse? Who knew? She looked back to Nelson.

"Don't rub his nose—that can be sensitive. But if you're okay with it, run your hand up his cheek."

Nelson demonstrated on the closest head to him. That horse enjoyed the attention.

Mariah turned her glance to Toby again. Slowly, she moved her hand up to his cheek, expecting him to bolt any moment. Bolt or bite. Instead, after a slight hesitation, he leaned into her caress.

Mariah stroked back and forth for a couple of minutes, then turned to Nelson. "It's working. I'm doing it!"

She felt a sense of accomplishment out of all proportion to the activity.

But Nelson grinned back, just as happy. At that moment she felt something.

Her smile faltered, but Nelson was pushing aside the heads next to him.

"Are you okay for a couple of minutes? I'm going to go grab some treats. We want to reward Toby for this."

"Sure." Mariah heard Nelson leave, while she focused back on Toby. She kept rubbing his cheek.

"Toby, it's nice to know that someone here likes me, but what the heck was that with Nelson? It was just weird. Don't tell anyone, okay, horse? Because Nelson might be happy that you like me, but he doesn't like me or my job, at all.

"Do you know why that is?" she continued, stroking the horse, hand moving to his neck, which he allowed, as well.

"Nah, you're new here, too, aren't you? Well, if he does tell you, would you mind sharing it with me? Because it would be a whole lot easier to fake date this guy if he didn't despise me."

He hadn't looked like he despised her a few minutes ago. But this thing with Toby? It was all Toby. She hadn't done anything to merit this. She was just the person Toby decided to trust.

It was too bad Nelson couldn't trust her, as well.

CHAPTER ELEVEN

NELSON WAS HAPPY that darts night was just the guys again. Ever since the engagement party had been greenlit, Jaycee had kept Mariah and Rachel busy with party plans. Unfortunately, the plans were stressing Dave, a lot.

"You're really dancing on skates." Nelson had a hard time picturing that.

Dave nodded. Instead of watching the hockey game over the bar, he was picking the label off his beer bottle.

"It's not that bad. It's more skating than dancing. But Jaycee is making such a thing of it. I mean, it's not like we're in the Olympics where someone is judging every little thing."

Nelson almost bit his tongue, but he managed to keep his comments to himself. It wasn't easy. He saw so much of himself in what Jaycee was doing.

This was what he had against these events. It could bring out a side to a person that could never be unseen. People could be hurt. Things were said that could never be unsaid.

Nelson had learned it all firsthand. But he'd learned other lessons, as well. One was that he didn't always know best. And that even though he could charm, argue or coerce people into doing things, that didn't mean he should.

He'd vowed to himself that he'd never do that again, and he

wasn't going to. He'd made a promise to his grandmother to stay out of the romance plan. He'd pushed those limits already, between his drunken diatribe and revealing Mariah's connection to Sherry Anstruthers to Rachel and Dave. He couldn't in good conscience do anything more.

Instead of telling Dave what to do, he asked him if he wanted another beer.

Dave shook his head. "No, I'm good. And sorry, didn't mean to whine. I want to ask you something."

Nelson had been about to go to the bar, but he waited.

"You've been spending a lot of time with Mariah."

Yes, the small-town grapevine was in fine form. He'd refused to tell Kailey and Judy anything except that Mariah was helping with the horses, but he knew they suspected there was more to it. Everyone did.

And there was. They had the proposal coming up in a couple of weeks. He and Mariah were spending most of their free time together, except for dart nights, and other planning emergencies with Jaycee. And it had been, well, not as horrible as he'd feared.

"I told you—when she's there, Toby is a different horse."

"That wasn't just a fluke?"

Nelson grinned. "Toby has a crush on her."

Dave blinked. "Is that a real thing with horses?"

"It is with Toby. Every time she shows up, he comes right over."

Dave had helped Nelson transport Toby to the farm. He understood just how big a deal that was.

"No kidding. So does she work with him?"

Nelson shook his head. "She doesn't know anything about horses. But while she's there, he sticks around, and I've been able to groom him, check his feet. It's been pretty incredible."

"It's just been about Toby?"

Nelson could feel the heat in his cheeks as he paused.

Dave started to grin.

"Oh, so maybe this wedding planner isn't so bad?"

Nelson would have loved to contradict him, but he couldn't.

It wasn't just that he was trying to make people believe that he and Mariah could be in love by Valentine's Day.

It was because they weren't just spending time with Toby together. And he didn't hate it.

Mariah, in a move that was typical, had come up with a program for their time together, one that would help them appear like a dating couple. Since they'd be learning about each other if they were really dating, they spent every free night together doing research.

Research in this case meant watching the other person's three favorite movies. And part of the other's favorite TV shows. And he had to read her favorite books while she read his.

They shouldn't have had too much time for talking, except that they managed to argue about the movies, TV shows and books. She was appalled by the lack of female representation in his choices. He thought hers were too serious and had no humor.

Needless to say, there was no overlap in their choices.

He enjoyed the sparring. He'd thought, after his wedding fiasco, that disagreements and arguments were the last thing he'd enjoy, but somehow, he did.

Because he was a Carter and had always been one of the smartest kids in school, and the most ambitious, people tended to defer to him. When he was treating his animals, no one contradicted him. When he made recommendations, for meals or movies or vacation spots, people listened.

Mariah, however, hadn't been impressed with him since they met. He suspected that sometimes she argued against him, not because she thought he was wrong as much as because she believed he needed to be put in his place.

Somehow, he liked it. And upon occasion, he'd argue a position he didn't honestly support, just to make her sit up, eyes sparkling, cheeks flushed, and go after him.

"She's…" She was what? How would he describe Mariah?

Aggravating and independent. Way too sure of herself. Pretty. Smart. Strong. Brave and patient with Toby. Kind and respectful with Grandmother.

Dave was waving a hand in front of him, waiting for an answer to his question.

"She's not so bad," he muttered.

Dave laughed, looking carefree for the first time in weeks. "You look like that was painful to say. I knew you weren't just spending time with her for your horses."

"Jeez, Dave, could you say that a little louder? I don't know if the kitchen staff heard you."

He squirmed on his seat, uncomfortable. But this was what he was supposed to do. And it made Dave laugh. It shouldn't bother him so much.

"Come on, spill. You aren't spending all that time with Nelson just working with his horses, now, are you?"

Mariah was impressed that it had taken this long before Jaycee and Rachel asked about what was going on between Nelson and her.

Rachel was nice. It wasn't a surprise that she hadn't pried. But Jaycee was different. It was only the pressure of the engagement party distracting her that had bought Mariah time.

She didn't need time, not really. But it had been a relief, all the same.

Mariah wasn't an actor, but she was trying to act. Whether she could convince these two women that she and Nelson were really falling for each other would be a real test.

Apparently, she was acing it.

"I asked him to take me to some places around here, things that might help with my planning."

"Sure. Is that why you've been spending nights at his place?"

How did Jaycee know that? Mariah was still getting used to small-town gossip.

"I have not been spending the night at his place." Not at all. She always came back to Abigail's to sleep.

"Okay, fine, spending the evening. I know he doesn't have any horses up there."

Mariah felt her cheeks flushing. This was good, really. She needed people to believe they were dating.

"We've been...hanging out." It would be better to be vague, and let people imagine what they wanted. Then she wasn't lying, and the rumors would still spread.

"Hanging out, as in making out on his couch?"

Mariah rolled her eyes, but she wondered if this is what she'd missed, with the way she'd been raised. The teasing, about boys and whatever else.

"None of your business." It was supposed to stop the conversation. Instead, it made Jaycee clap.

"Is he a good kisser? I've always thought he would be. I'm not sure why. I never thought Dave would be, but it turns out he's fantastic."

Mariah tried to get Jaycee back on track. "We're not here to talk about whether Nelson is a good kisser."

But now the question was in her head. Did Jaycee really have to bring it up? But then again, this was part of dating. If they really wanted to sell this...

Rachel was quiet. "You're leaving in the fall, right?"

Mariah nodded.

"Nelson knows you're leaving, too?"

Right. They needed to have a story for that to really sell the proposal.

"Nelson knows what my plans are."

Rachel smiled deprecatingly. "It's just, Nelson had a bad time, and it's taken him a while to get over it. He's my friend, and I worry about him."

Mariah appreciated that. She wanted friends like that, friends who knew you, knew where you'd been and what you'd done and worried about you.

"Rachel, I promise I'll be honest with Nelson. He may be an opinionated, arrogant know-it-all, but if he's your friend, I know there's good down there somewhere."

Jaycee offered her a high five. "You are exactly what Nelson needs. Rachel is way too nice to him."

Rachel smiled, but Mariah could see the worry underneath. Rachel was a lovely person. Quietly pretty, in a way that deflected attention. Kind, generous, helpful... Why had Nelson overlooked her? Nelson said they were friends—did Rachel want more?

Mariah hoped this proposal wouldn't hurt Rachel. But if Nelson didn't care for her, and she cared for him, it was better to know and deal with it.

Maybe, after Nelson broke up the engagement, something could work out between them. She didn't understand why that thought bothered her.

She wasn't here to play Cupid for the residents of Carter's Crossing. She was here to build a business. And that she would do.

After what Rachel said, she had to finally press Nelson on what had happened to him in the past. If they were going to sell this romance, it was something she needed to know.

She just hoped it wouldn't end the fun they'd been having together.

Despite Jaycee's imagination, Mariah and Nelson always sat a decorous distance apart when they were in his apartment, doing research.

Mariah could only imagine what Jaycee would think if she heard they were doing "research."

She hadn't pushed Nelson on his life story. If she was honest with herself, she didn't want to share her own in detail, so it hadn't seemed fair to ask him to do so. But she needed to know. There was something connected with weddings and romance and that was much too close to her job for her to ignore.

And, they needed to demonstrate some PDA. That wasn't going to be easy to bring up, but they were running out of time, and it wasn't going to happen organically. Not when they weren't really dating.

Since she hadn't been able to find a replacement event for the proposal at this late date, it appeared that they were going to have to do this thing.

Mariah had brought her laptop and notebook to Nelson's apartment. It was a familiar space by now. The first couple of visits, she thought he had cleaned up for her, but now she realized he just was that tidy. It was a trait she appreciated. Growing up with five people on a boat, the only way to find anything and stay safe was to have a place for everything and everything in its place.

Nelson turned on the hockey game. Mariah knew his favorite team, and more than she wanted about its history and how this season was going.

"You don't mind?" he had said the same the last time they got together, when she had some sourcing to do online, and they weren't actively "researching."

Then she'd said she didn't mind. This time she reached over and turned off the game.

He looked annoyed but didn't say anything. He wasn't stupid.

"I was talking to Jaycee and Rachel, and I realized…we have to work on kissing."

Nelson took a moment to hear what Mariah had just said and understand the meaning.

"Kissing? For this fake proposal, you mean? Is there a kissing part?"

Mariah shook her head.

He felt something drop in his chest. He was disappointed. Working on kissing sounded like fun.

"It's for now. If we want people to believe we're so in love that we want to get married, we have to show some affection in public. Unless that crosses some kind of line for you?"

That would be a no. He was a fan of kissing, and he'd missed it.

Mariah kept her eyes on her notes as she continued, "So that means hand-holding, touching and kissing. And yes, if two people are crazy about each other and one proposes, then there would be kissing at the proposal. I didn't script it—I just assumed it was going to happen."

Nelson didn't respond immediately. He hadn't thought about that part of the fake dating: her list of hand-holding, touching and kissing. Especially kissing. Not as far as actually making the moves necessary for their lips to meet. He'd thought Mariah was pretty, and, well, those lips had inspired some thoughts about how they'd feel...

Yeah, he'd thought about kissing Mariah. But not seriously. Always in the abstract. The idea of taking those thoughts and putting them into action? Not a place he'd allowed himself to go. Now he was going there, pushed on by Mariah herself.

"To be clear, you want me to kiss you the next time we're out together. Like, where there are people around." He didn't think the farm would count.

And, totally unrelated, he wondered if they should go out somewhere tonight, someplace where people were around.

"No, I think we need to practice first."

Practice? Nelson straightened on the couch. Oh, yeah, he was up for that.

"I'm good, but if you want a chance to make sure you're up to speed..." He raised his eyebrows. This research was sounding better all the time.

"Of course you think you're a good kisser. All guys do."

There she went, giving him grief again.

"I am a good kisser. Do you need references?"

Mariah waved off his assertion. "You really think any woman would tell you if you were bad? We're brought up to be nice."

If this was Mariah being nice...

"You think you need to teach me how to kiss?" Seriously, this woman was enough to drive a man to frustration. Frequently.

She was sitting upright, chin raised. "I don't know if I need to teach you or not. But I'd like to try it in private first, in case we need to work on it."

What, she was going to critique his kissing performance? Not happening. He'd make sure she had no complaints. And he needed to derail this line of thought right now.

"Mariah, I don't know what kind of 'working on this' you think we might need, but if you want to kiss me you could just say so."

Mariah lifted her hand and started counting off on her fingers. "Too much saliva, too much pressure, too much tongue, licking, scraping teeth, bad breath—"

"Okay, okay, I get it," Nelson broke in. She really did have a list on this. And then he wondered if he had breath mints around. What had he eaten for dinner?

He wanted to assure her he didn't do any of that, but now he began to second-guess himself. Would anyone have told him if he'd gotten it wrong? He couldn't remember any of his dates trying to avoid his kiss...

"It would look bad if one of us was flinching away from the other when we kissed in public. I just thought we should try a kiss in private first, so we can do it right."

Nelson looked at Mariah, her cheeks slightly pink, her gaze on her notebook and her teeth biting her bottom lip. Maybe it was all this talk of kissing, but right now he wanted to kiss Mariah.

Not theoretical, kissing would be great, but kissing the woman sitting there, the one trying to make kissing an item on her list, something they could practice in order to demonstrate to people that they were falling for each other.

Maybe some people kissed like that. But Nelson never had. He didn't kiss for anyone but himself and the woman he was interested in. He wanted to kiss Mariah but kiss her so that she wanted to kiss him again, not to impress anyone else or critique his technique.

He was going to make her love his kisses.

Being overeager was something that would be on the bad kissing list, so Nelson shrugged.

"Okay, then. Let's do it." He patted the couch beside him.

He watched Mariah. He saw her swallow. Her teeth were scraping her lip now. She set her computer and notebooks down on the floor beside her chair.

"I guess we should go ahead and get this taken care of."

Was she nervous? She totally was.

"Mark it off your list."

She narrowed her eyes, looking like she suspected something. He smiled back at her.

"Come on. No time like the present. Then I can get back to the game."

Her shoulders snapped back, and her teeth were no longer worrying her lip. He held back a grin. Unless he mistook the expression on her face, she was determined that he wasn't going to shrug off this kiss and turn on the TV.

Good. They were on the same page about it.

She stood and crossed to the couch, dropping on the cushion beside him. He watched the expressions swirling over her face. She was staring at his lips, and then she leaned forward, starting to pucker. He could almost read the checklist in her mind.

Uh-uh. Kissing wasn't a checklist.

He put a hand on her cheek, soft under his palm, and kept her at a distance.

"Hold on, Mariah. You all but accused me of being a bad kisser. I can't have that. We're going to do this right."

Her brow creased. "What do you mean?"

His thumb brushed over her cheek. She blinked. His other hand brushed her arm, fingers running up and down from shoulder to wrist and back. Her gaze followed his hand, her expression confused.

His fingers slid up her shoulder, across to her neck, gently stroking. He felt her soften under his touch. Soon he had both hands cradling her face. She drew in a breath, watching him intently. He caressed her bottom lip with one thumb, and her mouth parted.

Bingo.

He leaned forward and pressed a gentle kiss to her forehead. Her skin was warm and smooth under his lips. Her perfume tickled his nose, and he could hear her breathing. He felt his own breath speed up. Mariah's eyes fluttered closed as his lips traced a path down her nose, across her cheek, to one corner of the delectable lips.

She sighed, relaxing fully into his hold.

Then he touched her lips with his, softly. He pulled away, just enough to catch his breath, and she moved closer, seeking more.

He pressed forward again, brushing his lips against hers, back and forth, as she pushed closer to him. His hands slid into her hair, and hers moved up his chest, gripping his sweater.

Now he increased the pressure, feeling the texture of her lips, the brush of her breath, the slight moan that escaped her.

Or maybe that was him. Because kissing Mariah was a pleasure he'd have hated to miss.

Her lips parted, inviting him in, but he made himself pull back. It was more difficult than it should have been, because after all, this was Mariah, his fake date. But the kiss felt real, and that was a problem. It shouldn't. This was all pretend.

She was still there, eyes closed. Right, his hands, in her hair. He made himself loosen his hold, drop his hands, lean back to his side of the couch.

"So," he started, but his voice was rough. He cleared his throat. "Is that good enough?"

Her eyes were open now, and she was holding herself stiffly upright.

She took a trembling breath. "That...that will do."

Nice try. He'd felt her response, and it made the caveman in him want to sit up and beat on his chest.

"You're sure? You don't have any tips? Need to give me some lessons?"

He couldn't let her know how real that had felt.

Her eyes flashed. "Nelson, I'm not here to stroke your ego. We both did good enough. Lessons and further practice are unnecessary."

"All right. Have you got a schedule for kissing now? I'm sure you wrote down just how often we need to kiss in front of people to make this look good."

He wasn't sure why he was pushing this. If he was smart, he'd find a way to put kissing completely off the table. More kissing was just going to cause more problems.

Perhaps his intelligence was overrated.

"I'll let you know. After all, I can initiate a kiss myself."

Oh, that would be interesting.

"Good to know."

Mariah stood and crossed back over to her chair, picking up her notepad with shaking hands. Her hair was mussed from his fingers, and her lipstick smudged. Her cheeks were flushed.

Yeah, he felt confident that he could kiss her well enough.

Mariah could feel Nelson's smugness, see it on his face, hear it in his voice.

Yes, that kiss had been...unsettling.

Mariah would admit when it came to kissing, making out, she was inexperienced. Not completely, but she hadn't had a lot of opportunities to practice. There wasn't a lot for her to compare that kiss to.

She only knew that if Nelson hadn't pulled away, she'd have done her best to wrap herself as close to him as she could to continue that kiss. The one that made her forget where she was, what she was doing and why. The one she was already missing.

But even if Nelson was a more than adequate kisser, she couldn't let him have the upper hand. She had to do something so that she wouldn't throw herself back on the couch to continue that kiss.

Her notepad saved her, as it often had. "There's something I need to know if we're getting engaged. Why are you so against people getting married?"

Nelson stiffened, no longer relaxed. He appeared to choose his words carefully. "I'm not against people getting married."

Mariah raised an eyebrow. "Really. How can you even try to make me believe that?"

Nelson clenched his jaw. "I'm not against marriage, or dating, or love, or any of those things. I'm not a fan of elaborate weddings."

Hair splitting.

"Okay, tell me how you split that fine hair."

He narrowed his eyes. She kept her chin up.

"Can you honestly tell me that some weddings haven't been disasters? That some brides or grooms focus only on the big event, and bulldoze over everyone and everything in their way? They make life miserable for everyone around them in service for their big party? You've helped plan some of those, right?"

Oof. Mariah sat back. That was very...impassioned. Accusatory. And somehow, very personal.

"You're right. There are some people like that. But that isn't everyone, or even most people. My job was to try to find balance—make my clients' wishes come true, but as considerately as possible."

She could see the disbelief in his expression.

"Why do you look like you think I'm lying? What is your problem? Have I ever done anything to make you believe otherwise?"

"Don't you get paid to make sure the big event comes off, no matter what?"

She shook her head. "No, I don't make that my only focus.

I need people to refer me to friends, so it's not in my best interest to allow the wedding to make everyone miserable. I try to deliver the event they want, but it's not a thing in isolation. And I don't encourage my clients to believe their wedding is the center of the universe."

His expression hadn't changed.

"I heard you tell Grandmother, the first night I met you, that you'd worked for Sherry Anstruthers and learned everything you needed to know from her."

Mariah sat back. Okay, this might explain some things.

"You didn't hear exactly that. I did work for Sherry, but only for a short while. I didn't like the way she worked. What I told your grandmother was that I'd learned everything I needed to know about how *not* to do my job from her. She was a nightmare.

"But obviously, I don't need to tell you that. You know. You just assumed all wedding planners were like her. Why? What did she do to you?"

Nelson took a moment to consider what he wanted to say. And to consider what Mariah had said.

He couldn't remember exactly what he'd heard at his grandmother's, not at this late date. It wouldn't be hard to find out how long she'd worked for Sherry, or when. Grandmother probably had her résumé somewhere around. And the only way he could believe Zoey would have worked with Mariah was if she was the anti-wedding planner.

Unless Zoey had been steamrolled again.

"I knew someone who used her as their wedding planner. It didn't work out well."

Mariah was full of questions, but she restrained herself. This was important to work out with Nelson.

"I've heard some stories, about weddings that were nightmares. While I like to believe all of mine went well, I know

I'm not perfect. And I know some of Sherry Anstruthers's weddings went badly.

"The last wedding I worked on, before coming here to Carter's, was for someone who'd planned a wedding with Sherry, and she said it had been a disaster. Her fiancé turned into a groomzilla, and she ended up not showing for her own wedding."

"You mean Zoey."

Mariah opened her mouth, and then closed it again. He knew Zoey? Obviously. He must have known about her first wedding. That went a long way to explaining his attitude toward her. Zoey had interviewed Mariah five times before finally trusting her to take care of her wedding.

"Are you a friend of Zoey's? Were you at her wedding?" Had Nelson been there, and Mariah hadn't recognized him when she saw him again?

There was a bleak expression in his eyes. "No, I wasn't at her last wedding. And I can't say I'm a friend of hers, not anymore."

There was a wealth of meaning behind those words. Mariah tried to decipher it. Had he been a friend of the groom's? Had there been a break, after the wedding, between the groom's friends and Zoey's?

Zoey was such a kind, sweet, shy woman. It was hard to imagine her carrying a grudge. Unless Nelson had been close to her first fiancé. Nelson was a vet, and he'd said he worked with horses. Zoey's father had an equine veterinary practice. One of the best in the country. In vet circles, he was a big deal.

Zoey's fiancé had been a vet, too.

An idea flashed across her brain, but no. Zoey's fiancé had been a Theo, not a Nelson.

"Did you know Theo?"

Nelson shot her a glance, then stared at the blank television. "You could say that. I am Theo."

Mariah shook her head. "What? You're not making a lot of sense. Your name is Nelson. Zoey's ex was Theo—I know, we talked about her first wedding, and what we needed to do differently."

Nelson fiddled with the TV remote. "Grandmother was an only child. She was the last Carter of Carter's Crossing. When she married, her husband took her last name.

"His name was Theodore Nelson. After he married Grandmother, he became Theodore Nelson Carter. My father was Theodore Nelson Carter the second. I'm Theodore Nelson Carter the third."

Mariah felt like a vital part of her torso had taken the first dip on a roller coaster while the rest of her was still waiting at the top of the ride. She held up a hand, trying to come to grips with this information.

Nelson kept talking. "Grandfather was known as Teddy to everyone. Dad was Theo. I was named Theodore Nelson the third so that Grandfather's name didn't die out, but instead of confusing everyone with another Theo, they called me by my middle name. Nelson.

"Until I went to school in California. There was another Nelson in my class, so people called me Theo. When I graduated and was looking to work in some of the top veterinary practices, that 'third' helped with the snob value.

"I'm Theo, the groomzilla. And your former boss was the one who cheered me on, every step of the selfish, vainglorious way."

CHAPTER TWELVE

NELSON PULLED UP in front of the Goat and Barley. Tonight he and Mariah were on their first official fake date.

Mariah had planned out a schedule of dates. On a spreadsheet. This first one was to play darts, on a Thursday night. Nelson recognized immediately that she wanted to do something where she felt in control. She would easily win any dart competition against him. That would give her the upper hand.

Mariah had her lists, but Nelson had insider knowledge. And even though he was surprised that he enjoyed Mariah bossing him into this date, he'd insisted he got to plan the second one.

He had some surprises lined up for her tonight, as well.

It was cold outside, but he was waiting for her in the parking lot. Once her car pulled in, he walked over to open her door for her.

It was easy to read the surprise on her face. This wasn't part of her script. Neither was the kiss.

The kiss was purportedly to sell them as a couple. Nelson had his own reasons to surprise Mariah with some kissing action.

He'd hoped his memory had exaggerated how enjoyable their first kiss had been. After all, this was Mariah. They'd been at odds with each other for months. He didn't like the idea that she was holding on to the best kiss title he had to give out.

Unfortunately, when he pulled her shocked body close to his, it was his breath that hitched. When she looked up at him in surprise and licked her bottom lip, he forgot who was watching, and why he didn't want this to be so good.

Then their lips met, and he forgot everything but kissing Mariah.

Eventually, the pesky need for oxygen made itself known and he pulled back, his breath shaky. In the background he could hear comments from other patrons.

Right. This was to sell their fake date. He didn't dare let her know how much that kiss had rocked his axis.

"Appropriate use of PDA?" he asked, his voice husky.

It took her a moment longer to come back to the here and now. The kiss had thrown her off, and he liked a flustered Mariah. She could deny it all she wanted, but he knew she enjoyed the kissing, as well. She had opened to him, fitting herself against his body in a most satisfying way.

"Right," she finally said, looking around at their audience.

There were a lot of people arriving, and they'd all seen the kiss. That was a reason she couldn't argue. She'd resist any intimation that they were kissing because they enjoyed it.

He wasn't fond of the idea, either, but surely, they'd get used to it after some time passed.

She pulled away, her lips pleasantly pink, her breath puffing in the cold. "Yes, just what we wanted."

Mariah was a lot of things, but she wasn't ready to admit she liked him, for real.

"Come on, we don't want to be late."

She stopped, ignoring the tug of his glove on her mittens. Her brows lowered as she considered what he'd said.

"Late for what?"

"Trivia night."

"What?"

He grinned at her. "Yeah, on Thursdays no one plays darts. It's trivia night."

He pulled again on her hand, and this time she let him tug her forward. He could almost hear the gears in her head spinning. This was another case where having local knowledge was going to play in his favor.

Mariah liked planning. She liked lists. She liked the feeling of control. She knew that it was a result of the way she'd been raised, when so often it felt like she'd had none.

She'd carefully planned this first "date" with Nelson. By coming to the Goat and Barley, they wouldn't be in Carter's Crossing. It wouldn't be a blatant declaration that they were dating. It would look like they were trying to be discreet, but from what she'd heard, news would trickle back to Carter's Crossing. Then they could make a couple of dating appearances in town. People already knew they were spending time with Nelson's horses and at his place... It was a narrative that would work.

So how had she missed trivia night? She didn't miss things. She researched and double-checked. She made backup plans. Then she made backup plans for her backup plans.

Well, she wouldn't be caught out again. This was her job. It was important to her. Nelson couldn't mess her up.

Nelson had insisted on taking care of the second date, taking place in Carter's Crossing. With some reluctance she'd agreed. She hadn't realized he was going to derail her first date, as well.

There were a lot more people from Carter's Crossing in the bar than she'd expected on a weeknight. But she hadn't known about trivia night.

She had to absolve Nelson of sabotage. It's not like he could have asked the pub to set this up for the same evening she'd picked for their date. From the surprised looks being tossed his way, he obviously wasn't a regular for trivia night. He knew the routine well enough, though, that the two of them ended up at a table together with drinks and the paper lists that all registered teams received. He'd even given their team a name: Carter's Crew.

She mentally rolled her eyes at that.

Most of the other tables had more than two people. She resigned herself to making an embarrassing showing in this competition.

That was another miscalculation.

Nelson was smart. She should have known that. He hadn't completed his veterinary studies at the top school in the country because he was stupid.

She was surprised, though, that some of the time she was the one to carry the team.

Her education had been completed on the boat until she'd come on land to go to college. She'd done okay academically, but she'd been out of sync with her classmates when it came to pop culture and lifestyle.

It turned out that she had a good grasp of history, and her geography was totally on. She knew she was lucky such a big section of that night's quiz was based on bodies of water. It was almost as if whoever arranged the quiz had picked her brain for that section.

Sports? She was at a loss. Nelson aced that.

They both struggled with television and music. They didn't win, but they came in third. Since there were twelve teams, it was a respectable showing.

They high-fived each other and got a round of applause from the crowd as they went forward to receive their prize: a gift certificate for Moonstone.

It wasn't exactly the date Mariah had planned, but they certainly made a public splash, so she'd call it a win.

Mariah carefully tucked the Moonstone certificate in her purse. "We could use that for our next date."

Nelson leaned over the table. "You sound confident that I'm going to ask you out again."

Mariah leaned toward him. "I'm a big girl. I can ask *you* out."

Nelson's mouth quirked up in that grin that she was getting too familiar with, but someone stopped by the table to congratulate them before he could respond.

When they were left alone again, he ran his fingers over their quiz sheets.

"You know a lot."

The compliment warmed her.

"You were homeschooled, right? Since you were always traveling on your boat."

Mariah nodded. "Till I moved to land. My dad taught us."

Nelson leaned back in his chair. "What was that like? I always had boring regular school, like everyone else I know."

Mariah traced a pattern on the table with her finger. "I don't know if I can describe it very well. I have no idea what school is like for other people, only what I've seen in movies and read in books."

"Fewer pretty people, less drama and lots of boring lectures."

Mariah looked up with a smile. "Well, we had only the three of us, my two brothers and me, so the drama was limited to sibling fights."

"And the boring lectures?"

"There's not much point in lecturing your three kids. We already got that for chores around the boat and making sure we wore our life jackets. Dad was a good teacher. He made things interesting. And once we finished our assignments, our school day was over. It wasn't too boring.

"I always felt like I was the stupid kid, because I was the youngest, and as much as possible Dad would have us all study the same things at the same time."

"Now, that, I find hard to believe."

Mariah narrowed her eyes. "Which part?"

"I can't believe you let yourself think you were stupid. If you were keeping up with older kids, you couldn't have been."

She shrugged. "I did eventually figure that out." Maybe too late?

"Where did you have classes? Was there a special place on your boat?"

He sounded interested. Like this was something he'd been curious about.

"It varied, depending on what we were doing. There wasn't enough room on the boat for a separate classroom space. We usually sat either in the cockpit or the salon."

"That sounds cool. Did you run laps around the boat for gym? Climb the mast for recess?" Nelson had a teasing light in his eyes.

Mariah felt her expression go carefully blank. Their life on the boat wasn't cool, not at all. "We didn't really do gym. Dad always said we got enough exercise helping on the boat and swimming. And no, we didn't do recess, either."

"Was it weird to only have three students?"

"It's not weird when it's all you know. And sometimes, when we were with boats with other kids, we'd do classes together."

Mariah was ready to move on to another topic, but Nelson still had questions.

"Did you have friends on those other boats?"

Mariah looked away. "When they were around, we would play or hang out together."

"And when they weren't?"

"It was just us."

Mariah thought back over her words. She thought she'd sounded all right. Not too pathetic.

"That must have been rough sometimes. I mean, growing up, there were a lot of times I didn't want to be with my family, so it's hard to imagine not having Dave around."

Mariah squished down that envious pang she felt. She would have loved a Dave around. Or a Rachel, or a Jaycee.

She shrugged again, since it was her turn to respond. It was what it was.

"Is that why you're not navigating around the world with your sextant now?"

She glanced up at Nelson. The words were teasing, but there was too much sympathy in his eyes. He'd figured out that having only her family around hadn't always been enough. But he was also letting her off the hook.

She gave him a grateful smile. She'd rather he hadn't seen through her, but at least he wasn't picking into her psyche, either to figure her out or try to fix her.

She'd gained a lot, growing up on the boat, traveling the world. Her brothers appeared to have picked up that wanderlust. But for her, it had made her want something different.

She wasn't looking for pity. Her childhood had been unconventional, but it had its advantages, as well. She was an adult now. She was making the life she wanted for herself. A job she enjoyed. Her own community, one that could be constant. A home that stayed still.

This job in Carter's Crossing was a stepping-stone to all of that. It was showing her the things she wanted.

Her glance caught Nelson's, and for some reason she felt her cheeks heat up. He hadn't read her mind, and he wouldn't think of himself as one of those things she wanted.

At least, she hoped so.

CHAPTER THIRTEEN

"OH, NO."

Nelson had been secretive about this second date. Now Mariah knew why.

"Come on, you need to know how to skate. You're planning a skating party!"

She was also planning a vow renewal and didn't need to have been married fifty years to do that.

"How did you get my size anyway?"

Maybe not the best way to refuse.

Nelson was kneeling at her feet, holding out a skate. Mariah had her feet tucked safely under the bench; one she'd arranged to have installed here at the mill for the upcoming skating party.

"Your boots are in the closet at Grandmother's. I peeked."

She glared at him.

"Come on, Mariah! It'll be fun!"

That was Jaycee, already on skates and demonstrating that she was well able to handle blades on ice.

Dave was also on skates. And Rachel. Nelson's surprise date had been to bring her ice-skating. He'd told her to dress warmly, so she'd initially thought they might be going out to the farm.

Better the horses than skates.

Nelson had picked her up from Abigail's and driven her to

the mill. She'd seen familiar cars. Curious as to what the others were doing, she'd hardly noticed that Nelson had grabbed a duffel bag from the back of the car.

And now she was stuck here on the bench, everyone encouraging her to try skating for the first time. In her life.

The ice had been cleared of snow, making enough space for skating, but there were no boards around the sides, no railing, nothing to hold on to. There was no way she could do this. She'd fall and break something. She couldn't afford that, this close to Valentine's Day.

Now Mariah had a few things to add to her party to-do list. Because not having something like a board fence was just stupid.

"Come on, Mariah. I won't let you fall. I promise." Nelson was looking up at her, a glint in his eye.

That phrase. *I promise.* So easily said, so easily broken.

Nelson narrowed his eyes. "First fall, you can quit. How's that?"

With the others all egging her on, she finally pulled out her foot and allowed Nelson to take off her boot.

"Good girl!"

"I'm not a dog," she gritted out.

"Sorry. You gotta admit, though, this is a great date. People here to see us hanging on to each other. And a kiss would definitely be appropriate."

Mariah dropped her head, letting her hair cover her warm cheeks. The trivia night date had ended with another kiss in the parking lot. There may have been cheering from people passing by. And she may have enjoyed it, a little too much.

She flinched as Nelson gave a hard tug on her skate laces. "That's really tight."

He flashed a grin up at her. "You don't want floppy ankles."

"How do you know?" She had to push back. This was too much in Nelson's sweet spot.

"Because you don't want to embarrass yourself." He was working on her second boot now.

Mariah frowned. Big deal. No one wanted to embarrass themselves.

Another few tugs, and she had skates fastened tightly to her feet.

Nelson sat beside her and pulled out his own skates. While her borrowed footwear was white, his was black.

"Why do you get the black skates?" Hers were a little scuffed, so the dark color would have been nice to cover that up.

He pulled off a boot, and stuck his foot in a skate, bending over to lace it.

"Mine are hockey skates. We don't have a lot of women hockey players here, and they're a little proprietary about their gear. Yours are figure skates—you've got a pick on the toe of the blade. That can help you stop."

Being able to stop sounded good.

In no time Nelson had both skates on, and their boots safely stashed in his duffel bag. He stood up, easy and confident. He turned and held out a hand to her.

"You sure about this? First fall?"

He caught something behind her words. His gaze was serious. "I gave you my word."

He'd also promised Zoey, she thought, and wondered where that had come from. She shook her head and reminded herself this was just fake dating. She let him grab her hand and pull her to her feet, where she balanced precariously on the two narrow blades.

"I've got you."

She considered the ice surface just beyond them. The other three were crisscrossing the ice, confidently and surely. They looked like they were having fun. She took a breath and lifted her first foot.

Mariah wasn't comfortable without having control, and Nelson wanted her out of her element, at least for a bit.

He'd thought that bringing her skating, something she had no experience with, would shake things up a bit. And showing some affection, while he basically supported her around the ice, would give the other three lots to talk about. Word would get around that something was going on with Nelson and Mariah.

That was what they wanted, right?

The fake dating had turned into a lot more fun than he'd expected. And Mariah was...maybe not exactly a friend, but something. He knew a lot about her. He'd shared some things with her he didn't normally talk about. It gave them a bond.

He hadn't realized how much he did know her, until he promised to keep her safe while on the ice and he caught her reaction.

She almost flinched at that phrase—*I promise*.

He was going to ask her about that, but first, he was going to skate her around the ice, keeping his promise. Then he was going to kiss her.

He was looking forward to holding her on the ice while she had to cling to him to stay upright. And he was really looking forward to kissing her.

They might argue, but something, maybe that sparring, added to their kisses. He didn't think it was his technique, Mariah's list notwithstanding. Not that he was bad, but something happened when he touched Mariah's lips with his. Something extra.

She was hesitant, shuffling on the skates through the snow to the edge of the river. He kept hold of her hand, helping her balance. He stepped ahead of her onto the ice and turned back to take both her hands.

She glared at the ice, as if she could make it behave by sheer willpower. Then she put one blade on it, and almost went down.

Fortunately, Nelson was braced to support her. She had to grab his arms hard to stay upright. She had to trust him, even though she didn't want to.

He kept her upright.

She huffed a cloud of foggy breath into the cold.

"I don't like this."

"Don't give up," Jaycee encouraged.

She took a firm grip on Nelson's hands and put the second blade on the ice. Nelson kept her upright as she wobbled while trying to find balance.

"People really do this for fun?" she asked.

"Look at them." Nelson took advantage of her distraction to slowly skate backward, tugging her forward onto the ice.

She gasped but stayed up.

"What are you doing?"

"Skating."

"Backward?"

He nodded and pulled her out farther.

"How much does it hurt when you fall?" she asked, eyes focused on her skates.

"Doesn't matter." Nelson picked up his pace from snail to tortoise. "You're not falling, remember?"

She moved her gaze up to his face and stumbled. He brought her closer. "I've got you."

That shouldn't have removed the tension in her shoulders and legs. It shouldn't have relaxed her facial muscles and pulled up the side of her mouth in a half smile.

And he shouldn't have smiled back at her.

Because the next thing she knew, she was allowing him to drag her all over the ice, with Jaycee and Rachel and Dave cheering her on as they passed by. When Nelson held her hips and pushed her forward in front of him, as if she was actually skating, it was even fun.

Until he decided to teach her how to skate. On her own.

"Push with your right foot. No, not step. Push, leaving the blade on the ice."

"I am!"

"No, you're not. If you want to learn how to do this, you need to listen to me."

"If I want to learn how to do this, I need to find someone who can explain things properly."

The others laughed, and eventually Mariah was able to take a few shuffles on her own, Nelson close beside her.

"You don't need to hover."

"I promised I wouldn't let you fall."

That phrase again. *I promised.* It distracted her, and she caught the pick of the toe of her skate on the ice. She felt her balance go, and she started to topple forward.

A pair of hands caught her waist, keeping her from hitting the ice.

She caught her breath. "Thanks." His face was right there.

It was only natural that he brought her close and kissed her.

She almost forgot that it was for show.

Rachel had made thermoses of hot chocolate, and they enjoyed the warmth once they'd given up on skating. No one mentioned the kiss. Hadn't anyone seen it? He should have paid attention, been a little less lost in the kiss.

Dave and Jaycee got into a car together, and Rachel drove off, leaving Nelson and Mariah alone. There had been a lot of significant glances aimed their way, even if nothing had been said.

Nelson wasn't thinking of that right now. His mind wanted to linger on the kiss, on how good Mariah had felt in his hands and arms while he was guiding her over the ice.

But he also had a question to ask her. It felt important. He wasn't sure if he could convince Mariah that she should tell him, but he needed to know. For him. He needed to know why she got that look on her face when he'd promised to keep her from falling. Which, by the way, he had.

Nelson turned the car on, dialing up the seat warmers, but didn't put the car in gear. He looked over at Mariah, cheeks and nose pink from the cold. She looked like she'd had a good time after all.

"What's the deal with promises, Mariah?" He hoped to catch her off guard.

Her head snapped toward him.

"What do you mean?"

"Every time I promise something, you react."

She waved a hand. "You're imagining things."

He let the silence rest for a moment. "No, I'm not. I don't make promises lightly, and I do my best to keep them. Why do you flinch, like you're sure I'll break my word?"

She didn't respond.

"I mean, yeah, we all have to break a promise sometime, but we don't stop believing people unless there's a reason. Has someone broken a promise to you? A big one?"

Mariah looked out the car window. Her chin jutted out as she shook her head.

"My dad has never made a promise he couldn't keep."

"Never?" Nelson couldn't hold back the question. How did someone always keep a promise? Life happened, and sometimes you couldn't follow through.

Mariah shook her head again. "He wouldn't make a promise unless he knew he could keep it. All those nice soporifics people say to kids? He never did. Never promised we'd make it through a storm. He would promise to do everything he could, but he never promised we would be safe."

Nelson leaned back and considered. Was that the best way to talk to kids?

"He had a good reason for that. When he wanted to leave the family business, get out of the rat race, buy a boat and sail the world with my mom, my grandfather was furious. He said the only way Dad would be able to access his trust fund was if he promised to never marry 'that woman.' My mother.

"Dad promised. He got his money. Then he bought the boat and sailed away with Mom. But he never married her."

"That was harsh."

Mariah nodded, still not looking at him. "Still bothers my

mother. My grandfather apologized, took back the deal, but my dad won't budge. He made a promise, so he won't break it. Not for anything."

Nelson considered keeping his word a good thing. But that promise? Given under duress and kept even after the need was withdrawn? That was some messed up family dynamics.

It was no wonder promises made her skittish.

"When I was a kid, on the boat, and I'd make a friend...eventually, they'd travel in one direction and we'd go somewhere else. We always promised to keep in touch. But kids can't always do that, so those promises were broken easily."

She finally turned and looked at Nelson. "So yeah, I have a thing about promises. Most of them are worthless, and the ones that aren't? They can be devastating.

"I don't make promises now. I do my best, but I won't promise because it's too difficult to know I'll keep it. The costs might be too high."

Nelson put the car in gear and pulled out of the mill parking lot. Mariah didn't speak, and he let the silence stretch.

He was sure Mariah's father had meant well by his children, but based on Mariah, he'd still managed to mess them up. Just like every parent did somehow.

Mariah snapped to attention when he stopped in front of Abigail's porch. She shook her head when he reached to undo his seat belt.

"No, don't bother. I'll be fine. Tomorrow we'll use that gift certificate at Moonstone, right?"

Nelson hesitated but decided to let Mariah go into the house on her own. She'd given him a lot to think about. He was surprised she'd shared that much. Maybe she was, too.

He watched her go up the steps and open the door. Once she was safely inside, he drove back to the carriage house. Away from the woman who didn't believe in promises.

CHAPTER FOURTEEN

THE DAY EVERYTHING fell apart started like any other. Mariah woke up and checked the weather, like she did every morning. She hadn't been this conscious of climate conditions since she'd been living on the boat.

The weather was cooperating. The fourteenth of February was going to be clear and cold without crossing the line into brutal windchill that would keep everyone indoors.

There were no emails from vendors unable to fulfill their obligations. The morning passed with phone calls and to-do items checked off her list in almost monotonous regularity. The three events: anniversary/vow renewal, engagement and proposal, all planned for and on track.

She should have known everything couldn't go that well.

Abigail was the bearer of the first bad news. Gord had fallen and broken his hip. He was in the hospital.

Mariah was relieved that her first thought was about Gord and his health instead of how this would mess up her event. At his age, falls could trigger a slide into poor health. He'd been out throwing salt on the sidewalk to make sure no one slipped on the ice and hit an icy patch and gone down.

Gord, meet irony.

The doctors were going to operate, and every indication was

that he should make a full recovery. For his age, he was fit and healthy, and he was obstinate enough to get on his feet before he was supposed to.

He would not be on his feet before the fourteenth, however.

He would not be at the church where he and Gladys made their wedding vows fifty years ago, ready to meet her at the altar to repeat them.

After they'd covered all those caring-people issues, they had to focus on the party.

"How bad is this?" Abigail wanted to know.

Mariah considered. "This was probably the least marketable of the three events. It was definitely a feel-good story, and would make Carter's look good, but I wasn't expecting a lot of requests for fiftieth anniversary celebrations to come this way.

"But the work your committee did, finding the members of their wedding party and some of the guests, and arranging for them to come, that was impressive. It could inspire visitors. A video could have gone viral.

"Do we know when Gord will be back on his feet? Maybe we have the party a little later?"

They'd miss the publicity kick her grandfather was providing, but they'd still have material for the website and promotion. The out-of-town guests, however, might not be able to make it to a later event.

"I'll make some calls," Abigail said. "Find out when Gord is back home and mobile, and if we can rebook everyone."

Mariah thanked her. With less than a week to go before Valentine's Day, she wasn't sure they could cancel the food. Mariah pulled up her list for the anniversary party, ready to prepare a new list for cancellations.

It was closing in on dinnertime when her phone rang. Mariah frowned and pulled it up, expecting someone else was calling to tell her about Gord's fall. She'd had eleven calls to let her know already. The number on display was Jaycee's, however, so she pushed the talk button.

"Hey, Jaycee—"

The rest of her greeting was drowned out by a wail. Mariah pulled the phone away from her ear, hoping to be able to understand what Jaycee was saying if she wasn't being deafened.

It took a few minutes. Jaycee was crying. It was hard to make out words, and for a moment Mariah wondered if Jaycee had heard the bad news about Gord and was closer to him than Mariah had realized. But it wasn't Gord who was making her cry; it was Dave.

Dave had broken up with her.

"I'm on my way. What do you need?"

Mariah had no experience with breakups of this magnitude. Wine, ice cream and chocolate were the staples according to books and movies, so she arrived with those.

Jaycee answered the door with swollen eyes, a red nose and a voice so congested Mariah had a hard time making out what she was saying. But no words were needed to tell her that her friend was in pain.

Mariah peeled off her outerwear and followed Jaycee into the kitchen. "I brought rocky road, Snickers and pinot. What do you want first?"

Jaycee's response was indecipherable.

Mariah chopped the Snickers bar into pieces, swirled it in with the ice cream and poured the wine into a beer mug. She brought it into the living room, where Jaycee was curled up on the couch, an empty Kleenex box on the floor with a pile of used tissues, another half-full box on the coffee table.

Mariah put the ice cream and wine on the table in front of her and sat down beside her.

"Hug?"

Jaycee nodded. Mariah wrapped her arms around her. She felt the quivering in Jaycee's body and tightened the embrace.

"I'm so sorry. What happened?"

Jaycee's crying renewed. Eventually, she calmed enough to speak in words that Mariah could interpret.

Last night she and Dave had practiced their dance skate. She'd been frustrated that Dave still didn't remember the routine. She asked about the new clothes she'd told him to get for the party, and he hadn't gotten those yet. She'd been upset, and they'd said their good-nights on tense terms.

Today Dave had called her. He said things weren't working, and he thought they should put a halt on the wedding plans, including the engagement party.

Jaycee had asked him what exactly he meant.

They should cancel the engagement, and make sure they wanted the same things going forward.

Jaycee said if they weren't getting married, they weren't going backward to dating.

Dave had said if that was what she wanted…

Jaycee burst into renewed crying.

Mariah had rubbed her back, handed over more tissues and offered wine. She agreed that Dave was an idiot but also was the love of Jaycee's life. Jaycee wavered between joining a convent and plotting his murder.

Mariah could only offer comfort and caution about shooting someone in daylight in front of witnesses, but her mind had started making new lists.

Lists to cancel another event.

She felt bad for Jaycee. She thought Jaycee and Dave were a good, strong and committed couple. She thought it might even be possible that they could work this out between them. Eventually.

But things weren't looking good for the engagement party, and on top of the anniversary cancellation, and even the fake proposal, Mariah was looking at failure. She pushed the selfish thought to the back of her mind, but it lingered.

When Jaycee mentioned the name of Nelson in her ramblings, Mariah went on full alert.

"Nelson? What has he got to do with this?"

Jaycee snuffled into another tissue. "I don't know. Dave just said something about him. Maybe it was just because Nelson was stood up at the altar. Maybe Nelson talked him out of this. I don't know. I just…just…

"I just don't know how he could do this if he loved me. His mother…she's going to be thrilled. She never wanted us to get married.

"You're going to New York, right, Mariah? Could I go with you? I can't stay here, not now, not with everyone looking at me…"

Mariah wrapped her arms around Jaycee again and passed her another tissue.

"If you want, of course you can come to New York with me. But not yet. Rachel's coming over. We need to use those thumbscrews on Dave first."

It had been a bad day.

Two family pets had to be put down, and the rescue people brought in a dog they'd found. Nelson considered himself an easygoing guy, but when he saw what had been done to the dog, he was ready to put the hurt on whoever had done that to an animal.

He was grateful that this wasn't a night for dinner with his grandmother and Mariah. Until he'd put some of the day behind him, he was in no mind-set to make polite conversation. What he needed was a long punishing run, followed by a game on TV and some whiskey.

Not a lot. He couldn't put himself out of commission if an emergency came in, but he needed something to take the misery of the day away, and if not, at least move it to enough distance that he could sleep.

He'd had his run and dropped in front of the TV with the game and a shot glass before he bothered showering. His level of caring about that was in the negative numbers. So of course, someone pounded at his door.

He considered his options. Grandmother wouldn't pound, and she'd come in if she felt it necessary. Dave was supposed to be busy with Jaycee. The door pounded again, and he grimaced. Must be Mariah. He wasn't sure what he was supposed to have done this time, but that was angry pounding if he'd ever heard it.

He opened the door. Yep, Mariah on the warpath.

"Come on in," he said to her back as she stomped her way past him.

She stood, glaring at the half-empty whiskey glass.

"Are you drunk?"

"Unfortunately, no," he said, sitting down and taking another sip. "Did we have something planned this evening? Did I miss a scheduled PDA? 'Cause I don't remember one, and I'm not in the mood."

She crossed her arms. "Did you talk to Dave?"

He dropped his head on the back of the couch and looked at her. She was upset, for sure, but he was in the clear. He'd done nothing but his job all day.

"No. I haven't talked to him at all today."

"What about yesterday?"

Nelson frowned. "He was with Jaycee yesterday. I haven't seen him since darts night."

"You're saying you didn't talk him into this."

"Into what?" Obviously, Mariah was angry with him for something he'd done, or she thought he'd done, but he was pretty sure he was off the hook this time. And he was hurt. Weren't they past this now?

"He broke up with Jaycee."

"What?" Nelson jerked upright. Impossible. He knew Dave had been upset about some of the party stuff, but Nelson also knew without a shadow of a doubt that Dave loved Jaycee.

Mariah watched him, then, apparently reassured, dropped into his chair.

"Why don't you stay?" It wasn't polite, but he needed to process this news, and talking to Mariah was not going to help.

"I'm sorry. I thought you'd been talking..."

Nelson didn't have patience right now. And he couldn't believe Mariah was still so suspicious of him. He'd promised.

But she didn't put faith in people's promises.

"No, I haven't been trying to talk Dave out of marrying Jaycee. I've been too busy putting pets to sleep and dealing with animal abuse to start with people."

Mariah's face fell.

"I'm sorry, Nelson, really. I shouldn't have jumped to conclusions like that. It was just that Dave mentioned something about you to Jaycee when he broke up with her. I'm sorry you had a crappy day, as well. I'll go, unless there's something I can do?"

Nelson shook his head. "I think I'd better go see how my buddy is doing. I know he loves Jaycee, so something serious must have gone down."

"Jaycee right now is considering putting a hit out on him, so tell him to watch his back. And I am sorry, about—"

She waved her hand in a circle, indicating the whole mess that had been today.

He shrugged. Yeah, today was just a total crap show.

Dave didn't want to talk.

"There's nothing to say. You were right."

Nelson drew in a sharp breath. Maybe he *was* in trouble.

"What do you mean? She figured out she was too good for you?"

Dave tried to give him a smile, but it was a poor attempt.

"No, about these big wedding events. Jaycee is so focused on this party that she's forgotten about us. If she wanted a guy who could dance on skates, she should have gone looking for someone in the Ice Capades.

"I told her the party was getting out of hand, and we should just give it up. She threw a fit. I asked if the party was more important than us, 'cause from what I could see, the party was driving us further apart."

Dave picked up what looked like the latest in a line of beers. He held one up for Nelson, who shook his head. Dave shrugged and took a long swallow.

"She said that the party was a test of how we could handle things together. But this party has never been a together thing. I didn't ask for it, and she didn't ask me to plan it. I told her I didn't want a party, and that maybe she needed to figure out what was most important to her.

"She said the party was for us, and if I wasn't going to even try… I told her I'd tried, and I was done. She could have the party, or she could have me. She said she wasn't choosing, so I told her I was.

"It's just like you said. I thought we were solid, but Jaycee has been a different person with this party stuff. And maybe she's right. If we can't handle this, then maybe we can't handle other things. Better to end it now."

Nelson had time-traveled and was reliving his last conversation with Zoey. He'd made all the same points Jaycee had. But Nelson had been told this was normal for brides, so he'd ignored everything Zoey said.

And ended up with no bride at his wedding.

He felt guilty, as if he'd been prioritizing the wrong thing again. But he wasn't the one focused on the party, not this time. He'd learned his lesson. Not just about parties, and about weddings, but about manipulating and forcing people into doing what he wanted. He'd been good at that.

Not anymore.

He left Dave alone, once he made sure Dave had no more beer and was going to head to bed. He didn't try to talk him into anything. He wondered if Dave would have been as bothered by the engagement party planning and seen it as a breaking point if Nelson hadn't talked to him about his own wedding, but he'd never know.

He stopped by his grandmother's house, after texting Mariah that he needed to talk to her. She met him in the lounge, looking defeated for the first time since he'd met her.

That bothered him, more than he'd expected.

"I tried to talk to Dave. I don't know if he and Jaycee can work this out, but he's not interested in the party, and I don't think they can figure things out in time for it anyway."

Mariah nodded, her arms wrapped around her body.

"That's what I thought."

Nelson had to try to cheer her up. "You could still have the skating party. Take pictures, use it for some publicity. And you've got the anniversary and our proposal."

Mariah shook her head, eyes on the ground.

"Gord fell and broke his hip. He'll be in the hospital on the fourteenth."

"Oh." Not the greatest response, but Nelson wasn't sure what else to say.

"It's over. I'm going to tell Grandfather to cancel the press. I'll have to talk to the committee, see if they want to try again."

"You're giving up?" Nelson was shocked. He didn't think anything could stop Mariah once she was going.

"What else can I do? I told Grandfather we had a fiftieth anniversary/vow renewal, an engagement party and a marriage proposal. All happening here at Carter's Crossing, all designed to show how romantic this place can be. Now all I have is a fake proposal. That's not going to bring people here."

Abigail came into the room in her robe. "You've heard the news, Nelson?"

"I have, and I'm sorry." Seeing Abigail raise her eyebrow, he shook his head.

"I know, I haven't been a big supporter. But you're trying to save this town, and I shouldn't have let my hang-ups get in the way."

Despite the problems, the approving look from his grandmother was a touch of warmth.

"I should go call my grandfather now, let him know."

Abigail looked at Mariah, her posture drooping, her voice tired.

"I'll do that, Mariah. You go and rest. You've been working hard. Get a good night's sleep, and things might look better in the morning."

"Nice try, Abigail, but I'll let you talk to Grandfather if you want. I can wait to hear what he has to say. And we have vendors to cancel—"

"Tomorrow," Abigail said. "I've called a committee meeting tomorrow. Don't give up just yet."

Mariah gave Abigail a hug and nodded to Nelson as she left the room. He missed the embraces they'd shared, selling their fake dating.

That was probably over now.

It hit him then. Mariah was done. She'd be leaving. There'd be no more fake dating, no more time spent working together with Toby. No arguing, no annoying her. No kisses, no proposal. No Mariah.

It wasn't the best time to realize that the dating had become more real than he'd understood. Not with his grandmother watching, and Mariah ready to leave town.

Abigail poured herself a glass of scotch from the liquor cabinet that lived on the far side of the room. She raised an eyebrow, and Nelson nodded.

It had been a spectacularly bad day.

Nelson wanted to make it better. He couldn't change what had happened at work, but what about the rest of this disaster? For most of his life, he'd gone after what he wanted with a single-minded focus. Captain of the school hockey team. Valedictorian. USC. The best equine practice in the US. His drive and ambition had always been something people admired. He'd thought it was good.

Until his wedding. When he'd discovered just how much he would do to get what he wanted. How much he could hurt people he cared for, in order to get to his goal. He'd tried to justify it, to say it wasn't just for him, but he'd had to come to terms with how selfish he'd been.

He'd reined himself in after the debacle with Zoey. Part of that was guilt, part of it a need to punish himself. He couldn't go around spreading hurt like that.

When he started a veterinary practice in Carter's Crossing, it had been something that was just his. That success had been his, but it hadn't come at a cost to anyone else. He could focus all his drive into his practice without it spilling over on anyone else.

He was so bad at darts that there was no fear of going overboard there. He'd played rec hockey and baseball, but that was a team activity. And he'd always made sure to keep it on a fun level, not serious competition.

But since the wedding, since he'd decided he had to make some drastic changes and not to take things over, he'd never had anything he wanted as much as Mariah, here, fake dating him. He didn't want that to end.

Why did he feel that way?

The answer hit him hard and fast. Because he'd never be able to convince her to make it real otherwise. He needed more time with her.

His mind went right to finding a solution—a way to keep her here, at least through the fall when her year was up. That meant salvaging at least some of the Valentine's Day events. He could think of ways to do that. But those ways meant pushing himself into people's lives, playing God. Things he'd sworn not to do again.

He mentally struggled. He could do it, he was sure. If he went to Dave, he could convince him that Jaycee was right, that the engagement party was a test, and that things would be better after that. Dave trusted him. He could tell him all the ways that he, Nelson, had been different from Jaycee. Nelson knew, now, that he'd been driven by ambition. He saw the wedding as part of his career plan, and for that, he'd overlooked Zoey, and how she felt.

Which meant he hadn't felt for her what he should.

But he didn't want to manipulate his best friend just to get what he, Nelson, wanted. He didn't want to be that guy. Not anymore. He couldn't do that to Dave.

But he wondered, as he thought it through, what *was* Jaycee's reason for her fixation on the perfect engagement party? This party wasn't going to help Jaycee's career. She'd never been the kind of person who had to have the biggest and best of anything. This was costing her the man she loved. There had to be a reason.

If he could find that reason, then maybe they could still make this work. Without taking over or bending others to what he wanted. Could he? Could he put the brakes on once he started?

Nelson dropped his tumbler on the coffee table, untouched. "I'm heading out, Grandmother. Got some things to do."

She gave him a slight smile. "You do that, then. I think it's too late to call Gerry, so I'll wait till morning. Unless I hear from you."

His grandmother saw too much, but right now he had a mission.

Five minutes later he pulled up in front of Dave's house.

He'd changed his mind about asking Jaycee what the thing was, whatever was driving her to go crazy about this party. He knew what it wasn't, but he also realized, it wasn't his issue, and not his relationship. Dave needed to know why she was doing it. Not have Nelson tell him.

Dave had given up the beer to physically work out his frustration, Nelson deduced as his friend finally answered the door. He was sweaty, wearing ratty shorts and a faded T-shirt. His eyes were blurry and had a tendency to wander. He looked angry at being disturbed, a frown crossing his face. Nelson had taken a note from Mariah's book, and given the door a hard pounding, and refused to give up.

"Whatcha doin' back here?"

Nelson shoved his way in. Dave lurched back.

"Dude. Not cool."

"I need to tell you something."

Dave focused his gaze on Nelson. "Now?"

"Now. I should have told you before."

Dave stumbled into his kitchen and sat on a stool, a beer in front of him. Nelson thought he'd run out. Apparently not.

"Say it 'n' get out."

Nelson's fingers itched to put away the empty bottles and wipe the counter, but he restrained himself.

"I should have told you why I pushed Zoey so hard on the wedding."

Dave frowned as he looked at him, but he was interested. Nelson had kept most of the details of that disaster to himself.

"Why?"

"For my career."

Dave looked shocked. Bleary shocked. "Really? You used your wedding for that?"

Nelson nodded, feeling the shame that he should have felt three years ago.

"I know. I was selfish and stupid. But Zoey's dad was a partner in the practice, and so many of the guests were people that I needed to impress. I wanted to be partner someday, and I was already working toward that."

"That why you wanted to marry Zoey?"

"No. I loved her..." Had some part of him seen Zoey as a step on his career path? Just how self-centered had he been?

"I don't know. But Jaycee—"

"Not what Jaycee is doin'." Dave set down his beer bottle.

"I know," Nelson said. "The party isn't going to help her job, and it's not helping her with you. She's never been a diva. So why is this so important to her?"

Dave shrugged. "I dunno."

Nelson leaned toward him. "Then you should find out."

Dave stared at him. "Does it matter?"

"I don't know. But it might make a difference. And you don't want to throw away what you two have for something stupid, do you?"

Dave's gaze shifted to his beer bottle, but he didn't look like he saw it. Nelson waited, letting him think it through. He picked up a couple of empties and dropped them in the recycling box. Dave didn't notice.

He sat down beside his friend again.

Dave's lips tightened. "Yeah, I wanna know what's more important than what we have. It better be worth it."

Nelson relaxed. He didn't know what Jaycee's reason was, and he didn't know if finding out would make a difference, but this was something they needed to work out. It was good for Dave.

It might make a difference to Mariah. If the engagement was back on, then maybe the party would be. But Nelson was stopping now. Instead of pushing through to get what he wanted, he was just pushing enough to help his friends.

"Now," Dave said. "I wanna know now."

Nelson narrowed his eyes. "I don't think you're up to driving. This isn't something you want to do over the phone. And you might want to be sober."

"Not waiting anymore." Dave covered his mouth as he burped. "I need t'know. Drive me?"

Nelson saw the pain on his friend's face. Might as well find out while he was partially numb, if this wasn't going to work.

"You might want to put more clothes on."

Jaycee met them at the door with red eyes and nose, and flannel pj's that covered her from head to toe.

She shot Nelson a dirty glance. "What do you want, Dave?"

He pointed a finger, that just missed her nose. "I wanna know why."

Nelson thought Dave had sobered up on the cold ride over. Now he wasn't sure. He kept an eye on him.

"Why what?" She wiped a tissue across her nose.

"Why does this party have t'be perfect? Why do I have t'dance? Why can't you think about anything else but the stupid party?"

"It's not a stupid party!" Jaycee yelled back. "Why can't you see that?"

"I dunno! But I can't! Tell me, what is so important about it? We coulda just had a dinner, like Mom said."

Jaycee shrieked. Nelson covered his ears, wondering if her neighbors' dogs would hear that and cringe.

"Yes, your mother would have loved a dinner party with all her friends, where she could make nasty little digs all the way through the meal about how unworthy I was and how much better Nelson's sister would have been. That's why the party. I wanted to prove to your mother that I'm not trash. I'm just as good as the Carters."

Nelson knew he shouldn't be here for this, but he didn't dare interrupt.

"This party was going to be the best engagement party Carter's Crossing ever had, and then all her snide remarks about it would stop. All her friends were going to love my party. It was going to be so perfect…"

Jaycee started crying again. Dave, not that drunk, and not that stupid, quickly folded her in his arms.

"Oh, baby. No. Shhh, shhh. It's okay. I'm sorry about Mom. I'll talk to her."

"I wanted to handle her by myself. I didn't want to make you choose sides." Jaycee sniffled.

"I'm on your side, babe. Always. I'll tell Mom to back off or she's not invited to the wedding."

Jaycee raised tear-drenched eyes to Dave and hiccupped.

"Really?"

"Of course. I didn't know she was doing that. I'm sorry I

didn't notice. But the truth is, you're too good for me, and I know it."

Jaycee drew in a shuddering breath. "I'm sorry I was so awful. I just wanted everything to be so perfect... You don't have to dance. We don't have to have a party. Just you. If you don't mind if your mom—"

"I'm not marrying my mom. I'm marrying you. And we're making our own family. If she doesn't treat you with respect, then she's not invited to be part of it."

Jaycee's chin trembled. "I love you, Dave."

"I love you, too, Jaycee. I'm so sorry—"

"My job is over?" Nelson needed to extricate himself.

The two turned to him, having forgotten all about him.

"Thanks for the ride," Dave said. "But I think I can take it from here."

"You're letting him stay, Jaycee?"

She gave Dave a wobbly smile. "Yeah, I think we have some things to talk about."

"Enjoy your talk," Nelson said, winking.

"Go away, Nelson," Dave said, eyes fixed on Jaycee.

CHAPTER FIFTEEN

NELSON RETURNED TO his grandmother's house. He'd noticed the lights still on, and thought she'd want to be updated. That is, if her network hadn't already spread the news.

She met him at the door. "Well?"

Nelson stepped in, tugging his scarf loose. "Dave and Jaycee are back together. I don't know if the party is happening, but they talked, and figured out Jaycee was doing all this because of Dave's mother."

Abigail grimaced. "I can see that. I suppose Jaycee was trying to impress her. She's going to have a difficult time unless Dave is willing to support her."

Nelson gave a tired smile. "He told Jaycee that his mother isn't welcome if she doesn't treat Jaycee right, so that should help."

"Excellent." Abigail turned to go.

"I had a thought, Grandmother."

Abigail turned back and invited Nelson to sit down in the lounge with a wave of her hand.

"What kind of thought?"

"About Gord and Gladys. I know he's in the hospital, but can't they still have their vow renewal? Unless he has complications, he should be almost ready to send home by the four-teenth."

Abigail shot him a look. "That's an interesting point, Nelson. I had assumed he'd have a long recovery."

"Everyone is an individual, and their recovery will be, as well, but it might be worth looking into. If Gord is in good enough shape, could the anniversary party be moved to the hospital? It would take some work to make the place look right, but since you've arranged for everyone to be here, and I'm sure the food has been ordered…"

Abigail rested a hand on Nelson's. "That is a very good suggestion, Nelson, and I'm surprised I didn't think of it myself. I must be getting old. I'll look into it. I appreciate that you're helping out with this."

Nelson shot her a glance.

"Someone told me it was time for me to move on."

"Someone is rather clever."

"Yes, she is." Nelson leaned over and pressed a kiss to his grandmother's cheek.

"Good night, Grandmother." He stood.

"You've made it a good night, Nelson. Thank you."

Mariah woke to a few precious seconds of oblivion before everything came crashing into her head.

Gord had broken his hip. And Jaycee and Dave had broken up.

She pulled the covers up over her head. For just a few moments she wanted to entertain the possibility of staying in bed, forgetting her responsibilities and letting the whole mess go by without her. Perhaps a twenty-four-hour flu?

She couldn't do that. People were counting on her. But she wished they weren't.

It began to get uncomfortably warm under the covers, so she threw them back. It was time to face her day.

She unplugged her phone from the charger on her bedside table. She pushed herself to a sitting position and pressed it on.

At least, at this point, there wasn't any more bad news that could be waiting for her. Could there?

She had a text from Jaycee. Mariah drew in a breath. She'd left Jaycee with Rachel. She wondered if she was feeling any better. Or they might be committed to seriously hurting Dave. The text had come in at 2:00 a.m., so it could be interesting…

We're back together. We've got a couple of suggestions for the party.

Huh? When Mariah left last night, the convent idea was still being discussed. This was an abrupt one-eighty. Mariah wasn't sure how she felt about the suggestions part, but if the party was back on…

The party was back on! Mariah could feel her body energize as that realization sank in.

Okay, she wasn't done, not yet. She had an engagement party, and she still had the fake proposal to put on. She'd need to let her grandfather know about the anniversary/vow renewal, but that was totally a random problem. What were the chances of someone breaking their hip?

Well, probably good at Gord's age. That was something she'd need to factor in in the future.

Right now maybe there was even something she could do about that.

Abigail had been right. A new day, sleep, and things could look totally different.

Mariah didn't waste much time getting dressed. She had her laptop and notebook with her when she descended the stairs to the main floor and made her way to the kitchen.

Abigail was on her phone. The coffee maker was burbling, so Mariah helped herself to a cup.

"Let me know what you find out. Thank you, Mavis."

Abigail clicked off her phone. "Good morning, Mariah. You look better today."

Mariah couldn't hold back a grin.

"I got a text from Jaycee. The engagement party is back on."

"That *is* wonderful." Abigail tapped her phone. "I may have some good news for you, as well."

Mariah sat down. "Hit me. I could use it."

"We might be able to have the vow renewal at the hospital."

Mariah blinked. "Really?"

"Nelson told me Gord might be close to coming home by the fourteenth. Gladys confirmed that he should be home on the sixteenth, so she's checking with the doctor to see if he can handle a party. We're hoping it will be allowed as long as he stays in bed."

Whoa. Could they do that?

"Do they have space there?"

"They do have a room. Mavis is looking into whether it's available now. It's not going to be as pretty as it would have been at the church."

Mariah opened her notebook and turned to a fresh page.

"If it's available, I'll take a look at it as soon as possible and I can come up with ideas."

Abigail nodded. "Also, Gord and Gladys met when he was a patient. She was his nurse."

Mariah's mouth dropped open. "You're kidding. Oh, we can definitely work with that."

"I thought that might cheer you up."

Mariah took a long breath. "I cannot tell you how relieved I am. Last night I felt like it was all over. I…well, I didn't think we had a chance. I should thank Nelson for thinking of that option for Gord and Gladys."

"You have more than that to thank him for. He went to talk to Dave last night. I don't know what he said to Dave, but apparently, he and Jaycee had reconciled by the time Nelson left them. He didn't know what they were going to do about the party, but they were talking. Dave's mother is, I'm sorry to say, a snob, and she had been making Jaycee feel like she wasn't good enough for Dave. As a result, Jaycee had fixated on the party to prove herself."

Grateful didn't cover how Mariah felt. Nelson had gotten involved. On his own, despite his own history, his own dislike of big events, he had come up with an option for Gord and Gladys and brought Jaycee and Dave back together.

Nelson had changed from the angry man she'd first sat down with at the dining table. And that gave her mixed feelings.

Some of those feelings were warm ones. Gratitude, and maybe pride? Had he changed because of her? Had she convinced him that he was wrong?

But other feelings were problematic. *Had* he done this for her? They'd spent a lot of time together. She'd come to enjoy that time, not just because it helped them set up their proposal. She'd happily spend time with Nelson now just because she enjoyed his company.

In spite of their arguing, or possibly because of it, they had fun together. Maybe too much.

Mariah had her dreams. She was going to work for her grandfather, get her own place and make a home for herself. One with roots she could set down. She could make friends, friends who wouldn't sail away, unsure if she'd ever see them again.

She should have grown beyond that little-girl feeling of abandonment, but she hadn't. Not when making a circle of permanent friends and family was driving her dream.

There was more room for advancement and variety in the city. There were so many people, enough for her to find some who would like her. She wanted to work for her grandfather partly because she understood the advantage of connections and relationships.

And that meant leaving Carter's Crossing this fall. Once the groundwork was laid for the Center for Romance, there wouldn't be a job for her in Carter's Crossing. Her grandfather wouldn't pay for her to work here, and Abigail and her committee could keep the work going without her.

There wasn't enough work for her to stay.

She was making friends here, and she hoped to keep in touch with them. But she wanted her own community, and while she was leaving, these people were all staying here. Forgetting that would lead to more of the same disappointment she'd become so familiar with as a kid.

People didn't have to live on a boat to leave.

"What did you want me to see?"

Nelson's voice came from within the barn. "Just a sec. We're coming."

Mariah stomped her feet. The air was brisk and cold, and her toes were prickling. If she'd been spending another winter here, she'd need warmer boots.

She shook her head. Not happening.

She'd done her best to ignore Nelson. She'd had two days to rearrange the anniversary party, and to deal with Dave and Jaycee's suggestions. She'd kept herself busier than necessary. But when Nelson asked her to come to the farm, to see something with Toby, well, she had to say yes. She had a soft spot for Toby.

Part of her had been only too happy to have an excuse.

She heard a jingling sound, one that she now knew came from a bit of horse harness. Toby had been doing amazingly well the past couple of weeks, and she had stood holding his halter while Nelson tried stuff on him. Bridles, saddles...they all had metal bits that jingled like that.

Toby had not responded well to the saddles, so maybe Nelson had finally found one he was comfortable with.

The jingle was joined by the clop of hooves, and another strange swooshing noise, and they came around the corner.

Toby was wearing a bridle, and a harness over most of his body. Behind him was...it was a sleigh. An old-fashioned sleigh.

Like something out of a Christmas card or Norman Rockwell painting.

Nelson wasn't in the sleigh, but was walking beside it, holding the long reins that extended from the bit in Toby's mouth, to his neck where they passed through the harness and on to Nelson's hands.

"It's a one-horse open sleigh, isn't it?" Mariah had never seen one in real life. But this was the stuff of romance.

Nelson nodded, a big grin crossing his face.

"He didn't like the saddles, so I thought, let's try a harness. The Fletchers had this old sleigh, so once Toby was good with me driving him from behind, I hitched him up. He seems to like this."

Mariah crossed to Toby and stroked his neck. "Good boy. You look so handsome."

"Why, thank you."

Mariah rolled her eyes. "I was talking to Toby. I called *him* a good boy. I don't think you qualify."

Nelson pressed a hand to his heart. "You wound me. You wanted to have sleigh rides, and here, when I present one to you, nothing but insults."

Mariah ignored his teasing.

"Do you think Toby could give sleigh rides?"

He shrugged. "Not now. He's just getting used to the sleigh. I'd want to be sure that he's completely comfortable with that for a first step. Then we'd have to introduce him to crowds. He may never be able to handle that."

Mariah saw the concern in Nelson's eyes. Toby was in good hands. Nelson would never push him into something he couldn't handle. Nelson might not be a good boy, but he was definitely a good man.

She wasn't supposed to be thinking of things like that!

"Are you taking him out in the sleigh now?"

Nelson shook his head. "I'm going to drive him up and down

the driveway for a bit, see how he does. But he wanted you to see how handsome he was."

Mariah rubbed Toby's forehead, and he responded by snuffling in her chest. He'd come a long way in just a few weeks. It made Mariah feel like she'd accomplished something, something as important as reviving Carter's Crossing, to know she'd had a key role in his rehabilitation.

"He's a handsome and good boy."

"I'm only going to be about fifteen minutes more. Want to go for dinner after? You could visit Sparky inside—he's feeling neglected lately."

Mariah's cheeks flushed. It wasn't just Sparky who'd been neglected lately.

"I don't know… I've got a lot to do—"

Nelson narrowed his eyes.

"Is something going on, Mariah? I know you have a lot of work to prep for Sunday, but we're supposed to be so madly in love that I'm planning a proposal. Right now it's looking more like we're having a fight. Unless you've changed your mind—"

Mariah busied herself with straightening Toby's forelock. She couldn't tell Nelson she'd avoided him because she was catching some real feelings.

"No, you're right. We should—"

"Can you say that again?"

Mariah turned her gaze to Nelson, brows furrowed. "I said, we should—"

"No, the 'You're right' part. I love hearing that."

Mariah turned her attention back to the horse to hide her laugh. "Toby, this guy may be good with you, but honestly, the ego on him."

"Not fair. How can I have a big ego when I so rarely hear anything like 'You're right, Nelson'?"

"And yet, you do."

Nelson laughed. "Go on in and stay warm, Mariah. We'll be back soon."

* * *

They went to Moonstone, and Jaycee gave them the same table as their first dinner together. Jaycee was glowing these days and gave both of them credit for her rekindled romance with Dave. Now that she wasn't worried about impressing his mother, or not as much, she was looking forward to her party.

"What were the changes that she and Dave had for you?"

Mariah laughed. "The skate dance is out."

"I know that was Dave's idea. He hated it."

"I think he was purposely messing it up to try to get out of it."

Nelson shook his head. "No, he was trying, I swear. He wanted to make Jaycee happy."

Mariah swallowed. "I'm just glad they worked that out."

"Because your event is back in play?" His voice was suddenly serious.

"Well, I can't say I'm not relieved, but I'm mostly glad they're happy again. Parties come and go, but couples with a chance of making it are rare."

Nelson nodded.

"And the vow renewal is good to go?"

"Totally. We've been able to take over the cafeteria in the hospital. I know Abigail pulled some strings for that. We're providing food in the lounge for anyone who would normally use the cafeteria while we have it out of commission. Gord will be in a hospital bed, but since Gladys was a nurse when they met, the committee was able to recreate an old nursing uniform for her.

"When I first met the committee, I seriously underestimated them. They work hard and get stuff done."

Nelson grimaced. "I'm pretty sure they're not above using blackmail."

Mariah's eyes danced. "Have they blackmailed you?"

"Laugh now. You won't find it so funny when it's your turn to 'help them out.'"

Her eyes widened. "But I already am!"

"That's what you think."

She shrugged. "I can handle them. But that reminds me, we should finalize the proposal plans."

Nelson eyed her warily. "Have you made changes to that?"

He was supposed to have veto rights.

Mariah rolled her eyes. "Honestly, what are you so afraid of? We're just creating a romantic setting, and adding music, and a little firework display."

"There's no such thing as a *little* firework display."

"That is patently untrue. Besides, Abigail told me you like fireworks."

Nelson sighed.

"I liked fireworks when I was a kid. And I go to the Fourth of July display in Carter's Crossing, because everyone does. It's not like I travel the country to catch any firework display going."

"But at least this is something you might do. And something we can pull off here. I mean, if Toby was ready, and we could have him pull us in that sleigh? That would be great, but he's not, so we need something to make it special."

A picture flashed in Nelson's mind. Toby, pulling the sleigh. Mariah snuggled in with him, her coat red and cheeks pink. Nelson could almost imagine proposing to her in that setting.

Whoa. He was fake proposing. They were fake dating and fake falling in love.

But somehow, when he looked across the table at her, it didn't feel fake. He'd asked her to have dinner with him because he wanted to, not because it was part of their carefully orchestrated romance.

But maybe that was just him. Did Mariah even like him?

They argued. They didn't agree on many things.

But Nelson enjoyed what they did. He enjoyed bantering with her more than a regular conversation with anyone else. He liked knowing that he'd never maneuver her into doing what he wanted against her wishes.

No, he was in more danger of being manipulated by her. And he liked it.

Did she enjoy it, too? He thought so. Her eyes were bright, her cheeks slightly pink, and she had leaned forward, as if she was invested in their conversation. That look she used to give him, wary and suspect, was gone. He'd told her about his biggest failure, and she hadn't censured him.

She hadn't approved. But she'd been sympathetic.

She'd told him about her family, and her upbringing. He didn't know if many people knew how lonely she'd felt growing up. He suspected her parents and brothers didn't know.

Maybe she'd told him simply because they'd spent so much time together. Maybe it wasn't because she felt close to him and trusted him.

Like he trusted her. Something that was almost miraculous, considering.

The most telling thing? The kisses. The ones that were supposed to convince everyone else that something was going on between the two of them. They were convincing him.

Could someone fake those kisses? Nelson, if he was honest, couldn't. There was something there.

He needed to find out. He needed to kiss her, not for show, but for them, and see how she responded.

They were fake dating, and had a fake proposal in three days, but Nelson wanted to move their fake dating to real.

Smiling at Nelson across the table, Mariah relaxed. Everything was working out.

Not perfectly, not as originally planned, but this was her job. She had to take the bumps and potholes on the road and handle them to make things work. With three days to go, everything was on track.

She couldn't fix everything. If a couple decided not to get

married, she wouldn't try to force it. Her job was to provide the wedding they wanted, and if at the end, they wanted to not have one, that was what she needed to provide for them.

But things were going well here in Carter's Crossing. Even if one of her vow renewal people got sick, they were at the hospital, so barring an act of God, that one was good. Dave and Jaycee had worked out their problem. Dave's mother had been stunned by her son's anger over her treatment of Jaycee and was on her best behavior.

And she and Nelson were good. Good at the fake dating.

She thought, after all this time together, they were friends. After their rocky beginning, she was surprised by that, but it was true. They argued, but it no longer had any anger in it. They enjoyed it.

She thought he liked having someone stand up to him. And she liked that he didn't patronize her. He was arrogant at times, but when she knocked him down about it, he laughed.

So yes, they were friends. It made the fake dating easier. And the fake kissing.

Technically, the kissing wasn't fake...after all, their lips were really touching. It was just scripted. Still, she enjoyed it.

For some reason, that made her cheeks warm. Which was silly.

She shook her head to dispel those uncomfortable thoughts. Instead, she focused on Nelson across the table.

That didn't help. He was smiling at her, but it was a warm smile, intimate, unnervingly realistic for a man about to fake propose.

He was a better actor than she'd thought.

When they got up to go, he insisted on paying. When she tried to argue, quietly so that Jaycee wouldn't hear, he whispered back that he didn't allow his dates to pay all the time.

That silenced her.

Then he held her coat for her. Again, yes, it was selling the dating image, but it felt...real.

They drove back to Abigail's in silence. It wasn't an uncomfortable silence, but it wasn't comfortable, either. It was… it was like the silence was saying something, but she didn't know the language.

She didn't like not knowing.

When he pulled up at the front door, she reached for her seat belt. Before she could grab the door, Nelson asked her to wait.

She turned to him, slightly puzzled. If he'd wanted to talk, they'd just not talked for several minutes. And right now she was feeling on edge, thinking too much about kissing, and it would be better if she just got out of the car…

Instead, he reached over and cradled her face in his hands.

She was about to ask him what he was doing when he pressed his lips to hers and answered the unspoken question.

She responded without thinking. Her arms slid up to his shoulders, gripping them tightly, and she kissed him back.

She didn't know how long it was until the kiss ended, but in the dim light from the veranda, she could see that his lips were slightly swollen, his breathing ragged.

She didn't need a mirror to know she looked the same. And something inside told her this wasn't good.

She called on every reserve of self-control she had.

"Good night, Nelson."

She opened the door before he could get out of the car, but he followed her to the bottom of the steps and waited while she opened the front door of the house.

"Good night, Mariah."

She slid through the door, glad not to find Abigail waiting for her. She could tell Abigail they were kissing to sell their romance, but she didn't want Abigail to know just how well they were selling it.

Then, like a hammer to the head, it hit her.

That hadn't been a show for the town. No one had been there

to see it. The only one who could have was Abigail, and she knew it wasn't real.

Mariah pressed her fingers to her lips.

What was going on?

CHAPTER SIXTEEN

FORTUNATELY, MARIAH HAD lots to do the next day. She'd lain awake far too long, remembering the kiss and wondering about it.

She'd finally convinced herself it was just practice. Mostly. That was the only logical conclusion. Taking more meaning from it led to places she didn't want to go. It had still taken her too long to fall asleep.

She'd used extra concealer under her eyes and approached her day, list at hand, dressed in jeans for a day of decorating. She refused to think about Nelson. She shoved those thoughts down whenever they popped up. It gave her mental muscles a workout.

There were plenty of hands available to help with this, the first day of setup, even though it was a Friday. The committee, or Abigail in this case, had hired the local construction crew to help. The crew was led by a young woman named Andrea. Mariah had met her and admired her. It couldn't be easy to lead a team of men, especially in such a traditionally male field. But she did it, without any obvious difficulties.

Mariah could take notes.

The priority was the mill. The engagement party was the biggest event and would require the most work. Mariah had cornered the market on fairy lights, and they needed them everywhere: on the trees, suspended over the ice, on the side of the mill and around the parking lot. Having ladders and laborers at hand made things go faster than she'd expected. There was still setup for Saturday, but the hard labor was done.

Mariah then drove to the hospital to assist in the work to transform the cafeteria. Most of the committee was already there.

The committee got things done. However, they were mostly elderly women, so there were some obvious things they couldn't do. They couldn't do the heavy lifting, or reach up high, and they had a provoking habit of being sidetracked by chatter, but the largest pieces were moved out, thanks again to Andrea and her crew.

Mariah knew, but was supposed to pretend she didn't, that things were going on at the gazebo in the town square, as well. More fairy lights were involved there, but she was spending the evening with Jaycee and Rachel working on party decorations for the engagement party while Nelson supposedly supervised at the gazebo. Thanks to Abigail's personality, no one really expected Nelson to do much.

Frustratingly, Abigail refused to send her any pictures, so that Mariah would be surprised. Mariah didn't want to be surprised by an event she was responsible for.

Still, it meant she didn't have to see Nelson. And that was all for the best. She didn't need any more practice kissing. The kissing part was great, but unsettling. She didn't need any distractions.

Nelson had an idea but needed time. He asked Abigail if he could skip some of the event planning on Saturday.

He didn't like the look she gave him, but she agreed to tell the crew working on "his" proposal location that he was needed at the farm. That was exactly where he headed.

Toby would now come to him, even when Mariah wasn't

around, to get treats, but it was obvious that Toby was disappointed when Mariah wasn't there.

Nelson scratched the horse under his forelock. "Me, too, buddy. But let's give her a surprise. A nice one."

He tied Toby in cross ties in the barn, and spent some time grooming him, tidying up his mane and tail and smoothing out the thick winter coat. Then he put on the freshly polished harness. Toby didn't react when the leather gently settled on his body, which gave Nelson a warm feeling. Thanks to Mariah, Toby was going to be okay.

He led Toby to the sleigh and hitched him up. Toby tossed his head a couple of times but didn't jerk away. Nelson gripped the reins and encouraged Toby to move forward. After a look back at Nelson, he walked forward, down the driveway again.

After fifteen minutes of completely uneventful pacing up and down the drive, Nelson pulled him to a halt. Then, moving slowly and keeping up a constant low-pitched conversation with the horse, he slid into the sleigh.

Toby didn't move.

"Okay, Toby. Let's do this for Mariah."

Nelson flicked the reins, encouraging him to move forward. After a short pause, Toby did as requested.

The sleigh was heavier this time, and Toby's head jerked up.

"I know, boy. This is a little different. You're pulling me, as well. But do this nicely, and we can put Mariah in the sleigh, and we both know that's what you'd really like."

With a shake of his head, Toby took another step. And another. And then they were walking smoothly down the drive.

Nelson grinned. They'd done it. This time when they came by the barn, he didn't stop Toby, but let him continue along the old laneway that headed down through the trees.

Toby, having accepted the idea of the sleigh, continued a steady walk. After a quarter of a mile Nelson turned him into the field, and, pivoting the sleigh, they came back the way they'd come. This time he coaxed Toby into a trot, and the trip back to the barn was quicker.

Nelson drew Toby to a halt. He climbed out of the sleigh and came forward to rub Toby's neck.

"What do you think, Toby? Ready for a show tomorrow?"

The whole town, it appeared, had come on Saturday to help Mariah and her Romance Committee make Valentine's Day a success. Most of the time she was able to stay on the sidelines, supervising her crew of volunteers. With the big items done yesterday, things were being ticked off her list with impressive speed. And anytime something needed to be picked up, Mariah was gently encouraged to stay put while someone else did the run.

Mariah knew she was being kept away from the gazebo in the town park, but she pretended not to notice. In the meantime, the two venues she was overseeing were transforming.

Thanks to her volunteers' enthusiasm, everything on Saturday's list and a good portion of Sunday's were done by the time pizza was served to the volunteers in the empty mill. Space heaters, some of which would remain there tomorrow, some of which would be placed closer to the skating ice, kept the interior warm. Abigail, or the committee, had provided the pizzas and drinks to thank the volunteers.

Watching Abigail, Mariah could sense her satisfaction with how things were going. The town was pulling together, supporting this new business she was trying to launch. This was the kind of community Carter's Crossing was, and why she wanted to save it.

Mariah wanted this to be a success, too. It was no longer just for her own future. She'd grown attached to the people here. She wanted success for them.

Her future was in New York City. And success here meant that she'd have a good foundation on which to base her work for her grandfather. But she was learning more than how to plan and organize different events.

She wanted a community like this for herself. It had been her dream as long as she could remember. But now she knew it was also a dream she could realize.

If she could make friends here, she could do the same in New York. It would take time and effort, but she was slowly learning to trust people. People in this town might not be able to keep every promise, but their intentions were good, and they stayed. Mariah could live with that.

She was too aware of Nelson's return to the mill. He'd been away most of the day, busy at the gazebo, she assumed. She knew the basics of what was happening: the gazebo decorated, the live music, the flowers and the fireworks. Abigail insisted they needed to add some surprises for Mariah, since it was her "surprise" proposal, and Mariah was on edge, wondering just what those surprises might be.

Surprises were rarely good when planning events.

But Nelson was here now. Something inside relaxed when she felt him beside her.

He placed a hand on the small of her back, and her whole body warmed. She turned to look at him to say hello and felt her cheeks flushing.

She saw several knowing looks being cast her way.

It made her nervous.

It shouldn't. After all, they'd only had a few weeks to sell this romance story, and it had worked. People thought they looked like a couple. A serious couple. It wouldn't shock them when Nelson fake proposed.

The problem was that it didn't feel like work. It didn't feel fake. It felt…real.

Mariah kept a smile on her face, but inside a shiver of ice was dispelling the warmth of Nelson's touch. And that cleared her mind.

This wasn't real. She'd set this up with Nelson as fake. But somehow, something inside her, that lonely girl, had grabbed on like it was real.

This was bad. This feeling wasn't real. And if it was, it wasn't going to last. It would turn out the same as it had been on the boat, people drifting away. Promises left unfulfilled. She wasn't putting roots down in Carter's Crossing; this was temporary.

When she'd arrived here in the fall, she'd considered this a pit stop on the road to her final goal. She couldn't allow herself to linger in another place that wasn't going to be home.

Sunday Mariah woke up with an unusual feeling on event day.

She didn't have more to do than hours in which to do it. In fact, last night Abigail had taken her list and removed most of the items, transferring them to other people on the committee.

Even more surprisingly, Mariah had let her.

Mariah wasn't good at that, loosening the reins and letting someone else take the lead. That meant trusting someone else to do the work. But no one could describe Abigail as anything but competent and intelligent. As well, she'd agreed to let Abigail take most of the to-do items from her list because people in Carter's Crossing needed to handle this all on their own.

The sooner Carter's Crossing became Cupid's Crossing, the sooner Mariah would be able to transfer responsibilities over to the residents of this town, the sooner she'd be able to end her fake engagement and go to New York, and then the sooner she could start her next life working for her grandfather and finding what would be *her* place in the world.

She didn't have to stay a full year if she got the job finished.

Last night, to keep herself focused, she'd started a new list of rentals in New York. The place she'd end up staying.

She shook her head. Enough navel gazing. Time to work.

Mariah stopped by the mill. The fairy lights weren't visible in the daylight, but she'd done this often enough to be able to picture how they'd look when darkness settled.

The mill was...well, still the mill. They wouldn't take photos of the building until it was renovated. But once she followed the path down to the river behind the building, she saw her vision of an old-fashioned skating party come to life. She checked and double-checked, and everything was under control.

Leaving the mill taken care of, she stopped by the hospital and found the same smooth operation underway.

The cafeteria had been transformed to replicate a hospital from fifty years ago. They'd been careful to bring in items thatt would have been available at the time. The menu was based on the simple one Gord and Gladys had had at their wedding. Out-of-town guests had already arrived and been safely settled. Costumes, attire from the decade of Gord and Gladys's dating and marriage were already tried on, altered and were waiting in a side room to be donned as guests arrived.

It was confirmation that Mariah was good at her job. She'd worked really hard, wanting everything to go off smoothly, both to impress her grandfather, and the press he was bringing with him, and also to give these people she'd come to know and like the events they deserved.

It also meant that now the only thing she hadn't checked out was the proposal site, since she wasn't supposed to know it was happening. She could feel the urge to surreptitiously drive by the park, just to be sure everything was going as planned there, when she got a message, saving herself from an unpopular decision.

Nelson wanted to see her at the farm. Mariah let Abigail know where to reach her, in case of problems, and asked her to let her know when her grandfather arrived. Then she got in her car and drove away from the park and toward the farm.

She noticed several people watching to make sure she drove off in the right direction: away from the town green.

She really liked this town.

Nelson was nervous. This was undoubtedly the craziest thing he'd done in a long time, possibly ever.

He remembered his proposal to Zoey. He'd booked reservations at the best restaurant in town and asked her to marry him between the main course and dessert. He'd talked to her father beforehand. It was all organized, by the book, and he'd been as certain that she'd say yes as anyone could be.

This was...crazy. He'd never met any of Mariah's family. He had no idea how she'd answer. He was sure there was something, something special between them. It was stronger than any connection he'd felt in his life. He was sure she felt it, too.

She wasn't indifferent, but whether she'd be willing to take a chance...he had no idea.

He just knew he couldn't do the staged, elaborate proposal they'd planned as a performance piece, not before he did something real. Because for him, the time they were spending together wasn't fake. Not anymore.

He wasn't an event planner. And he didn't want to try to manipulate Mariah into the response he wanted by staging an elaborate setup. Especially when he might not get that response.

He needed to know how she felt, and he wanted her to know what he was offering.

He was all in.

Toby was hitched up to the sleigh. Nelson had stashed a couple of warm blankets inside. He had the family ring that Abigail had provided for the staged event this evening in his pocket.

That was all he had. That and the way he felt.

He felt an awkward lurch in his chest when her car pulled into the driveway. Something inside him warmed when he saw her heading his way. She was smiling, but it might just have been at the sight of Toby and the sleigh.

"He looks so good!" Her gaze was on the horse.

Okay, the smile was for Toby. He remembered what he was doing, and the tension ratcheted up. He took a breath, determined to make the most of his moment.

"Want a ride?"

Her eyes widened and sparkled. "Really? He's ready?"

Nelson nodded. He stood by the sleigh and watched her greet Toby.

She accepted his hand as he helped her in. They didn't touch skin, both bundled in winter clothing, but Nelson felt a responsive tingle. His breath was shallow, his palms clammy, and he had a horrible suspicion his stomach was ready to hurl the contents of his breakfast. This was nothing like last time.

He drew in another deep breath and settled into the sleigh beside Mariah.

He gently slapped the reins, and Toby started at a walk. He didn't bolt, and his ears were forward. He looked proud of himself, and Mariah told Toby what a good boy he was.

She turned her shining expression to him.

"Thank you for this, Nelson. Your grandmother took over most of the jobs I had left, and I was getting nervous without anything to do."

Nelson cleared the lump in his throat.

"I thought you'd like to see how Toby was doing and enjoy a one-horse open sleigh ride, just like the song."

"It's incredible. I've never done this before." Her eyes were sparkling, her smile wide. She was beautiful.

He felt it like a jolt of lightning. It scared him. He took a breath.

"I wanted to talk to you, so, um, it seemed like a good idea."

Mariah's gaze skittered over his face, then returned to Toby. "Okay."

Was her voice breathless? What had she seen on his face? Nelson told himself to quit stalling.

"Mariah, I know we got started on the wrong foot, back when you came to town."

Mariah bit her lip. "Yeah, but we're past that now, right?"

He was.

"I've had more fun fake dating you than I expected."

He saw her forehead crease. He pushed on, the words awkward on his tongue.

"A lot more. I know we disagree on some things…"

"You mean we argue."

"I don't know if it's really arguing. More like bickering."

Mariah looked at him, the corners of her lips clenched from holding back a grin. "Are we arguing about how we argue?"

Nelson felt his own mouth quirk up. "I guess so. But I like that you don't back down."

"Really?" Her voice was skeptical.

"Well, most of the time. I know you'll tell me how you feel, and you won't let me talk you into doing something you don't want to."

"Well, duh. No one is going to do that to me."

"I know. It's good. And even though we disa—argue, we have fun."

"We do. And we've done a good job. People believe we're really dating."

This wasn't as difficult when it had been Zoey. He knew why. He was risking more this time.

"Right. I think people believe it because we aren't acting. We get along."

Okay, just shoot him. *We get along.* He'd expressed his feelings better back in high school.

"Where are you going with this, Nelson?" She looked confused.

How could he be messing this up so badly?

Nothing ventured…

"Will you marry me, Mariah?"

Now Mariah looked worried. That hadn't come out as smoothly as he'd wanted. None of this had.

"Are you practicing, Nelson? Is that what this is about? Because I thought you'd have a better speech. But it's okay, we can work on it."

Nelson pulled Toby to a halt.

"No. I'm not practicing. I did work out a speech for later, just like you wanted. This isn't a practice."

"But what… I don't understand."

Nelson found he couldn't meet her gaze. With heated cheeks, he said, "It's a proposal. A real one."

There was a long, awkward silence. Nelson couldn't think of a way to break it. He could jump in and say it was a joke, but he wasn't sure he could sell that.

He needed to know.

She was going to turn him down as soon as she understood he was serious. He could see that now. But he wanted it said. He didn't want to have to second-guess, worry that he hadn't been clear.

He needed to *know*.

He waited for her to let him down nicely. Mariah wouldn't be cruel, not after the time they'd spent together. But while she didn't give him the answer he wanted, she spoke seriously.

"Nelson, how can you possibly do that? You tried this before and it didn't work out."

A vise had wrapped around his ribs. But at least she was talking about it.

He turned to her, hoping his face showed that he meant what he was saying.

"This is different."

Mariah rolled her eyes.

"Don't do that. It's exactly because I've been in this place before that I know that this is different. It's real. It's real in a way it wasn't with Zoey. I don't hold back with you. And I like it. I can be myself, but better."

Mariah looked away. He couldn't blame her. This was a mess. He was a mess.

"Nelson, you can't know, not for sure. You can't keep a promise like this. Things change. People change, and how they feel changes. I'm sorry, but I just…can't believe you. I mean, even my dad…that promise of his hurt my mom so much…"

She swallowed.

Nelson knew that this would hit him later, but right now he was still numb.

"Mariah, I know there aren't a lot of things people can promise and keep their word every time. Either those are little things, things that don't matter, or they're big things. And yeah, I can't promise that I won't be hit by lightning, or that we'll always get along. I mean, in real life, things aren't easy.

"But people make promises, and they try, and sometimes, sometimes that turns into something stellar. I think we could be that. I love you, and I want to spend my life with you, whether we bicker or argue or disagree every day. I'd rather have that every day, than wait for some perfect thing that will never happen."

He paused, drawing in a shaky breath. Mariah was still staring determinedly to the side. She shook her head.

He thought he saw tears in her eyes. He was sorry to have put them there, but he wasn't sorry he'd tried.

He would be later. Later he'd realize how awkward he had just made things. His feeling, that there was something between them, something that needed to be out there before the fake proposal, was wrong. But he was still sure he'd done the right thing.

He sighed and nudged Toby to start the turn back to the barn. He'd thought he was right before, with Zoey. He'd forced what he wanted to make it happen.

This time he hadn't pushed and shoved, but again, he was on his own.

This time, he knew, it wasn't professional embarrassment that was going to be the hardest part. But he shoved that thought aside.

He had to return Mariah to her car, and then meet her in the gazebo tonight. To make a romantic, scripted, totally phony proposal.

It was all wrong. He should just give up on romance.

No matter what Mariah and his grandmother might do, this was not the place where romance lived.

Mariah desperately wished for the ability to teleport. If she could just get away from Nelson, away from the farm, out of this lovely sleigh, with Toby proudly pulling them through the snow…then she could get somewhere safe before she started crying.

She could feel the tears in her clogged throat, the burning in her eyes, the clenched muscles in her stomach.

What was wrong with Nelson? They had a perfectly good time together. This wasn't an actual romance. She wasn't really feeling things; she'd just been searching for that sense of belonging she'd always wanted.

He wanted to make it real. Really real. Commit to each other real. That terrified her.

She knew people did that. Made the promise, took the leap. Jaycee and Dave, Judy and Harvey… Gordon and Gladys. No, forget Gord and Gladys. They had succeeded, but there was too much risk.

Mariah didn't want promises. She wanted things she could control. That way she couldn't be disappointed, not again.

Losing friends as a kid? Nothing compared to losing someone you loved—

No, not loved. She didn't truly believe in that.

Or did she? Her parents were still in love, she knew. But her dad had put his promise ahead of her mother, and she'd seen how much that hurt her mom. If you promised, you couldn't break it. And how could you promise a feeling? Feelings changed. And if you promised, and didn't break that promise, what did you do when those feelings changed?

It was just…messy. Painful. Better avoided.

Maybe she was missing out. She could be missing something good, but it also meant she was missing the chance of something monumentally bad.

Her phone rang, and she pulled it out in relief. She didn't want to stay here in silence—heavy, disappointed silence—while they returned to the barn and she had to speak to Nelson again.

"Hi, Abigail! What's wrong?" Abigail would only call if there was a problem. She wanted a problem. Something that meant she had to go and solve things and not think about this last half hour.

"Oh, right. He's here now. I'll be there as soon as I can. Thank you."

She'd completely forgotten her grandfather was coming. How could Nelson do something like this now? Now, when so much was at stake? She couldn't afford to be distracted.

"My grandfather is here. I should go see him."

She saw Nelson nod from the corner of her eye. She didn't dare look at him.

She scrambled out of the sleigh with more haste than dignity when they got back to the barn. She fled to her car, quickly starting it up.

Nelson had exited the sleigh, as well. He had hold of Toby's bridle and was leading him to the barn.

For a moment she wanted to call out to him. She wanted to go back to that easy relationship they'd had. To forget the parties she had planned, the fake proposal, and just go in and help him settle Toby. To have nothing more to do than argue about what they should have for dinner and what they should watch on TV after.

No. She had her plans. Plans she was in control of. They were safe. They were sure. That was what she wanted.

CHAPTER SEVENTEEN

MARIAH NEEDED THE whole drive back to town to get her mind focused on her job again. Truthfully, she probably could have driven back and forth a couple more times, but once was going to have to do.

Her grandfather and Abigail had arrived at the skating party. Mariah had some last-minute details she wanted to check, but when she arrived, Abigail had everything under control. Including her grandfather, it appeared.

Jaycee and Dave were there, buzzing with excitement and obviously in love. The creek was strung with fairy lights, ready to bathe the skating area with romantic light when the daylight faded. The high school students had arrived to oversee parking. Music was playing over speakers near the ice. The bonfire was lit, with her approval, so there would be glowing embers for toasting marshmallows later. The makeshift bar was preparing hot chocolate.

There were skates available to borrow for those who didn't have any. Benches carefully arranged around the creek, and Porta-Potties tactfully set back. And a fence around the section of ice set aside for beginners.

For those who got cold, the mill interior was warmed with heaters and more seating.

And now, people. People skating, talking, drinking hot chocolate and selecting sticks to use for s'mores. Exactly as she'd imagined.

"Abigail, everything looks beautiful."

"Thank you, Mariah, but it's thanks to your careful planning." Abigail smiled warmly at her.

"Looks good, sweetheart," her grandfather said, but his attention was focused on the woman he'd been talking to, rather than the party set up around him.

Mariah couldn't blame him. She wasn't entirely focused on the party, either.

"Everything here is under control. I should go check on the vow renewal now."

Abigail glanced at Mariah. "Why don't we all go? The press will be here soon, so we might as well make sure it looks effortless when they arrive."

If Abigail hadn't been running a mill, she'd have been an awesome event planner.

Mariah found herself in the back seat, with her grandfather and Abigail up front. Mariah felt very much a third wheel.

She hardly noticed. Her mind kept playing back her conversation with Nelson. What was he— How could he— And why did this upset her so much?

Why did she feel like she'd made a mistake? The decision she'd made was a no-brainer. She had her plans. She was creating a romantic destination. She wasn't here for romance for herself.

As always in Carter's Crossing, it didn't take long to get anyplace. The three of them were soon walking down the hallway to the hospital cafeteria, now repurposed as a hospital room from five decades earlier.

Mariah had seen everything yesterday, but it still surprised her. She could almost believe it was fifty years ago. The women on the committee had found furniture and clothing from that period.

Gord was in the hospital bed, looking alert and pleased. Mariah had learned over the past few months that that was not his normal expression. Gladys was wearing a nurses' uniform from fifty years ago and appeared happy to be bossing Gord. Members of the committee were bustling around, in costume, making sure the food was just so. They had even recreated the wedding cake from Gord and Gladys's wedding.

It was perfect. She could see that her grandfather was impressed. With the limited resources and budget they had, they'd made an incredible setting.

Then the guests started to arrive.

Except for Gord and Gladys's children, the guests were all older. It was touching to watch the reunions among friends who hadn't seen each other for years. There was a problem with the coffee maker, and Mariah kept herself busy for a few minutes, getting everything set.

Gladys came over to get a cup for Gord.

"Thank you so much, Mariah. This is…perfect." Her eyes were glistening with tears of joy.

"I'm so pleased you like it." This was the real reward for her work.

Gladys surprised her with a hug.

"It's not just the food, and the room…but all these people, some I haven't seen for so many years…it just means so much."

This was the part of her job Mariah loved. Making people happy, making the big moments of their lives memorable. Doing the work so that they could simply experience it.

"I'm happy to do it, Gladys. You and Gord and your friends enjoying yourselves is all the thanks I need."

Gladys looked over at Gord and shook her head. "Even Gord is loving this, despite the hip. If there's anything you ever need…"

Mariah hadn't planned it, but the words shot out. "Can I ask you a question?"

"Of course." Gladys held the cup in her hands but turned to Mariah.

"How did you know?"

Gladys's brow furrowed.

"Know?"

"That you and Gord were real. That it would last, this long."

Gladys's eyes widened. "Ah, that." She narrowed her gaze and looked over at Gord.

"Part of it, we were crazy about each other. Head over heels. The way that man could kiss…"

Mariah stole a glance at Gord. Nope, not the guy she would have pegged for a great kisser. Now, Nelson… She shook her head to rid herself of distractions.

"But also, we were determined. And realistic." Gladys's expression was serious.

"Some days he annoyed the snot out of me. Still does. But with compromise, commitment, love and sometimes just plain old mule-headed determination, we got through the tough days. And it was all worth it."

Mariah watched Gord catch Gladys's eye. She saw the smile on his normally grumpy face.

She could easily imagine that there were days Gladys wanted to give up on him. But they'd made it work.

She didn't know what the secret was that made some couples last and some not. But she understood determination. She was good at making things happen, and not giving up. She thought Nelson was, too.

Nelson certainly made her crazy. They could argue or bicker or whatever he wanted to call it. But they never crossed the line into deliberate meanness. She could picture them still arguing when they were the same age as Gladys and Gord.

And yes, he could certainly kiss.

Her stomach muscles tightened, and she had a hard time breathing in enough air. Maybe Nelson was right. Maybe this didn't just seem real. Maybe it was.

Could she make a promise? She didn't want to ever break her word.

Maybe she just had to make a promise she knew she could keep.

Nelson thought he might be an idiot.

No, he was sure of it.

Why else would he be showing up at the town gazebo, ready to pretend propose to the woman who had turned down his real proposal?

He closed his eyes. Tried to forget the afternoon.

He'd promised Mariah that he would do this. He'd salvaged the anniversary party for Gord and Gladys. He'd talked to Dave to get the engagement party back on track. This was it, the last of Mariah's three events.

He should be doing this for Grandmother. This was the final event to get Cupid's Crossing launched. He knew she'd invested money and time and brain power to make this happen. But as much as he loved his grandmother, he wouldn't be here, offering his heart on a platter only to be crushed again, for her.

Oh, this time Mariah would say yes. But it wouldn't be real. And after tonight he was going to have to pretend for who knows how long that they were in love and getting married, when he was the only one in love, and a breakup was already programmed into Mariah's calendar.

He could have canceled. Had a fake bout of colic for Sparky or one of the other horses. Claimed a flu bug. Anything to avoid this painful farce.

But he wasn't breaking a promise to Mariah. She might not value it, but he would give her this last gift.

The gazebo looked beautiful. It was covered with white and red fairy lights, lending it a soft glow. The seats inside had cushions that he'd never seen before, red and white, of course. There were roses, deep red and white, in a tall vase thing, braving the freezing weather.

There was music, too, a string quartet by the sounds of it, playing out of sight. He wondered how they kept their hands and instruments warm, but knew Mariah would have planned for that, and told his grandmother how to take care of it.

It was beautiful, romantic and fake. He hated it.

He patted his pocket, checking that the ring was there. It was the only element that would be a true surprise for Mariah. He'd hoped she'd like it. She'd pretend she did, in any case. Just like she'd pretend to say yes.

Making himself take the first step, Nelson slowly walked toward the gazebo. There was no point in showing up if he wasn't going to go through with it.

He heard footsteps behind him, just before he reached the steps. He turned, and saw Mariah, rushing toward him.

She was early. She was also wearing that red coat. Her dark hair shone beneath the white cap, and her cheeks were flushed above the scarf wrapped around her neck. She looked beautiful, all red and white, with shiny black hair and boots.

It was for the cameras, though. Not for him.

He forced a smile.

She looked at him, then at the ground between them. "I wasn't sure you'd come."

He swallowed over a lump in his throat. "I promised."

She flinched. He looked away. It wasn't his intention to hurt her.

"Can you take this?" She passed him a piece of leather, which he noted was a leash. Attached to Tiny. He'd been so absorbed in her that he'd totally missed the Great Dane at her side.

Before he could ask why she had Tiny, she'd turned to go, with a quick comment over her shoulder. "I'll be right back."

He stared down the path where she'd disappeared. What was going on? She'd promised to let him know the details of this proposal. Since it was being recorded, it was all programmed, the timing of everything set. He had his script and was here to follow it.

Tiny had not been part of it.

He and Mariah were supposed to meet at the gazebo, dance, then he'd go down on one knee. Tiny wasn't going to help with that. If Tiny didn't trip anyone during the dancing, he'd mess things up for the camera by licking Nelson's face when he kneeled.

Maybe that wasn't why Tiny was here. He looked at the dog. Had Mavis called Mariah because Tiny had eaten something?

Tiny was sitting on his haunches, tongue hanging out. Patiently waiting for the next fun thing. No digestive complaints.

Nelson looked again. Tiny was wearing a sweater. A red sweater, with white blobs on it. Seriously, it was a homemade sweater, done by someone who wasn't very good at knitting. Probably Mavis. Didn't bother Tiny, though.

Nelson had no idea how long he was supposed to wait, so he tugged on Tiny's leash and climbed the steps to the gazebo.

There were heaters under the seats, keeping the space warm, and the roses from freezing and drooping. Nelson sat, and Tiny sat beside him, chin on Nelson's thigh. He was drooling, but Nelson couldn't see that it much mattered.

He heard hoofbeats. That caught his attention. Had Mariah found a horse-drawn sleigh to add? He looked away, blinking his eyes rapidly. A short time ago they'd been in his horse-drawn sleigh. Not a memory he wanted to revisit.

With his emotions back under control, he turned to where the hoofbeats were louder and couldn't stop his jaw from dropping.

Mariah was leading Sparky up the path. Sparky, wearing a big red bow.

Nelson found himself on his feet. He headed down the steps, toward his horse, dragging Tiny behind him.

Tiny was a dead weight. Apparently, he wasn't fond of horses.

Nelson stopped, ten feet between him and Tiny, Mariah and Sparky.

"Why do you have Sparky? And why do I have Tiny?"

Mariah looked down, then off to the side. She took a deep

breath and tugged on Sparky's lead. She crossed the ten feet separating them, Sparky clopping behind her, glad to see Nelson. Nelson had to brace himself, since Tiny was trying to back away. He tugged the leash.

Mariah dropped on her knee in front of him. He reached out to catch her, not having seen her slip. But she pushed his hand away.

"Theodore Nelson Carter the third, will you marry me?"

Nelson looked around, trying to understand the change in plans. He didn't see anything to clear up the confusion.

He reached for Mariah's hand again. She was staring up at him, eyes shining with what looked like tears.

He tried to tug her up, but she tugged back. Then Tiny gave his own tug, and Nelson fell on his butt, losing the leash.

Tiny took advantage and ran back to the gazebo, sticking his head under a seat.

Mariah was biting back a grin. Nelson, flat on his back, felt pain running down to his frozen posterior, but it was nothing compared to what he was feeling inside.

"What are you doing, Mariah? We're supposed to be in the gazebo. I'm the one who 'planned' this. I was the one going down on one knee, remember?"

Mariah crawled over to him, and held herself up over his chest, staring at him intently. There was an expression on her face—he didn't dare try to label it. It was too tempting to read things into it, and he'd already fooled himself enough.

He closed his eyes. He couldn't look at her this closely if he was going to get through this.

"Nelson, this isn't the proposal for Carter's Crossing. The one for the pictures. This is for me."

"I don't understand."

"Nelson. Look at me."

He drew a long breath and opened his eyes.

"Nelson, I, Mariah fraidy-cat Van Delton, have fallen in love with you and want to marry you. I'm hoping you haven't fallen out of love with me since this afternoon."

He felt Sparky nudging his foot. It grounded him. This wasn't some weird dream or imagination. Tiny and Sparky? Not part of anything he would make up.

"What happened? This afternoon—"

Mariah put a white mitten over his mouth. "This afternoon I was scared. You know I have a problem with promises.

"Then, at Gord and Gladys's party. I asked Gladys how she knew. How they could last. And she said it was not just feelings but sometimes hard work and determination."

Her eyes blinked back tears.

"I can do that. I can work hard, and I'm stubborn. You are, too. So I promise you, Nelson, that I'll work my hardest to love you for the rest of my life, if you'll promise that, too."

She took her hand from his mouth and paused, watching him. Nelson looked up at the face of the woman kneeling over him. The woman he loved. And this time he saw the same thing in her face.

She also looked ready to cry. He reached a hand to her cheek, drawing her down for a kiss. She collapsed on top of him, returning his kiss with fervor.

He didn't know how long they stayed there, making promises with their hands and lips, but he finally couldn't ignore the cold creeping up from the frozen ground below him.

He pulled away, smiling at the dazed expression on her face.

"Yes." He felt light, despite the cold seeping into his bones. "Yes, I'll promise to work with everything I have to love you for the rest of my life. Are we being recorded, by the way?"

Mariah took a moment to focus. "I don't know. Maybe. The press is here."

"Then I have proof that *you* proposed to *me*."

A smile crossed her face. "Really? You're going there?"

He traced her nose with a shaky finger.

"If we don't get up, I'm going to have frostbite."

Mariah shoved herself up and off him. "You know, you proposed first."

Nelson pushed himself to a crouch and then stood up, pulling Mariah up with him.

"You turned me down." This time it didn't hurt the same.

"It still counts."

"Nuh-uh."

"It absolutely does."

He cut her off with a kiss. Best way to win an argument.

Sparky interrupted that one, almost knocking Nelson over with a hard shove of his head. Nelson pulled back with reluctance, and curiosity.

"What's with Sparky and Tiny?"

Right now he just wanted to be alone with Mariah, but they had two large animals to take care of. It wasn't what he'd expect from Mariah's meticulous planning.

Mariah turned to Sparky, surprised, as if she'd completely forgotten the horse was there.

"I didn't have a lot of time, and I wanted to make this proposal something for us. Something real. And well, we met with Tiny, and we spent all that time with the horses. But I couldn't bring Toby, or any of the others, so…"

Nelson laughed, a happy, full sound.

"I love you, Mariah. But you are a little bit nuts."

Mariah wrapped her arms around him. "Well, obviously. I just messed up a beautiful proposal…"

Nelson tugged her toward the gazebo. "We can still have a dance. And I have a ring in my pocket."

Her eyes lit up. She tugged him to the gazebo steps, Sparky clopping behind.

"Okay, Nelson. Sweep me off my feet."

It was a challenge. One he planned to meet every day for the rest of their lives.

"I'm confused," Gerry said. He and Abigail were with the photographer, watching her shoot pictures of Nelson and Mariah dancing.

"This part I get." He nodded toward the gazebo. "But what's with the dog and the horse? And whatever they were doing on the way to the gazebo?"

Abigail smiled. "I think that was 'the real thing.'"

His brows drew down, putting a frown on his forehead.

"What does that mean?"

"I think there might have been a real proposal in there."

Now his eyebrows flew up. "What? I thought this was a publicity event. Fake."

"It started out like that, I know, but I think they actually like each other."

He shot her a sharp glance. "Does this mean you've poached my granddaughter?"

Abigail threw out her hands. "This was all Nelson, not me."

Gerry had a skeptical expression on his face. "I have more respect for your abilities than that, Abigail."

She turned her head to the couple in the gazebo again. From this distance, she could hear their voices. She suspected a lot of arguing would be involved in that relationship, but Nelson needed someone strong enough to stand up to him.

"Is your grandson going to move to New York?"

Abigail shrugged. Gerry had enough to deal with now.

"Mariah is only supposed to be here another seven months."

Abigail nodded. "That's the plan."

"Have you got another plan, Abigail?"

She turned to Gerry and raised her eyebrows.

"Me?"

He scoffed. "Of course you have a plan. Give me the news, I can handle it."

"If Mariah wants to stay, the committee could cover her salary. If she's not going to end up in New York City, for whatever reason, it wouldn't be reasonable for you to cover those expenses. We would reimburse you."

Gerry leaned back. "So you *are* poaching my granddaughter. But if she stays here, what will you do?"

Abigail pursed her lips. "I needed to know that Carter's Crossing will survive. That people can work here, raise their families here, and if their children wish, they have the opportunity to stay here. I have a lot of faith in Mariah. If she can implement her plan, the way she has begun, then I'd be happy to step aside and let her run everything."

"Then what are you going to do—knit?"

A corner of her mouth tugged up. "No, not knitting. I'm not sure what I'll do."

"There's not that much else you can do here."

"You might be surprised. Who said I'd be staying here?"

Gerry was staring at her now, expression serious. "You'd consider leaving Carter's Crossing?" There was doubt in his voice.

"If I know it's thriving, then yes, I've done my job. I've already started the process to change the name officially to Cupid's Crossing, to support the romance initiative."

She shrugged. "Then I could do something else. I deserve some fun."

"You're serious."

Abigail didn't respond.

"If Abigail Carter can leave Carter's Crossing behind, maybe there's hope for me yet. Maybe I can step back, have some fun, as well."

Abigail gave him her serene smile. He narrowed his eyes, suspicious.

"I guess we'll see."

* * * * *